W9-ACY-697

SILENT MELODY

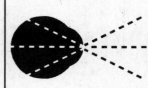

SILENT MELODY

MARY BALOGH

THORNDIKE PRESS

A part of Gale, Cengage Learning

GALE
CENGAGE Learning·

Farmington Hills, Mich • San Francisco • New York • Waterville, Maine
Meriden, Conn • Mason, Ohio • Chicago

GALE
CENGAGE Learning®

LIBRARY OF CONGRESS CATALOGING-IN-PUBLICATION DATA

Balogh, Mary.
    Silent melody / Mary Balogh. — Large print edition.
        pages cm. — (Thorndike Press large print romance)
    ISBN 978-1-4104-7816-0 (hardback) — ISBN 1-4104-7816-5 (hardcover)
    1. Large type books. I. Title.
PR6052.A465S523 2015b
823'.914—dc23   2015017014

Published in 2015 by arrangement with New American Library, an
imprint of Penguin Publishing Group, a division of Penguin Random
House LLC

Printed in the United States of America
1 2 3 4 5 6 7 19 18 17 16 15

Dear Reader,

Of all my books, *Silent Melody* seems to be a reader favorite, mainly because of the heroine. She is a deaf-mute living in the eighteenth century, when there was no standard sign language and deaf people were often considered mad and consigned to insane asylums. Lady Emily Marlowe is fortunate enough to belong to a family that loves her and wants her, and she has taught herself to lip-read. However, most of her life is lived internally. I did not see her as a victim or as handicapped. I tried to show how richly her life is lived even though she cannot share that richness — until she meets Lord Ashley Kendrick.

When Emily and Ashley fall in love, he has much to offer her. Because she had hearing for the first few years of her life, he is able to teach her to speak. And he is able to protect her from all the dangers that threaten over the course of the story. But Emily has at least as much to offer Ashley. She teaches him that silence is rich and teeming with life and color and joy, and she teaches him that companionship and love do not need the medium of words.

Writing a love story without any real dialogue between the hero and heroine was incredibly challenging, but it was rewarding too. I am delighted that the book is being republished in this lovely edition so that it will be available again to those of you who have read it before as well as those of you who will be discovering it for the first time.

Mary Balogh

PROLOGUE:
1756

It was hard to leave. But it was impossible to stay. He was leaving from choice because he was young and energetic and adventurous and had long wanted to carve a life of his own.

He was going to new possibilities, new dreams. But he was leaving behind places and people. And though, being young, he was sure he would see them all again someday, he knew too that many years might pass before he did so.

It was not easy to leave.

Lord Ashley Kendrick was the son of a duke. A younger son, and therefore a man who needed employment. But neither the army nor the church, the accepted professions for younger sons, had appealed to him, and so he had done nothing more useful with his twenty-three years than sow some wild oats and manage the estate of Bowden Abbey for his brother, Luke, Duke

7

of Harndon, during the past few months. Business had always attracted him, but his father had forbidden him to involve himself with something he considered beneath the dignity of an aristocrat — even of a younger son. Luke felt differently. And so Ashley, with his brother's reluctant blessing, was on his way to India, to take up his new post with the East India Company.

He was eager to go. Finally he was to be his own man, doing what he wanted to do, proving to himself that he could forge his own destiny. He could hardly wait to begin his new life, to be there in India, to be free of his dependence on his brother.

But it was hard to say good-bye. He did it the day before he left and begged everyone to let him go alone the following morning, to drive away from Bowden Abbey as if on a morning errand. He said good-bye to Luke; to Anna, Luke's wife; to Joy, their infant daughter; to Emmy . . .

Ah, but he did not really say good-bye to Emmy. He sought her out and told her he was leaving the following day, it was true. But then he set his hands on her shoulders, smiled cheerfully at her, told her to be a good girl, and strode away before she could make any reply.

Not that Emmy could have replied

verbally even if she had wanted to. She was a deaf-mute. She could read lips, but she had no way of communicating her thoughts except with those huge gray eyes of hers — and with certain facial expressions and gestures to which he had become sensitive during the year he had known her, plus others they had agreed upon as a sort of private, secret, if not entirely adequate language. She could not read or write. She was Anna's sister and had come to Bowden soon after Anna's marriage to Luke.

Emmy was a child. Though fifteen years old, her handicap and her wild sense of freedom — she rarely dressed or behaved like a gently born young lady — made Ashley think of her as a child. A precious child for whom he felt a deep affection and in whom he had been in the habit of confiding all his frustrations and dreams. A child who adored him. It was not conceit that had him thinking so. She spent every spare moment in his company, gazing at him or out through the window of the room in which he worked, listening to him with her wonderful, expressive eyes, following him about the estate. She was never a nuisance. His fondness for her was something he could not put satisfactorily into words.

He was afraid of Emmy's eyes the day

before his departure. He did not have the courage to say good-bye. So he merely said his piece and hurried away from her — just as if she were no more to him than a child for whom he felt only an indulgent affection.

He regretted his cowardice the following day. But he hated good-byes.

He got up early. He had been unable to sleep, his mind tossing with the excitement of what was ahead of him, his body eager to be on the way, his emotions torn between an impatience to be gone and a heaviness at leaving all that was familiar and dear behind him.

He got up early to take a last fond look at Bowden Abbey, his home since childhood. But not his, of course. It was true that he was heir to it all, that Luke and Anna's firstborn had been a daughter. But they would have sons, he was sure. He hoped they would. Being heir was not important to him, much as he loved Bowden. He wanted his own life. He wanted to build his own fortune and choose his own home and follow his own dreams.

But he loved Bowden fiercely now that he was leaving it and did not know when he would see it again. If ever. He strode away behind the house, watching the early-morning dew soak his top boots, feeling the chill wind whip at his cloak and his three-cornered hat. He did not look back until he stood on top of a rise of land, from which he had a panoramic view down over the abbey and past it to the lawns and trees of the park stretching far in all directions.

Home. And England. He was going to miss both.

He descended the western side of the hill and strode toward the trees a short distance away and through them to the falls, the part of the river that spilled sharply downward over steep rocks before resuming its wide loop about the front of the house.

He had spent many hours of the past year at the falls, seeking solitude and peace. Seeking purpose. Seeking himself, perhaps. A little over a year ago, he had been in London. But Luke had returned from a long residence in Paris, rescued him from deep debts and a wild and aimless life of pleasure and debauchery, and ordered him to return to Bowden until he had decided what he wished to do with his life.

He climbed to the flat rock that jutted over the falls and stood looking down at the water as it rushed and bubbled over the rocks below. Emmy had spent many hours here with him. He smiled. He had once told her that she was a very good listener. It was true, even though she could not hear a word he said to her. She listened with her eyes and she comforted with her smiles and with her warm little hand in his.

Dear, sweet Emmy. He was going to miss her perhaps more than any of them. There was a strange ache about his heart at the thought of her, his little fawn, like a piece of wild, unspoiled nature. She rarely wore hoops beneath her dresses and almost never wore caps. Indeed, she did not often even dress her hair, but let it fall, blond and loose and wavy to her waist. Whenever she could get away with doing so, she went barefoot. He did not know how he would have survived the year without Emmy to talk to, without her sympathy and her happiness to soothe his wounded feelings. He had felt despised and rejected by Luke, his beloved brother, and his own sense of guilt had not helped reconcile him to what he had considered at the time to be unwarranted tyranny.

He drew a deep breath and let it out slowly. It was time to return to the house. He would have breakfast while the carriage was brought around and his trunks were loaded, and then he would be on his way. He strode back through the trees in the direction of the house. He hoped everyone would honor the promise not to come down to see him on his way. He wished that he could just click his fingers and find himself on board ship, out of sight of English shores.

He wished there did not have to be the moment of leaving.

Ashley had told her yesterday that he was leaving today. It had not been unexpected. For weeks past he had been excited over the prospect of joining the East India Company and going to India. There had been a new light of purpose in his eye and a new spring in his step, and she knew that she had lost him. That he no longer needed her. Not that he ever avoided her or turned her away. Not that he stopped talking to her or smiling at her or allowing her to walk about the estate with him or to sit in his office while he worked. Not that he stopped holding her hand as they walked or stopped calling her his little fawn. Not that any of the affection had gone out of his manner.

But he was going away. He was going to a new life, one that he craved. One that he needed. She was glad for him. She was genuinely glad. Yes, she was. Oh, yes, she was.

Lady Emily Marlowe curled up on the

window seat in her room and gazed out on a gray and gloomy morning. She tried to draw peace from the sight of the trees and lawns. She tried to let them soothe her aching heart.

Her breaking heart.

She did not want to see him today. She would not be able to bear seeing him actually leave. It would hurt just too much.

And yet instead of peace, the only feeling that would come to her was panic. Had he left yet? She could not see the driveway or the carriage house from her room. Perhaps even now the carriage was before the doors. Perhaps even now he was stepping inside after hugging Anna and Luke — would they have taken Joy down too for him to kiss? He would be looking about him for her. He would be disappointed that she was not there. Would he believe she did not care? Perhaps he was driving away — now. At this very minute.

It could well be that he would be gone forever.

It was possible she would never see him again. Ever.

She leapt up suddenly and dashed into her dressing room. She shoved her feet into a pair of shoes and grabbed the first cloak that came to hand — her red one. She flung

14

it about her shoulders and rushed from the room and down the stairs. Was she in time? She felt that she would die if she was not.

Ashley. Oh, Ashley.

There was only one footman in the hall. And a mound of boxes and trunks by the doors, which stood open. There was no carriage outside.

Emily sagged with relief. She was not too late. Ashley must be at breakfast. She took a few steps in the direction of the breakfast parlor, and the footman hurried ahead of her to open the doors. But she stopped again. No. She could not after all see him face-to-face. She would shame herself. She would cry. She would make him uncomfortable and unhappy. And she would see the pity in Anna's and Luke's eyes.

She ran outside and down the steps onto the upper terrace and on to the formal gardens. She ran fleet-footed through three tiers of the gardens and then down the long sloping lawn to the two-arched stone bridge over the river. She ran across the bridge and among the old trees that lined and shaded the driveway for its full winding length to the stone gateposts and the village beyond. But she did not run all the way to the village. She stopped halfway down the drive, gasping for breath.

She stood with her back against the broad trunk of an old oak and waited. She would see his carriage as it passed. She would say her own private good-bye. She would not see him, she realized. Only his carriage. He would not see her. He would not know that she had come to say good-bye. But it was just as well. Fond as he was of her, to him she was just a type of younger sister to be indulged.

She could remember her first meeting with him, the day she arrived at Bowden Abbey to live with Anna, feeling strange and bewildered. She had instantly liked Luke, though she had learned later that her sister Agnes was terrified of his elegant appearance and formal manners. But he had been kind to her and he had spoken with her as if she were a real person who had ears that could hear. And incredibly she *had* understood most of what he said — he moved his lips decisively as he spoke and he kept his face full toward her. So many people forgot to do that. But she had felt uncomfortable during tea in the drawing room until Ashley had arrived late and demanded an introduction. And then he had bowed to her and smiled and spoken.

"As I live," he had said, "a beauty in the making. Your servant, madam." She had seen every word.

Tall, handsome, charming Ashley. He had gone to sit beside his sister, Doris, and had proceeded to converse with her after winking at Emily. He had taken her heart with him. It was as simple as that. She had adored him from that moment as she had adored no one else in her life, even Anna.

Ashley had a loving heart. He loved Luke, even though they had been close to estrangement for almost a year. He loved his mother and his sister, who were now in London, and he loved Anna and Joy. He loved her too. But no more intensely than he loved the others. She was Emmy, his little fawn. She was just a child to him. He did not know that she was a woman.

He would forget her in a month.

No, she did not believe that. There was nothing shallow in Ashley's love. He would remember her fondly — as he would remember the rest of his family.

She would hold him in her heart — deep in her heart — for the rest of her life. He was all of life to her. He was everything. Life would be empty without Ashley. Meaningless. She loved him with all the passion and all the intense fidelity of her fifteen-year-old heart. She did not love him as a child loves, but as a woman loves the companion of her soul.

Perhaps more intensely than most women loved. There was so little else except the sight of the world around her with which to fill her mind and her heart. She had somehow made a life of her own dreams before meeting Ashley. It had not always been easy. There had been frustrations, even tantrums when she was younger — when perhaps she had remembered enough of sound to be terrified by its absence. She had no conscious memories of sound since it had been shut off quite totally after the dangerous fever she had barely survived before her fourth birthday. Just some fleeting hints, yearnings. She did not know quite what they were. They always just eluded her grasp.

Ashley had become her dream. He had given her days meaning and her nights fond imaginings. She did not know what would be left to her when the dream was taken away — today, this morning.

She was beginning to think that she must have missed him after all. Perhaps he had gone ahead and his luggage was to follow later. She was almost numb with the cold. The wind whipped and bit at her. But finally she heard the carriage approach. Not that she could hear it in the accepted sense of the word — she often wondered what sound must have been like. But she felt the vibrations of an approaching carriage. She pressed herself back against the tree while grief hit her low in the stomach like a leaden weight. He was leaving forever and all she would see was Luke's carriage, which was taking him to London.

Panic grabbed her like a vise as the carriage came into sight, and despite herself she leaned slightly forward, desperate for one last glimpse of him.

She saw nothing except the carriage rolling on past. She moaned incoherently.

But then it slowed and came to a full stop. And the door nearest her was flung open from the inside.

There had been a feeling of mingled sadness and relief as the carriage lurched into motion, drew away from the house, and turned at the end of the cobbled terrace to take the sloping path beside the formal gardens and past the long lawn to the bridge.

He was on his way. Soon now he would be beyond the park, beyond the village, and leaving Bowden land behind him. He could look ahead with pleasure and excitement. Ashley set his head back against the comfortable upholstery of his brother's carriage and closed his eyes with a sigh of relief. It had been easier than he had expected.

But he did not keep his eyes closed. When he heard the rumble of the bridge beneath the carriage wheels, he opened them again for one backward glance at the house. He looked at the trees of the driveway and beyond. He could see a small group of deer grazing peacefully off to his left.

And a slight flutter of red.

It caught his eye when the carriage was already on a level with it and for a moment he could not identify it. But then he knew.

Emmy's cloak!

He leaned forward without thought and rapped sharply on the front panel for the coachman to stop. Almost before the carriage had come to a complete standstill, he flung open the door and jumped down onto the driveway. He looked back.

Ah. He had not been mistaken. And only now when it was too late did he realize that it might have been better if he had kept on going. He was not going to escape painful good-byes entirely after all.

She was standing against a tree trunk, holding it with both hands behind her as if she feared falling. Her face was all eyes and ashen paleness despite the slight color the wind had whipped into her cheeks. He walked toward her slowly and came to a stop only when he was a few inches in front of her. He felt guilty. He was off on an adventure, off to begin his adult life. All of the world, all of life were ahead of him. But Emmy, his close companion for almost a year, was to be left behind to — to what? What would life hold for a child who would grow into a woman who could not always understand others or communicate with them?

"Little fawn," he said softly. He clasped his arms together and shivered. *You must be cold,* he told her in one of their private signs — as if physical comfort was of any significance at this moment.

She made no reply. Her eyes gazed back into his — and filled with tears.

Ah, Emmy.

He leaned forward until his body pinned her against the tree. He wished — Lord, but he wished he had not noticed the flapping of her red cloak. What could he say to her in either words or gestures? He knew she was desperately unhappy, and her unhappiness clouded the exhilaration he had been feeling. He tilted back his head and closed his eyes. He clenched his hands tightly at his sides. He should have done this properly yesterday instead of just telling her cheerfully to be a good girl.

When he raised his head and opened his eyes, he found that she was looking at him. Her face was only inches from his own.

There were no words. And no gestures, except one, which was no part of their private language. There was only one way to say good-bye.

Her lips were cool, soft, and motionless beneath his. She had been chilled by her wait for his carriage. He warmed them with his own, softly and gently. He warmed them until they pushed back against his, and he realized in sudden shock that what they were sharing was undoubtedly a kiss.

A kiss, not of a brother and sister, but of a man and woman. Her body against his, he noticed now that he had been alerted, was slim, coltlike, soft with budding woman-hood.

He felt a flush of heat, a rush of tightness to his groin.

He lifted his head, feeling disoriented. She was Emmy. She was a child who needed comforting. She needed some sign of affection from him, something to wrap about herself until she had grown accustomed to his absence. She certainly did not need . . .

He framed her face with gentle hands, keeping one still while the other smoothed back her windblown hair.

"I will be back, little fawn," he said softly but distinctly, as he always spoke to her, noting that the tears had gone so that she was able to read his lips. "I will be back to teach you to read and write and to teach you a more complete language you can use — not just with me but with everyone. One day, Emmy. But by that time you will have found other friends to love, other friends who will love you and learn to find meaning in your silence. You must not mind my going too deeply, you know. I am a careless sort of fellow. There will be others far more worthy of your affection." He smiled gently at her.

She gazed at him in such a way that he was given the impression that her whole soul gazed out at him. Her right hand, clenched loosely into a fist, lifted and pulsed lightly over her heart. *I feel deeply. I am serious. My heart is full.* It was a gesture he used sometimes when talking, a sign that he was speaking the deep emotions of the heart. It was a gesture she had picked up from him and added to their all-too-inadequate language. He wondered if the gesture was involuntary at this particular moment.

"Ah," he said. "I know, Emmy. I know. I'll be back. I'll not forget you. I'll carry you here." He stepped back from her at last and touched a hand to his own heart.

And then he turned and strode back to the carriage. He vaulted inside, shut the door firmly behind him, and sat back as the vehicle lurched into motion. He blew out his breath from puffed cheeks.

Emmy. His dear little fawn. Sweet child.

He tried to convince himself that that was how he had seen her, how he had treated her right to the end. He had put his body against hers and his lips to hers in an almost instinctive gesture of comfort. Brother to sister, uncle to niece, man to child. But he was uncomfortably aware that his chosen method of giving comfort had been unwise and inappropriate to the occasion. He had discovered a body and a mouth that would very soon belong to a woman.

He did not want Emmy to be a woman — foolish thought. He wanted her always to be that wild and happy child who had brought him peace when his life had been in turmoil. He wanted to remember her as a child.

He was ashamed of himself for reacting to her for one startled moment as a male. He loved her. But not as a man loves a woman. The feelings he had for her were quite unique in his experience. He loved no one else as he loved Emmy. He wished — ah, he *wished* he had not sullied his feelings for her by reacting to her physical closeness as a man reacts to a woman. He would not remember her *so*. He would remember her standing on the rock above the falls, her skirts loose about her legs and short enough to reveal bare ankles and feet, her blond hair in a wild tangled mane down her back, her lips smiling, her lovely eyes telling him that, incredible as it might seem, she had found peace and harmony in her silent world.

The village was already behind him, he noticed. He was well on his way. His future had already begun. His thoughts turned ahead to India and his new life. What would it be like? How well would he meet the challenge? He could feel the exhilaration of youth and the thirst for adventure humming in his veins.

Emily stood where she was for many long minutes after she had felt the vibrations of the carriage moving off again. Her head was back against the tree trunk. Her eyes were closed. And then she pushed herself away from the tree and began to run recklessly, heedlessly, through the woods, over the bridge, in among the trees again, faster and faster, as if all the fiends of hell were at her heels.

She stopped only when she came to the falls and had bounded up the rocks beside them so that she could cast herself facedown on the flat rock that jutted out over the water. She buried her face on her arms and wept until her chest was sore from the weeping and there were neither tears nor energy left.

Behind her closed eyes she could see him as he had appeared when he vaulted out of the carriage, before she had been blinded by tears, tall and slender and handsome, his long dark hair tied back with a black silk ribbon and unpowdered as usual. He had been elegant in cloak, frock coat, waistcoat, and breeches. But elegant in his own almost careless manner — quite unlike Luke, with his Parisian splendor.

She lay on the cold rock beside the falls, spent and passive, for hours until at last she felt a hand on her shoulder. She had neither seen nor sensed anyone coming, but she was not surprised. She turned her head to see Luke sitting beside her, his eyes intent and sympathetic on her. She set her face back against her arms while his hand patted her shoulder.

There was nothing left to live for. Ashley had gone. Perhaps forever. Taking her heart, her very life with him.

And yet there was Anna, her eldest sister, who had been more of a mother to her than anyone else in her life. And there were her brother, Victor, the Earl of Royce — and Charlotte, her sister, though both lived far away with their spouses. And Agnes, Lady Severidge, the sister next in age to herself, who would be living close by at Wycherly Park after she returned from her wedding trip. There was Joy, her niece, on whom she doted. And there was Luke.

She loved Luke dearly. He loved Anna and Joy, and Anna loved him. Emily would love anyone who loved Anna. And he was Ashley's brother, though he was not as tall as Ashley, nor was his face as good-humored or quite as handsome — at least not to Emily's partial eyes. But he was Ashley's brother.

When he turned her finally and lifted her onto his lap and cradled her just as if she were a child, she cuddled against him, trying to draw comfort from him. He too must have hated seeing Ashley leave this morning. Ashley had used to say that Luke was cold and did not care for him. But she knew that it had never been true. Luke was

27

neither cold nor unloving.

Luke had made it possible for Ashley to find purpose in life. He had arranged for Ashley to join the East India Company. And he had given her a home here with Anna instead of forcing her to live with Victor and Constance, who felt awkward with her silence even though they loved her well enough.

She felt some warmth creep back into her body as Luke murmured comforting words to her. She could tell he was doing so by the vibrations of his chest.

She loved Luke. She loved her family. But it was going to be very difficult to live on. Ashley had found purpose in life. How was she to find purpose in hers? Could it have meaning without Ashley?

But she knew, emerging as she was now from the blackest depths of despair, that she must live on and that she must do so without him. For he would not come back. She knew that. He might return at some distant time in the future. But the Ashley she knew and loved would change. And she would change.

She *would* change. She would grow up into the womanhood that was already changing her both physically and emotionally. And she would learn to live without him. She would not mope and pine her life away for what could not be had.

Ashley could not be had. He loved her, but she was not in any way central to his very being. He would soon consign her to nothing more important than a fond memory. She knew that. She had no illusions about what she meant to him.

She would grow up without him. She would live without him. No one would ever know how much he would always be a part of her. She would live as if her heart had not broken from love for him — although it had.

She would always love him, but from this moment on she would take her life back and live it as fully as she had before she set eyes on Ashley a year ago — and all else had faded into insignificance. And it *had* been a full life, even if it had necessarily been an almost totally solitary one.

Even at its darkest moment, life was a precious gift.

1
1763

"Faith, child," Lady Sterne said, "but you are as lovely as all your sisters put together. With no offense meant to the two who are present." She laughed, clasped her hands to her bosom, and let her eyes sweep once more over the young lady who stood in the middle of the dressing room.

"Oh, but she really is," Lady Severidge said generously. "She really is *beautiful.*" At the age of six-and-twenty, seven years and two children after her marriage, Agnes was still pretty, though she had grown almost plump.

"Of course she is as lovely as all of us put together," Anna, Duchess of Harndon, said, smiling her bright, warm smile. "And lovelier even than that. Oh, Emmy, you look *wonderful.*" But in truth Anna herself looked equally lovely. Although she was well past her thirtieth year and had given birth to her fourth child only three months before, her face was still youthful and unlined, and her figure was again as trim as it had been before her marriage.

"You will be the belle of the ball tonight, as I live," Lady Sterne said. She was in the dressing room only partly by right of the fact that she was Anna's godmother. Although she was no blood relation, she had assumed the role of favored aunt to Anna's sisters as well as to Anna herself. After all, she always reminded them, when a woman had no daughters of her own, then she simply had to adopt a few. " 'Tis a pity you cannot dance, child. But no matter. Dancing merely makes a lady flush and sweat — and smell."

"Aunt Marjorie!" Agnes said, shocked.

Lady Emily Marlowe's eyes followed their lips for a while, but it was a weary business and she knew she had missed at least half of what had been said — as she always did in a conversation that involved more than one person. But no matter. She had caught the trend of the conversation, and it pleased her to for once be called beautiful — as other women were beautiful. She turned her head to steal another glance at herself in the pier glass of Anna's dressing room. She scarcely recognized herself. She was dressed in pale green, her favorite color, but all else was unfamiliar. Her petticoat, with its three deep frills, was held away from her legs by large hoops. Her open gown was trimmed with wide, ruched, gold-embroidered robings from bosom to hem. Her stomacher, low at the bosom, was heavily embroidered with the same gold thread. The three lace frills that edged the sleeves of her chemise flared at the elbows below the sleeves of the gown. Her shoes were gold. Her hair — ah, it was her hair that looked most unfamiliar.

Anna's maid had dressed her hair rather high in front, in the newest fashion, and curled and coiled at the back. In the glass Emily could see the frills of the frivolous lace cap that was pinned back there somewhere, its lace lappets floating down her back. Her hair was powdered white. It was the first time she had allowed anyone to do that to her.

Beneath the gown she could feel the unfamiliar and uncomfortable tightness of her stays.

At the grand age of two-and-twenty, she was about to attend her first real ball. Oh, she had occasionally — when Luke, Duke of Harndon, had insisted — attended local entertainments with her sister and brother-in-law, and there had sometimes been dancing, which she had sat and watched. And she had always been present at the occasional balls held here at Bowden Abbey, though usually she had watched unseen, looking down from the gallery. Dancing had always fascinated her.

She had always wanted, almost more than anything else in the world, to dance.

She could not dance. She was totally deaf. She could not hear the music. Though sometimes she imagined that once upon a time she must have heard it. She could not remember music — or any sounds at all — but there was a feeling, an inner conviction that music must be more beautiful, more soul-lovely than almost anything she had ever seen with her eyes.

Tonight she was to attend a ball, and everyone was behaving as if the whole occasion were in her honor. Almost as if this were her come-out. In reality the ball was in honor of Anna. There was always a ball at Bowden a few months after Anna's confinements, following the christening of the baby. There had been balls after Joy's birth seven years ago, and after George's and James's more recently. Now there was to be this one, following Harry's birth. He needed to demonstrate to his neighbors, Emily had once seen Luke say as he bent over Anna's hand and kissed her fingers, that his duchess was just as beautiful now as she had been three months before, nine months swollen with child.

"Lud," Lady Sterne said now, taking Emily's hands in her own and bringing both her eyes and her mind back from the glass, "but you have not heard a word we have said, child. I vow your head has been turned by your own beauty."

Emily blushed. She wished Aunt Marjorie would speak more slowly.

"Luke will approve, Emmy," Anna said with her warm smile, cupping Emily's chin with one gentle hand and turning her head so that she would see the words.

That would be no small accomplishment. Although Luke loved her unconditionally, Emily knew, he also did not always approve of her. He paid her the compliment of treating her as if she had no handicap. He often pushed her into doing things she had no wish to do, assuring her briskly that she could do anything in the world she set her mind to doing, even if she must do it silently. He was unlike Anna in that way, and the two of them sometimes exchanged hot words over her. Anna felt that her sister should be allowed to live her life in her own way, even if doing so made her unsociable and totally unconventional. The implication, loving though it was, was that Emily could never be quite as other women were. Luke was more capable of bullying.

There had been the time when she was fifteen, for example, and he had decided that it was time she learned to read and write. And she had learned too — slowly, painfully, sometimes rebelliously, with Luke himself as her patient but implacable teacher. After the first week, he had banished Anna from the schoolroom and had never allowed her back in. Enough of foolish tears, he had told her. Emily had learned in order to prove something to him — and more important, to herself. She had had everything to prove to herself at that painful stage of her life.

She had proved that she could learn, as other girls could. But she had learned the severe limits to her world. Books revealed to her universes of experience and thought she had never suspected and would never properly understand. She *was* different — very different. On the other hand, there was in her intense relationship with the world close at hand something unique, she believed.

Luke's approval, Emily thought now, smiling back at her eldest sister, was worth having. Sometimes she almost hated him, but always she loved him. He had been both father and brother to her during the almost eight years since she had come to live at Bowden.

"And Lord Powell will be *enchanted*," Agnes said. "Oh, Emmy, he is such a very distinguished-looking gentleman. And he seems genuinely not to mind the fact of your affliction."

Lord Powell liked to talk. He rather enjoyed the novelty of having a silent listener, Emily suspected. But indeed he was rather handsome and his manners were polished and charming. It was hardly a surprise, of course. Luke had chosen all of her suitors with meticulous care. All four of them had been eligible in every possible way. She had rejected the first three without making any effort whatsoever to become acquainted with them — or so Luke had claimed. He had regarded her with pursed lips and a look of mingled exasperation and amusement in his eyes after each had left.

"Emily," he had said on one of those occasions, "if you would merely cultivate a different image while you are being courted, my dear. If you would only *not* do your best to appear before the flower of male, unmarried society as the witch of the woods."

It was unfair, as she would have told him

if she had had his advantage of a voice. She might have written it, but she never enjoyed holding such awkward conversations. It was unfair, because it was *she* who had rejected them, not they who had taken fright and left her. Besides, she did not look like a witch. But it did not matter.

And now Lord Powell was here, paying court to her. He had been here for five whole days. Luke had decided to invite him while other visitors were here for Harry's christening and for the ball that would follow it. Perhaps, he had reasoned — Emily was well acquainted with his mind — the formality of the occasion would force his sister-in-law to stay in company and to behave in a more conventional manner than was usual with her.

And she had stayed in company and behaved herself and worn stays and hoops and shoes and curls and caps — though nothing as elaborate as tonight, it was true. But not just because of the house guests and the christening.

This time she had decided to allow herself to be courted.

"I vow 'twould be strange indeed if he did not come to the point tonight," Lady Sterne said. "He will make you his offer, child, and Harndon will make the announcement before the night is over. But mercy on me, I almost forgot that Victor is here. 'Twill be Victor who will make the announcement — mark my words."

Victor, the Earl of Royce, was Emily's brother. He was here for the christening with Constance, his wife, and their child. So was Charlotte, Emily's other sister, with the Reverend Jeremiah Hornsby, her husband, and their three children. Charlotte was in the nursery now, nursing the newest baby before attending the ball.

"Will you say yes, Emmy?" Agnes looked eagerly at her. "William says that Lord Powell has spoken privately with both Victor and his grace. It can mean only one thing. How splendid 'twill be to have a wedding in the family again. But would it be here or at Elm Court? Victor will want it at Elm Court, I do declare. How provoking of him. *Will* you say yes?"

There was a feeling of breathlessness and panic at seeing on the lips of her sister and Lady Sterne what she had really known already in her own heart. Lord Powell had come to court her — Luke had arranged it all on a visit to London. He had walked with her and sat with her and talked with her and had seemed pleased with her. She had not discouraged his attentions. Tonight there was to be a grand ball. And she had been fully aware of the private meeting this afternoon involving Lord Powell, Victor, and Luke. Everyone had been aware of it.

Tonight in all probability she was going to be called upon to make her final decision. Not that there was any decision still to be made. She had already decided to have him. She was going to be Lady Powell. She was going to marry and have a home of her own where she would be dependent upon no one. She was going to have children of her own. She was going to have a warm, cuddly baby like Harry to hold, but he would be all her own.

She was going to change — again. She was going to be more than just half respectable. She was going to be entirely so. Anna and Luke and all her other relatives were going to be proud of her.

But Anna was hugging her suddenly, as far as the combined widths of their hoops would allow. She let Emily see her lips before she spoke. "You are frightening her," she said. "Emmy does not have to do anything she does not want to do. She is different, but very special. She belongs here. We love her. You must marry no one just because you think you ought, Emmy. You may stay here forever. I hope you *will* stay here. How would I live without you?"

Very well, Emily thought, watching her sister blink back bright tears. Anna had Luke, whom she loved dearly and who loved her with an equal intensity, and she had her four children, on whom they both doted. Emily had — no one. She belonged nowhere. It was true that her brother and sisters issued frequent invitations for her to come and stay and always urged her to remain indefinitely. And it was true that even Luke had explained to her — it was just before the appearance of the first suitor — that Bowden was her home as much as it was his and Anna's and their children's, that he was thinking of her lasting happiness, but only she could know where that happiness lay.

"You must never feel that I am urging marriage on you because I wish to be rid of you," he had said, looking at her with keen eyes. "Even though your sister, my wife, has accused me of just that." He had thrown a stern look at Anna, who had protested the introduction of a suitor. "I will present you with marriage possibilities, my dear, because I feel it is my duty to do so. You will decide if you want marriage and all it can bring with it or if you would prefer to remain with us here, as much a member of our family as

Joy or George or James. Have I made myself clear, Emily? Madam?"

He had made both her and Anna reply.

"But Lord Powell is very handsome," Agnes said now. "I do not know how you could resist him, Emmy. I could not if I were still young and unmarried and he paid me court, I declare." She smiled kindly. But Agnes, who had had choices, had married the very plain and portly William, Lord Severidge, for love and had long ago settled into dull domestic felicity with him.

"And Lud," Lady Sterne said, clapping her hands, "if we stand here for much longer, admiring the child and anticipating her betrothal, the ball will be over and Lord Powell will have gone home. And no one will have seen Emily in all her finery."

"Come, Emmy." Anna smiled and took her by the hand. "Tonight you will stand in the receiving line with Luke and me. And my nose will be severely out of joint because everyone will be looking at you and will not notice me at all."

"Pshaw!" Lady Sterne said as she strode to the door to lead the way downstairs to the ballroom. "Harndon has eyes for no one but you, child. He never has had since he first laid 'em on you at just another such ball."

Anna laughed as she slipped her arm through Emily's, and Emily could see the happiness sparkling in her eyes. Emily herself fought bewilderment. There had been so much talk, most of which she had missed, though she had determinedly kept turning her head from one speaker to another, trying to concentrate. She often noticed the fact that other people did not find conversation wearying and did not seem to share her all-too-frequent urges to be alone and undistracted — it was just one more thing that set her apart . . .

She drew a few deep, steadying breaths. This evening was so far beyond anything in her past experience that her mind could contemplate it only as a complete and rather terrifying blank. She was dressed as formally and with as much glittering splendor as Anna. She was going to attend a full-scale ball. She was to stand in the receiving line, smiling and curtsying to all of Luke's guests. And she was to receive the continued attentions of Lord Powell and possibly — probably! — his marriage proposal too. She was going to accept.

By the time she came back upstairs in several hours' time, much would have changed in her life. Everything would have changed. She would be betrothed. As good as married.

There was something resembling panic in the thought.

Ashley. Ah, Ashley.

He had forgotten just how cold England was. He shivered and drew his cloak more closely around him. He sat in a darkened carriage, looking out on darkness — though the landscape was not pitch-black, it was true. There were moonlight and starlight to illuminate the way. Although the coachman had been reluctant, he had agreed to continue the journey after dark. The man had even commented on what a pleasant warm evening it was for late April.

Warm! He shivered again. He had had time to get used to the coldness during the long voyage home from India, of course, but somehow he had expected that he would be warm again once he reached land.

Perhaps, he thought, setting his head back against the cushions, he would never be warm again.

And yet Lord Ashley Kendrick still clung to the notion that there was warmth to be had. At Bowden. If he could but get there. For months he had been living for the moment that was now only an hour away, if that long. He must be almost on Bowden land already, he reasoned. The thought of Bowden had sustained him through all the months of his voyage, through calms and storms, through the sleepless nights.

Luke, he thought. If only he could reach his brother. Luke was a pillar of strength. And Anna. Sweet, warm Anna. And their children, three now. Joy would be seven, George five, and James three. Luke had been almost apologetic in his letter announcing the arrival of George, Marquess of Craydon, his heir to the dukedom. Ashley had been delighted, and even more so when he had read of the birth of James two years later. Luke was secure in his line. There could never be any question now of Ashley's breathing down his neck.

He longed for Bowden and for Luke and Anna. Almost as if they could make all right for him. Almost as if he were not a man capable of ordering his own life and handling his own emotions and purging his own guilt. Almost as if there were warmth to be had. And peace.

Ashley rolled his head on the cushions as if to find a comfortable position for sleep. But he soon opened his eyes and stared out onto darkness. And inward into deeper darkness.

Peace! He had had the strange notion that

it was to be found at Bowden. And only there. Now that he was approaching it — yes, he was sure now they were on Bowden land; they would pass through the village very soon — he stared at the truth. There was no peace to be had anywhere. Not even here. Why had he thought there was? What was it about Bowden that always brought with it the illusory idea of peace? As if it were a place unlike any other on earth. A place of escape, a refuge, a home, a belonging.

What was it about Bowden?

He had come back from India with the desperate idea that if he could but reach home all would be well again. Yet now, even before he had quite reached the house — the carriage was passing along the village street and slowing to make the turn between the massive stone gateposts onto the winding driveway through the park — he knew that he had deceived himself.

There was no home for him. No end to his journey. No end of the rainbow.

Even so he found himself leaning forward in his seat, eager for his first glimpse of the house as the carriage emerged from the trees to cross the bridge at the bottom of the long sloping lawn that led upward to the terraced formal gardens and the upper cobbled terrace and the house beyond.

But he sat back abruptly as the wheels of the carriage rumbled over the stone bridge.

Deuce take it, but they were entertaining. The house was lit up by what had to be a thousand candles. There were carriages outside the carriage house and stables.

Damnation, but what rotten bad fortune.

He should have stayed in London for a few days, he thought. He should have sent word ahead of him. Zounds, but they did not even know he had left India. They did not even know . . .

He set his head back against the cushions again and closed his eyes once more.

No, they did not even know.

"Well, my dear," the Duke of Harndon said to his wife, their first duties in the receiving line with his mother and Emily at an end, their secondary duty of leading off the opening set of country dances about to begin, "you may as usual have the satisfaction of knowing yourself by far the loveliest lady at the ball. 'Tis almost shameful with Harry in the nursery for only three months and you already — ah, nine-and-twenty, is it?"

"For the fourth year in succession," she said, laughing at him. "Luke, you have been shopping in Paris again. Your coat is such a splendid dark shade of blue, and there is so much embroidery on your waistcoat that you put my gown to shame."

"Ah, but 'tis the woman inside the gown who dazzles the sight, madam," he said.

She laughed again. "I am glad you remembered your fan," she said. "It still scandalizes a few people."

He fanned her face with it. "My cosmetics I have abandoned with the greatest reluctance, my dear," he said, "in deference to country tastes. But a man must be allowed to retain some of his pride. Without a fan at a ball I would feel quite naked, by my life."

" 'Tis what comes of those ten years you spent in Paris," she said. "Luke, what will Emmy do?"

"Emily," he said, "is looking so fine that every other lady's face, except yours, is tinged with green. And as I told her earlier, if she dressed thus all the time, I would by now be beating back all of His Majesty's army and navy and the single portion of his civilian male subjects as well from my doors. Perhaps I should be thankful that she is more often the witch of the woods."

"Oh, Luke," she said reproachfully.

"If you must quarrel with me, madam," he said, "let it be later. Much later, in your bedchamber. But I will not play fair, I would warn you."

"Will she have him?" There was acute anxiety in her voice.

"She would be a fool if she did not," he said. "Powell has everything to recommend him to a bride below the rank of princess, I believe — looks, breeding, wealth, mildness of manners. And he is remarkably eager to bring the matter to a point. There are Emily's dowry and her connections to attract him, as well as his openly expressed determination to please his mother and do his duty by taking a wife and setting up his nursery. I believe too he is somewhat captivated by the prospect of a wife who will not prattle. There is the small question of love, of course, and experience has demonstrated to me that in reality it is no small matter at all. But I believe we can trust your sister to order her own destiny, my dear. There is nothing abject about Emily. One can only hope that Powell does not see her as someone who will be passive and biddable, poor man. The musicians and all our guests await my signal to start the ball. Shall I oblige them or would you prefer to indulge in a fit of the vapors?"

"No one else will understand Emmy as you and I do," she said. "What if he does not like her when he learns more about her? As you say —"

" 'Tis what marriage is all about, madam," he said. "Have you not realized it? 'Tis about discovering unknown facets of the character and experience and tastes of one's spouse and learning to adjust one's life accordingly. 'Tis learning to hope that one's spouse is doing the same thing. 'Tis something only the two persons concerned can deal with. Let us dance." He looked toward the leader of the orchestra, raised his eyebrows, and lifted one finger.

The music began.

"Egad," Theodore, Lord Quinn, Luke's maternal uncle, said to Lady Sterne, his longtime friend and lover, "but the young gels grow lovelier with every passing year. As do the mature ones. That is a fine new hairdo, I warrant you, Marj, m'dear. Takes ten years off your age."

"Mercy on me," she said, "but that would make me more than ten years too young for you, Theo."

He threw back his head and laughed heartily before speaking again. "So will she have him?" he asked.

The two of them were sitting rather than dancing the opening set, which they had agreed was somewhat too lively for their aging bones. They looked across the ballroom to where Lord Powell was seated on a sofa beside Emily, talking to her despite the loudness of the music and conversation.

"Do they not look splendid together?" she asked. "And her affliction really does not signify, Theo. The dear man likes to talk, and Emily is well able to listen with her eyes. I had no notion that she would dress up so fine, though she has looked well for the past number of days, I declare."

"Zounds," Lord Quinn said, "but it would be hard, Marj, to be tied to a woman who could not answer one back. One hopes that is not her chief attraction to the man. One has the notion that there is more to little Emily than receptive silence. But how is one to know what she is saying with those big eyes of hers?"

"My dear Anna has always worried about her," Lady Sterne said, her eyes softening on the sight of her goddaughter dancing opposite her duke, her face smiling and animated. "She has always taken the full burden of her family on her own shoulders even though Royce is the head of the family. 'Twill be good for her to know that the last of her sisters is well settled. Anna can be finally and fully happy."

Lord Quinn patted her hand, though he did not leave his own on hers. They were ever discreet in public. "And so can you, Marj," he said. "Anna is like the daughter you never had. You love her to distraction. I might almost feel jealous."

"But you do not." She turned her head to smile at him.

"But I do not," he agreed. "I am fond of the gel m'self, Marj, and of Luke too. He has always been my favorite nephy, though one is not supposed to have favorites."

"Ah, look at them," she said, returning her attention to Emily and Lord Powell across the room. "As I live, Theo, she is smiling at him and he is dazzled enough to move back six inches. 'Tis just like my Anna's smile, I vow. If only they can be one half as happy as Anna and Harndon."

Lord Quinn patted her hand again. "Leave love to take its course," he said. "By suppertime he will have got up the courage to speak and she will have given him her answer with those eyes of hers and the announcement will have been made. Then our dear Anna will be happy, and you too. And hark ye, Marj, m'dear: 'Tis your happiness that concerns me more than all else."

She smiled at him once more.

2

Emily sat beside Lord Powell on the sofa and longed to dance. But no one had ever asked her to join a set, and she supposed that no one ever would. People had a strange notion of deafness. They assumed that because one could not hear, one could not really see either. More important, they did not seem to notice for themselves how much of sound came in vibrations that could be felt. Sound was not just a thing of the ears. It affected the whole body.

She could feel the rhythm of the dance. And she knew every step of every dance. She had watched with attentive longing for many years.

Lord Powell was telling her about his mother and about his younger brothers and sisters — a sure sign, she supposed, that he was moving closer to a declaration. There was a whole brood of them — his own word. Three of his six sisters were married, as was one of his three brothers. He had two nieces and a nephew already. He considered family, commitment to one's home and one's domestic duties, important. He had noticed how well Lady Emily was loved by her own nephews and nieces and how she loved to play with them. Children, he had observed, never needed words when they were able to see affection at work. And children almost never returned love that expressed itself only in words.

It was a compliment to the way she handled her deafness, Emily supposed. She smiled. Indeed, she had not stopped smiling since leaving Anna's dressing room.

There was a great deal to smile about, though she felt the strain of having to watch a man's lips when she longed to gaze about her, and even so missed many of the details about his family that he tried to share.

His eyebrows were dark and thick. A little too heavy for perfection of looks, perhaps, but they were the only small defect to an otherwise handsome appearance. His nose was well shaped if a little prominent. His eyes were dark and compelling. His hair, she supposed, was dark. She had not seen him without his carefully powdered wig, but thought his own hair must be short beneath. His teeth were good and only a little crooked — and not unattractively so.

She had noticed several of the other young ladies present gazing at him admiringly and glancing at her in envy. He was a handsome man, moderately tall and well formed. He dressed elegantly. Tonight he wore dark brown and gold.

"I am engaged for the second set with her grace," he said, leaning toward her slightly as if to be heard above the noise that Emily could not hear, "and for the third with Lady Severidge. I have not engaged the supper dance with anyone, Lady Emily. Will you sit with me for that half hour? Perhaps after we have eaten, you will allow me to send a maid for your cloak and step out onto the terrace with me?"

Emily opened her fan. The room suddenly felt suffocatingly hot. She kept her eyes on Lord Powell's lips. They were rather full lips, well shaped. He had spoken slowly and precisely, she guessed, so that she would know the final request was important to him.

"I observed earlier," he said, almost as if he felt his invitation needed explanation, "that it is a fine spring evening."

She nodded and smiled.

"Perhaps," he said, "you will allow me to speak on a matter of some importance?

When we are on the terrace, that is."

She held her smile and nodded again.

"Splendid," he said, and looked enormously relieved as he rushed on with an account of his youngest sister's tyranny over her governess in the schoolroom. Emily could not understand most of what he said. She longed suddenly and illogically to be alone. Anywhere — alone. "I believe she would like you, Lady Emily. I believe you will — *would* like her."

She liked *him,* Emily decided. Not just because she had determined to like him, but because he was a pleasant and earnest young man. She just wished he did not talk so much. Was silence so unnatural to those who could hear that they felt obliged to fill it without ceasing? But how could she dislike any man who loved his mother and his brothers and his sisters? And who was willing to accept a wife who was handicapped — though she did wonder why. She wished she could ask him exactly why he wished to marry her. Did he think her beautiful? Did he like the fact that she was Victor's sister, Luke's sister-in-law? Did the mystery of her character intrigue him?

She looked down briefly at his hands. They were blunt-fingered, capable-looking hands. She imagined them touching her, touching her body — beneath her clothes. She imagined his mouth against hers, his body. Imagination forsook her after that. She was not really quite sure . . .

She looked up to find him telling her more about his sister — he had demanded that she apologize to the governess. He seemed to believe that because she could read lips she could understand everything he said. Would he be disappointed when he learned that she did not?

She had often wondered about physical love. Was it something that added a dimension to life? Or was it an intrusion, the ultimate invasion of privacy? By both necessity and inclination she had always been an excessively private person. She knew enough to understand that a husband would come right inside her body.

This man. Lord Powell. She did not yet know his first name, she realized.

On their wedding night she would have to allow him inside herself. Only so could she be a wife. Only so could she have the babies she wanted. Would it be wonderful, magical? Or would it be demeaning?

She knew sometimes during breakfast that Anna and Luke had loved the night before. They would be horrified if they knew that she knew, but she did. Perhaps it was the absence of one of her five senses that had sharpened the others. Certainly it was nothing very obvious. Just something about the softened look in Anna's eyes, something in the slight droop of Luke's eyelids. Or perhaps not anything even as overt as that. But whatever it was, it was something that told Emily that what they shared was more wonderful than anything she could yet imagine.

Perhaps she would know soon. Or perhaps she would be disappointed. Would it make all the difference, she wondered, that she did not love him, though she liked and respected him?

But there were other things to imagine. This man would become as familiar to her as her own image in the glass. He would be her companion for the rest of her life. Her friend, perhaps. She would live in his home. It would become hers, and his family would be hers. She would learn to run his household. Would she be able to do it? She had watched Anna run Bowden Abbey. She would have to write things down, she supposed. She would visit his tenants and his neighbors. She would not be able to allow herself to be daunted by the fact that she could not speak to any of them or even understand all that was spoken. Indeed, it was the exhilaration of the challenge that was one of the main inducements to her accepting the offer that was about to be made.

She would become like Anna. She would have a marriage like Anna's. Or was she deluding herself? Was such a thing possible for her? But she would have a chance at happiness. At last. After so long. And she would be happy. She had learned through hard experience that the will was a powerful thing. She would will herself to be happy, and she would be.

"The set has ended," Lord Powell was saying, bent slightly toward her again. "More is the pity, I vow. I shall dance each set until the supper dance, Lady Emily, but I shall look in envy at each gentleman who occupies this sofa with you."

It was the closest he had come to a declaration of ardor, though Emily, sensitive to the language of the body, guessed that he spoke what he thought she expected him to say. She smiled at him.

But something was wrong. The music had stopped, of course. She had felt that even before Lord Powell had mentioned it. There was something else. She felt something almost like panic and looked over her shoulder to the doorway.

A man was standing there. No one else

appeared to have noticed him yet. He was wearing a long dark cloak and was only just removing a three-cornered hat even though he must have entered the house downstairs and passed numerous footmen before climbing the two flights of stairs to the ballroom. He was tall and thin. Beneath his dark unpowdered hair, which was neatly curled at the sides and bagged in black silk behind, his face was thin and pale. Pale to the point of being haggard. His expression was dark, morose.

She did not recognize him with her eyes. Only with her heart. Her heart lurched and left pulses beating erratically in her throat and in her temples. It left her breathless and gasping for air. She got to her feet and turned and stood still, watching.

Lord Powell, everyone, everything, no longer existed.

Only Ashley.

Ashley was home.

It had been his intention as his carriage approached the house to avoid whatever entertainment was proceeding within — by the number of lights and carriages, it appeared that it must be nothing less than a ball. It had been his intention to have himself shown to a room — his old one, it was to be hoped — and to remain there until the morning. It certainly had not been his intention to make a grand, theatrical entrance.

But Cotes, his brother's butler, was in the hall when he entered it, apparently giving some instructions to one of the footmen standing there. And Cotes had looked at first stiff with suspicion of the stranger who had arrived apparently ill-dressed for the occasion, then shocked as he recognized the new arrival, and then his usual dignified, impassive self. And Cotes informed him, when he asked, that there was indeed a grand ball in progress and that the occasion was the christening of his grace's new son, Lord Harry Kendrick.

Ah, a new child. Another son. Ashley bowed his head and closed his eyes and swayed on his feet. One of the footmen had taken a step toward him, arm outstretched, by the time he opened his eyes. He held up a staying hand.

But he was close. So very close. Was he now to go to his room and shut himself inside and postpone everything until the morning?

"They are in the ballroom?" he asked.

"Yes, my lord," Cotes said. "If your lord-ship would step into the salon, I shall fetch his grace myself."

But Ashley turned as if he had not heard and made his way to the archway that led to the grand staircase. He would wait in no salon. He would retire to no bedchamber. Luke was close.

"My lord?" Cotes sounded surprised, even perhaps a trifle alarmed.

It was indeed a grand ball, considering the fact that it was taking place in the country, where most of the guests must have had to travel a long distance. The ballroom seemed filled with light and noise and laughter, with color and movement. Ashley stood in the doorway, unaware of the inappropriateness of his appearance, of his cloak and travel-creased clothes and top boots. He removed his hat, more from instinct than conscious thought. His eyes scanned the throng of people. He was unaware that a few of them were already beginning to look at him curiously. He was looking for only one person.

And then he saw him. A set of dances had just concluded, and he was bowing over the hand of his partner and raising it to his lips. Luke, looking as richly splendid and fashionable and elegant as he had looked on his return from Paris eight years ago. Luke, looking familiar and solid and dependable. Ashley stood very still.

Luke raised his head and looked toward the doorway. And raised his eyebrows in an unconsciously haughty expression characteristic of him. Ashley watched the expression become fixed and frozen on his face. Then Luke took a step toward him, stopped, frowned slightly, and came hurrying across the ballroom. He kept on coming, opening his arms when he was near, then closing them hard, like iron bands, about his brother. Ashley returned the embrace and closed his eyes very tightly.

"Good God!" Luke said after what felt to Ashley like minutes but was probably only seconds. "Dear Lord God. Ash!" His voice sounded dazed, shaken.

"Yes." Ashley swallowed. He did not want to open his eyes.

But Luke ended the embrace and took a step back. He set his hands on Ashley's shoulders. "By God, Ash, it really is you. What the devil?" He patted his brother's shoulders as if to assure himself of the reality of his presence. "What the bloody devil?" Clearly he had forgotten his surroundings.

Ashley, facing into the ballroom, had become suddenly aware of them. Noise, or rather the surprising lack of noise considering the occasion and the largeness of the gathering, assaulted his ears. He was aware of people, of the very public nature of this reunion. He was aware of Anna, who came hurrying up behind Luke, looking scarcely a day older than when he had left and every bit as lovely, looking as sweet and as sunny as she had ever looked.

"Ashley," she said, and Luke stood aside and she was in his arms. "Oh, Ashley, my dear, you are home."

And then his mother was there, looking her usual composed, dignified self even though her eyes were wide with surprise. He had recovered some of his control and bowed formally over her hands and kissed her cheeks.

"Madam," he said, "you are looking well."

And then a lady in pink satin and silver lace was hurtling across the room and throwing herself into his arms, and he closed his eyes again briefly as he hugged his sister to himself.

"Ashley." She said his name over and over again. "Oh, Ashley, you wretch. You have not written to any of us for over a year, so that we have been almost beside ourselves with worry. And all the time you have been coming home. How could you!"

Doris, Lady Weims, looked a vibrant and

lovely woman rather than the pretty, sometimes petulant girl she had been when he left. She had married Andrew, the Earl of Weims, five years ago. They had two children.

But Luke was recovering control of both himself and the situation. He turned to face his guests in the ballroom and raised his arms, though the gesture was unnecessary. The attention of almost everyone was already focused upon the drama playing itself out in the doorway.

"My apologies for the delay in the festivities," he said. "As you can see, Lord Ashley Kendrick has arrived home from India unexpectedly. You will pardon my family group for withdrawing for a few minutes? The music will resume as soon as the sets have formed." He nodded to the leader of the orchestra.

"Ashley." Anna had taken his arm and was leading him away from the ballroom. "Where have you left Lady Ashley — Alice? And Thomas? Are they downstairs? Or did you have Cotes or Mrs. Wynn show them to a room?"

He was aware of his family about him. A stranger had joined Doris — presumably Weims. They were all beaming with happiness. They were in the middle of celebrating a new baby's christening with a ball. And he was tired. Bone weary. Soul weary.

"My wife and son are at a hotel in London," he said. "They were exhausted after the long voyage. I came on alone. I wanted to come home."

He was desperately tired. Perhaps tomorrow there would be peace. Not tonight. There was too much turmoil tonight.

Perhaps tomorrow.

A hand touched her elbow and she came back from a long way away to find herself standing in the ballroom at Bowden Abbey. Lord Powell was smiling at her and gesturing to the sofa beside her. She sat.

He stood looking down at her, his hands clasped at his back. The hilt of his dress sword, she noticed, was studded with rubies. They did not match his coat. But perhaps, unlike Luke, he did not have a sword to match each outfit. Or perhaps, unlike Luke, he was not so meticulous about such matters.

He bent forward and waited for her eyes to focus on his lips. "Her grace will not now be here to dance with me," he said. "I may spend the time sitting here talking with you, Lady Emily."

She nodded, not quite sure to what she

was agreeing.

"If 'tis your wish," he said. "If you do not consider it improper. Or an imposition. If you have not promised to spend the time with another gentleman."

She shook her head and he seated himself beside her again. He smiled. He looked very pleased with himself. She wished he would go away. She wished she could be alone. Lips moved wherever she looked but she could understand nothing. She was like an alien in an alien country.

She did not want Ashley to come home. Not now. Not ever.

"Lord Ashley Kendrick?" Lord Powell was saying. "From India? He is his grace's brother, is he not?"

She nodded. Yes, Ashley. Yes. But she did not want it to be Ashley.

"What a happy chance," Lord Powell said, "that he has arrived tonight of all nights. They all seem exceedingly happy."

She nodded. She wanted simply to close her eyes, to shut out everything.

"I have observed," he said, "that this is a close and loving family, Lady Emily. You must consider yourself fortunate to be a part of it."

Yes. Yes, Ashley was home.

Lord Powell leaned a little closer. "I am

reminded of my own family," he said. "You will find — you *would* find a similar closeness with us, Lady Emily."

She smiled, stretching the corners of her mouth upward with a conscious physical effort. He was speaking of his family again. She tried to concentrate, to remember what he had told her of its members. She tried to think as his lips continued to move. And she tried not to think.

She did not want Ashley to be home. She wanted to be able to look at this man and see in him her future husband and life's companion. She wanted to make a rational decision about her future. She wanted a husband and a home and a place of her own in society. She wanted babies. And perhaps beyond rationality, she wanted hope, the hope that an affection would grow, even love perhaps. She wanted to have control over her own destiny. She wanted the impossible — she wanted to be *normal.*

And she wanted the hope that her soul would be restored and healed and made whole again. So that she might take this man inside it.

She had to blink her eyes suddenly and saw when she could do so clearly again that he was looking at her with concern.

"Yes, you would, on my life," he said, tak-

68

ing one of her hands in both of his. "And they would be willing to take you into their midst, Lady Emily. I know it. They love me, and they will love you. That is, they *would* love you if . . ."

She wondered if she would have tumbled into love with him during the past week if her heart had been whole, if her soul had not been shattered long ago. She rather thought she might have. But a heart and soul could not be mended by the power of the will, she had discovered over seven years. And so she had accepted reality and moved on. She watched Lord Powell raise her hand to his lips and hold it there for a few moments. She was aware that other people must be observing them — probably with indulgence — and that he knew it. She was aware too that the announcement of their betrothal must be a common expectation tonight.

And then, before the set was at an end, Anna was there and Lord Powell was scrambling to his feet and bowing. She smiled warmly at him and took the seat he had vacated. She took both of Emily's hands in hers.

"Ashley has come home," she said unnecessarily. "He took passage from India without sending us word. He did it quite impulsively, he said. He was homesick. He has left Lady Ashley and their son in London. Luke is beside himself with joy. 'Tis a wonderful surprise for him, Emmy."

Yes. There had always been a special bond between the brothers, even though they had been estranged for much of the year between Luke's return from Paris and Ashley's departure for India. Yes, Luke would be overjoyed.

But Anna's eyes were keen on hers, and Emily knew why she had returned to the ballroom before the rest of the family and had come to talk to her sister. Anna knew. So did Luke, though not a word had been spoken on the subject since that dreadful day when he had found her and comforted her at the falls.

"Luke plans to send our carriage for them tomorrow," Anna said. "I daresay he might even go himself to fetch them. 'Twill be good to meet Alice at last. And Thomas. The children will have yet another cousin with whom to play. Though Harry will doubtless sleep through it all. He seems content to sleep his life away, except at three o'clock each morning, when he thinks 'tis time for a leisurely meal and a play. His papa had a stern word with him about it just last night, but Harry merely yawned at him and blew bubbles and tried to pull his nose. Luke says he must learn greater respect." She laughed, but her eyes were still on Emily's and were still almost anxious.

Emily smiled. Anna was saying more than she usually did all at once to her sister. Anna was worried about her — about how she would behave, how she would feel.

"Lord Ashley Kendrick must be exceedingly weary," Lord Powell said. "But at the same time he must feel great pleasure at being back in the bosom of his family."

"Yes." Anna smiled warmly at him. "But he *is* weary. And so pale and thin that he looks almost emaciated. Traveling such a long distance by sea must be dreadful indeed. My husband has taken him to his room. Doubtless he will return to his guests soon. Ashley will want to sleep."

Emily had wanted to die when news came three years before that Ashley had married Alice Kersey, the daughter of Sir Alexander Kersey, his superior in the East India Company. She had literally wanted to die. She had not wanted to live any longer. There had been nothing left to live for. It had been frighteningly easy after four whole years to regress to the terrible self-pity and feeling of isolation she had felt on the day

71

of his departure.

She had dreamed during those four years. Of course, she had known the difference between dream and reality. Deep down she had known that Ashley had never loved her as she had loved him, that he would not come home to her, that there would never be a happily-ever-after with him. But it had been a sweet dream. It had sustained her through the pain and loneliness and emptiness she had felt deep within even while outwardly she set about living an active and fulfilling life. Her deepest, most private self might have lived on the dream for a lifetime, even if ten, twenty, fifty years had passed and he had not returned.

But the news of his marriage had shattered the dream beyond repair. And life without the dream had seemed insupportable to her. She simply could not live without it. She had wanted to die. She had had to begin all over again the lesson of self-reliance.

Soon afterward, Luke had presented her with her first suitor. Luke, she had realized, understood. He really did know her remarkably well. Better, perhaps, even than Anna. Luke had never offered her pity, except perhaps during that dreadful hour at the falls. Luke offered her solutions and then stepped back so that she could accept them or reject them as she chose.

Lord Powell had taken her hand again and was raising it to his lips once more. "I shall return for the supper set, Lady Emily," he said slowly. The dancing had stopped, she noticed, and the dancers were preparing for the third set. "I shall look forward to it."

"What a very pleasant young man," Anna said after he had left.

Emily smiled at her and nodded.

"And a very attentive young man," Anna said. "You could be happy with him, Emmy?"

Emily nodded.

Anna touched her arm. "You could love him, Emmy," she said. "Oh, my dear, marry him if you have any feelings for him at all. I have told you repeatedly that you do not have to marry anyone, that you can stay here for the rest of your life and be as welcome as my own children. Luke has told you the same thing. We both mean what we say. But, Emmy, what you will miss if you do not love and do not marry. The closeness and the contentment, the . . . Faith, but this is not the time or place. I want you to be happy. You know that. I want you to be happy as I am."

There was passion in Anna's face. She was

speaking with an earnestness that she would not normally have shown in such a public setting, and Emily had understood her even if she had not seen every word. Ashley had come home. But Ashley was married. He was a father. And during those moments when he had stood in the ballroom doorway, looking about him and then hugging Luke and Anna and the other members of his family, he had not once looked at her. Having greeted them all, he had been content. He had looked about no longer.

He had not looked for her.

Anna was afraid that Emily would forget reality.

She would not forget. Now that she had had a few minutes to recover herself, she would not forget again. She looked deliberately about the room until her eyes found Lord Powell leading Agnes out to join the third set. She smiled and knew that Anna saw both the direction of her eyes and her smile.

He was home. He was here at Bowden. He was upstairs, preparing for sleep.

He was thin and haggard. Exhausted from his long journey.

Tomorrow she would meet him again.

Ashley was home.

3

" 'Tis madness, by my life," Luke gave as his opinion as he sat in his brother's dressing room, one leg crossed elegantly over the other, his eyes watching the powder in a cloud above Ashley's head, then lowering to watch the valet gingerly remove the powdering gown Ashley had donned over a full-skirted evening coat of burgundy brocade.

Ashley grinned at him. " 'Tis not every day one arrives home after a seven-year absence," he said, "to be reunited with one's brother and sister and mother and to find a ball in progress celebrating the birth of another nephew. A third now between me and the dukedom, Luke. Well done."

Luke raised his eyebrows. " 'Tis in the nature of marriage," he said, "as you have discovered for yourself. One's brood tends to expand in number."

Ashley laughed as he stood and buckled his dress sword at his side and slipped his stockinged feet into heeled and buckled shoes. He was feeling rather wild and reckless. What was the point in going to bed, as his mother and Luke and Anna had urged him to do? He would not sleep anyway. He rarely slept. But the absence of sleep was worse when one lay alone in a darkened room. No, he would go down to the ballroom and dance.

"I shall look forward to meeting your sons and Doris's children tomorrow," he said. "And Joy. She was but a babe when I left."

"And is now a little girl who favors her mother in looks to such a degree," Luke said with a sigh, "that she has her papa wrapped very securely about her little finger and knows it. Wait until you have a daughter, Ash."

Ashley laughed gaily. "Lead on to the ballroom," he said. "One would hate to arrive too late to dance. I shall dance with all the prettiest young ladies. Are there any?"

Luke pursed his lips and looked keenly at him. "There are," he said.

"Then present me to the prettiest first," Ashley said, opening the door and bowing with mock courtliness as he grinned and gestured his brother to precede him. "Who is she?"

" 'Tis a matter of personal taste, Ash,"

76

Luke said. "For myself, I can never look past Anna. But 'tis an affliction that does not affect all men, I am glad to say. 'Twould not be good for any other man's health."

Ashley laughed again. "Anna is spoken for, then," he said. "I will have to settle for second best."

His tiredness was forgotten. Suddenly he was filled with energy. Suddenly he wanted to dance all night and all tomorrow too. He wanted noise and laughter and movement and flirtation. Above all, flirtation.

He was standing inside the doorway of the ballroom again a few minutes later, his brother at his side. A vigorous country dance was in progress. He resented the fact that he would have to wait for it to finish before he could dance himself. He felt drunk with exuberance and gaiety. He looked about him with interest. He saw the members of his own family, who looked surprised to see him all decked out for the ball, and then smiled at him. He saw a few familiar faces from the neighborhood. He saw Agnes, Anna's younger sister, who was dancing. She was Lady Severidge now, he remembered, of Wycherly Park close by. She had grown plump.

Then his eyes lit on a young lady who was sitting on a sofa some distance away, half turned away, though he had the impression that she had looked away from him the very moment his eyes moved in her direction. He smiled. He had noticed the same thing with a number of other people in the room. Doubtless he was the sensation of the hour.

"That one, egad," he said to Luke, indicating the young lady on the sofa. "The one sitting with — with Will Severidge, by thunder. He has grown more portly with age. Who is she? And pray do not devastate me by telling me she is married."

Luke did not answer, and Ashley swung his eyes to him and laughed.

"Zounds," he said, "but you will not keep the secret. Who is she? Present me to her, Luke. I mean to dance with her. Without delay. This particular set is ending, by my life."

"She is Emily," Luke said. " 'Twere better . . ."

Ashley did not hear what would be better. Emily. Emily. *Emmy?*

"Emmy?" His voice was almost a whisper. "She is Emmy? Little Emmy?"

"Yes," Luke said.

He stared at her blankly. She was totally unrecognizable. Though that was not the real reason he stared. She was the one person he had *not* thought about during his journey home. He had not really thought about her in years. And yet now he remembered all in a rush how very . . . *precious* she had once been to him. He had carried her in his heart for many long months after his departure, half with pleasure, half with heaviness, until the heaviness had outweighed the pleasure. He had missed her. He had wanted her. Not sexually — she was a child. Nonetheless he had needed her — her companionship, her acceptance, her devotion, her happiness, her peace. But he had despised his need for a child. And he had been uneasy with some guilt over it. He could no longer remember quite why he had felt guilty. But he had put her very effectively from his mind.

And then he had met and fallen in love with Alice. And had married her when he had found his feelings returned. It had been a love based on need — perhaps on both sides — just as his love for Emmy had been. But with Alice it had been reassuringly sexual in nature. She had been a woman and not a child. His lips tightened with memory for a moment.

But by God, how could he have all but forgotten Emmy? And not even given her a thought during the voyage home? And not thought of seeing her in Luke's ballroom? It was as if he had pushed her ruthlessly from his consciousness and slammed the door on her. He could no longer remember why he would have done so.

"Take me to her," he said even as he watched another man step up to her and take her hand in his. William Webb, Lord Severidge, got to his feet.

"We are expecting an announcement tonight," Luke said, "of her betrothal. To Powell, the man who is with her now. He has spoken with both Royce and me. She seems enamored of him."

"Does she, by Jove?" Ashley had not taken his eyes off her. In full profile she was stunningly beautiful. He still could not believe she was Emmy. Emmy, all grown up, a woman and not a child. "Take me to her."

He did not even notice his brother's reluctance. Or if he did, he did not care about it. He had come here to dance. To dance with the prettiest young lady in the room. And she was the prettiest, by Jove. Emmy. He would dance with her. He had forgotten her deafness.

She seemed to know he was coming. She stood and turned to watch him come. But Emmy, he remembered with a jolt of recognition, had always seemed to possess that extra sense. She had always seemed to know when he was approaching from behind her. Even though she could not hear. Ah yes, there was that. He recalled it with a shock of memory. Emmy could not hear. Or speak. Or communicate except with her eyes and certain gestures he had grown adept at interpreting. And had they not devised something resembling a language between the two of them? Zounds but he had forgotten so much.

"My dear," Luke said, "here is Ashley come home to us."

She was Emmy, right enough. Emmy masquerading as a grand lady and doing magnificently at it. But Emmy all the same. There were the eyes, large and expressive, leaving one with the impression that one could look through them straight into her soul. But she was a *woman*. He felt strangely sad.

"Emmy." He took her hand from her side. It was limp and icy cold. He smiled. "Hello, little fawn." He had forgotten his old name for her until he heard it coming from his own lips. And how inappropriate it seemed now. She was an elegant, fashionable, beautiful woman. Again he felt that flashing of sadness. The name had used to fit so well.

Her mouth quirked into the most fleeting of smiles. But she was pale and serious. He brought her hand to his lips.

"Tell me you are glad to see me," he said, almost instinctively speaking to her in the old way, mouthing his words carefully, speaking a little more slowly than he did with other people. "I have come all the way from India. It has been a weary journey. Tell me you are glad."

She stared mutely at him and there was nothing in her eyes that he would instinctively have recognized. Ah. She was not glad. Seven years had passed. He wished unreasonably that she of all people and places and things could have remained the same — a wild and lovely and happy child. What a selfish thought!

"May I present Lord Powell to you, Ash?" Luke was saying. "My brother, Lord Ashley Kendrick, Powell."

Ashley made his bow, as did Lord Powell, briskly, the annoyance unconcealed on his face. So this was to be Emmy's husband? And he was already possessive of her? Even jealous, perhaps? Ashley turned back to Emily with a grin.

"They tried to put me to bed," he said. "They tried to tell me I was tired. But I wanted to dance, Emmy. I am determined to do so. I promised to dance with the prettiest lady in the room. She is you. Come and dance with me." Her hand still lay in his. He covered it with his free hand. "You see? The sets are forming."

"This set is mine," Lord Powell said stiffly. "Lady Emily has agreed to sit with me."

"Besides, Ash," Luke said, "Emily cannot dance."

"Because she cannot hear?" Ashley grinned at her. "Is it true, Emmy? Does your deafness make it impossible for you to dance? Do you not know the steps? Can you not watch the other dancers? Do you not long to dance?"

Her eyes had taken on depth and he realized with some satisfaction that he could still read them, just as if seven years had not passed since he had last looked into them. Yes, of course she longed to dance. She always had. He knew it as surely as if she had put her feelings into words. Had no one else this evening seen the longing there? The longing to dance to the silent melody she could hear in her heart? And he was drunk with longing himself.

"Ashley." His brother's voice had taken on the firmness of authority. "Emily cannot hear the music. Besides, this set is promised to Lord Powell. Come, allow me to find you another partner."

But Ashley was gazing into Emily's eyes.

"Let Emmy choose," he said, smiling at her. "Which will it be, Emmy? Will you sit here, where I will wager you have sat all evening? Or will you dance with me? *Will* you dance with me?"

For several moments she merely stared. Her nod, when it came, was almost imperceptible. But they all saw it.

"Emily," Luke said, but she was looking at Ashley, not him. "Ash —" But Ashley took no notice of him. He was still smiling at Emily, a look of triumph and recklessness in his eyes.

Lord Powell bowed. "I shall return to take Lady Emily in to supper," he said.

"Come," Ashley said, squeezing the cold little hand that lay in his own. "We will dance, Emmy. We will prove to these unbelievers that a man who is weary through to the marrow of his bones and a woman who cannot hear music or anything else can dance without missing a step."

She walked beside him to take their places in a set. Emily had not grown taller since the age of fifteen, he noticed. She had been slightly above the average in height then, and slim and agile as a young colt. She had developed womanly curves since then, accentuated by the fact that she wore stays and hoops. But she had not really changed in any other way. Not physically, anyway.

He wondered if they really had tamed her during the seven years of his absence. If they had imposed all the trappings of civilization upon her. He hoped not. By God, he hoped not.

She looked up at him and he smiled at her as the orchestra began to play. Ah, yes. And her face was no longer that of a pretty child, but that of a lovely young woman.

He knew he had just done a dastardly thing. He had taken her from the man who was apparently to propose to her and announce his betrothal to her tonight. He had interrupted the set the man had reserved with her. He had stolen her away with the temptation of fulfilling a dream he knew very well she must always have had. Emmy would always have wanted to dance; anyone who had ever known her must surely understand that, he reasoned. He had not known her for seven years, but he remembered her as a child who was born to dance. He was drunk with emotion. He did not pause to analyze the strange thought.

He had done a dastardly thing. Another heavy burden to add to a dauntingly long list.

But he did not care the snap of two fingers. Tonight he had arrived home.

Tonight he was going to enjoy himself. Tonight he wanted to dance with Emmy. And Emmy wanted to dance. And dance they would, by God. Together.

It was only later that she realized what she had done, how very unmannerly she had been. She was remorseful then, for herself and the selfish weakness she had portrayed and for Lord Powell, whom she must have humiliated. But it was only later that she felt those things.

She had been caught up in some magical spell, and reality did not exist for her. He was there before her, speaking with her, holding her cold, cold hand in his strong warm one, smiling at her, calling her his little fawn as he had used to do, just as if seven years had rolled back and they were as they had used to be. He was here again, real flesh and blood.

Ashley.

He was the same and different. His eyes were the same, his blue eyes that searched desperately for meaning, for peace. His smile was the same — boyish, mischievous, reckless. His restless energy was the same. He was the Ashley she had known and adored. But he was different. Peace had forsaken him, and with it . . . hope? Was it despair that impelled him forward now? It looked very like despair to her searching eyes. And he was no longer a boy to whom restlessness and eagerness were appropriate. He was a man, hard and harsh beneath the surface gaiety. He was thin, haggard. Not with the paleness of one who has traveled long and far, but with the paleness of one who has suffered almost more than he can bear.

He looked like a man who was close to breaking and who might yet break.

Ashley!

Yet he was there before her. He had come home. And he needed her to dance with him. Not only wanted it, but needed it. She sensed his need like a tangible thing. Even such a small thing as her refusal might snap him in two.

But despite that realization, there was magic. Irresistible, wonderful magic. He was asking her to *dance.* He did not doubt for a moment that she could dance. And he knew instinctively that she wished to dance, that she had always wanted to dance. She had almost forgotten how well Ashley had always understood her. Perhaps it was one reason she had loved him so dearly. He had seemed so nearly the other half of herself.

He was asking her to *dance.*

How could she possibly resist? How could she possibly say no? The temptation was just too powerful. Though at the time she did not even think of it as temptation. If she had, perhaps she would also have paused to realize that there was something wrong about accepting. But she did not realize it — until later.

And so she danced. A minuet. With Ashley.

It was not as easy as she had expected. Now that she was moving herself, she was not at liberty to watch as she always could when she sat at the edge of the floor, sometimes with her eyes half closed, seeing the rhythm and patterns of the dance as an ordered, visual kaleidoscope. Feeling them in the pulsing of her blood. Although she knew the steps, now that she was part of the kaleidoscope, she was not quite sure of the timing. But Ashley grinned encouragement at her and the magic caught at her again. She closed her eyes for several moments, not even trying to watch the other dancers, merely feeling the vibrations of their feet on the floor and of the instruments playing the tune. And then it was almost easy. She could feel the rhythm pulsing in her body. She moved her feet in time to the pulse, using the remembered steps and patterns of the minuet. As if she had stepped into a painting and had become part of the perfect symmetry of its composition.

It was, she thought, the most glorious moment of her life. She was dancing. With Ashley. And then she was smiling at him, feeling all her happiness flowing out to him, feeling all the joy of the music she had never consciously heard and never would hear.

"Ah, Emmy," he said after a half hour, when sadly the set was coming to an end, "you need to throw off the disguise of fashionable woman and become again my little fawn. Though you never can be quite that again. You are all grown up. *Is* it a disguise you wear? Or is this what they have done to you? Have they tamed you and your heart has not cried out for the wild? Do they have you singing prettily here, like a linnet in a cage?"

She saw his words. In addition she could see the harshness and bitterness in his face. Ashley's face, also in disguise. Like a grotesque mask that needed to be peeled away.

"Ashley." Doris had come up to them and had taken her brother's arm. She was laughing. "You came back downstairs. I thought you were exhausted. And Emily, you can *dance.* How very clever of you. How do you do it when you cannot hear?"

"Emmy can feel the music," Ashley said. " 'Tis inside her, Doris, whereas 'tis merely outside you and me."

"Oh, fie," she said, laughing, "how strangely you talk, Ashley. You are to take me in to supper. I have a thousand questions to ask, eight hundred of them about young Thomas. Here is Lord Powell for Emily."

It was then that Emily too saw Lord Powell approach and that the magic was broken. She realized what she had done. She turned to smile uncertainly at her suitor.

"Egad, but the lad has the energy of a twenty-year-old," Lord Quinn said to Lady Sterne as they sat at the supper table, watching Ashley talking and laughing with his sister and her husband, with his mother, and with Agnes and William. "One would have sworn when he first arrived, Marj, that he was on the verge of collapsing with exhaustion. He is happy to be home, I warrant you."

"Lud, but so thin," Lady Sterne said. "He looks ill, Theo, though he is as handsome as the devil when he smiles, it must be admitted."

"Aye, but 'tis the voyage that has done that to him," Lord Quinn said. "A few English dinners and a few draughts of English ale will soon coat his ribs and plump him out again."

"Is he here to stay?" she asked. " 'Twill mean much to Anna and Luke if he is. He has been sorely missed."

"I daresay," Lord Quinn stated. "He has made his fortune in India, or so 'tis said, and he has married a rich wife into the bargain. Her papa has died and left everything to her, and therefore to my nephy too. They have come home to stay, I warrant you, Marj. There is the young lad to be considered, after all. England is the place to raise children."

"Yes." Lady Sterne smiled. "And so I may drift into old age and know my adopted family and yours to be happily settled, Theo. 'Tis a comfortable feeling. All will be complete by the time this night is out, think you?" She raised her eyebrows and nodded in the direction of the dining room door. Lord Powell and Emily, having finished their supper early, were leaving the room together.

"Aye, by my life," Lord Quinn said. "A

wedding in June, would you say, Marj? And Lady Powell will be delivered of a boy come nine months following that same night?"

Lady Sterne sighed, too accustomed to the bluntness of her lover's language to be shocked by the indelicacy of his remark. "Faith, but 'tis to be hoped," she said. "My little Emily settled. I did not think to see the day, Theo. I thought no man would be willing to overlook the affliction."

"Nay, but the gel is as pretty as a picture, Marj," he said, handing her a large linen handkerchief, with which she dabbed at her eyes. He chuckled. "And not daunted by her affliction. She can dance, by Jove. Egad, but my nephy had some audacity to lead her out into the set as he did."

"Dear Emily," Lady Sterne said. "And dear Anna. Who will make the announcement after supper, do you think, Theo? Luke or Victor? I can scarce wait."

4

"Luke?" Anna touched his arm and looked in the direction of the dining room door. "They are leaving."

He stopped cooling her face with his fan for a moment. "And so they are," he said. "Neither is hungry and both find the indoors stuffy and long for air and exercise. 'Tis nothing to be alarmed about, my dear. 'Tis called youth and young love, I believe." He smiled at her.

She gazed at him as if all the answers to life's worries might be found in his eyes. "She will have him, you think?" she asked. "She feels an affection for him, Luke? She will be happy with him?"

He raised his eyebrows. "Your questions become progressively less possible to answer, madam," he said. " 'Tis my belief that the answer to all three may be yes. But only Emily and Powell can answer them for sure — and only with the passage of time.

Are you intent upon creasing my cuff by gripping so hard?"

She released her grip immediately. "Luke," she said, "why did he come back downstairs? He was so very tired."

"I believe for that very reason," he said. "He was too tired to sleep. Too emotionally excited, perhaps, at being home again after so long. I may have trouble sleeping myself, Anna — unless you can be persuaded to help me, of course." His eyelids drooped over his eyes for a moment.

"Why did he dance with Emmy?" she asked. "And why did she dance with him, Luke? She *danced* with him. I had no idea she could."

Luke shrugged elaborately. "He wished to dance with the loveliest lady at the ball," he said. "Emily is the loveliest — after you. She danced with him because, apparently, she has wished all her life to dance. She did remarkably well, my dear. She did not make a spectacle of herself."

"Luke." She looked at him with appeal in her eyes. Yet she seemed to have no words for what she wished to say. "Luke . . ."

He drew his closed fan along one of her arms to the ends of her fingers. "Emily is receiving her offer at this very moment," he said. "She has appeared somewhat enamored of him, my dear. Certainly she has grown into a sensible young lady who is unwilling to pine her way through life as either Victor's dependent or mine. And she is not near the untamed creature she once was. Ashley has his wife and his son staying at a London hotel. Tomorrow I shall go and fetch them home. I will persuade him to stay here and rest instead of accompanying me. You must not upset yourself unnecessarily. There are realities to dictate everyone's behavior."

"I am so very happy to see him at home again," she said. "Happy for you, Luke, because he is your only surviving brother and there is a close bond between you. And happy for him. I cannot believe that India is the place to spend more than a few years of one's life. It is certainly not the place in which to raise a young family. I am happy."

"But you could wish that his timing had been a little better," he said with a smile. "That he had arrived at least a few days later, or preferably a few weeks."

"Yes," she said lamely.

"You have ever been overprotective of Emily, my dear," he said. "You persist in seeing her as delicate and more than usually vulnerable merely because she lacks one of the five senses most of us take very much for granted. Emily is not delicate. Merely different — *very* different, I will confess. But she has a strength of character beyond that of almost any other woman I know, I do believe. Since the day he left, has she given one sign that she cannot order her life without him?"

She shook her head. "But we knew —," she began.

He interrupted her. "Even on the day his letter announcing his marriage arrived?" he asked.

"I remember how you avoided for hours reading it aloud to her," she said, closing her eyes briefly.

"Or on the day the letter came telling of Thomas's birth?" he asked.

She shook her head again.

"Yes," he said, "of course we *knew,* my dear. But Emily is a strong person. You can safely allow her to live her own life in her own way."

She smiled ruefully at him. "He is dreadfully pale and thin."

"Yes," he agreed.

"I hope Alice and Thomas are well," she said.

"Doubtless," he said, "if they are back in England to stay, they will wish to remove to Penshurst without too long a delay since 'tis

Alice's home and now belongs to Ashley. In the meantime, you will persuade them to stay here, my love, and you will fuss over them and feed them and tuck them into their beds to your heart's content. They will look quite human again by the time they leave here."

She smiled.

"That is better," he said. "I thought the sun had disappeared behind a cloud. And of course, my dear, you will have a wedding to prepare too. Royce seemed agreed that this would be the better place for it. You may plan and spend as lavishly as you wish. I shall not ask for an accounting."

"Luke." She leaned slightly toward him. Her cheeks were flushed and her eyes were shining again, her more normal expression. "All will be well, will it not?"

"All will be well," he told her, covering her hand with his own. "But we neglect our guests, madam. Shall we lead the way back to the ballroom?"

"Lady Emily." He leaned toward her at the supper table until her eyes focused on his mouth. "May I send a maid for your cloak? Will you step outside with me?"

Her heart was heavy with guilt and other things. She had been unable to do anything more than toy with her food. And rightly or wrongly, she felt that much attention was being directed at her. Probably rightly. She would be under observation for two reasons. It was expected that Lord Powell would declare himself tonight. And she had just danced for the first time in her life. Besides, she felt suffocated. She was very aware of the group clustered about Ashley not far distant and of Ashley himself, brightly chattering in their midst.

She still could not quite grasp the reality of his return home.

She would give anything in the world, she thought, to escape to her room. Or better still, to escape alone outdoors. She always found crowds and conversation overwhelming. She missed so much. She was always so aware of her differentness, of her inability to understand more than a fraction of what was being said, of the impossibility of communicating her own thoughts beyond the simplicity of smiles and nods. But she could not escape — she *would* not. She had pledged herself to be like other women as far as she could.

She smiled and nodded. Lord Powell drew back her chair as she got to her feet, and offered his arm. She took it and felt the eyes of everyone in the room follow them to the door and through it. Or so it seemed.

It was not really cold outside, although it was only April and late at night. The slight breeze even felt refreshingly cool. They strolled the length of the cobbled terrace and back again. There was no one else outside. He stopped at the top of the steps leading down to the upper terrace of the formal gardens, perhaps thinking it would be too dark down there for her to be able to read his lips. He turned to her.

"Lady Emily," he said, "I believe you must know why I came to Bowden Abbey at his grace's invitation."

She gazed mutely at him. If she could have stopped this moment, delayed it for a day or two, she would have. Her head was pounding in a tight band just behind her eyes. But it could not be delayed. Every moment since his arrival five days ago had been leading to this one. She wished suddenly that she had a voice, that she could apologize for her bad manners in dancing with Ashley when she had promised the set to him. His own manners had been too polished to allow him to refer to the matter during supper.

"I came here not knowing you," he said. "Not knowing if . . . You are beautiful.

Poised and elegant and perfect in every way."

And a fraud. And without a whole heart to give. But perhaps he did not want her heart.

"You cannot speak," he said. " 'Twould be thought by many men to be an insuperable handicap in a w-wife. But not to me. I have always preferred quiet women. And my mother will gladly continue to run my household and entertain our guests — 'tis what she does best. You would merely have to charm everyone with your beauty and your smiles." He smiled at her.

No. Oh no. So she would merely be another protected child in another household that would run very well without her. He merely wanted an ornament for his home, a — a breeder for his children? He was choosing her because she was quiet and biddable — and because she would allow his mother to continue dominating his household? Did he believe that what he saw, what he had seen in five days, was everything that was her? She felt a stabbing of fear. He saw only a smiling, placid, reasonably lovely woman? Was she nothing more to him?

But when it came to the question of what she meant to him — what did *he* mean to *her*? And what really did she know of him beyond certain facts she had read from his lips? Was she merely using him to give purpose and a measure of independence to her life? Was it enough? Was it even fair?

She had believed she had thought through her decision very sensibly and very carefully. Suddenly she felt that she had not thought it through at all.

"Lady Emily." He had possessed himself of her hand. Unwillingly she noticed the difference between his touch and Ashley's. His hand lacked the warmth, the strength of Ashley's. She shook off the unwelcome thought. "Will you do me the honor of marrying me?"

He had said nothing of love. That realization at least brought relief with it. But only for a moment. He was offering her everything else — his name, his home, his family, a place at his side for the rest of her life. He thought she was poised and elegant and perfect.

Have they tamed you and your heart has not cried out for the wild?

She could see in her mind Ashley's mouth forming the words.

But Ashley was married. He had forgotten her — or rather, she had never been of any importance to him as a woman — and he

101

had married someone else. He had been married for three years. The fact that he had come home and had danced with her made no difference to anything at all. She had learned to live without Ashley. She had taken her life back for herself and had pieced it together again. She had enriched it, making it more deeply lived than it had been even before she met him. The fact that Ashley would be a part of her for as long as she lived mattered to no one but herself.

She wanted marriage. She wanted a home of her own. She wanted children. She wanted to be *normal.* She could fight for the right to run her own home and entertain her own visitors. She could show that she was capable of doing both. It would be the new challenge of her life. And she could do no better than Lord Powell. Luke had chosen well.

"Lady Emily?" He was peering at her anxiously in the near darkness. "Will you? Do you understand what I have said? Is it too dark out here?"

For one who had made up her mind quite deliberately over the past five days, she reasoned, she was alarmingly hesitant. There was no reason to hesitate. There was every reason not to. She had no reason to feel guilty. Her heart was no less whole than it had been five days ago. Her love for Ashley was her own private concern — always had been and always would be. Lord Powell had neither offered his own heart nor asked for hers. He had merely offered an arrangement that could be comfortable for them both. And as for the loneliness of not being known — well, she had never been known by anyone. Though almost by Ashley, an unwilling part of her mind whispered. She half nodded.

"You will?" He smiled broadly. "Zounds, but I was not sure. Not sure at all. You *will* marry me?"

She nodded a little more firmly, though his lips were moving faster now and she could not see every word. But he looked so very pleased. She resisted the temptation to close her eyes, to block out everything except herself. She had made every effort over the past few years to live outside herself as well as deeply within, to be a part of the social world in which she had to live her life.

He had taken her other hand, and kissed the back of each before holding her palms against his chest.

"You have made me the happiest of men, Lady Emily," he said. "My mother will be pleased. So will all my family. They have made me realize in the past year or two, you see, that 'tis my duty to bring home a bride and to set up my nurs— Well." He looked embarrassed.

But she had stopped making the effort to follow the rapid movement of his lips.

"I knew as soon as Harndon approached me," he said, "that you would be the perfect choice. You are the daughter and sister of an earl, sister-in-law of a duke, the possessor of a competent dowry. You are the right age." He smiled. "Pardon me, but I did not want someone directly from the schoolroom. I wanted someone who has proved that she knows how to behave in society. I have a position to maintain. I have brothers and sisters yet to marry. I wanted someone I could trust." His smile became almost boyish. "And someone quiet. I could scarce have done better on that score, could I?"

From tonight on her life would have to change more drastically, she thought. But could she bear to live every day as she had lived the past five? Could she do this? Could she live permanently in the wearying world of other people merely because she wanted . . . well, merely because she *wanted*!

"And in addition to everything else," he said, and her eyes read his lips again, "I have conceived a fondness for you."

Ah. She had not wanted that. She lowered her gaze and looked at his hands holding hers against him. And yet it was what she must want, for him as well as for herself. A relationship without fondness would not prosper. There could be fondness even if there could not be love. Very deliberately she turned her hands to clasp his, to squeeze them.

He waited for her to look up. "May I have your brother make the announcement tonight?" he asked her. "Now?"

She swallowed involuntarily. Tonight. Now. Once the announcement was made, it would be irrevocable. It would be like being married. There would be no going back from a public announcement. She would be bound to him for life. But that was what she wanted. That was what she had decided for her own future. It would be a good future. The best she could ever expect. Luke had helped plan it. She could trust Luke. Besides, she had already given her consent.

But when she looked at him to nod her head, she found herself shaking it instead.

"Lady Emily?" He frowned. "Not tonight?"

She shook her head again.

"Tomorrow, then?" he asked.

Tomorrow. Yes, tomorrow. Not tonight, so very publicly. Tomorrow, when there would be just the family to hear — and Ashley, a treacherous part of her mind said. She thrust the thought back.

She nodded and smiled. Yes, tomorrow. By tomorrow her mind would be calm. Good sense would have returned. By tomorrow she would have forgotten that she had danced tonight. With Ashley.

She would never forget dancing with Ashley. It would be etched on her memory like his departure for India. Like the first time she ever saw him. But by tomorrow she would have put it all away again in that deep recess of her being where it would not intrude on daily living or cause suffering to anyone except herself.

"Tomorrow, then," he said. "Perhaps 'twill be better then. I have not relished the thought of going back into the ballroom and becoming so much the focus of attention. You are cold."

She had shivered though she did not feel cold at all.

"Let me escort you inside," he said. "I long for tomorrow. To be able to write to my mother. To know that the future is finally settled."

She wondered what his mouth would feel

like on her own. But she was glad he had not kissed her. Not tonight. Soon enough she would know his kiss and a great deal more. Tomorrow she would think about it. Tomorrow she would begin to prepare for it. Tonight she was weary. So very weary.

Waiting until today had not perhaps been a great idea after all, Emily thought as she lay wide awake in bed. It was very early — or very late, depending upon the perspective from which one viewed the time. She had been in bed for only a few hours — the ball had ended very late and she had forced herself to stay to the end. She had not slept at all.

It was daylight. She would not sleep now.

There had been an embarrassing air of expectation when they had returned to the ballroom. She feared she had deeply mortified Lord Powell by her insistence that they postpone the announcement. Perhaps Luke's guests thought she had refused him. She still did not know his given name, she thought. Yet they were betrothed.

Yes, they were. She had said yes. Even though they had told no one and no announcement had been made, she had said yes. They were betrothed. He would probably want to be married before the summer was out.

She wished now that she had agreed to allow him to speak to Victor so that the announcement might have been made. It would all be finally irrevocable.

It was irrevocable now.

Emily pushed the bedclothes back from the bed and got out to cross the room to the window. It was the very loveliest time of the day, now when no one was yet up except perhaps a few grooms in the stables. It was the time of day she loved best, the time of day when she felt most free.

She had promised herself, she thought, but she was tempted anyway. She gazed longingly across the side lawn over which her window looked toward the line of trees in the distance. She could not see the river or the falls, but she knew they were there, just beyond the limit of her vision. Her favorite place in the world. Her haven of peace.

It was the way in which her differentness showed. Her need for solitude, for the living things of nature that were as content as she to communicate without demanding reciprocity. To give and to receive without obligation. Her contentment. Her happiness.

Her *loneliness*. Why had she had to grow

up? Why had she had to *need*?

Was it Ashley who had taught her unwittingly about loneliness? About the needs of a woman?

She had promised herself that she would not go to the falls while Lord Powell was at the house. It was not a *normal* activity. She had promised herself . . . But it was very early. And no one would be up much before noon anyway after such a late night. Besides, she would not have many more chances for freedom. Once she was married, she would have to be much more careful to behave respectably — normally. She owed him that.

But surely just this once . . .

Less than ten minutes later, Emily was leaving the house and turning in the direction of the trees and the falls. She had paused only long enough to pull on an old and loose sack dress and to drag a brush through her hair. She had hesitated over her shoes. She knew that, lovely as the day looked from inside her room, in reality it would be chilly at this hour of the morning. And there would be dew. But she could not bear the thought of being shod. She had to feel the earth beneath her feet. She had to feel the connection.

Beneath her arm and in her hands she carried her easel and paper and paints and brushes. She had tiptoed into the schoolroom to get them, hoping that she was not making noise that would disturb the children sleeping in the nursery rooms.

She was going to paint.

She had discovered painting fairly recently. She had been taught long ago to paint pretty watercolors by a very competent governess, of course. But she had always found the lessons and the exercises tedious. Why paint something that, however pretty, could not even begin to rival the real thing? Why attempt to reproduce what only God in his majesty could create? But she had discovered real painting, and it had become something of an obsession with her. Something so deeply necessary to her that she wondered how she was to leave it alone when she married Lord Powell.

She would have to leave it alone, at least most of the time. But this morning was hers. Later today he would tell Victor that she had said yes, and Victor would tell everyone staying at Bowden that they were betrothed. Later today she would no longer be free. She would exchange freedom for conformity and the greater independence she would enjoy as a married lady. But this morning she was still free. Or if that was not strictly true, then she would cheat a little.

She would steal one more hour of freedom.

She set her things down when she reached the falls and stood for a long time, as she usually did, looking, listening with her body, smelling, feeling. She let it all seep inside her, the beauty, the wonder, the glory of it. Beneath her bare feet, cold and wet from the dew, she could feel the pulse of the world. The pulse of life.

Idleness was so often seen as a vice. Every moment had to be occupied with busy activity and endless conversation even if one never stopped to ask what purpose was served by a particular task or by a particular communication. Idleness was so often despised. And yet it was in idleness, she knew, that one touched meaning and peace. Sometimes she put the name God to what it was she touched, but the name was too evocative of rules and restrictions and sin and guilt. In the Bible, which she had tried to read since Luke taught her how, she had noted with interest how the great meaning and peace behind everything had instructed Moses not to name it. It had called itself merely the I AM. Emily liked that. It was in idleness that one came face-to-face with the I AM. With simple, elemental Being.

She stood still for more than fifteen

minutes before setting up her easel and starting to paint. She worked slowly, even hesitantly, at first, not sure what the paper and the paint and the brush in her hand had to show her today. But soon enough she was absorbed in what she was doing. All else receded.

She was free. She had found a way to pour out all the wordless, unformed passions that were inside her.

5

Ashley had slept for maybe a couple of hours, and woke up disoriented, believing he was still in India. He was surprised he had slept at all. He had still been filled to the brim with nervous energy when he went to bed.

He marveled at the coolness of the morning. The blessed coolness. Through the window that he had opened before lying down he could hear birds singing. And somewhere far in the distance, probably in the stables or the carriage house, the faint ringing of a hammer on metal.

He was in England. He was home. He drew in a deep breath of cool English air through his nostrils and let it out slowly through his mouth. Then he threw back the bedclothes and jumped to his feet. He shivered as he crossed the room to the window. He had always slept naked, but perhaps it was not such a good idea now that he was back in a cooler climate.

He was in his old room, one of the few bedchambers that looked out on the front of the house. The terraces of the formal gardens were still bright with spring flowers. Beyond them the long lawns stretched to the stone bridge and the trees in the distance. The trees were bright with their spring foliage.

He was here, where he had longed to be. The thought of Bowden had sustained him through the long, tedious voyage. If he could but get here, he had thought. Irrationally, he had expected to find peace here. He had expected to be able to put everything behind him. Including himself. Or perhaps not. In reality he had known very well that there was no peace to be found — anywhere.

He should get dressed, he thought, and go riding. Luke must have some decent mounts in the stables. A good gallop would blow cobwebs away, if nothing else. Suddenly he craved the recklessness of speed, the feel of a good horse between his thighs. It was early. He was unlikely to encounter anyone else, especially today of all days, after the ball. It had been well into the morning hours before any of them had gone to bed.

He turned to stride into his dressing

room, but he did not ring for his valet. Poor Bevins had been up as late as he despite the fact that he had been instructed not to wait up.

An hour later he had completed his ride. He had taken out a powerful and skittish stallion, which his grace allowed no one but himself to ride, the most senior groom on duty had explained pointedly. On the grounds that it was dangerous? Ashley had asked.

"Aye, m'lord," the man had confirmed.

Ashley had laughed and led the horse from its stall into the stableyard in order to saddle it up himself. And so had begun a grand battle of wills that had lasted the whole of the hour. But he and the stallion understood each other very well by the end of the hour, he thought, patting it on the rump before turning it over to a groom's care and leaving the stables.

He wondered if anyone else was up yet. He stood still, looking toward the house, tapping his riding crop absently against one boot. He was reluctant to return. Reluctant to face anyone. There was something that had to be told this morning.

He drew a deep, slow breath.

And then he remembered something — somewhere. A place that had been gone from his memory until this very moment. Completely, almost as if he had deliberately blotted it out. Strange, really, considering the fact that it had been his favorite part of Bowden, the place where he had spent so many solitary hours. The place where he had always been most likely to find peace. Especially during that last year . . .

The falls. He turned his head toward the trees to his left, and his whip tapped harder and faster. He was strangely reluctant to go there. Although he had forgotten it with his conscious mind, he knew now that in some way it had been the focus of all his longings during his journey home. All his hopes for peace and forgetfulness and oblivion were centered on the falls. An absurd thought. An absurd hope.

It was a hope impossible to be realized. But for as long as he did not go there . . .

His jaw set grimly.

He was going to be even more disappointed than he had braced himself to be, he thought a few minutes later as he made his way through the trees and realized that someone was there before him. He could hear a voice. Luke's? But by the time he had stopped to listen, the man had ceased talking. Perhaps it had been merely a gardener passing by and talking to his dog.

But he picked his way more carefully. He had no wish to be seen, to be engaged in social conversation before he had properly braced himself. Even with Luke. Especially with Luke.

He saw Powell first. He was immaculate for so early in the morning, in dark blue frock coat and knee breeches, with embroidered cream cotton waistcoat. His wig was carefully styled and powdered — it was not last night's powder, at a guess.

He was standing silently in front of an easel, his hands clasped at his back. He was frowning. The easel was turned away from Ashley, so he could not see what was displayed there.

Ashley drew back behind a tree. He had no wish to encounter the man he had treated rather badly last night. Emmy's betrothed. Though now that he came to think about it, no announcement of a betrothal had been made, even though Luke had predicted it.

And then he saw her. She was standing some distance away, on top of the pile of rocks that ascended the bank beside the falls. On the flat one that jutted out over the water. She was looking across the water, very still. A gust of wind had flattened her dress against her and sent it billowing out

117

behind. Her hair was blowing out behind her too.

God, he thought. Lord God, Emmy. The dress was a loose sack dress. Very loose. Shapeless. It looked as if it might once have been a rich blue in color, but now it was a nondescript gray-blue. It must have shrunk from repeated launderings; it ended at least two inches above her ankles. Her feet were bare. Her blond hair, unconfined and unpowdered, fell in wild and unruly curls to below her waist.

God, he thought, memory stabbing at him. His little fawn. Except that she was no longer a child. Yet she did not seem quite a woman. She was more sprite than either child or woman. More a graceful and beautiful creature of the wild.

How many times had he seen Emmy standing or sitting on that rock? And yet he had forgotten every single one of them. Just as he had forgotten the falls. Just as he had forgotten her. Yet he could not have forgotten what had been so important in his life. Why had he suppressed the memories?

It was a lovers' tryst, he thought. He felt a moment's resentment over the fact that his first visit to the falls had been spoiled thus. But perhaps it was as well. This was a mere place, after all. There was no magic here.

And they had the right, the two of them, to meet where they would. They were to be married. And Emmy was of age. Seven years had passed since those days of his memory. Yes, of course she was of age. She had been fifteen when he left, had she not?

A child then. A woman now.

But instead of turning immediately away, as he knew he ought to have, he watched as Powell removed a handkerchief from a pocket, touched it to his brow, and turned to stride the few steps to the bottom of the pile of rocks.

"Lady Emily?" Lord Powell called.

She could not hear him, of course, but she must have seen him with her peripheral vision and realized that he was speaking. She did not turn her head to see what he said.

There was silence for a few moments. Ashley turned away. He had no wish to eavesdrop on lovers' words. He had even less desire to watch a lovers' embrace.

"Lady Emily," Lord Powell said again, loudly and distinctly, as if he thought she was only partially deaf. "I shall return to the house now. I shall see you at breakfast? I shall — Perhaps we may talk further?"

Despite himself, Ashley paused and looked back. She had not turned. Powell stood where he was for a few moments, and then turned to stride away through the trees. He was still frowning, and watched the ground at his feet. He did not see Ashley.

A lovers' spat? But how could one quarrel with Emmy? Ashley mused. What could she say to make one angry? She could, of course, ignore one when one was talking to her. Emmy could more effectively ignore someone than most other women. All she had to do was refuse to look at one. It would be a trifle annoying, to say the least.

Ashley grinned and set one shoulder against the trunk of a tree. He crossed one booted foot over the other. Good old Emmy. She was not after all allowing them to walk all over her just because she was deaf. He watched her.

She did not move except to clench her hands at her sides and tip back her head and close her eyes. Her hair cascaded all the way down to her bottom. She looked, Ashley thought, a hundred times more lovely than she had looked last night with her elaborately powdered curls and her silks and lace and her stays and hoops. And yet even last night she had been the loveliest lady at the ball.

His little fawn really had grown up, he thought regretfully. It was strange how one could come back after seven years, totally and dreadfully changed oneself, and yet imagine that everything and everyone one had left behind had somehow been happily frozen in time. If he had pictured Emmy at all during those years, it was as a slender, coltish child.

He had made no sound. Even if he had, she would not have heard it. And he was well behind her line of vision. But after a minute of stillness she opened her eyes and raised her head and looked over her shoulder directly at him. Being Emmy, of course, she had sensed his presence. She had known he was there. She had known he was not Powell — she had refused to turn her head for him.

She had known he was there.

The years had somehow rolled back after all. For the first time, there seemed to be a thread of warmth in the morning.

Usually she sensed someone coming up behind her, especially when she was alone. But sometimes that intuition failed her. It happened most often when she was absorbed in some activity and lost all sense of time and place. Painting had had that effect on her for the past year or so.

She turned with a start of guilt only when

whoever it was was very close behind. She expected to see Anna or Luke. Anna would merely smile and hug her and commend her on her painting and pretend not to notice her appearance. Anna perhaps did not realize that she still treated her youngest sister as a child. Luke would raise his eyebrows and purse his lips and look at her painting and make some satirical remark about witches in the wood.

But it was Lord Powell who was standing there, looking perfectly immaculate. Even his wig had been freshly powdered, she noticed. If only she had heard him coming, she might at least have hidden her painting. Preferably, she would have hidden herself too. She felt suddenly naked. Not physically so but emotionally. He had come unexpectedly upon her other self. The very private self she could explain to no one.

This morning he looked more handsome than usual. Even with the frown on his face and the aghast look in his eyes. He looked very . . . civilized.

"It *is* you, by my life," he said. His perfect manners appeared to have been left behind at the house, at least for the moment. His eyes moved down her body, from the topmost hair on her head to the tips of her toenails. It was a look of sheer horror.

Emily saw herself through his eyes. She saw her shapeless, shabby dress, with neither stays nor hoops beneath. And her bare ankles and feet. And her wild, tangled hair. In her embarrassment she felt and resisted the totally inappropriate urge to laugh. This was *her* world, she might have told him if she had been able. So very different from his own. Why was she the one called upon to make all the adjustments?

But for five days she had been so very careful. So very determined.

She smiled.

He recovered his lost manners then and made her a hasty but elegant bow. "Lady Emily," he said.

She tried to picture him without his wig, with dark, close-cropped hair. She rather believed he would look more handsome yet. Though quite undressed by current standards of fashion and propriety, of course. She hated fashion and propriety. Last night she had been dazzled — and wearied — by them. This morning she hated them.

"There are servants up and abroad," he said. "House servants, grooms, gardeners. 'Twas his grace's butler who informed me that you were up and outside already and had come this way. He also informed me that his grace and Lord Ashley Kendrick are up. You may be *seen,* Lady Emily."

She had been seen. By him. She could not tell if he was warning her of possible embarrassment to herself, or whether he was scolding her.

She smiled again and raised her shoulders in acknowledgment of the fact that she had been caught out and was perhaps sorry. Yes, she was sorry. This morning was in the nature of a swan song to freedom, she would have told him if she had had words. She must work on some sort of shared language with him, she thought suddenly. As she had with Ashley. But then perhaps she did not want anyone else to know her. Perhaps she hid deliberately behind her deafness and muteness. Perhaps she was too frightened by — or attached to — her differentness to expose it to someone who might not understand or accept. But this man was to be her *husband.*

"Zounds, but it *does* matter." His frown had returned, and his heavy brows almost met over the bridge of his nose. "The careless shrug does you no credit. Appearances do matter, especially in one who is the daughter of an earl and one who is to be a baroness and wife of the head of a family. I have younger sisters, who will look to you as a model of appearance and behavior. I do not believe your deafness can be used as an excuse for such shocking impropriety."

Emily frowned in incomprehension. Why was he angry? She looked into his eyes and raised her chin. She did not often feel anger, but she felt it now in response to his. Though she realized that her appearance *was* improper and that after five days it must be a shock to him to see her thus on the sixth. He was speaking hastily, before he had given himself time to digest what he had seen and to react more rationally.

She watched him draw a deep breath and watched his frown lessen in ferocity. Perhaps he had realized his mistake. Perhaps he would apologize for his hasty and hurtful words, beg her pardon. Perhaps he would smile at her and she at him. Perhaps they would even laugh together. And perhaps she would run back to the house ahead of him and change into more acceptable clothes, and there would be an end to this unfortunate encounter.

But his eyes had moved beyond her shoulder and focused on her painting. Her first instinct was to move across in front of it, to block it from his view. But she did not do so. It struck her suddenly that through her painting she could communicate with him for the first time beyond smiles and nods. She could show him something of her inner self. She felt terribly afraid and almost breathless in anticipation. She moved to one side and watched his face.

His brows snapped together again. He gazed at her painting rather as he might at a poisonous snake. He turned to her after he had gazed long and hard.

"*You* did this?" he asked.

She nodded. Why was he angry?

"But what *is* it?" His polished manners seemed to have deserted him yet again.

It was not obvious, then? Her painting was no substitute for words? She lifted her arms and indicated the trees around them. Then she raised her arms to the sky, stretching her fingers tautly upward, and closed her eyes. Then she looked at him again.

"I see no trees or sky in the painting," he said. "Did his grace not hire a drawing master or a governess capable of teaching watercolors when you were in the schoolroom, Lady Emily?"

She nodded.

"My sisters have had the good fortune to enjoy the services of a very superior governess," he said. "They all paint charmingly. I have paintings of theirs hanging in my study and my bedchamber. They have been taught to create gentle beauty out of the world around them." She watched him intently. It seemed important to see every word he spoke.

God had created gentle beauty. And ferocious beauty too. She had no interest in slavishly copying what had already been done. But perhaps to people who could hear — and talk — it was not so important to be able to speak through a painting. She wondered if he would understand even if she could explain to him. She had the rather alarming notion that he might not. The burden of understanding was always on her. *She* was the odd one, the one who lacked speech and wits. Or so it seemed sometimes. But she was being unfair to Luke and Anna and a few other people.

"This," he said, indicating her painting and turning his face to it, "is the ravings of a madwoman."

She was not sure if he had meant her to see his lips. But she had. She had been watching intently, and her eyes widened in shock and hurt and anger.

"I beg your pardon," he said too late, looking again at her. " 'Tis not entirely your fault, perhaps. I am beginning to understand that his grace might have been too lenient with you, Lady Emily, because of your affliction."

She thought of Luke leaning over her desk as she learned to read, firm and implacable despite her frequent tears and occasional tantrums, telling her that the effort might well kill him and shatter his marriage but that she *would* read and write and that they *would* persevere for one more hour before stopping for tea. And yet never for one moment — she had never quite known how he did it — had she doubted that he loved her dearly. If she had, she would probably never have learned.

" 'Tis understandable," Lord Powell said, his eyes softening somewhat. "He must pity your affliction. My mother will help you when we are married."

But she had been too deeply shocked, too deeply hurt to be soothed by his apology or his assurances, though she saw his lips offer both. And now indignation had been added to everything else. His *mother* would help her to learn what was what? As if she were a gauche and ignorant, somewhat spoiled child. Or a half-wit perhaps.

She turned sharply away from him even though she realized that he was speaking again, and darted along the riverbank and up the rocks that took her almost to the top of the falls. She stood on the top one, looking out across the fast-flowing water that rushed and bubbled downward over the steep, rocky slope to the level below. She deliberately did not turn her head, though she knew that he was still there. She wanted him to go away.

Fortunately he did not try to come after her.

Luke would have understood her explanation about her painting, she thought. He might not have approved of it, and he might well still have made his remark about witches, but he would have understood. And if he had not, he would merely have shrugged and suggested that perhaps it was time for breakfast. He would not have raved. More important, he would not have condescended. Luke treated her as if she were a real person.

And Ashley. Ashley had asked her to dance even though he knew very well she could not hear music. But she did not want to think about Ashley. Not now.

Lord Powell, she could see though she did not turn her head, had moved from in front of her easel and had gone to stand at the foot of the rock pile. She willed him not to come up. She needed to recover from her hurt before she could smile at him again. He needed to see her again as she had been for the past five days before he said more. They both needed time.

Go away, she told him silently, without looking at him. *Please go away.*

And finally he went. She had the feeling that he had said something first, but she had no curiosity to know what.

It was very clear to her, even clearer than it had been before, that her life would change completely on her marriage. Even if the wedding was not to take place immediately, even if there was still time here alone with Luke and Anna and the children before it, she must accept the fact that life was to change, she told herself. She must prepare for it. There must be no scenes like this after her marriage. None.

She had not really expected that the changes would have to be so very sweeping. Much would have to go. This freedom, this communion with the natural world around her. Her solitary wanderings. Her painting. Everything that she had held most dear all her life. Everything that had given her life meaning and texture. It was what was called growing up, she supposed. And it was probably about time. Anna lived very well within the bounds of convention and propriety. So did Agnes and Charlotte and Doris. So did every other woman of her acquaintance. It could be done. It *would* be done, even if she did have a handicap that made her situation not quite comparable to theirs.

But *should* it be done? she wondered. Must she sacrifice herself in order to conform, in order to achieve the respectability and relative independence of marriage? Was it in the nature of womanhood that one had to amputate oneself for the sake of a man? She rather thought it must be.

Emily clenched her hands at her sides, closed her eyes, and lifted her face to the morning sun. Yes, she would change from this moment on. Everything from the past would be gone, and she would accept the challenge of the future. She would fit in. She would be normal. She would learn to smile and nod and endlessly read lips.

But everything would be gone . . .

Ashley . . .

Even as she thought his name, before she could push it firmly away from her, she felt him. He was there. Not just at Bowden. He was there, here, close by, watching her. She had but to open her eyes and turn her head to see him.

For a few moments she hesitated. If she did not look, he would perhaps go away. And there would be an end to it. For once she left the falls, she knew, she must never come back. In many more ways than one, she must never come back. Ashley would be gone. Gone forever, even though she would see him at the house over the coming days, with his wife and his son.

And so this was the end. Or not quite. There was this now, this final moment. And she could not resist it. She was not yet strong enough in her new commitment. She opened her eyes and turned her head and looked at him.

He was dressed for riding, with the old careless elegance that had always character-ized him. His long dark hair, unpowdered, was caught at the back of his neck with a black ribbon. His three-cornered hat was in one hand. He was leaning lazily against a tree, smiling at her.

And yet she was aware that beneath the relaxed, careless stance was the haggard weariness that had translated itself into frenzied gaiety the night before. His thin, haunted body pretended to a well-being this morning that might have fooled everyone but Emily.

She was not fooled for a moment.

6

She did not move. She stayed where she was, unsmiling. But there was nothing unwelcoming in her stance either. She merely looked at him.

He remembered then that the first time he had met her here he had been alone, hurrying toward this place to find solitude and peace. But she had been here before him. And had bounded down the rocks to take him by the hand and lead him back up to join her. They had sat side by side on the flat rock and she had asked him to talk to her — yes, she had, even though she had not been able to ask in words. And so he had talked.

There was an ache of something in the memory — of a friendship lost.

She did not come down now. Or invite him to join her. But she did not tell him to go away either, as she had just told Powell. He pushed his shoulder away from the tree and lessened the distance between them. He stopped at the foot of the rock pile.

"I should have known I would find you here," he said. "Where else would you be so early on a lovely spring morning?"

But she was not to be amused. Her eyes, which watched him unwaveringly, gained depth, but she still did not smile.

"Emmy," he said, reaching up one hand, "come down."

But he wanted to go up to her. How many hours had they spent sitting together on that rock while he talked and talked, pouring out his heart to her? And yet, strangely, those monologues had felt more like conversation. Though silent, she had seemed like a participant. He longed for her friendship again. But she was no longer a child. Was friendship with this woman possible?

It was as if she had read his mind. She shook her head slowly and beckoned once — and then touched the fingers of her beckoning hand to her heart.

He felt a fluttering of memory. It had been one of their secret signals. Not just *Yes, please join me,* but *Yes, do join me. I want your company.* Without that extra sign they knew that the other was just being polite and therefore had not intruded — not that that had happened more than once or twice

134

in the year they had known each other.

He wondered now if she remembered —
if the gesture had been conscious.

He must not try to recapture the past, he
told himself. She was a woman with a life
of her own, not a child willing and even
eager to listen while he unburdened himself
of all his troubles. He grinned at her as he
strode quickly up to stand beside her. "He
said he would go back to the house and
perhaps see you at breakfast," he told her.
"He said that the two of you must talk
further. Did you wonder what he was saying, Emmy, when you would not turn your
head? 'Twas nothing more significant than
that."

She looked down at her hands for a moment and then back at him.

"I did not hear it all," he said. "You must
not fear that I was eavesdropping. Was it a
quarrel, Emmy?"

She did not answer him.

"Do you wish to talk about it?" he asked,
smiling at her. He meant what he said. She
could tell him if she would. Emmy had
always been able to make herself understood
to him — on some things at least. But then,
that had been a long time ago. "As to an
old friend, Emmy? As to a brother?"

The thought of listening sympathetically

to someone else's concerns, to *her* concerns, was strangely seductive. To be able to give back a little of what she had once given him so unstintingly. To forget for a few moments about his own concerns.

Her eyes went beyond him, down the slope, and back to him again. She raised her eyebrows.

He turned his head and looked. "The painting?" he said. "You quarreled over the painting? He did not like it? What a scoundrel he was if he said so. No gentleman would do so, Emmy. Shall I go down there and give you my judgment?"

But she caught at his arm and shook her head, and then dropped her hand quickly. He caught the look in her eye. It was one of dismay, even fear. She was *afraid* to let him see the painting?

She pointed in the direction of the house and then at herself. She indicated the whole of herself with hands sweeping downward from her head. And she took a step back so that he could have a good look at her. She looked at him ruefully. The truth was, he supposed, that if she had been anyone else but Emmy he might have been almost shocked. Her body was softly and revealingly feminine beneath the loose dress. Her legs were bare to well above the ankles. Her hair was displayed as no woman's hair should be except to her husband in the privacy of their own bedchamber.

"He objected?" He chuckled. "I cannot understand why, Emmy. He must be a fool. Last evening, before I even recognized you, I was knocked over by your beauty. But this morning you are many times lovelier. Today you are yourself. Does he not *know* you, Emmy? Does he know only last evening's lovely woman?"

She looked lovelier still with a blush of color in her cheeks. It was such a relief to him this morning to see that she was still the old Emmy, a creature far more suited to the wild than to a ballroom — though he really had been dazzled by her beauty there last evening before he knew it was she. But she was not as other women were. To try to make her so would only emphasize her handicap and make her feel both unhappy and inadequate. She was different, but she was not inferior. Did none of them understand that? Not even Anna — or Luke? But what did he know of her now? He had not seen or thought about her for seven years. She had undoubtedly become a woman.

"You are to marry him, Emmy?" he asked. Powell certainly understood and was willing to live with her inability to hear and speak, Ashley reassured himself. It had probably been unfair to judge him on the displeasure he had shown a few minutes ago, apparently over what was on that canvas.

She nodded.

But the man had objected to her appearance too; she had just indicated so. Yet this was Emmy, far more surely than that dazzling beauty of last evening. Powell's disapproval did not bode well.

"You love him, little fawn?" It saddened him that the old name no longer suited her.

She would not answer him. Her feelings for her betrothed were none of his business, of course. He was a stranger to her — as she was to him. They stood there for several moments, looking at each other. He realized that he was feeling more relaxed than he had felt for days. Weeks. Months. There was something about Emmy . . . There had always been something about her.

You, she said then, holding both hands palm up and beckoning quickly with her fingers — the old gesture. *Tell me about you.* It was no mere polite inquiry. He could see the light of real interest and sympathy in her eyes. The temptation to do what he had done all those years ago was strong in him. He longed to open his heart, to pour out everything to her. *Everything.* Emmy had always understood him. He had been aware that she did not see every word that he spoke. He was never sure quite how many she had missed. But she had always understood him.

With one hand she indicated the edge of the rock where it protruded over the water. She seated herself there without waiting for his comment, and very briefly dangled one bare foot in the water. As he lowered himself beside her, she drew up her knees, clasped her arms about them, then rested one cheek on them, so that she could watch him.

Memory rushed at him again. She looked once more almost like the girl she had been. He felt almost like the very young man he had been.

"I went to India for the challenge," he said. "I went to work to make my fortune. But most of all I went to acquire a sense of my own worth. I wanted to prove that I could make my own way in the world. You remember all this, Emmy."

Yes. She needed neither to nod nor to smile. Yes, she told him, she remembered.

"I did it all," he said. " 'Twas like a dream come true. I was very happy. There was the war with France, of course, and it touched us in India. There was always danger and the threat of danger. But somehow it merely added to the challenge, the exhilaration. I had — I have — some close friends in the military." Major Roderick Cunningham, for example, who had come to fetch him . . .

She gazed at him and then invited him with those beckoning fingers to tell her more. She knew there was more.

"And then I met Alice," he said. From the way he had worded it, he had made it seem as if meeting her had put an end to the happiness, the exhilaration. "Her father, Sir Alexander Kersey, was my superior in the company. She was newly arrived in India — she had been at home with her brother until he died suddenly. I met her when I was in the middle of a raging fever. My valet had sent word to Kersey, and when I came to myself from the delirium, she was cooling my face with a damp cloth. She tended me tirelessly for a number of weeks, her old nurse always hovering in the background. She was exquisitely lovely, Emmy — small, dainty, dark, soft-spoken. Is it any wonder I tumbled head over ears in love with her?"

No, she told him with large, calm eyes and a half smile. He knew from the intentness of her gaze that she had read every word from his lips. No, it was quite understandable.

Perfectly understandable. Alice had been gentle and patient. She had been deeply grieving for her dead brother. She had responded to his sympathies and his attentions. She had fallen in love with him. And so they had married.

"And so we married, Emmy," he said, "on a few weeks' acquaintance, during which time I knew her as a nurse and she knew me as a patient. We set about living happily ever after."

She reached across and touched his hand for a moment. Perhaps something of the bitterness in his voice must be visible in his face, he thought. *Why are you not happy?* her searching eyes and her puzzled frown asked him. *Why have you come home?* She did not need words or even gestures. He had never known anyone with as expressive a face as Emmy's.

"Her father died," he said, "and so through my wife I inherited property and another vast fortune. And then there was Thomas . . . Perhaps the challenge went, Emmy. Perhaps I was homesick and wanted to return to England. After all, I always said I would come back when I made my fortune — to settle on my own land, to live in contentment with my own family."

She knew it was not as simple as that. She

told him with her steady, intelligent eyes that she knew something was wrong, that she knew he was in pain even if she did not understand its source. Perhaps she had not even understood all he had told her. But she had sifted out essentials. She knew he had not told all.

He would tell her no more. She was a woman now with a life of her own to live. With a suitor of her own — and some sort of quarrel to patch up, it seemed. She did not need the burdens of a virtual stranger. Besides, he was no longer that boy who had selfishly loaded all his troubles onto the shoulders of a willing listener. He had learned to bear his burdens alone. Though he had come running back to Bowden, back to Luke, even back to Emmy, he had known even before his arrival that none of them could help him — partly because he would not allow any of them to do so. He was a man for whom self-reliance had been learned the hard way.

He looked over his shoulder down at her easel and then back at her. He grinned.

"May I see the painting?" he asked. "I confess myself curious, Emmy."

She bit her lip and flushed again. She raised her cheek from her knees.

" 'Tis so very dreadful?" he asked.

He could see her hesitation. She looked downright embarrassed.

"I'll not insist," he said, laughing. "Or keep you from your solitude, Emmy. I'll take myself off back to the house. Perhaps I will have breakfast with Powell."

But she relented then and shook her head and bounded to her feet to move lightly past him and down the rocks to lead the way to her easel. She turned to watch with wide and wary eyes as he approached.

It was not anything he might have expected. Indeed, it was difficult to know what it was she had painted. There were greens and browns and blues, all bright. Her colors appeared to have been thrown at the canvas rather than smoothed on. He could see bold brush strokes moving up through the paint in wild swirls that drew the eye upward to where they all almost converged. He had seen nothing like it before. He could almost sympathize with Powell's frown. Except that there *was* something he could see. Whatever it was she had painted, she had done it with passionate conviction. It was a painting that pulsed with feeling. It *spoke* — though he could not understand the language.

"Emmy?" He looked at her curiously. "Explain, if you will. I can feel the painting, if that makes sense, but I cannot understand it."

Oh, she told him with eyes and hands, and he knew that she was spilling over with eagerness to tell him what the painting was all about. She showed him the trees around them and the sky above and stretched her arms and her hands and her fingers upward. Her head tipped back and her eyes closed. There was a look of near agony, near ecstasy, on her face. Her arms moved in small spirals.

He looked back at the canvas. Yes. Ah yes, he could see it now, though it was unlike any other painting he had ever seen. It was like music. Wild, passionate music that exalted the spirit. He could imagine himself lying on the forest floor and gazing heavenward to that point where tree trunks and branches reached up and met the sky and merged with it. Emmy had seen that in her mind? And somehow reproduced it on canvas? She had been that close to — to what? To understanding the meaning of it all? He looked back at her, intrigued, almost awed. The wary look had intensified in her eyes.

Powell had not understood, he realized, or been willing to try to understand. Powell had hurt her. He had expected her to read his lips but had been unwilling to read her painting. Perhaps he had thought there was no meaning there. Perhaps he thought Emmy would be an empty receptacle, a comfortable but unchallenging life's companion.

"You see life spiraling through everything," Ashley said. "It comes through the soil and bursts upward, through everything and on out into the whole universe. Life is too powerful to be contained in one living thing but must be joined to all other living things. Life is a passionate celebration — a dance, perhaps. Is that what you saw this morning, Emmy? What you painted?"

Her eyes were bright with tears then and she closed her right hand into a loose fist and pulsed it against her heart. Ah yes. He remembered immediately. *I feel it deeply.* She bent to gather up her paints and brushes.

He felt somewhat awed, somewhat humbled. He had always known that there were depths to Emmy that all but a few of those who loved her had never even suspected. He had experienced her sympathy, her happiness, her peace. He had devised a very rudimentary language of signs with her so that they had some form of two-way communication. But for the first time he had glimpsed something of the complex depths of her vision. He felt . . . privileged.

"Emmy, my dear," he said, sensing that he had entered one of those rare moments of insight in his life. "If you could but speak." But she could not, and she would not be the person she was if she could, he realized. Besides, she was not even looking at him to know that he had spoken. Or to know that bitter despair had welled up suddenly inside him.

When she did look up, the rush of tears had gone and she raised her eyebrows and gestured toward the house. Was he ready to return with her?

"Go," he told her. "Leave me here. I am not good company for you this morning. Or for anyone else, either. You must guard your innocence and your happiness and your inner peace from such as me, Emmy. I could only destroy them."

She did not look startled or hurt, as he had half expected she might, though he knew she had seen his words. She looked calmly at him, but the sadness in her eyes almost had him grabbing for her. He had spoken the truth, though: If once he gave in to the lure of confiding completely in

Emmy, unburdening himself to her, as he had used to do, he would destroy her. He would cling and pull her into his own darkness and never let her go free.

It terrified him that he was tempted.

"Go," he told her again, and heard with surprise the harshness in his voice. He wondered if it showed in his face.

She went, taking her easel and her painting with her.

She was in communion with all that was light and joy and life-giving, he thought, or so it seemed to him. He had felt it in her painting, strange and wild as it was. He had seen it in her silent explanation.

And he was all darkness. The very antithesis of what she had found.

Emmy had grown up, he realized. And grown beyond him in the process. She had taken the limited opportunities that life had offered her as a woman, and a handicapped woman at that, and had used them to make herself into a mature and interesting person — he was sure she would be fascinating to know. He longed to know her as he had once longed for her to know him.

He was suddenly appalled by the selfishness of that former self of his. And by something else too: He had taken the limitless opportunities that life had offered him and used them to discover — hell.

He must stay away from Emmy, he knew. If there was something good he could still do in life, he must do that. He must stay away from her.

She was a woman now — beautiful, fascinating, alluring. Oh yes. He closed his eyes and smiled twistedly. Even that demon had found him out. There was no point in denying it. She was alluring.

Luke embraced his brother when Ashley entered the breakfast parlor, there being no one else present.

"Harry has decided to kick his heels and exercise his lungs," Luke explained. "An unusual time of day for him. 'Tis the advent of teeth, Anna swears. She has stayed in the nursery to help Nurse soothe him. Zounds but 'tis good to see you, Ash." He indicated a seat at the table.

Ashley smiled crookedly and sat. "I have been up these two hours or more," he said, "riding and walking. English air is more conducive to exercise than to sleep."

"Yes." Luke had seated himself and picked up his coffee cup. But he returned it to its saucer. "Sultan was in something of a lather when you returned him to the stables, Ash. I was obliged to take him out again to calm him and to cool him gradually."

Ashley laughed. "Deuce take it," he said, "have you taken to trotting sedately about the park, Luke, at a pace to suit your children? 'Tis time, perhaps, that your mounts knew that there is a pace known as a gallop."

Luke pursed his lips. "There is such a thing as respect for one's horse," he said. "Sultan is particularly difficult. 'Tis my theory that he was abused by his previous owner. I *had* advised my grooms that until further notice no one was to ride him but me. One of my grooms received a tongue-lashing from me this morning — probably unfairly."

"I beg your pardon," Ashley said somewhat frostily, turning to indicate to the footman at the sideboard that he was ready to be served. "I had forgotten that I am a mere stranger here now."

Luke sat back in his chair, one hand playing absently with his cup and saucer until Ashley's plate was heaped with food and the footman had been informed with a mere lift of the ducal eyebrows that he might withdraw.

"We have quarreled," Luke said with a sigh when they were quite alone together. "On your first morning back. 'Twill not do,

Ash. I refuse to quarrel further. What brought you back to England?"

Ashley laughed again. "An inhuman climate," he said. "Inhuman for Englishmen, anyway. Wealth — I must almost rival even you in riches, Luke. The desire to move on to the next chapter of my life. Homesickness."

"And the desire to settle your family in their homeland?" Luke said.

"Ah." Ashley laughed once more. "And that too." He pushed away his heaped plate, the food scarcely touched, and got restlessly to his feet. "And your family has expanded since I was last here, Luke. I must see your sons today. And Joy. And Doris's two are in the nursery here as well? Egad, but we have been a prolific family. Mother must be ecstatic."

" 'Tis never the way of our mother to show any emotion to excess," Luke said. "But she is fond of each one of us. And her grandchildren too. She will be pleased to see young Thomas at last. We all will. Speaking of which —"

But the door opened at that moment and Anna came inside. She smiled warmly at her husband, who got to his feet and smiled back, and hugged Ashley and kissed him on both cheeks.

"Ashley," she said, "I feared I had dreamed you up during the night. But you are really here. Dreadfully thin though. I fear the voyage was too much for you. Is that your plate? Do sit and eat."

"Every mouthful, Ash," Luke said, his lips quirking with amusement. "Anna's wrath is dreadful to behold when one of her children refuses to be coddled. I have the notion that you are to be one of her children during the coming days and weeks. Until she has fattened you up."

"What nonsense you speak," Anna said, smiling sunnily at her husband. "But Ashley, *if you* are this worn and thin, what must Al—"

"I have been drawing good English air into my lungs this morning at least, Anna," Ashley said. "I have been riding — galloping Sultan, actually, and incurring Luke's wrath in the process. And walking. I found Emmy and Powell at the falls, quarreling."

Anna bit her lip and looked at Luke.

He raised his eyebrows. "Emily and Powell?" he said. *"Quarreling?"*

"I saw her just now before I came downstairs," Anna said. "She went early to the falls, Luke. To paint."

"Ah." Luke sighed and looked pained. "She was able to remain inside her cage, singing, for five days, was she, but had to break loose on the sixth? I suppose, Ash, she was not dressed demurely for the eyes of a lover and executing a picturesque water sketch?"

Ashley grinned.

"No," Luke said. "I thought not. Well, my dear." He leaned forward sufficiently to pat Anna's hand. "I suppose he had to find out sooner or later that there are two quite distinct sides to our dear Emily. Better sooner than later. And they were quarreling. How can Emily *quarrel,* pray? Ash?"

"She can lift her chin in the air and refuse to look at the one who has the advantage of a voice," Ashley said. "She can refuse to acknowledge his very existence."

"Dear me." Luke drummed his fingers on the table.

"Emmy does not have to marry anyone," Anna said fiercely. "She can remain here for the rest of her life if she wishes, dressed in her favorite rags and painting her strange paintings. I will love her no matter what."

"No one, my dear," Luke said with raised eyebrows, "is arguing with you. Ah."

He got to his feet again as the door opened to admit a seeming flood of late breakfasters. He bowed over his mother's hand, kissed Doris's cheek, bowed to Lady

Sterne, and acknowledged Lord Quinn and the Earl of Weims with a nod. There was a great deal of noise and bustle as the ladies hugged and kissed Ashley and the gentlemen shook his hand.

"I expected," the dowager Duchess of Harndon said when they were all settled at the table, "that you would be on your way to town by now, Lucas. Lady Ashley and her son must be anxiously awaiting their removal here."

"You are quite right to scold me, madam," Luke said. "Blame a late night and a teething infant, if you will. Or blame Ashley, who has been elusive this morning and who did not tell me last night at which hotel in London I might find my sister-in-law and my nephew. But I shall be on my way within the hour."

"I would go too," Anna said with a warm smile for Ashley, "if 'twere not for Harry. There are a maid and a nurse, are there not, Ashley? Even so, will Alice and Thomas be well enough to travel as early as tomorrow? You certainly would not be well enough. I hope you have no notion of accompanying Luke."

"No," Ashley said, smiling about the table. "And there is no need for Luke to go either."

There was a chorus of protest, but he held

up both hands. He chuckled.

"There is something I neglected to mention last evening," he said. "It seemed somehow unbecoming to the occasion."

"Oh," Anna said, her hands clasped to her bosom. "Alice is *ill*. Or *Thomas*. Oh, Ashley, are they having the proper care? How could you bear to leave them?"

"Hush, my love." Luke covered her hand with his and kept it there.

"I traveled to England alone," Ashley said. He was laughing. "I did not bring my wife or my son with me."

"Egad," Lord Quinn said, "then you will be going back soon after all, lad."

"No, Uncle." Ashley smiled at him. "There is nothing to go back to, you see. I have resigned my post with the East India Company."

"You have *abandoned* Alice and Thomas?" Doris's words were spoken in a near whisper, but they sounded loud in the breakfast parlor.

Ashley looked at her with a crooked smile. "It has to be spelled out, by my life," he said. "No one understands. Or no one wants to understand. They are dead. They died together when my house burned to the ground a little more than a year ago. I was fortunate enough to be from home at the time."

The only discernible movements were Luke's hand gripping Anna's more tightly and the Earl of Weims's hand going to his wife's shoulder.

"It seemed an appropriate moment to tell it," Ashley said, "with the whole family gathered for breakfast. Pardon me for blurting such shocking news without sufficient preamble. As for myself, I have had a year in which to grow accustomed to the facts. A year in which to shrug off grief. I am free and I am wealthy. And I am home."

He got to his feet and made them all a bow that seemed almost mocking in its elegance. He left the room as Luke, the first to react, got to his feet. But Luke did not follow him. He had a wife and a mother with whom to concern himself.

Emily did not go down to breakfast. She did not often do so. She preferred to eat alone. But since the arrival of Lord Powell six days before, she had been behaving as any normal young lady would. She had taken all her meals in the breakfast parlor or the dining room, watching the conversation about her, dazed by it, but smiling pleasantly to indicate that she was a participant, not merely a dumb spectator.

This morning, however, she could not face Lord Powell at the breakfast table. Or Luke. He would know by now. He would look at her with pursed lips and narrowed eyes and she would feel more dreadful than if he scolded her roundly for five whole minutes. That was the trouble with Luke. He had learned early in their relationship that a few well-chosen looks were far more effective with her than a thousand words.

And she could not face Ashley either.

She dressed herself carefully in her dressing room, without the assistance of a maid. She had no personal maid. What was the point, Anna had said some time ago with affectionate exasperation, when Emmy never made use of one? She wore one of her pretty open gowns, with its accompanying petticoat draped over small hoops. She dressed her hair smoothly in front and knotted at the back. She covered the knot with a lace-trimmed cap, and made sure that its long lappets flowed freely down her back to her waist.

There, she thought, she looked civilized again, if not particularly grand.

When she got to the nursery, she returned Anna's smile and saw that Harry was lying quietly in her arms, his eyes fluttering closed. Beyond them Joy was lifting James off the rocking horse while Amy, Doris's daughter, waited to be lifted on. George was doing something at the table with two of Charlotte's children. James and the other children rushed toward Emily, demanding to be entertained. She laughed and obliged them. Soon Amy was scrambling down from the horse and joining them.

Children readily accepted abnormalities, Emily had realized long ago. Even the youngest of her nephews and nieces knew that they had to thrust their faces almost against hers and talk with slow clarity if she was to respond to their unceasing demands. They knew too that she always *did* respond. Soon she was crawling on all fours, hoops notwithstanding, with two small infants drumming their heels against her sides.

Luke had once told her that she was more foolishly indulgent of infant tyranny than even he and Anna. It always pleased Luke to pretend to be under the thumb of his children. In reality Emily knew that a mere look from his cool gray eyes could quell inappropriately high spirits, and that a mere lifting of his eyebrows could put an instant end to incipient rebellion. Love there was in abundance in Luke's family, but there was also total obedience.

Anna had just set a sleeping Harry down on his cot in an inner room and left the nursery when the door opened to admit Lord Powell. Emily felt hot and disheveled, but he smiled at her as she got to her feet and checked that her hair was still confined by its pins and her cap was still where it should be.

"Lady Emily," he said, "will you do me the honor of stepping out into the garden with me?"

He had recovered from his frowns, she

saw. She wondered if he had any inkling of exactly what he had witnessed that morning — a deaf woman in her own world, a world very different from his own. A world of sensation and feeling and thought, though not quite as people with hearing thought, perhaps. Did they think in words? She wondered if Lord Powell understood that she did not. Probably not. Probably he never would. But she would not feel hurt or angry. She had decided to marry, to move into that other world. The burden of adjustment was hers alone.

The children looked disconsolate. But ever resilient, they went in search of Joy, the eldest, the substitute playmate now that Aunt Emily was being taken away from them.

The sun was still shining. The air was considerably warmer than it had been when Emily had left the house earlier with her easel. Lord Powell led her down the steps onto the first terrace of the formal gardens, and they strolled together along the graveled walk there, her arm looped through his.

"I would make my apologies to you," he said, drawing her to a halt at last and turning toward her. "You are in your own home. 'Twas unpardonable of me to be critical here of your appearance and your behavior. Forgive me?"

Critical *here*? Would he feel justified in being critical elsewhere, then? In his own home, perhaps? But it was a point too complex to be considered now. And it was a handsome apology. She nodded.

"You look remarkably lovely this morning," he said. "It pleased me to see you playing with your nephews and nieces even at the risk of the perfection of your appearance. It pleases me to imagine you playing thus with your own children."

Your own children. Yes, the effort, the sacrifice would be worthwhile. She ached with longing somewhere in the region of her stomach. *Your own children.*

He had taken her hand in his. He raised it now to his lips.

"I would ask only," he said, "that when we are wed, Lady Emily, you will appear as you did earlier this morning to no one but me. I would not have my mother or sisters or — worse! — my brothers see you thus and think you wanton. Or even mad." He smiled.

Mad. He had thought her mad. Merely because her dress had been too short and her hair had been down her back. She felt a flaring of anger again for a moment. But it was merely a word — mad. It meant essentially the same thing as improper. And she would admit that her appearance had definitely been that. She would not quarrel again over a word.

"For myself," he said, "I could find your appearance thus almost appealing. If the gown were but richer . . . But 'tis improper to indulge such imaginings yet when we are merely betrothed."

She saw the look in his eyes — admiration? He found her attractive? She wondered again what his lovemaking would be like. Would he, even then, be concerned with what was right and proper? But she did not know herself what was right and proper — or what was wrong and improper, for that matter.

She just hoped there would be some — oh, some *passion*. The thought took her quite by surprise.

"I know now," he said, smiling at her, "what I will give you as a wedding gift. Something unusual, perhaps, but something I am sure will please you. I shall engage the services of the best drawing master I can find for you. I could see this morning that you very much wish to paint but do not know how. I shall see to it that you learn how — from an expert. And I will predict that before a year is out I shall be replacing my sisters' paintings in my bedchamber with paintings of my wife's."

She had watched intently. She had understood what he said. But he had so totally *not* understood that she could only stand now and stare at him. And feel the hurt and frustration again despite herself. What was worse, he did not even realize that he did not understand. She thought unwillingly of Ashley. He had understood instantly when she had explained that there were both passion and meaning in that wretched painting. And afterward he had put into words exactly what she had been telling him with her hands and her body.

But Ashley had always understood. He had always known that there was a person behind the silence — not just a person who listened with her eyes and would have responded in similar words if she could have, but one who inhabited a world of her own and lived in it quite as richly as anyone in his world. With Ashley there had always been a language. There had always been a way of giving him glimpses of herself.

"I could see the anger in your painting," Lord Powell said. "The impossibility you felt of ever painting what you wanted to paint, of ever reproducing what you saw

162

with your eyes. 'Tis something you feel often?" His eyes were warm with sympathy.

She saw his words — and his intended kindness. He had entirely misinterpreted the emotion that lay behind her painting. How could she marry a man who knew her so little that he believed her unhappy and frustrated, all locked up inside herself, wanting only to be able to hear and to speak?

"Harndon told me you can read and write," he said. "When you are in my home, Lady Emily, as my wife, I shall give instructions that there are to be paper, ink, and quill pens in every room in the house. You must write down what you wish to express. I would not have you unhappy with suppressed anger and frustration. I would know what you have to say. I would listen to you — to the writings of your hand — as you listen to the motions of my lips."

But he was a kind man. He wanted to help unlock her from her perceived misery. He was willing to give her a voice and to listen to her. He could not know that when Emily wrote it was for merely practical purposes, not for the revelation of self. She did not have enough skill with language to translate her world into written words.

But he *was* kind. She smiled at him.

Their attention was distracted. Someone

had come hurrying out of the house and down the steps into the garden and almost collided with them before he saw them. Ashley. He stopped abruptly, said nothing, laughed, and skirted around them to go scurrying on down through the terraces and over the low hedge at the bottom to the lawn beyond. He was hatless.

"Strange," Lord Powell said, looking again at Emily. "Lord Ashley Kendrick is rather peculiar. It must be the effect of a foreign clime."

Ashley had been different this morning, she thought. He had been as friendly toward her as ever. He had listened to her and understood what she had said to him. He had accepted her, both her appearance and her painting. He had neither condemned nor covertly criticized. But he had not talked to her as he used to do. He had spoken to her, yes — even at some length. But it was more what he had not spoken of than what he had actually said that had put the bitterness, the tautness, the haunted suffering in his face. There was a great deal shut up inside him. Once he would have sat there with her, time forgotten, and poured out his whole heart to her. But no longer. He had sent her away this morning. He had told her to go.

She was aware of him striding away down the lawn in the direction of the stone bridge.

It was as well. This morning at the falls had been the end. The end of everything that was past. This now was the beginning of everything that was future. Perhaps she would not so easily be able to put the past behind her, where it belonged, if she carried the burden of Ashley's confidences in her heart.

Yet even now, knowing nothing, her heart ached for him. She had seen him laugh just now, but the look on his face had not been one of amusement. It had been a grimace. There had been wildness in it.

Lord Powell had both her hands in his, and she gave him her full and determined attention. "I was very annoyed with him for forcing you against your will to dance last evening," he said. "I was almost ready to call him out, but I would not create a scene and embarrass you or my host. If he had succeeded in drawing you into making a spectacle of yourself, though, I believe I would not have been able to contain my anger. But you acquitted yourself well. I was proud of you." He squeezed her hands.

Against her will. He thought she had danced against her will. She knew that she would never ever forget the exhilaration and the sheer wonder of that half hour and that minuet. Her heart already ached with the memory.

"I would have our betrothal announced today if you will," he said. "Your family is almost all gathered here, and Lord and Lady Severidge are to come from Wycherly later for dinner, I believe."

Yes, it would be a good time for the announcement. Suddenly she wanted it to be soon. She regretted that she had not allowed it last evening. She wanted her future to be final and irrevocable.

Ashley, she was aware though she did not look in that direction, was standing on the bridge.

"May I speak with Royce?" Lord Powell asked.

Victor would make the announcement at dinner. Everyone would be pleased. Even Anna, who kept insisting that Emily did not have to marry anyone.

She nodded and smiled and was rewarded by a wide smile in return.

"You have made me very happy, Lady Emily," he said. "The happiest man in the world."

She had to share her news. Lord Powell had gone to the library to write to his mother.

Anna and Luke often spent a half hour or so together in Anna's private sitting room in the middle of the morning, between the hour they spent playing with the children or taking them outside and the separate duties they busied themselves with for the rest of the morning. The household was not following quite its normal routine this week, of course, what with all the guests. And Luke was supposed to be setting out for London this morning. But perhaps he had not left yet.

She knocked on the door and, after a decent pause, opened it gingerly and peered around it.

At first she was embarrassed. She thought she had walked in on a very private moment. Luke and Anna were standing in the middle of the room, clasped in each other's arms. But then she saw the pallor of Luke's face and the shaking of Anna's shoulders.

"My dear." Luke held up a staying hand. "Do not go away, I beg of you."

Anna lifted her head, apparently only just becoming aware of Emily's presence. Her face was red from crying.

"Oh, Emmy," she said, "Emmy. Ashley's Alice and Thomas are *dead.* They perished in a fire more than a year ago and we were not there to comfort him. He has borne the burden entirely alone. And the burden too of having been from home himself when it happened. How he must blame himself. He has come home for comfort, Emmy."

She saw every word, as if she really could hear and could not stop hearing.

Luke, as was to be expected, was in command of himself, though only just, Emily guessed as her eyes widened and turned to him.

"Emily," he said, "stay here with Anna, my dear. She has need of you for a while. I must find my poor Ashley. He has offended my mother by *laughing* as he told us about it, the foolish man. He is deeply, deeply hurt. You will stay?"

There was a faintness in Emily's head, but she nodded as Luke transferred Anna from his arms to hers and then hurried from the room.

Ashley, she thought. Ah, Ashley. Why had he not told her? Had he thought her arms not strong enough, her heart not big enough? Seven years was an eternity after all. The distance between them had grown vast. He had not told her.

Ah, Ashley.

As she sat down on the sofa with Anna, their hands clasped tightly together, she forgot why she had come to the sitting room.

"Emmy," Anna said, her reddened face a mask of grief, "we are going to have to be very gentle with him and very kind to him. Poor Ashley."

Emily raised her sister's hands and set them against her cheeks.

Luke had come to stand beside him on the bridge. He said nothing, as he rested his arms on the stone parapet and gazed down into the water of the river flowing beneath. Ashley was throwing stones into it, trying to skip them, but the angle was too sharp. They all sank quite decisively.

"I suppose," he said, breaking the silence at last, "you left Anna and Doris in tears, and Mother *not* in tears?"

"Theo and Lady Sterne bore our mother off between them," Luke said, "and I left Doris to Weims's care. Anna was in tears, yes."

"For something that happened more than a year ago," Ashley said, throwing the next stone farther than the others. It still sank. "To people she did not even know. 'Tis foolish. Ah, well. I noticed that Powell had Emmy almost in an embrace in the garden a short while ago. Anna must be in high hopes of having a summer wedding to plan."

"Ash," Luke said, "you need to talk about it, my dear."

Ashley laughed. "Zounds," he said, "I remember how disconcerted and indignant I was when you first called me that, Luke. You have still not abandoned all your Parisian ways, I see. I noted your fan last evening. 'Twas a glittering occasion, by the way. I am thankful I came in time for it."

"You are as brittle as glass," his brother said quietly. "And I believe you could shatter into as many pieces."

Ashley tossed his last stone over the parapet into the water and turned to rest one elbow on the wall. He looked at Luke with some amusement in his eyes.

"No longer," he said. "Look at me, Luke. I am quite relaxed. 'Twas merely the ghastly prospect of having to break the news to you all, you see. I was sorry in my heart I had not written to you before dashing off home. I knew very well that Anna and Doris would dissolve into tenderhearted grief, that Mother would stiffen her upper lip and accompany it with a face of stone, and that you would square your shoulders and attempt to take my burdens upon them. You play the part of head of the family exceedingly well."

"I did not come down here as head of the family, Ash," Luke said. "I came as your brother. Who loves you. You are in pain."

"Am I?" Ashley smiled. "It was a long and a tedious voyage. I ate poorly and slept worse. Both will be rectified now that I have my feet on firm earth."

"You came home," Luke said. "Not just to England, Ash. You came to Bowden. You might have stayed in London. You might have gone to Penshurst — 'tis yours, I assume? But you chose to come home. Why? Just so that you might hold us at arm's length? So that you might spurn help?"

"Help." Ashley laughed.

Luke turned his head and looked assessingly at him before directing his gaze back at the water. "I have been trying to imagine," he said, "how I would feel if 'twere Anna and one or all of my children. You are right: There could be no help, no comfort. Not immediately. Perhaps never. But I believe that after a year I might turn to my family. Yet I can see that even then I might be afraid to allow them inside the shell I would have constructed about myself."

"Damn you," Ashley said.

"I would be bitter and brittle. I might laugh from behind my shell."

"You know nothing," Ashley said. "You

know *nothing.*"

"No, I do not," Luke admitted. "Tell me, Ash. Tell me what happened."

"I told you," Ashley said. "They died. They burned with the house. I did not know until a friend came to fetch me. I came home to smoking ashes. I had been away — at a business meeting."

"How did the fire start?" Luke asked. "Was the cause ever determined?"

Ashley shrugged. "A candle caught the draperies," he said. "A lamp was tipped over. Who knows? There was a war in progress. There had been any number of sporadic and inexplicable atrocities."

"There was a suspicion of arson, then?" Luke asked.

"But no proof," Ashley said with another shrug.

"Did you have enemies?" Luke asked.

"A nationful," Ashley said with a laugh. "I am an Englishman, Luke. Englishmen were at war with Frenchmen. And there were Indian men fighting on both sides. 'Twas not a wise time to leave one's wife and son alone at home."

"Anna said that you must be blaming yourself," Luke said. "She was right. Were there no servants, Ash?"

"My valet was with me," Ashley said. "Alice had dismissed the other servants for the night except her faithful nurse and companion, who had been with her since she was a girl. She died with them."

"Only one servant." Luke frowned. "Why did she dismiss the others? Was it customary? Even when you were from home?"

Ashley merely shrugged. "There were those, you know, who said I did it," he said. "When a wife dies in inexplicable circumstances, the husband is always suspect."

"Zounds," Luke said.

"They were, of course, wrong." Ashley laughed and drummed his fingers on the parapet of the bridge. "I should not have come here, Luke. I should have gone straight to Penshurst. Yes, 'tis mine. I was penniless seven years ago, but I am now in possession of two sizable fortunes: the one that I amassed for myself and the other that my wife brought me. And I am free to enjoy both, unencumbered by wife or child. What more could any man desire?"

"Stay here for a while," Luke said. "Let yourself be loved, Ash. Let yourself be healed. I cannot know what you have suffered or what you still suffer — 'tis beyond imagining. But there is love to be had here. And perhaps healing too if you will but give it a chance. If you will give it time."

"I will stay for a few days," Ashley said with a shrug. "And then I will be on my way to Penshurst. To my new life. 'Tis the one I have worked toward since joining the East India Company, Luke. And now 'tis within my grasp. And so he lived happily ever after."

Luke turned his head to smile at him. "And perhaps 'twill do the trick, too," he said. "But stay here for a while. Anna will want to fuss over you. The children will wish to become acquainted with you and discover how indulgent you can be when wheedled. And I have missed you. Come back to the house with me? I will have toast and coffee brought to the study, unless you wish for something stronger. I noticed you ate almost no breakfast after all."

"Later," Ashley said. "I still revel in the coolness of English air. I would not willingly exchange it so soon for the indoors."

Luke nodded and after a moment turned to walk back to the house alone. Emmy, Ashley noticed when he looked after him, was no longer in the formal gardens with her beau.

He should have written to them a year ago. And when he returned to England, he should have gone straight to Penshurst. He

174

was a mature man now, independent, confident, assertive, resourceful. He had spent six years achieving that effect, overcoming the handicap of having grown up as a dependent, irresponsible, bored younger son of a duke. So he had lost a wife and a child. Every day men lost wives and children.

He should have continued with the life he had made for himself and by himself.

But he had resorted to instinct rather than to cool judgment and good sense. He had come running home — home to Bowden and to Luke. And, without consciously realizing it, to Emmy. To a wild and happy child who no longer existed.

He should have told her this morning, he thought. It somehow hurt to know that she would learn it from someone else. She would be sad for him. He should have told her himself. But he knew that he could not have done so. He could not have told her the bald facts as he had to his family at breakfast. If he had said that much to Emmy, he would have grabbed for her and poured out everything else too. Somehow with Emmy words could never be used as a shield. She seemed to know them for the inadequate vehicle of truth they were. Emmy saw to the heart.

But he had no desire to use a woman as an emotional crutch.

He had a sudden unbidden image of Thomas with his soft down of gingery hair. It was an image he often held behind his sleepless eyelids when he lay down. Poor child. Poor innocent little baby. The sins of the fathers . . . No! It had been an accident. A tragic accident. That was all. No one, least of all God, would punish a child . . .

8

The Earl of Royce was delighted by his talk with Lord Powell. He had begun to have doubts when nothing had been said after all last evening during the ball. Now he was happy and relieved for his youngest sister, whom he had not really expected to be able to settle in life. And he was grateful to his brother-in-law, who had made such efforts to find her a husband of suitable rank and fortune and one who would be kind to her. Powell seemed genuinely fond of Emily.

The earl did, though, hesitate about making the announcement on this particular day. It had not taken long for the news to spread through the house, to those who had not been present at breakfast, that Lord Ashley Kendrick's wife and child had perished in a fire a year ago in India.

But the Duke of Harndon was pleased too to hear that the betrothal had been agreed upon and that Powell was both ready and eager to have it made public. The duke insisted the gloom that had descended on the house must be lifted and that his brother certainly had no wish to wallow in it. The celebration of a betrothal in the family would be just the thing to lighten everyone's spirits, he maintained.

And so the announcement was made during tea, when everyone was gathered in the drawing room, including the children. Even Lord Harry Kendrick was there, asleep with open mouth against his father's shoulder. Agnes and William had come from Wycherly Park with their children. The mood of the gathering was subdued, or rather determinedly cheerful, until Victor rose to his feet, cleared his throat for silence, and informed them that Lord Powell had offered for his sister, that Emily had accepted, and that there was no more to be said on the matter except that making the announcement gave him the greatest pleasure and that the nuptials would be celebrated some time during the summer. And that really he was no great speech maker.

There was general laughter.

Emily, standing beside her betrothed, watched her brother's face intently and felt a sense of finality. A calm contentment. It had been done now. The words had been spoken to all the people who mattered most in her life. There was no going back now. Not that she felt any wish to go back. She needed this marriage. She might be deaf, she might be different, but she was a woman.

Lord Powell had taken her hand and was bowing over it in a touchingly courtly manner and bringing it to his lips.

She could not hear the noise that the announcement aroused, but she could see its effect. Everyone looked at her, and everyone looked suddenly joyful. It had to be right, she thought, smiling. What she had done had to be right. Her family and Luke's were happy for her; they believed Lord Powell would make an excellent husband. But there was no chance to think further. She was being engulfed in hugs. And her betrothed, she saw when she was able, was receiving his fair share as well. At the moment, Constance, Victor's wife, was embracing him, tears in her eyes.

Yes, it had to be right. It *felt* right.

Ashley was sitting in a far corner of the room. He had sat there all through tea, smiling, laughing, James on one knee, Amy on the other, Joy beside him. But they had abandoned him now, Emily saw, though she did not look directly his way, in order to join the general bustle of excitement about herself and Lord Powell. He sat there alone, still smiling.

"How can he smile and laugh?" she had seen Agnes say earlier to Constance. "Has he no feelings?"

But Emily, even without looking directly at him, had been able to feel the unbearable tension behind his smile. His wife and his son had died. Between leaving for a meeting and returning, he had had his whole family wiped out.

Ashley. She wished desperately that he had confided in her out at the falls that morning. Though that was not quite true either. For if he had told her, she would not have come back to change into pretty clothes and listen to Lord Powell's apology and agree to have their betrothal announced. She would have been caught up in a past that would have overshadowed her present and her future. Besides, she would have been unable to comfort him as she had used to do. Nothing could comfort him for what had happened to him. It would have hurt to know that she was powerless to ease his pain.

Ah, but she wished — with her heart she wished — that he had told her.

And then, while Jeremiah — the Reverend Jeremiah Hornsby, Charlotte's husband —

was congratulating her and Lord Powell and hoping that they might do him the honor of asking him to conduct their wedding service, Ashley touched Emily on the arm.

"Well, Emmy." He took her hands in his and kissed her on both cheeks. "It seems I have returned home just in time to say good-bye to you. You were always like a dear sister to me. I hope you will continue to think of me as a kind of brother."

Like a dear sister. That was all she really saw. Yes, she had been that to him. That was how he had seen her. Like a sister. It was good to have been seen thus. Closer than a friend. A sister. And she was to continue to think of him as a brother — yes, he had said that too. Oh, Ashley. She smiled at him, but she squeezed his hands very tightly as well and spoke to him with her eyes. He understood her. Of course he understood. But lest he did not, she closed her hand into a fist and pulsed it against her heart.

"Yes, I know," he said. "I know it makes you sad, Emmy. But I have come home to give up sadness. Seeing you happy is good for me. 'Tis hard to believe you are no longer the child you were when I went away. You are all grown up. Be happy, little fawn. Promise me always to be happy."

Yes. She smiled again. *The child you were*

when I went away. Ah, Ashley. Yes, she would promise. She would promise to try.

And then Joy was smiling sunnily up at her — she was so like Anna, even in her smiles. "Aunt Emmy," she said, "may I be your bridesmaid? I am seven and a half years old."

Emily laughed and touched the child's hair.

It had been a difficult evening. Agnes and William had stayed, toasts had been drunk at dinner, everyone had gathered in the drawing room afterward for conversation and cards and music — Constance and Charlotte and Doris played the pianoforte; William and Jeremiah sang. The tea tray was ordered later than usual and they all went to bed late.

But none of them had known quite if they should be sober and solemn out of respect for Ashley or bright and merry in celebration of the betrothal they had toasted at dinner. The only one of them who was unashamedly cheerful all through the evening — he had even suggested that the carpet be rolled back for dancing — was Ashley.

Luke had said quite firmly that the carpet would stay where it was. They had all had quite enough of dancing the evening before. And of course they were all rather tired after the evening before, and thus it was more difficult to keep up their spirits. At last, an hour after Agnes and William had left for home, the dowager duchess got to her feet and the rest of the party took her doing so as the signal to go to bed.

Emily changed into her nightgown without assistance and brushed out her hair and was thankful that the day was finally at an end. It had been an unbearably eventful day, and the evening had been almost intolerable. Everyone talking. Everyone focusing on her, expecting her to listen and understand. She had been unable to leave early, to relax into her own solitude as she had longed to do. Her eyes *ached* from such intent watching. And one foolishly insignificant fact had dominated her thinking all evening: She still did not know his name. She was to be his bride in two or three months' time, yet she did not know his name. The thought struck her as funny, and she laughed softly. It did not matter anyway. She could never speak his name.

He knew hers. It was almost all he knew of her. Another foolish, insignificant thought.

She was tired. She remembered suddenly

that she had not slept at all last night and had snatched only perhaps an hour's rest this afternoon between tea and dinner. She was very tired, but she was not sleepy at all. There was a difference, she thought, wandering from her dressing room into her darkened bedchamber and standing before the window, still absently brushing her hair.

She did not believe she would sleep even if she lay down. She was betrothed, she thought, trying to feel different. She was going to be married. There were going to be form and purpose to her life. A totally new direction. Even her home and her companions would change. She would spend her days with his mother and his younger brothers and sisters. And with him.

He was going to have paper and pens and ink set in each room. Without them she could not hope to communicate in the simplest ways with all those strangers.

He was a stranger too, she thought. And she would never be able to communicate with him. He would never know her. Such intimacy but no communication, because words — even if she could speak or write them — could never explain her world to him.

She rested one bent knee on the window seat. It was a lovely night, bright with moonlight and starlight. It was a tempting night, one that beckoned her. How lovely it would be to throw on a dress and a cloak and to slip outside to wander. Down across the lawn, along by the river. But it could not be done. She had made the decision. She had promised herself this morning. He would never understand a wife who wandered outside alone at night. If she were to, he would soon be echoing Luke's words, but in all seriousness. He would be calling her a witch.

Emily sighed. Her new life was not going to be easy. But it was one she had chosen deliberately.

She longed for it to begin. She looked back involuntarily at her bed. She wanted that too. It was strange how her body had come to crave it during the past couple of years or so, even while her head had been unable to fix upon any man — until now — and her heart had been faithful to an impossibility. Her body wanted to know . . .

She lifted her shoulders and turned her eyes back toward the window and the shadowed lawns and trees beyond it. How she yearned to go out there, to wander quietly, not doing anything in particular. Merely being. That was the heart of the difference, she thought. In her world she had learned to *be.* Other people seemed to gain their sense of identity and worth from *doing.* They pitied her idleness, believing it denoted emptiness, boredom. But now she had chosen to enter the world of doing.

She wondered if it would disappear with time and perseverance, this yearning to be free, to be a part of everything that was natural and beautiful and timelessly turning with the days and the seasons.

And then her brush stilled against her head and she leaned forward, her lips parting.

He was not strolling. He was not out there with any thought of enjoying his surroundings or of merely taking the air before retiring to bed. He was hurrying with purposeful strides, his head down. He looked almost as if he thought himself pursued, though he did not look back either.

He looked haunted.

He was going to the falls. Of course he was going there. He was close to breaking. All last evening, all today, his smiles, his laughter, his gaiety had scandalized some of the family and aroused the pity of others.

"How very brave the poor boy is being, Theo," she had seen Aunt Marjorie, Lady Sterne, say to Lord Quinn.

Emily had known that the gaiety had been

no more than skin-deep. She had known that the company of his family had not helped him at all but had possibly had the opposite effect. She had known that he was close to breaking and that he might very well break.

She could not help him. She leaned forward until her forehead was against the glass of the window, and closed her eyes. Ashley. *Ashley, I cannot help you.*

But she would not believe it. Nothing had really changed. She was here and he was here. She could still listen to him. And he could still talk to her. Luke had come back to Anna's sitting room that morning, pale and weary, and said that he had tried to talk to Ashley, had tried to assure him that there were love and healing to be had at Bowden for the taking, but that he was not sure he had accomplished anything. Ashley had built a wall about himself.

Luke had *talked* to Ashley. Perhaps what Ashley really needed, as he had more than seven years ago, was someone to listen. Someone who could not give him verbal consolation or advice. Someone like herself.

Perhaps he would talk to her if they could be together at the falls again, as they had so often used to be. As they had been this morning. Perhaps he would feel some of the old magic return. Perhaps some of the burden could be lifted from his soul. Perhaps he could be saved from breaking apart.

She had been like a dear sister to him, he had said just that afternoon. His words had hurt. They still hurt. He had been so much more to her than a brother. But her feelings did not matter. Besides, she no longer could be more to him than a sister. And perhaps a friend.

But was she fooling herself? She kept her eyes closed and looked honestly at the question. Could she go to him there, break the promise she had made to herself just that morning, and not be deeply hurt herself? Would she be going only for her own sake? Because she wanted to go to him?

But she did not matter, she thought. It was Ashley who was hurting. Even though she would allow her feelings for him to make no difference in her life from now on, she was never going to deny to her inmost self that he mattered to her more than anyone or anything else in her life — herself included. If she was hurt, it did not matter. She would heal, as she had healed before. And his pain was so much worse than her own.

She wanted to go to him, she decided,

because he needed her. If she was mistaken, if he spurned her, then she would bear the humiliation. But she did not believe she was wrong. There had always been an extra sense where Ashley was concerned — almost as if it had been given her in place of the sense of hearing. She *knew* that he needed her.

And so promises and propriety and common sense and the very real possibility of being hurt mattered not one iota. Lord Powell, her betrothal, were forgotten.

Ashley needed her.

She was hurrying after him, in the direction he had gone, less than ten minutes later, having donned a dress and a warm cloak. She was wearing shoes against the chill of the night, and had tied her hair back with a ribbon at the nape of her neck.

He stood for a while on the flat rock, looking down into the almost black water beneath his feet as it spilled and bubbled over the stony basin of the steep descent. He was enclosed by trees and night and the rushing sound of water. He breathed deeply and remembered how he had always been able to come here and feel that he had left the world and its cares behind. But his cares had been insignificant things in those days.

Even so, it was good to be alone. He had been alone in his bedchamber, of course, but it was not the same. He had felt surrounded by people, by family, by those who cared for him. He had felt suffocated by them. It had been a mistake to imagine that people would be able to help him. Least of all his family.

He had felt the depth of Luke's love this morning and it had weighed heavily on his heart and his conscience. He had felt the love and concern of all of them. He had been unable to reach out and wrap it about himself. It had felt more like a heavy burden pressing down on him, stifling him.

But how could he feel otherwise? How could he take comfort from his family when his wife and Thomas had died and he had not been there? And when he had wished a hundred times for their deaths? No. No, that was not true. He shook his head from side to side, denying the terrible thought. He had never wished for Thomas's death. Never. He must never burden himself with that untruth. And never seriously for Alice's either.

But he had not come here to be plagued by memories or by guilt, he thought, closing his eyes, listening to the soothing sound of the water, trying to let it seep into his soul. He had come here for an hour's forgetfulness. He wanted to be able to go back to the house later to sleep.

If only he could sleep.

He had been wildly, passionately in love with Alice. As she had been with him. Two strangers, who had mistaken an initial attraction for love. He had loved her because she had nursed him through a lengthy illness. She had loved him because he had needed her nursing. It had been almost inevitable. Neither could be blamed, perhaps.

And she had married him for another reason too — one he had discovered twenty-four hours after their wedding. After a difficult and disappointing wedding night. The passion with which his bride had responded to his kisses had changed to panic as soon as his hands touched her body and — it still made him shudder to remember — to revulsion as he entered her. He had finished the consummation quickly, unsatisfactorily.

And she had not been a virgin bride.

Her lover, she had told him when confronted the next morning, had been left behind in England. She had even told Ashley his name — Sir Henry Verney, a neighbor, her brother's closest friend. And yes, she loved him still. She would always love him. *Always.* The fierce, almost fanatical, light in her eyes had left Ashley in no doubt of the truth of her words.

Ashley had been left wondering exactly why she had married him and exactly how he was to make anything of this marriage.

She had answered the first question, though he had not put it into words. He had reminded her of her lover, she had told him with bitter defiance. She had thought he looked a little like him. She had been mistaken — dreadfully mistaken. He had not *felt* like the lover, Ashley understood her to have meant.

Love had died an instant death on both sides.

It was the only time they had been together as man and wife, he and Alice. Though fidelity to Verney was certainly not her reason, or chastity its result. She had taken lovers and not even tried to hide her infidelities from him, though she had been otherwise discreet. He had tried to reason with her, to persuade her to give their marriage a chance, since they were bound to it for life. But she had hated him with a passion equal to the love she had shown him before their marriage, perhaps because she had realized too late that her lost lover could not be re-created in him. He asked why she had not married Verney. Perhaps he was married already? She had refused to answer his question.

He had thought she was with a lover on the night she died. She had given her usual lame excuse, which she never even expected him to believe — she and Thomas were to visit her friend, Mrs. Lucaster, overnight. And she had left the house before he did. But inexplicably both she and Thomas had been at home when . . .

And yes, numerous times he had wished her dead. He had imagined the enormous relief he would feel to be free of her.

Ashley laughed harshly.

And then he turned his head sharply, some instinct warning him that he was no longer alone. Devil take it, but he did not want company. He had come here to be alone.

Emily was standing at the foot of the rocks, looking up at him. She was wearing a long dark cloak. All he could really see of her was her face and her fair hair, falling in thick waves down her back from the ribbon that confined it at her neck.

Emmy. Part of him leapt with hope and with gladness. But the saner part of him knew that she was the last person he wanted to see at this moment. He was not in a mellow mood. However, there was little point in saying anything. In the darkness and at this distance it was unlikely that she would be able to read his lips.

She came up the rocks toward him, her eyes on him the whole time. She stood in front of him, close to him, looking at him. She made no attempt to say anything, as she could have done with her eyes and her hands. He knew very well why she had come. It was why she had always come. She had come to listen. She had come to give of herself.

"No, Emmy." He shook his head. "Go back to the house. Go back to bed."

But she touched her fingertips to his chest and then to her own heart. *Speak to me.* It was a gesture that had been part of their silent language. Not just *Talk,* but *Speak to me; tell me more than facts; open your heart.*

"There is nothing to say." He laughed harshly. "You heard it, Emmy. They died and I blame myself. I am filled to the brim with bitterness and self-pity and am no decent company for anyone. Least of all you, on this of all days. The happiest day of your life. Go away."

But she shook her head. She was watching his lips intently. She touched them very briefly before beckoning with her fingers.

194

Speak to me. Tell me. She touched his heart with her fingertips again.

He felt a sudden, shocking, and quite unexpected stabbing of desire. And realized fully the danger.

"Listen to me, Emmy." Desire converted quickly into anger — annoyance against her dangerous innocence in coming to him alone like this, in the middle of the night; fury against his unwanted response to her. "We are out here alone together, a single man and a single woman in the dead of night. The impropriety of it would be obvious to an imbecile. The danger of it should be apparent even to an innocent like you. Go home while you have the chance."

But being Emmy, she could see beyond his anger. Her eyes, gazing deeply into his, told him so. *Let me share it,* she begged him without having to use her hands at all. But then she did lift her hands to cup his face gently in her palms. One of her thumbs brushed his lips. *Speak to me.* This had never been part of their language. But it was very eloquent.

She was incredibly, foolishly generous, as she had always been. This surely must have been a deliriously happy day for her, and yet she had made room in it for him. This morning and again now. For old times' sake she was offering all her understanding and sympathy. She was offering her deaf ears for his dark secrets. She was offering her ability to probe beyond words. She wanted to soothe his pain.

And all he could do in return was — desire her. He felt himself harden into uncomfortable arousal. He took her hands from his face and held them tightly in the space between them.

"I have no use but one for you tonight, Emmy," he said harshly. "Go away while you may. Go!" And yet he clung, without realizing it, to her hands.

She raised their joined hands and set the backs of his against her cheeks. Emmy. Dangerously innocent or dangerously courageous or both. Feeling his need and not really caring how that need showed itself. Prepared to give all that was needed to comfort him. Prepared to give until there was nothing more to give. Emmy, his savior — the forgetfulness and the peace he had sought single-mindedly since leaving India, not knowing that it was she he sought.

He groped blindly for her mouth with his own, his eyes tightly shut. Her lips were cool, closed, trembling, pushing back against his. He pressed his tongue urgently against the seam of her lips and she opened to him, so that he tasted all the warmth and moistness and sweetness of the inside of her mouth. He withdrew his tongue and thrust deeply inward again. Desire was one strong, insistent pulse in him. He was still gripping her hands. He had lowered them from her cheeks and was using them to keep the rest of their bodies from touching. He raised his head.

" 'Tis your ruin you have come to tonight, Emmy," he said. " 'Tis the only use I have for you. Go away. Leave me." He felt unfamiliar and unexpected tears spill down one cheek and then the other.

She removed her hands from his, but even as he felt a mingling of panic and relief, expecting that she would turn and bound away down the rocks, she stepped closer and set her arms around his waist. She leaned lightly against him, turning her head to rest one side of it against his shoulder. He could feel all the warmth of her generosity. All her incredible foolishness. He wondered if she fully understood.

He drew a deep breath and wrapped his arms about her. He shuddered.

"Damn you," he said, lowering his face to her hair. "Damn you, Emmy. Damn you." He knew she could not hear him. He swallowed — and swallowed again.

And then he had a hand beneath her chin, lifting her face so that she would see his lips. So that there would be no doubt of her *knowing*.

"If you wish to give me comfort tonight, Emmy," he said, "it must be as a woman. My need for you tonight is physical." He took her hand in his, turned it palm out, and brought it against the front of his breeches, beneath his cloak. He was trying desperately to shock her. Her eyes widened, but there was no real alarm in them. "Go now. Go while you still can. While I can still allow you to leave."

With all his mind he willed her to go. With his eyes he begged her to stay. She heard only what his eyes had to say. And she had come to give — whatever he needed. He knew that and did not have the strength to reject her gift.

He scooped her up into his arms suddenly and strode downward with her. Part of him — the cold, rational, intellectual part — could still not believe that this was going to happen, that one of them would not impose sanity on a dangerous situation before it was too late. But his body burned for hers; with blind instinct he yearned for her.

He set her down on her feet on the grassy bank beside the river, removed his cloak and spread it on the ground, removed her cloak, and laid her down.

"Emmy." He came down beside her, leaned over her, brushed his lips lightly over hers, touched a warm, firm breast through her dress, and tried to tell himself that it was still not too late. But it was. It was far too late. He lifted her loose dress with both hands, and her shift with it; then she raised her arms so that with one motion he could remove the garments entirely. He dropped them above her head. She was wearing nothing else; she had kicked off her shoes when he had laid her down. Ah, rash, innocent Emmy.

He made love to her with urgent, ungentle hands and lips, touching, stroking, pressing, sucking. She touched him with warm, gentle hands and made strange low sounds in her throat. He had no time to undress. Need was a pulse that drowned out even the sound of the falls, and a pain that drove him onward to release and oblivion and obliterated conscience. He undid the front of his breeches, his fingers fumbling with the buttons.

He tried to mount her slowly. She was slick with wetness, but the passage was tight and virgin. He felt the barrier. He felt it stretch and thought it would never give and release her from pain. But then it was gone, and he eased his full length inside her. He could hear someone sobbing. Himself. She was crooning to him with unknowing sounds.

He waited in an agony of patience, giving her time to adjust to the hard and painful invasion of her body. He had his hands spread beneath her in an unconscious attempt to cushion her against the hardness of the ground. His face was buried in her hair, which had come loose from its ribbon.

He tried to take her slowly, but she had lifted her legs and wrapped them about his own, and pivoted her hips, so that his pain was enclosed in a cradle of soft, warm womanhood. He drove into her, far too deeply, far too fiercely, half aware that this was all wrong. It was all give on her side, gentle, generous giving, and all take on his side, harsh, selfish taking.

But she gave.

And he took.

He heard himself shout out as he burst and spilled into her. He heard himself sobbing as one of her hands smoothed over his back while the other softly played through his hair.

And then for a few blessed moments or minutes or hours he lost himself. For a few moments he found what he had blindly sought for a whole year and longer, and rested in it.

9

She gazed up at the stars, finding the formation that always reminded her of a giant soup ladle with a slightly bent handle. She lay still and quiet and uncomfortable, cradling his too-thin body with her arms and legs while he slept. She would hold him all night if necessary.

She knew she had deceived herself. She knew she had come because she loved him. She knew she had come to comfort him. She had known and admitted those facts before she came. But she knew now that she had come with the sole purpose of giving — of giving herself, if that was what he needed. And she had known deep down that her mere sympathetic presence would not be enough, as it had used to be. She had known that the passing of the years would have made all the difference. Even then, seven years ago, when he had been leaving her, the change had been coming. He had begun to be aware of her as a woman, and so the possibility of pure friendship had been disappearing.

Of course, she had always loved him as a woman loves a man. Even at the age of fourteen she had known that her love for him involved the whole of her person, body as well as mind and emotions.

She had come tonight to give her body for his comfort if that was what he needed.

And so she had betrayed the promise she had made to herself just that morning. Worse — far worse — she had betrayed another promise. She had involved another person in her betrayal. Other people. She thought of her own family, and of Lord Powell's. He had written to them that morning and sent the letter on its way.

Tomorrow she would know bitter remorse. She would live with guilt and remorse for the rest of her life. She doubted she would ever forgive herself.

It was all her fault. Entirely. He had been completely frank with her. He had not only given her the chance to stop it and to escape to the house, he had urged her to do so — more than once. And she did not have the plea of innocence. She had known — deep down she had known — almost from the first moment. Perhaps before the first moment. Perhaps she had known it before she left her room.

It had been different from what she had expected. Not sweet union, sweet romance. It had hurt. Constantly, from the first moment. From the moment he had started to push into her. He had felt too big. She was still sore. He was still inside her, though she was no longer stretched painfully by his hardness. There had been no shared emotion, no shared tenderness, as she had dreamed there would be in such an intimate act. It had not been an act of love — not in the romantic sense, anyway. She did not believe he had enjoyed it. But then it had not been done for enjoyment.

She could not feel sorry. She could not feel the wrongness of it. She could only *think* about her own guilt and *think* about her sorrow for those innocent people she had wronged tonight. But she could not feel sorry.

He was at peace. For these few moments at least he was at peace.

She thought of the kind of grief and guilt that could still torment him so even after a year. Of the kind of love there must have been to have left such a storm of darkness behind it. *She was exquisitely lovely, Emmy . . . Is it any wonder I tumbled head over ears in love with her?*

She stared upward at the stars, her fingertips still absently massaging his head through his hair.

And then she knew that he was awake. There was tension in his body, a vibration in his chest. He had said something. He drew free of her body and lifted himself to one side of her, sliding an arm beneath her neck and about her shoulders as he did so. Cool air rushed at her naked body, but he reached over and drew his cloak about her. She could see his face quite clearly in the moonlight.

He gazed at her for a long while before he spoke. "You have given a great and reckless gift this night, Emmy," he said at last. "I cannot condemn you. I am too touched by your enormous generosity. I can only wish that I had had firmer control over my desires. I will forever regret what I have just done to you."

No, not that. No regrets. It had happened. And it had happened because he had had need of her and the need had shown itself in physical form. She had come to bring him comfort, not more guilt. No, not regret. Not forever. Forever was too long a time.

"No," he said, "I know you will never blame me, Emmy. You never did. You never asked anything for yourself, did you? You encouraged selfishness in me, and I readily took advantage of what you offered. All those years ago and again tonight. Well, it will be my turn now. My turn for the rest of my life."

Though she did not catch every word he spoke, she could see the bitterness in his face. But he did not give her the chance to reply. He set his mouth to hers, his lips closed, and kept it there for a long time, one hand firm against the back of her head.

"I hurt you," he said when he finally put a little distance between them.

She did not reply. It had been merely a physical thing. He had not *hurt* her.

He put a handkerchief into her hand, but she looked at him, uncomprehending. And so he took it from her and used it himself, setting it gently against her sore and throbbing flesh, cleansing away what she guessed must be blood, folding it, and pressing it lightly but firmly against her again, soothing her.

She turned her face in against his chest and closed her eyes. She was soothed by the vibrations, though she did not know what he said. If it had been important he would have lifted her chin so that she could see his lips. His hand massaged her head as hers had done for him just a few minutes before.

She wondered what the future would be like now that there had been this between them. She wondered if it would be more or less bearable than the past seven years had been. But suddenly she knew she would be fooling herself if she imagined even for one moment that it would be more bearable. She knew him now with her body as well as her heart. She had loved him with her body. She had given herself with the whole of her being, but it was her body he had taken, coming inside her and using her as a woman.

She did not regret it. She knew that tomorrow and perhaps for the rest of her life she would bitterly regret many aspects of what had happened tonight. But she knew equally that she would never regret loving Ashley. With her body as well as with every other part of herself. She always had loved him. She always would.

Without even realizing that she was close to doing so, she slept.

She had slept, he guessed, for well over an hour. Perhaps two. Deeply. As he might have expected Emmy to sleep, warm and relaxed and trusting.

But finally she stirred and looked at him

and smiled — how could she *smile* when she had been so misused tonight? — and moved away from him in order to sit up and pull on her shift and her dress. He adjusted his own clothing, shook out their cloaks, set hers about her shoulders and buttoned it at her throat, pulled his own about him, and led the way through the trees back to the house.

He considered sending her on ahead of him when they came to the open lawn and keeping an eye out for her safety — for her *safety*! — but he rejected the idea. If they were seen together, what difference would it make now anyway? Tomorrow everything must change. He walked beside her, not touching her, not saying anything. He had not spoken a word since she woke up.

He took her to the door of her room and opened it for her. But there was not enough light for her to see his lips. He put his arms about her and set his lips to hers. Without passion. Merely a goodnight embrace.

"Thank you, Emmy," he said afterward, though he knew she could not hear him. "For what you tried to do and for what you did, thank you. Good night, little fawn."

He took a step back and waited until she had closed the door between them.

He spent most of the rest of the night

standing fully clothed at his window.

He had debauched Emmy.

Through all the darkness that had engulfed his life in the past three years, he had finally touched the very heart of darkness. He had taken sweet and bright innocence and destroyed it, pulling it into the darkness with him.

And perhaps she did not even know it yet. Emmy!

The Earl of Royce had walked with his wife and child and some of his nieces and nephews out to the hill behind the house. Ashley was strolling alone on the terrace when they returned. He declined the children's eager invitation to play, and Constance, throwing him a look of sympathetic apology, herded them into the house. Victor would have followed them after nodding amiably, but Ashley stopped him.

"I would have a word with you, Royce, if I might," he said.

"Certainly. 'Twould be my pleasure," Victor said, making to stroll along the terrace instead of accompanying his wife and the children indoors. He schooled his features to quiet sympathy.

"In greater privacy," Ashley said. "Luke is

209

out riding. The study will be unoccupied."

"Certainly." Victor looked somewhat surprised, but he followed Ashley willingly enough.

Ashley closed the door of the study behind them and half smiled as he stood against it. "This is going to come as something of a shock to you," he said. "Especially in light of some of yesterday's events. But I must ask you for Emmy's hand."

Victor, who had been in the process of seating himself, changed his mind. He stared blankly. "Emily," he said. "Her hand?"

"In marriage." Ashley clasped his hands behind him.

"In marriage." The earl still looked blank. "She is already betrothed. To Powell."

"But 'tis me she will marry," Ashley said quietly. "She is of age. I do not need your permission except as a courtesy. But there is the matter of a marriage settlement. I am well able to give her the sort of life the daughter of an earl might expect."

Victor appeared to be recovering himself. He frowned. "Emily is *betrothed,* Kendrick," he said. "The announcement was made yesterday. You were there. A betrothal is as binding as a marriage. Besides, you have been back at Bowden less than two days.

You came a little too late for such maneuverings, did you not?"

His manner had become stiffer, more disapproving. It was hard to believe, Ashley thought, that Royce was younger than himself. The responsibilities of his position and family life had put dignity and the illusion of years on him.

"Her betrothal must be ended," Ashley said. "She will marry me."

"I am well aware," Victor said, now sounding downright irritable, "that you have suffered a severe loss, Kendrick, that coming home and having to break your news has put great stress upon you in the past couple of days. But —"

"But she *will* marry me," Ashley said. "She has no choice. Neither do I."

The Earl of Royce went very still and looked at him fixedly for several long moments before coming toward him.

"What exactly do you mean by that?" he asked.

"Just what you think I mean," Ashley said.

He saw it coming. He might quite easily have avoided it. He did not move, even to the extent of taking his arms from behind him. The back of his head crashed against the door, pain exploded in the right side of his jaw, and his vision blackened for a few

211

moments. He kept his hands where they were.

"You swine!" There was fury and contempt in Royce's voice. "You will meet me for this, Kendrick."

"If I must," Ashley said. "But perhaps it would be more rational to talk business. If I lived through a duel, nothing would have changed. If I died and there were . . . consequences for Emmy, she would be in an impossible situation."

He watched the other man fight his fury as he considered the sense of what had just been said. His nostrils flared.

"It was ravishment?" he asked.

Ashley did not immediately answer him. "If she says so," he said. "You must ask Emmy. But her answer can change nothing. We will marry."

"Powell may feel less concern than I about whether you live or die," Victor said.

Ashley inclined his head. "That will be his choice," he said. "I shall find him as soon as I have left here."

"No!" Victor said sharply. "You will leave that to me, Kendrick."

Ashley considered the matter and nodded. "Let us proceed to business, then," he said, indicating the desk that faced him across the room.

But Victor did not turn. "You will pardon me if we postpone this discussion until later today," he said. "This matter is hard to digest. And by my life, 'tis hard to accept. 'Tis not enough that you are scarcely out of mourning for one wife, but you must be stealing another from under the nose of a perfectly decent man?"

Ashley's head went back, but he said nothing.

"If you will excuse me," Victor said coldly.

Ashley stood away from the door, but he spoke again. "I would have no harsh words spoken to Emmy," he said. "She is under my protection now, and I will allow no one to upset her."

The Earl of Royce paused with his hand on the doorknob. He did not look away from it. "Zounds," he said, "but if you were a man, Kendrick, you would have been there with your wife and child. You would have saved them from the blaze or perished with them."

Ashley said nothing. His jaw was throbbing like a giant toothache. He did not touch it.

Emily found Lord Powell in the morning room conversing with Charlotte and Jeremiah. Emily smiled at all of them and

213

beckoned Lord Powell. He followed her from the room, looking half embarrassed, while Charlotte looked archly at Emily and Jeremiah looked somewhat disapproving.

Emily led the way to the library, opened the door before either Lord Powell or a footman could get there to do it for her, and waited inside to close it. Lord Powell looked decidedly uncomfortable by the time she had done so.

"Good morning, my dear," he said, reaching out both hands for hers. "How delightful to have a private greeting from you. But we must not be too long alone. We are as yet only betrothed." He smiled at her.

She did not smile back or take his hands. She reached through the slit of her petticoat to the pockets taped about her waist and removed the letter she had written that morning after she had woken up. She had been enormously surprised to discover that she had slept — and apparently for several hours. She awoke feeling sore and uncomfortable and heavy of heart.

The remorse she had anticipated the night before had been there in full force. Guilt and sorrow and shame — they had assailed her from all directions. But she had refused to lie there and wallow in any of them. She had known what she did. She had known what the consequences would be. She had no right now to nurse her suffering. She had no right to suffer.

And so she had written the letter. And then two more.

She handed the first letter to Lord Powell and noted with a stabbing of pain that he looked pleased.

"For me?" he said. "You have *written* to me, Lady Emily?"

She had not anticipated his expecting that it was some sort of love letter she had written. She lowered her eyes for a moment, but she would not give herself that comfort. She watched him as he unfolded the paper and read, and then watched as his eyes moved up the page so that he could read it again. There was no discernible expression on his face.

"My lord," she had written. She could remember every word — she had taken a whole hour to write it. Words — even written words — did not come easily to her. "Forgive me if you ever can. I cannot continue our betrothal. I cannot marry you. The fault is not yours. It is all mine. I have written to my brother and to the Duke of Harndon to tell them so. With regret, Emily Marlowe."

His eyes lifted and met hers and held them.

"Why?" he asked.

She could only stare mutely at him.

"Your promise has been given," he said. "The marriage papers have been signed by both Royce and myself. The betrothal has been announced to your family — and to my own."

She bit her lip.

"Is it fear?" he asked. "Fear of leaving here where you are loved and understood? Fear that your affliction will cause insuperable problems when you go to live among strangers? Is that it?"

No. She had felt that fear, but she had been willing to accept the challenge. She shook her head.

"Why, then?" He was frowning now. "Two evenings ago the answer was yes. Yesterday the answer was yes. Why is it suddenly no this morning when 'tis too late for no? There must be a reason. Write it for me." He looked about the library and strode toward the desk by the window. He pulled a piece of paper to its edge, tested the nib of a quill pen, dipped it in the inkwell, and held it out to her.

She moved reluctantly toward him and took the pen from his hand. What had he said so quickly and so angrily? What did he want of her? How could she marshal thought and feeling into words? Writing was almost as impossible to her as speech. Her mind did not think in words.

"I cannot," she wrote. But he already knew that. He deserved more. She wished she could explain, but she could not.

"Because of this?" he said. "Because you cannot speak? Because you cannot hear? I knew these things before I came to Bowden Abbey. I was prepared even before I met you to accept you as a bride. You are eligible in every other way. Explain yourself."

She could see that the anger in his face was almost explosive now.

"I am sorry," she wrote after dipping the pen in the inkwell again. She kept her gaze on the paper. She could not continue the conversation — if conversation it was. As it was, she would see his bewildered, angry face in her memory and feel his humiliation for days and weeks to come. Perhaps longer. She had no illusions about that.

What she had done to him was unforgivable. She would never forgive herself. She did not even have the excuse of having been so caught up by emotion that she had not thought of all the implications and consequences of what she was doing.

She had known.

But he had not finished with the conversation. His hand came beneath her chin and raised it and even turned her head to the light from the window. It had started to rain, she saw. It had looked this morning as if it might rain. Heavy clouds had covered the sky since she had been lying outside, looking up at the stars.

"There is someone else," he said when her eyes came to rest unwillingly on his lips. "There has to be. And it takes no genius to discern who that someone must be. Lord Ashley Kendrick."

She frowned and closed her eyes and shook her head. But his hand tightened on her jaw and lifted it higher so that her head was at an uncomfortable angle. She opened her eyes again.

"He danced with you," he said. "You gave him the set you had granted to me. You had nothing but smiles for him. He calls you 'Emmy.' There was the fondness of brother and sister between you, I thought. I begin to believe I am a fool. But he will not marry you. He is a duke's son. He is enormously wealthy, from all I have heard in the past day or so. He is somewhat above my stamp, Lady Emily. He will look for more in a bride than I am able to. Besides, he lost a wife just over a year ago and has been devastated by her loss. Perhaps you dream of comforting him and replacing her in his affection?"

It hurt her to see the sneer on his face. It was not a pleasant or a becoming expression. And she had put it there. She could not grasp what he was saying. She read only the hurt and humiliation behind his words.

"Perhaps," he said, "he will take the comfort if you offer it blatantly enough. But he will not marry you. You will be sorry you did not have me when you had the chance. I will take my leave of you. I will be gone from this house before the day is out. Believe me, it cannot be soon enough for me."

He had removed his hand from her chin at last. He made her now a deep and mocking bow before hurrying past her. She did not turn to watch him leave the room. She lowered her head and stared downward for a long time, her eyes directed unseeing on the carpet beneath her feet.

10

She was not at the falls, though he walked there in the rain to look for her. She was not in the nursery, where the children played with loud enthusiasm. He found her in the conservatory, seated among the large potted plants, almost hidden from view. She did not look up when he came into her line of vision.

He stood looking down at her, not even attempting for a while to speak with her. Her hair was neatly dressed this morning. It was smooth over her head and knotted at the back. She wore no cap. She was wearing stays and small hoops beneath her simple, unadorned open gown. Her face was pale and composed. The hands in her lap were still.

He remembered the smiling, exuberant girl who used to bound about outdoors like a young colt — or a little fawn. He remembered the smiling, trusting eyes as she watched him speak. He remembered her warm, responsive hand, her cheerful patience as she mended his quill pens when he worked for Luke. Dear Emmy. Sweet child.

This was what she had come to, this pale, calm, beautiful woman. This was what he had done to her. He could still scarcely believe how all the tender brotherly feelings he had always had for her had been converted into unbridled lust last night. He had tried to fight it, it was true. He had urged her several times to leave. But the fault for what had happened was entirely his. Emmy had had only two faults — a vast innocence and an unbounded generosity. She had seen him suffering and she had come to comfort him.

She had not understood that he could no longer take comfort from her in the old way. And yet when she had realized it, she had not taken fright. She had given anyway. She had given the ultimate gift.

And now her betrothal, her future, her life, were in ruins. There had been a fondness — perhaps more — between herself and Powell.

He remembered with deep shame how he had used her the night before. He remembered how she felt inside, how he had been less than gentle there with her. How he had taken and taken and taken. He did not want such memories of Emmy. He wanted her to be that sweet child again. He did not want to remember how he had lusted after her, how possessing her body had driven him wild with the desire for release. He wanted the gentle memories, not the harsh reality.

He went down on his haunches in front of her and looked into her face. She gazed steadily enough back at him, though color crept into her cheeks.

"Emmy," he said, "how are you?" Foolish question. How did he *think* she was?

Her mouth smiled fleetingly.

"Are you hurt?" he asked, realizing the ambiguity of his words even as he spoke them. He had meant physically. He could remember the seemingly endless moments of stretching before the virgin barrier had broken. He could remember the involuntary vigor with which he had worked to his climax soon after sheathing himself in her newly opened depths.

She shook her head slightly. He felt a moment's relief about that at least, but he could hardly expect her to admit to soreness or pain even if she felt either, he supposed. If there was soreness, she should at least have had the consolation of this being the morning after her wedding night.

It should have been Powell . . .

"I will not insult you by asking for your forgiveness," he said. "What I did was unforgivable."

There was light in her eyes suddenly. She shook her head vigorously.

"I know," he said, "without having to ask you, that you consider yourself equally guilty, Emmy. But you were not. You came to help me. Even through your happiness yesterday, you saw that I was unhappy. And so you came last night to comfort me — as you always used to do when you were no more than a child. Your generosity was boundless, and I was scoundrel enough to take advantage of it. And so I have destroyed your happiness. You do not intend this morning to continue with your betrothal?"

She frowned briefly in that characteristic way of hers when someone was speaking too fast or too long. But she understood his final question. She shook her head.

"You have already spoken with Powell?" he asked.

She nodded, her eyes huge and sad.

"Poor Emmy," he said. "I am so very sorry. How did you do it, I wonder. But you can always make yourself understood when you want to. I have spoken with your brother already."

Her eyes asked the question. She still did not understand, of course. Her sense of honor had led her to breaking her betrothal, but she did not fully understand. Perhaps she had thought she could retire quietly into her old way of life.

"I shall wait to talk with a few other people today," he said, speaking more slowly. "Luke. Your sister — your sisters. Your clergyman brother-in-law, perhaps. And I shall stay to lend you some moral support today. But I will leave at first light tomorrow. I should be back the following day with a license. Our wedding can be solemnized three days from now."

Her eyes were wide with bewilderment and then disbelief. She shook her head.

He rested one knee on the floor. "Yes," he said. "Oh yes, Emmy. We will marry."

She tried to get to her feet, but he was kneeling too close to her and would not move. She sat down again. *No,* she told him. *No, no, no.* Her eyes gave him no reason, only the adamant refusal.

His smile was somewhat twisted. "You loved him, Emmy?" he asked. "You *love* him? And only yesterday you were facing a happily-ever-after with him. 'Twas an evil day for you when I came home. But it signifies nothing in what must now happen. In three days' time you will be Lady Ashley Kendrick. You will be respectable again."

The very idea of Emmy's not being respectable was preposterous. Innocence shone from her eyes despite last night's dark deed.

No, she told him again. But now her eyes and her expressive hands said more. He did not *need* to do this. She had given freely. She wanted and expected nothing in return. There was no need of this.

"Emmy," he said, and for the first time he touched her. He set his fingertips against the back of one of her hands. "I had your maidenhood last night. Your brother knows it this morning. Everyone in this house and at Wycherly will know it before the day is out. Thanks to my perfidy, you are a fallen woman today." The absurdity of his words was clear to him — as was their truth. "You must allow me to do what is honorable."

He saw her eyes move to his jaw, which was doubtless darkening into a bruise. And he watched them fill with tears and knew that he must wait. There could be no conversation, no communication while she could not see. None of the tears spilled over.

She loved him, he knew. Only the deepest

love could have prompted her actions of last night. But it was not a sexual love, even though paradoxically that was the form it had taken last night. She did not love him as a woman loves a man. Her love was purer than that — and he had sullied it. And now, he knew, he must forever shackle it to himself, and perhaps destroy it and her in the process.

And so he had to destroy himself as well. He had been loved unconditionally, and he had selfishly squeezed the life and the joy out of that love. It was a heavy burden. The heaviest of all.

"Did you understand me?" he asked when he could see that her vision had cleared. She had to understand that there was no choice whatsoever. "We will marry. My seed might bear fruit."

He watched awareness come into her eyes and color to her cheeks. He watched understanding dawn — that they had been together as man and wife, that perhaps they had begotten a child. Even to him, though he had thought of it before, the idea was dizzying.

Not Emmy. Not in Emmy.

He could not think of her so. He did not *want* to think of her in sexual terms. He did not want her as his wife, his woman. He loved her too dearly. Sexual passion and marriage were foul things.

She lowered her head and looked at her hands for a long time. When she looked up at him again, her eyes told him nothing. They were unlike Emmy's eyes. There was a blankness in them, as if she had shut herself away from him.

It was the worst moment of all.

But he guessed she had accepted the inevitable. He covered both her hands with his own. "We will marry in three days' time, Emmy," he said, smiling at her. " 'Twill not be so bad, you will see. I will devote my life to your happiness."

She shook her head slowly, her eyes still blank.

"You think I should not so devote my life?" he asked her.

She shook her head again. But he knew now that she was not answering his question.

"You will not marry me?" he asked her.

No, she told him quite firmly. She would not marry him. And she motioned away from herself with her hands. She was telling him something she had never told him before: *Go away from me; leave me.*

Lord Powell was leaving. It had certainly

not taken him long to have his bags packed and to summon his carriage. Luke and Anna were seeing him on his way — a grim-faced Luke and a tearful Anna. Ashley was careful to stay well out of sight. He was the last person any of the three of them would wish to see at that moment. He had half expected a challenge from Powell, but it had not come. Perhaps he did not know the truth behind his broken engagement after all.

But Luke and Anna surely did. He was standing in the stairway arch when they came inside. Anna bit her upper lip when she saw him.

"Ashley," she said. "Oh, Ashley, what have you done?" There was no accusation in her eyes, only a huge misery.

"You will oblige me by going to your room, madam," Luke said, "where you may have some peace. I will come to you there later. You and I will walk outside, Ashley."

There was chill command in his voice. He was at that moment every inch the Duke of Harndon, the man who had been respected and feared for ten years in Paris for his prowess with sword and pistol. Anna disappeared without another word.

They walked in silence through the rain, which had settled to a steady and chilly drizzle. Luke wore a cloak. Ashley did not. Dampness seeped into his skirted coat, into his embroidered waistcoat and shirt, and into his hair, which was tied back and bagged in silk. He did not even notice. They walked out behind the house, past the hill, to the no-man's-land between it and the river. They were out of sight of the house there.

Luke stopped and removed his cloak. He dropped it carelessly to the grass and sent his coat to follow it — and then his waistcoat. Ashley watched him, a half smile on his lips.

"Remove yours," Luke said, ice in his voice. "I am going to thrash you."

"I'll not fight you," Ashley said quietly.

"As you would not fight Royce?" Luke said. "I suppose the bruise comes courtesy of him. I noticed no matching sign of violence on his face when he spoke to me a short while ago. Very well, then. You may take your punishment without defending yourself, if that is your choice."

Ashley fought only one fight during the minutes that followed. He fought to stay on his feet, not to take the coward's way out and crumple to the ground to avoid the punishing blows of his brother's fists. His hands balled at his sides, but he did not use them. Luke's strength had not diminished with age, Ashley quickly realized, though he was well into his thirties.

Finally Luke took the edges of his coat in both hands and backed him against the lone tree that stood in that barren place.

"She is my wife's *sister*," he hissed. "She is here under my *protection*. And yet, under my very nose, my brother has ravished her and ruined her. Be thankful that you will escape this morning with your life, Ashley. You do so only because now she needs *your* miserable protection and because I would not deprive her of that dubious comfort."

Ashley said nothing. He was concentrating on his physical pain, which was a welcome relief from a far worse pain.

"But by my life I swear this, *brother*," Luke said. "If you mistreat her, if you give her one moment of anguish, your life is forfeit. I will not ask if you understand me. You understand very well."

He released his hold on Ashley's coat as if he might contaminate himself with such contact, then turned his back. He stooped down for his discarded clothes and began to pull them back on.

"She says she will not marry me," Ashley said quietly.

Luke paused in the act of bending for his

cloak. He turned to look over his shoulder. "What?" he said.

"She says no," Ashley said. "She is quite adamant about it. I will persist, of course, but somehow I do not believe she will be moved."

Luke walked toward him and stood examining his own handiwork. Ashley did not avert his face or try to dab at the blood that was dripping from his nose onto his cravat.

"Well, my dear," Luke said, "perhaps you will be justly punished. Not in being forced to marry the woman you have ruined, but in being forced *not* to marry her. I have always had great respect for Emily. That respect has just increased tenfold."

He turned to stride away in the direction of the house, not pausing to see if his brother would accompany him.

They all knew or would soon know. The whole family would know why she had put an end to her betrothal just the day after it had been announced. Because he had foolishly spoken to Victor and had foolishly assumed that she would marry him. He might have asked her first. They might have spared their families the sordid, painful truth.

But perhaps not. Perhaps they would have

suspected — Lord Powell had — and questioned and cajoled. And then they would have thought the worse of Ashley for keeping silence. They would have thought, perhaps, that he was trying to avoid doing what was honorable.

What was honorable! Emily, still in the conservatory, stared down at her hands. She had given her promise two days ago. Yesterday she had consented to a public announcement. And last night . . . She sighed.

And she had been so very wrong. She had thought to give comfort. When she had understood what he needed of her, she had gone ahead anyway. She had sacrificed everything, including honor, in order to give comfort. And she had failed miserably.

But she would not make matters even worse. She would not take the coward's way out. She would not marry him. Ashley. She spread her hands on her lap. There was not a part of her that did not ache, she thought. Even her fingers. Even her heart. Especially her heart.

Anna was the first to find her, a long time later or five minutes later — time meant nothing to Emily this morning. Her sister drew up a chair and sat down beside her. It was tempting not to look up, to remain hidden inside her very private and silent life.

And she did not look up for a while. But she could not hurt Anna more than she already must be hurt, Emily told herself. Anna had been a mother to her. She raised her eyes.

Anna's face still showed the red marks of dried tears. "Emmy," she said. "Oh, Emmy."

Emily reached across and touched her hand. But it was too late to be offering anyone comfort.

"Lord Powell was so stiff and angry on the outside, so hurt on the inside," Anna said. "But you did the right thing meeting him face-to-face instead of having Victor do it for you. I must admire you for that."

Dear Anna. Always so reluctant to condemn. Always looking for good, even when there was none. Emily patted her hand.

"Luke just came to me," Anna said. "He told me you will not marry Ashley. Is it true, Emmy? And is it true that . . ." She shrugged her shoulders, and color flooded into her cheeks. "But that is none of my concern. He told Luke that he will ask you again. Will you not have him?"

Emily shook her head.

"But you love him." Anna had taken her sister's hand in both of hers. "You always have. Even during the years he was away.

Even after he married and after his son was born. That is the only explanation for — for what perhaps happened last night. It must have been dreadful for you to have watched the suffering he tried so very valiantly yesterday to hide from us. Now you could marry him, Emmy. Indeed, many people would say you have no choice but to marry him."

Emily shook her head.

Anna squeezed her hand tightly. "Then I will support you in your decision," she said. "I will not allow anyone to bully you. I have always told you that you need not marry anyone, that you may remain here for the rest of your life. You are my sister, but you have always felt like one of my own children. You were just a child when Mama was so ill, and even when she died. I love you like one of my own, Emmy. You are as dear to me as Joy or any of the boys."

That was the trouble, Emily thought. Oh, that was the trouble. She would have no choice but to stay here, a burden for the rest of her life on people who had lives of their own to live. Ashley's own brother. There would be no escaping now. She had lost her chance with Lord Powell. She had refused her chance with Ashley. And there could be no other man.

"Come and have something to eat," Anna said. "I would guess that you have not eaten all day."

She shook her head. She could not eat. Even less could she go back into the house and face other people. They would all know by now. They would all look at her, perhaps with condemnation, perhaps with pity, perhaps with embarrassment. They would all know that last night she had lain with Ashley. How very public it had become, what they had done together at the falls. Ashley, she thought, would have the additional embarrassment of having it known that she had refused to allow him to retrieve his honor.

And she had thought to comfort him!

Anna left her, but had a tray of food sent in a short while later. Emily ate an apple and sipped a cup of tea.

"She will have to be made to see reason," Charlotte said. "The trouble with Emily is that she has always been allowed to do whatever she wishes because of her affliction. No one has ever taught her any sense of duty. Perhaps you would explain it to her, Jeremiah. Perhaps she will listen to you, considering the fact that you are —"

"I hardly think, my love —," the Reverend

Jeremiah Hornsby began.

"If anyone is to speak to Emily," the Earl of Royce said sharply, " 'twill be me."

Everyone, with the exception of Emily and Ashley, was gathered in the dining room, though very little food was being consumed. A family conference was in progress.

"No one will speak to Emily," Anna said. "She has made up her mind. We would do well to remember that she is of age, that she is no longer a child."

"Pox on it," Lord Quinn said. "My own nephy is the villain of this piece. As I live, I would draw his cork for him this very minute if he were to walk through that door."

"There are ladies present, Theo," Luke said.

"Lud, Theo," Lady Sterne said, "have you not noticed what Luke is hiding beneath the table by keeping his hands in his lap?"

Luke pursed his lips and raised his eyebrows. "My dear," he said, "I have already explained. I skinned my knuckles while playing roughly with my sons and nephews and even a niece or two this morning."

"Pshaw!" Lady Sterne said.

"You must talk to Emily, then, Victor,"

236

Charlotte said. "But you must be firm with her."

"Lookee here," Lord Quinn said, wagging a finger about the table. His brows were knit together in a ferocious frown, marring his usually good-humored expression. " 'Tis my nephy who must be firm with her. And I shall tell him so the next time I see him. Egad, she is such a sweet little gel, and with such speaking eyes. He has doubtless frightened her to death. He has to be made to convince her that he has put behind him grief for that unfortunate wife of his and will devote himself to her comfort. Did he do that this morning, eh? I will wager not, as I live."

" 'Tis a dreadful thing," the Reverend Hornsby said, "and a reflection on the honor of the whole family. Broken vows, seduction, a refusal to accept the consequences of sin. Pardon me, my love and Anna, but the blame must be put squarely on Emily's shoulders. It does not signify how Lord Ashley expressed himself this morning, Lord Quinn. The fact is that he *did* express himself and did offer to do the honorable thing."

"Perhaps," Lady Sterne said, "she will change her mind. Ladies like to be persuaded. Perhaps Lord Ashley forgot this morning to mention the fact that he is fond of her. Faith, but 'twould be a disastrous omission."

"Perhaps," Luke said, sounding infinitely bored, "we should eat the food that has been set before us. Perhaps we should allow the two people most central to our discussion to order their own lives as they see fit." He held up a staying hand when Charlotte opened her mouth and drew audible breath. For a moment everyone had a shockingly clear view of the raw knuckles he had skinned while playing with the children. "I shall speak with Emily myself before the day is out. I believe I have some influence with her."

"Luke —," Anna said, reaching out to touch his arm.

"Madam." He turned his steady gaze on her. "Will you have some cold beef with your bread? Or would you prefer the chicken?"

11

Emily had changed into the very old dress that had so shocked Lord Powell only the day before. She had taken the pins out of her hair and shaken it loose down her back. She had kicked off her shoes and removed her silk stockings. It looked wet and dreary outside, though the rain had stopped. She did not care. She slipped down the servants' stairs at the back of the house and out through a side door.

She would not go to the falls. She was not sure she would ever be able to go back there, to the place where she had made the biggest mistake of her life. All of her memories of Ashley would be tied up in that one spot — all of them. Culminating in the memory of how she had hung herself about his neck like a millstone just at the time when she had been trying to free him from suffering.

Gifts were dangerous things, she thought.

Sometimes one succeeded only in taking far more than one gave.

She ran lightly in the other direction, across wet and chilly lawns, among trees whose branches dripped large drops of water onto her head and face and arms, and through to the meadow beyond. She had always loved this place — for the opposite reason to her love of the falls. The falls closed her into a small and private world; the meadow opened the world before her in a long and wide vista across fields and distant rolling countryside.

She stood for a long time and gazed at the world beyond herself. At order and beauty and peace. The grass was wet beneath her feet. But she would not be deterred by it. She went down on her knees and then lay facedown on the ground, her head tilted back so that she could gaze across the meadow almost from ground level. She saw the grass and the wildflowers as they would see themselves, rooted to earth and growing upward toward light and rain. She could see droplets of water on individual blades of grass and petals of flowers.

Then she rested her forehead on her arms. Her hands were flat against the ground, her fingers spread. She could feel the world spinning with her. She could feel the pulse of the universe against her own heartbeat. She lay still and relaxed, feeling the connection.

She felt no alarm, no unease when she realized that she was not alone. She did not even move for some time. She knew who it was. He would not disturb her or go away. She turned her head eventually and looked at him. He was sitting cross-legged on the grass a short distance from her. His elegant brown skirted coat and the breeches beneath were going to be soaked, she thought. She studied his battered face — one eye swollen half shut, both cheeks red and raw-looking, a swollen, cut lip. Victor had given him the bruise beneath his jaw. Who was responsible for the rest? Lord Powell? Luke?

"Luke," he said, almost as if she had asked the question out loud.

She sat up and noticed how her dress was dark with wetness and clinging to her all the way down the front. It did not matter. She raised her knees and clasped her arms about them.

"I saw you from my window," he said, startling her by signing the words with his hands in the private language they had started to devise long ago, "and followed you. There is no peace for you today, is there?" He smiled at her and then winced

241

before touching a finger gingerly to his lip.

She wondered if Luke looked as bad. Why was it, she thought, that no one had come to beat her? She deserved a beating more than Ashley.

"We need to talk, Emmy," he said, still signing the words. "It never even entered my head that you would refuse me. And so I nobly blurted out the whole truth to Royce, and he spread the glad tidings to everyone else in the house. Doubtless it did not enter his head either. I have put you in a very awkward position — to put the matter mildly."

She wished he would stop taking responsibility for her. What she had done she had done freely. He had offered her respectability and she had refused. He owed her nothing else. He owed her nothing at all. She wanted to smooth her fingers very, very gently over his hurt cheeks and lip.

"Ah, those eyes," he said. "They speak volumes, but sometimes even I cannot translate the language. And we never did invent enough signs for deeper thoughts and feelings. 'Tis not fair that all the burden of listening and understanding be on you. I remember once telling you that I would come back to teach you to read and write. Do you remember?"

He had said it when he was leaving. On that most painful of all mornings — even more painful than this morning.

"Perhaps," he said, "I should remain here for a while, Emmy, and teach you. Forget about last night. Forget about this morning. And just be dear friends again. Brother and sister, as we used to be."

She smiled sadly. But she pointed to herself, spread her palms flat before her, and read them as if she were reading a book. Then she dipped an imaginary quill pen into an imaginary inkwell and wrote an imaginary word with a flourish. She looked back at him.

"You can already read and write," he said. "Who taught you, Emmy? Luke?"

Yes, Luke.

"Damn him," he said.

She lifted her shoulders.

"And so there is nothing I can do for you, is there?" he said. "Strong, self-sufficient Emmy. You were always the same. It was always a ridiculous fallacy to believe you weak and vulnerable because you could not hear or speak, yet many people believed it. And probably still do. Perhaps I should ask what I can learn from you. We always think of teaching you, Emmy. Teaching you to communicate. Perhaps we should do the learning — and learn *not* to communicate, or to do it in a different way. Now there is a thought. Perhaps we could learn your peace if we could share your silence. What is it like? 'Tis not a dreadful affliction to you, is it? You have found meaning in silence. You are almost like a different being. You have perhaps the strongest character of anyone I have ever known."

He had stopped signing. And he had spoken at great length, as he had always used to do. She had always understood him, perhaps because she had loved to gaze at him. She felt anything but strong. At this moment she almost wished she had given in this morning and let life happen to her for the rest of her days. She would have had Ashley — for the rest of her life. As her companion, her lover, her husband. No! No, she would never have had him. Even if she had agreed to marry him, she could never have him. Ashley's heart was given, buried with his dead wife. She could never be happy with just what was left — especially when it was offered out of a sense of obligation, an obligation she had placed him under.

"Perhaps one day I will learn silence," he said, and his one good eye smiled gently at her, making him look like the old Ashley despite the mutilation of the rest of his face. "But in the meantime perhaps I should teach you to speak, Emmy. Now that might be a gift worth giving."

She caught her lower lip between her teeth.

"Have you ever tried?" he asked. He leaned slightly forward toward her. "I suppose 'twould not be impossible. You make sounds, you know, Emmy, especially when you laugh. You could probably speak if you could only hear. Have you ever tried?"

When I was a small child, she told him with busy and eager hands, *I did speak a little.*

He gazed at her. "You?" he said. "You could speak? You could hear, Emmy? What happened?"

I had a fever, she told him as best she could. *And then I could not hear.*

"Zounds," he said, "I did not know that. Do you remember sound, Emmy? Do you remember speech?"

No, she told him sadly. *No. I was very small.*

"You should be able to speak again then, Emmy." He had leaned forward, looking eager and almost boyish despite his battered face. "*Have* you tried?"

She had often sat before a looking glass forming with her mouth the words she read on other people's lips. She had even tried making sound. But she had no way of knowing if the resulting effort was speech. She had never tried it out on anyone. And she could not remember how it felt to speak.

"Zounds, you *have.*" He smiled broadly and then fingered his lip again. "Admit it."

She nodded, feeling embarrassed.

"Say *yes,*" he said. "Let me hear you."

She felt breathless, as if she had been running for five miles without stopping. She should never have admitted the truth. But he would have known.

"Say *yes* to me." His smile had softened.

She drew breath and moved her lips in careful formation of the word. At the same time she forced what she thought was sound. Then she hid her face in her hands.

There was laughter in his face when she gathered enough courage to remove her hands and peep up at him. He had been *laughing.* "The word was correctly formed," he said, "and there was sound. But there was no communion between the two, Emmy. I believe you blocked the sound — perhaps with the back of your tongue? It came through your nose."

She bit her lip, horribly mortified. What had happened to his idea of learning silence? Would *she* laugh at *him* if he got it wrong?

"Try again," he told her. "Let the sound come through your mouth. Let the air come through your lips."

She did not know how. She could not remember. *Say the word to me,* she demanded with one hand. But when he did so, she still did not know how. She wriggled closer to him until their knees almost touched. *Again,* she commanded.

"Yes," he said while she stretched out one hand and set her fingertips lightly against his throat. She could feel the vibrations. *Again,* she motioned, frowning in concentration.

"Yes. Yes. Yes."

She set her fingers against her own throat and tried to make vibrations. He had told her to let the air out through her mouth. She set the other hand before it. She could feel the air — and then the vibrations. She darted a look up at him.

"You have it, by my life," he said. "Sound, Emmy, coming through your lips. Now say *yes.*"

"Yyaaahhhzzz," she said.

The gleam in his good eye was not exactly amusement. It was . . . triumph. The type of look she had seen in Luke's eyes when Joy took her first step.

"Yes-s-s," he said, stretching his swollen,

cut lips and showing her that the final sound was a more violent one than the one she had produced.

"Zzzzsssss," she said.

He was enjoying himself. The old Ashley, though somewhat battered. But she was concentrating too hard for the thought to be conscious.

"Yes," he said.

"Yyaazzss."

"Yes-s-s."

"Yyaassss."

"Yes."

"Yyass."

"Yes."

"Yass."

He was laughing. "Yes, Emmy, yes," he said, and he opened his arms to her.

She was laughing too, helplessly, excitedly, like a child with a hard-won prize. She could speak! She could form words and make sound and be understood. She could speak all of one word. She could not stop laughing. She swayed forward a couple of inches — and stopped.

The laughter went from his face even as she felt it drain from hers. His arms dropped back to his knees.

"Emmy," he said, "marry me. Marry me and make me laugh again. Marry me and teach me your silence, your serenity. Marry me and let me teach you to speak — to hold a whole conversation. To drive people distracted with your constant chattering. Marry me."

The temptation was almost overwhelming. For a few minutes seven years had fallen away and they had been purely happy together as they had always used to be. In a rare two-way communication he had stepped into her world as surely as she had stepped into his. The temptation to believe that those few minutes could be expanded to a lifetime was powerful indeed.

She shook her head.

He had sat looking at her for a long time before she gave in to a small temptation. She lifted one of his arms from his knee, nestled her cheek against the back of his hand, and turned her head to kiss it. Then she set his arm back over his knee.

"Yes, I know," he said when she looked into his face again. "You love him, Emmy. And there have been Alice and Thomas in my life. Our fondness for each other will not overcome those barriers. Have it your way then."

She smiled at him.

"But Emmy," he said, and he was signing again, "if there is a child — and there may be a child — you must marry me. You must. Do you understand? 'Twould not be just you and me then. There would be someone else, more important than you or me. Children are so very fragile, and so very innocent. Protecting them must always come before any other consideration. Promise me?"

She could see in his face the rawness of memory. The knowledge that there had been one child — his own son — whom he had been unable to protect. His hands made a baby seem a tender, precious being.

She nodded. "Yass," she said.

"Thank you." He reached across and took both her hands in his. He raised them one at a time to his lips. "If you do not catch a chill, Emmy, in that soaked dress, there is no justice in this world. Come back to the house with me."

"Yass," she said, getting to her feet and grimacing as her dress clung wetly to her. She walked beside him, glad that he did not offer his arm. When they reached the lawn, she smiled at him, gathered her wet skirts about her, and ran off alone in the direction of the side door.

A maid answered the bell she had rung, and she signaled to the girl that she wanted hot water. When the maid returned, she carried a large jug of steaming water and a message.

"His grace wishes to see you in the study at your earliest convenience, my lady," she said, bobbing a curtsy.

Emily felt a fluttering in her stomach. Of all of them, Luke was the one she most dreaded having to face. Not that he had ever been harsh with her. He had never chastised her — or any of his own children. But then Luke never needed to use either harsh words or violence in order to impose his will on his household. His very presence was enough. His eyes were worse. The study! It was a formal summons, then. And her "earliest convenience" meant now, or sooner than now.

She washed quickly, pulled on a clean, dry gown over small hoops, dressed her hair in a hasty knot, and drew a few steadying breaths.

A footman opened the study door for her. Luke was seated behind his desk, writing. He neither looked up nor got to his feet for the whole of one minute. Emily stood silently facing him across the desk. This was deliberate, she knew. She was being made to feel like a recalcitrant servant about to be disciplined.

He set his pen down at last and looked up. As she had expected, his eyes were cold. Also as she had expected, he did not speak for so long that she had to make a conscious effort not to squirm and not to drop her eyes — she, who did not deal in words, was suddenly cowed by their absence. He did not invite her to be seated.

"Well, Emily," he said, "you have made a young man very unhappy and very angry today. You have humiliated him in the eyes of your family and his own. 'Twas not well done."

She swallowed.

"You have made your family very unhappy," he said. "Including Anna. Anna's happiness means more to me than anyone else's in this world. I do not feel kindly disposed toward you."

She had glanced down briefly as he had lowered his pen. She had seen his knuckles. There were no marks of violence on his face. It had been punishment pure and simple, then. Ashley had not fought back. Just as she would not fight back now.

"I would ask one question," he said. "What exactly you did with my brother last night and how it came about is a matter for the two of you alone. I am without curiosity. But I would know if it was by mutual consent, Emily. Were you in any way coerced?"

No. Oh no, she told him. They would never be allowed to think that of Ashley. Had he asked Ashley if *he* had been coerced?

"Thank you," Luke said. "I did not believe so, but I felt it necessary to ask. And so, Emily, you have freely and rashly given what you had no business giving, and now you choose not to allow Ashley to make restitution. Is that correct?"

She nodded.

"And there is no chance that you do not fully understand? That when you do you will change your mind? That we may prepare for a wedding within the next week?"

Only if she was with child. But she would not know that within a week. She shook her head.

Luke set his elbows on the arms of his chair and steepled his fingers. "Then you have won back a modicum of my respect," he surprised her by saying. "It takes character to refuse a man you love more dearly than life merely because marrying him would be the wrong thing to do."

She had been prepared to stand stony-faced through a scolding and through an argument to allow Ashley to do the proper thing. She felt a rush of tears to her eyes at

253

Luke's unexpected approval.

He waited for her eyes to clear.

"You are dismissed," he said, nodding curtly, and he lifted his pen and lowered his head again.

On the whole, she thought, stepping from the room and closing the door behind her, she felt almost as if she had been severely punished. Her legs trembled beneath her and her palms felt clammy. It was a strangely comforting feeling.

It was no longer pleasant to be at Bowden with his family, Ashley discovered. And that was stating the case very mildly indeed. He wandered into the drawing room, where his mother, his uncle, the Hornsbys, the Severidges, and Lady Sterne were taking tea, and felt that he had collided with a wall of frosty silence. He wandered out again. He climbed to the nursery, where all the children with the exception of the Hornsbys' newest, who was sleeping, and young Harry, who was taking his private tea with Anna in an inner room, were ecstatic at seeing a potential new playmate and were instantly buzzing with questions about his face. But Doris made him feel decidedly unwelcome, and even Weims merely raised his eyebrows and turned away to deal with a tug at his coat skirts from a tiny son, who clearly wished to be picked up. Ashley smiled at the children, drew roars of delight from them by telling them he had run into an angry bull, which now looked infinitely worse than he did, raised a hand in farewell, and withdrew.

He would stay, he had decided while walking back to the house with Emily, and help her somehow to face down the terrible scandal that had erupted during the day. At least it had been confined to the family. He doubted that Powell had been treated to the full truth — unless Emmy had been rashly honest with him. He would stay, Ashley thought, and court her more slowly. Given time, she would realize that she had no alternative but to marry him. There could be no other husband for her now.

He would stay and teach her to speak. He would do something useful with his life for a change. It seemed an eternity since he had last done that. He closed his eyes for a moment and remembered how very busy and how very happy he had been during most of his years with the East India Company. Learning to speak would be wonderfully liberating for Emmy. And with one word, slightly mispronounced and spoken in a strange little contralto voice, she had shown him that it was possible.

Staying, teaching her to speak, courting her, would be good for him too. They would take his mind off a past that could not be remedied and could not be atoned for. Perhaps. And perhaps too he would stay and learn from her. There was at least as much to learn as there was to be taught, he suspected.

But soon after returning to the house, he changed his mind. Emmy had set her own course today. She had broken off her betrothal with Powell, and she had refused his marriage offer — twice, even though he had tried, and he was sure other members of her family had tried, to explain to her the inevitability of their marrying. She would not change her mind. Emmy was someone who never took the easy course if it was not the course she wished to take. She recognized the inevitability of nothing.

One could only respect her — and wish sometimes to shake the living daylights out of her. He smiled despite himself. He was fonder of Emmy than of anyone else in his life, strange as the thought might be, especially considering the fact that he had almost completely forgotten about her while he was away. Though he was no longer so sure of that — there had been that urgent, quite irrational urge to come home to

Bowden. However it was, his fondness for Emmy was the main problem today. He did not want to marry her, if the truth were known. He was as relieved by her stubbornness as he was alarmed by it.

He hated to think of Emmy as a wife, a lover. He remembered her warm, soft, shapely body, naked beneath his own. He remembered her tight virginity. He remembered the urgency of his need driving into her. And he felt something that was definitely not revulsion, but was . . . a great sadness. A deep shame. He had known what he had no wish to know. He had known her as a woman. Yet he wanted to know her only as the sprite he had seen yesterday morning, when she had stood on the rock at the falls, refusing to listen to Powell. And he wanted to remember her as his little fawn of seven years ago.

"Where may I find his grace?" he asked a footman in the hall, looking him directly in the eye, scorning to try to hide his face in the shadows. One could be very sure that what the family knew abovestairs, the servants knew in even greater detail belowstairs. That was in the nature of life in a great house. The servants probably knew exactly how many punches Luke had thrown, even though Ashley himself had not kept count.

"He is in the study, my lord," the footman informed him.

"Ask him if Lord Ashley Kendrick may have a word with him," Ashley said formally, and waited in the hall until the footman reappeared and beckoned him.

Luke was seated behind his desk. He looked up coolly when his brother came inside but neither rose to his feet nor offered Ashley a chair. Ashley recognized the tactic, which had always been damnably effective. Seated behind his desk, Luke was the Duke of Harndon, undisputed master of Bowden and all its properties, undisputed head of his family. Eight years ago, as a wild, rebellious young man who had been going nowhere in life except to possible ruin, Ashley had stood thus before Luke's desk more than once. Now he felt like that young man again. He had become an independent, successful, highly respected businessman in India. But he had let his life fall apart, and it had continued its decline in the few days since his return home. It was time he did something about it. The resolve he had made within the past half hour was strengthened.

"You wished to speak to me?" Luke asked.

"I will not ask if she may stay here," Ashley said. " 'Twould be an insult to the love you and Anna have always shown her. I would ask only that you ensure she is left in peace. There are to be no recriminations, no insults, no coldness. She is blameless."

"And yet, my dear," Luke said, "she has assured me that she was not coerced."

Ashley's jaw tightened. "She was blameless," he said. "You will promise me something, Luke."

"I will?" No one looked more haughty than Luke with raised eyebrows.

"You will send for me," Ashley said, "if she is with child. I will come immediately, bringing a license with me."

"You are going somewhere?" The eyebrows were still up.

"Where I should have gone as soon as I set foot in England," Ashley said. "To Penshurst. To Alice's home. My home. There will be work to do there. A steward has been running the estate single-handed for over four years, since the death of Alice's brother. 'Tis time I took the reins into my own hands."

"Yes," Luke said. "You were always good at that."

"I will leave at first light tomorrow," Ashley said. "But 'tis not far. Only in Kent. I can come back here quickly."

"Yes." Luke nodded.

"I am fond of her," Ashley said. "I want you to know that. 'Twas not — ugly. I am fond of her."

"Yes." Luke's eyes coolly examined his face. "You always were, Ash. Fond of her. Sit and have a drink with me. When my eyes alighted on you in the ballroom two evenings ago, and when I had convinced myself that they did not deceive me, I was more delighted than I can possibly express in words. My brother — my only surviving brother had come home. I pictured myself having long conversations with you, taking long walks and rides with you, while our wives and children became acquainted. 'Tis a picture that has been dashed into a thousand pieces since then."

He came around the desk, set a hand on Ashley's shoulder, and indicated two chairs by the fireplace.

12

Ashley was leaving. He was going to Penshurst, the estate in Kent he had inherited through his wife. It was not as far away as India. Indeed, it was only a day's drive away. Closer than Victor's or Charlotte's. But Emily knew as she sat on the window seat in her room, hugging her knees, the side of her head resting against the cold glass of the window, that it was as far away as India. Farther. When he had gone to India, there had been the hope, however faint, that he would come back someday. This time there was no such hope.

He would not come back to Bowden. Not while she was there.

It was altogether probable that she would never see him again.

She gazed out over lawns and trees. It was a day very similar to the one on which he had left before. Gray and blustery. She could not see the front of the house or the stables or carriage house. She did not know if he had left yet. She remembered the feeling of panic that had clawed at her stomach the last time. It had driven her finally to rush outside and down to the driveway so that she might hide among the trees and see his carriage pass. She felt the same panic now. But this time she could do nothing about it.

She lowered her forehead to her knees and closed her eyes. This time his leaving had been entirely of her own choosing. And if she had the choice to make again — if he came now to ask her one more time — she would not change it. He was going because she would not have him. Because she loved him.

She wondered if her suffering was sufficient to atone for what she had done to Lord Powell. She did not feel sorry for herself; she deserved this feeling of black despair. She hoped Lord Powell would find someone else. She hoped he would be happy. She hoped he would look back at some future date and be fervently glad that she had rejected him. She concentrated her mind on him, picturing the dark handsome face with its heavy eyebrows and rather large nose and slightly crooked teeth. She tried to analyze why it was that handsomeness did not always require perfection of features. She tried to distract her mind.

Ashley was leaving.

She would never see him again. And if she did, seeing him would make no difference to anything. It would only make her feel worse.

No, there was no worse way to feel.

She had not gone down to dinner last evening. Nor had she joined the family in the drawing room afterward. Anna had come to her later, after she had been to the nursery to feed Harry, and had told her that Ashley was leaving.

"Everyone will be returning home soon, Emmy," she had said, taking her sister's hands in hers and smiling her sunny smile. "Everything will be back to normal again. There will be just Luke and me and the children and you — the way I like it best. Even Mother is going, with Doris and Andrew. You can live your life as you wish again. You can paint again. You can be at peace again. You will be happy, Emmy, once the rawness of these few days has passed. Lord Powell was pleasant, but he would not have understood you as Luke and I do or loved you half as much. You did the right thing."

Dear Anna. No mention of Ashley or of

what had caused her to break off her betrothal.

And so today he was leaving. Had left. There had been more than an hour of daylight already. Anna had said he was to leave at first light. He was gone. He was an hour on his way. Emily's arms tightened about her legs and she squeezed her eyes more tightly closed. Shutting herself in — totally.

The rest of her life had begun. So be it, then. And she would not cower in her room forever or escape outside merely for the sake of escape. She was going to dress respectably, just as she had almost every day since Lord Powell had first arrived, and she was going to go down to breakfast. There was the danger, of course, that everyone would be there. It did not matter. She would go anyway.

"Yass," she said, getting determinedly to her feet and crossing to her dressing room.

She stood in front of her looking glass. "Yass," she said. No, it was not quite right. Her lower jaw dropped too far. He should have told her yesterday, as he had told her about the *s* sound. This was the way the mouth and jaw should look. "E-e-e," she said. "Yess." That looked better. She would scold him for not scolding *her*. She smiled

264

at her image.

And then her face crumpled before her eyes. She dropped her face into her hands and sobbed with unabashed self-pity.

"Emily will come home with Constance and me," Victor said. His face was unsmiling, almost grim. " 'Tis only fitting. I am her brother, head of her family. Elm Court is where she belongs. I will be able to keep an eye on her there."

"And Charlotte and Jeremiah will be close by," Constance said. " 'Twill be a consolation to her to be close to the church."

Jeremiah added, "I have always said — have I not, my love? — I have always said that an unmarried daughter's place is in the home of her birth with whoever is head of that home. Emily can be taught to be useful at Elm Court. And Charlotte will help Constance to provide moral guidance."

"La, it sounds almost," Doris said, "as if Luke is not considered a responsible guardian."

The Earl of Weims laid a hand over hers on the table and she subsided into silence.

"Emily would probably be happier away from here," the Dowager Duchess of Harndon said. "With her own family and away from all members of mine."

"Emmy will stay where she belongs," Anna said, her cheeks flushed with color. "Where she has always been happy and loved. She will not go with you, Victor, to be made to feel that she is somehow a child who needs to be disciplined."

Luke did to Anna what the earl had just done to Doris. He set a hand over hers. "You need not upset yourself, my dear," he said.

"If truth were known," Victor said, "Luke will be only too glad to be rid of Emily, Anna. It cannot be comfortable for him to know that his brother was the one to dishonor her or that our sister was the one who refused to allow Lord Ashley to retrieve his honor."

" 'Tis true, Anna," Constance said, looking as if she was on the verge of tears.

Anna already was in tears.

"And you must consider your husband's feelings before your own or Emily's, Anna," Jeremiah added. "He is your lord and master."

" 'Tis remarkable, by my life," Luke said, his eyebrows raised haughtily, though the eyes beneath them looked more lazy than cold, "to find that so many people are privy to my inmost thoughts and feelings and choose to speak for me."

He had not finished. But Emily, who had been sitting at the breakfast table, watching herself being spoken of in the third person, watching her future being decided for her, though she had kept her eyes determinedly on her plate for much of the time, did not wait for the rest. She got to her feet, folded her napkin and set it neatly beside her plate, and left the room. She resisted the urge to run.

There was nowhere *to* run. There was nowhere to go. Whether she wished it or not, they would decide for her. She was now and forever the spinster member of the family, a burden on them all whether or not they ever admitted it, even in the privacy of their own minds. It was the desire to avoid that very situation that had made her decide upon marriage. Better an unexciting marriage in which there was no deep love, she had decided, than dependence upon her relatives for the rest of her life.

Now she had no alternative to dependence.

And worse now was the fact that she was not even a *maiden* relative dependent upon them. She was a fallen woman. Perhaps they would never describe her as such, but every word that had been spoken at the breakfast table this morning had presupposed that fact. And the fact that she was subnormal, incapable of managing her own life. How weary she was of the sight of sound — too weary even to be amused by the thought. Sound, it seemed — voices — ruled the world. It was the only sanity.

She went upstairs for a cloak and then walked outside. She walked all the way down through the terraces of the formal gardens and across the lawn below them. She crossed the bridge and walked down the driveway into the trees. Strangely, in seven years she had never come back to that particular tree. But she knew it unerringly. She stood against it as she had stood that morning. She set her head back against the trunk and closed her eyes. Shutting herself in again.

This morning she was several hours too late.

Luke waited for Emily to leave. He curled his fingers about Anna's hand. Like Emily, she had remarkable control over her emotions. Rarely did she become openly and publicly upset.

" 'Twould seem to me," Luke said, "that two important facts have been ignored both yesterday and today. Perhaps three. First, Emily is a person, with intelligence and a

will of her own. Second, she is an adult —
two-and-twenty years of age. Thirdly, she
has already taken responsibility for her own
questionable actions of two nights ago and
has already decided her course. Perhaps
discussing her future among ourselves,
especially in her presence, is not the right
thing to do. Perhaps we should consult Emily's wishes."

"Bravo, my lad," Lord Quinn said.

"Emmy will wish to stay here, Luke,"
Anna said.

"Emily must learn that she gave up her
right to choose yesterday," Victor said.

"Emily needs to learn that she must be
ruled by the men in her life," Jeremiah said.
"In this case, by Victor."

"I shall offer Emily a choice that has not
been mentioned yet," Lady Sterne said,
entering the discussion for the first time. "I
shall offer it, not dictate it. And I would
remind anyone who speaks of the men in a
woman's life" — she looked severely at the
Reverend Hornsby — "that some women
manage very nicely without such a disagree-
able watchdog. Harndon has already
reminded us that Emily is of age. If she
chooses, she may return to London with
me. 'Tis the Season, when all the fashionable world will be assembled for enjoyment.

I shall take her about and have the happiest spring since I had Anna and Agnes to bring out. 'Tis time that Emily was no longer coddled. She is *deaf,* not a mindless infant."

"Bravo, Marj, m'dear," Lord Quinn said.

Luke pursed his lips and looked amused.

"Aunt Marjorie," Anna said. "Oh, Aunt Marjorie, you are a *dear.*"

"Impossible, madam," the Reverend Hornsby said. "I would remind you that Emily is a fall —"

"Complete that thought, lad," Lord Quinn said in perfectly agreeable tones, "and you will be licking up the blood from your nose."

"Theodore!" The dowager glared coldly at her brother.

"Might I suggest the weather as a topic of conversation?" Lady Sterne said, getting to her feet and gesturing with both hands to indicate that she did not expect the gentlemen to scramble to theirs. " 'Tis dull but invariably safe. I shall go and search for Emily. Faith, but the coming spring begins to looks brighter to me already. If I can but persuade her."

Luke patted his wife's hand.

"The clouds are low and heavy, egad," Lord Quinn said. "But they are white rather than black. Or perhaps gray, to be strictly accurate. Will it rain, d'ye think? Hornsby?"

270

■ ■ ■ ■

Lady Sterne watched from the lowest terrace of the formal gardens as Emily trudged, head down, up the sloping lawn from the bridge. She was not wearing stays beneath her gown this morning, but even without she had a trim and pleasing figure. Her hoops were small, but then large hoops were falling out of fashion. She was not wearing a hat, and her lace cap had slipped so far to the back of her head that it was hardly visible from the front. There was, of course, all that glorious hair, which might have been described as either golden or blond without too much stretching of the truth.

And then, of course, there were her eyes, by far her best feature. Men would fall in love with her eyes alone, Lady Sterne mused, even if the surrounding package were but moderately pleasing. And Emily was more than moderately lovely.

She dressed up to look quite superb. The older lady recalled how she had looked for the ball just three nights ago.

Lud, but she would do very nicely indeed, Lady Sterne thought, feeling her spirits lifting by the minute. She had begun on occasion to catch herself feeling old. At the grand age of fifty. That was what had done it, of course. Fifty sounded a whole decade older than nine-and-forty. She needed something to keep her young. There was Theo, of course, but he felt more like a dear old habit than a force of rejuvenation.

If she could but take Emily to London with her. If she could but be given the challenge of bringing the girl into fashion despite her affliction. No, *because* of it. Much could be made of the novelty of a beauty who could neither hear nor speak — except with those eyes.

As for virgin brides . . . Pshaw! Lady Sterne thought. If truth were told, any man would be thankful to avoid blood and skittishness on his wedding night.

Emily had seen her, had realized that it was too late to take a different course and avoid the encounter, and came onward, smiling. Lady Sterne came face-to-face with her across the low hedge that separated the terrace from the lawn.

" 'Tis like this, Emily, my love," she said slowly and distinctly. "They would divide you up like a bone if they could and take you in a dozen different directions. Each for your own good, of course. Lud, men and their ideas of what is for a woman's own good! 'Tis time more women stood up to them as you did yesterday to Lord Ashley and demanded to decide for themselves what was in their own best interest." She forced herself to slow down again when she saw the slight frown on the girl's face. "Become a bone if 'tis your wish, child. Or take your life in your own hands and bring it to London with me. We will enjoy the Season together. We will have every man in the kingdom groveling at your feet. What do you say?"

Emily looked gravely at her for such a long time that Lady Sterne felt her dream fading. The girl had not understood. And how could she possibly function in London, where all was noise and conversation and music and dancing? It was madness to have imagined . . . But then Emily smiled, first with her eyes and then with the rest of her face. She began to laugh in her strange, rather ungainly way, tipping back her head and looking more vividly lovely to Lady Sterne than she had ever appeared before. There were wildness and recklessness and animation and sheer beauty in her face. She was a true original. Yes, that would be the secret of her success. She was an original.

Every man in the kingdom? Lady Sterne thought. Nay, but it was no exaggeration.

She joined in Emily's laughter. It was

madness. But madness felt good. It felt . . . youthful.

Penshurst was situated in a pleasant valley, rounded and wooded hills behind, the park with its sloping lawns and copses in front. A wide river flowed to the east of the house. On the opposite bank was the village, clustered about a church with a tall spire. The house was squarely classical, set between a smaller matching stable block to one side and an office block to the other. It all looked still new and rather splendid.

Ashley drew his horse to a halt on the road, which afforded a wide view across the park to the house and the village and the hills — his carriage with his valet and his baggage were coming behind him. It was all very beautiful and very peaceful. He felt sad for Sir Alexander Kersey, who had purchased the land, pulled down the old house, and built this one. He had built it with the fortune he had made with the East India Company. He had intended to retire here, set up his dynasty here. But the dynasty had ended very soon after him. His son had died before him, Alice soon after, and Thomas with her. So already Penshurst had passed into new hands — his.

And he did not want it. Grand and lovely

as it was, much as he had always wanted to settle on an estate of his own here in England, it had come to him in the wrong way and too late. Throughout his voyage home and in the days since, he had several times thought of selling it, going somewhere else, starting fresh. If Emmy had married him, perhaps he would have done so. He would not have wanted to bring her here.

Emmy. He felt a sinking of the heart whenever he thought of her — and she was constantly in the back of his thoughts, no matter how much he tried to concentrate his mind on the challenge ahead of him. He had ruined her life; he did not believe he was overdramatizing, especially since there was still the chance that he had got her with child.

But he could not think of that now. He nudged at his horse and continued on his way. Each time he had thought of it, he had realized that he could not sell Penshurst. Not yet, anyway. He had to go there, see the place where she had lived, where she had grown up. For her sake and her father's he had to see that the estate was well run. He felt somehow tied to it, like a millstone about his neck.

He remembered something his friend Major Roderick Cunningham had said to him in India when he had announced his intention of resigning from his post and returning to England. Roderick had advised him to come back, to marry and have children, to put the past behind him. But finally he had set a hand on his friend's shoulder and squeezed hard.

"But you will not, Ash," he had said. "You will go to Penshurst and you will find her there and punish yourself with memories. You will make it the best-run estate in England as a kind of penance and you will be miserable. Well, do it. But not forever. Forgive yourself at last, sell the place, go somewhere else, and get on with the business of living the rest of your life."

Rod had been right — at least on everything except that last point. Ashley did not know how he would ever be able to forgive himself. But self-pity would serve no purpose. Look where self-pity had got him in Bowden. He winced at the memory of how Emmy had found him just when his spirits had been at their very lowest ebb, when he had touched the very bottom of despair.

He had grasped for peace and had shattered it.

Ashley smiled and touched his hat to several people he passed in the village. It was a pretty place. At the far end of the main street a humpbacked stone bridge crossed the river. At the far side of it was a cottage, somewhat larger than those in the village itself. And beyond that were the high gates leading into the park. They stood open.

But he paused beside the cottage. A young child was swinging on the gate leading into the well-kept garden. He stared at Ashley with large blue eyes. His dark hair was short and curly.

"Good day to you, lad," Ashley said. "And who might you be?"

"I am Eric Smith," the boy said. "Who are you?"

"Eric!" a voice called from behind him. A woman stood in the open doorway of the house. She was dressed plainly but decently. She was young and rather lovely. Ashley thought she must be the child's mother, though her hair was lighter.

"Madam." He touched the brim of his three-cornered hat. "Good day to you. May I present myself? Lord Ashley Kendrick of Penshurst."

She half inclined her head to him, though she did not curtsy as he had expected she would. Her face, which had looked embarrassed when she first called out to her son, was now expressionless.

But before Ashley could ride on, someone else appeared in the doorway, an older man, who stepped around the woman and came walking down the path toward the gate. He was smiling, though he looked at Ashley with shrewd, perhaps wary eyes.

"You are expected at the house, my lord," he said. "Ned Binchley at your service. My grandson, Eric." He set his hands on the shoulders of the child and stopped his gate-swinging, then turned his head to look back at the doorway, which was now empty. "My daughter, Mrs. Katherine Smith."

"I am pleased to make your acquaintance," Ashley said. The man was dressed as a gentleman, even if his coat and breeches had seen better days. He also spoke as a gentleman.

"I was Sir Alexander Kersey's steward for fifteen years," Mr. Binchley explained. "I have an interest in the estate, my lord. If there is anything in which I can assist you, I am here."

"But you are no longer the steward?" Ashley asked.

"I retired," Mr. Binchley said, "almost five years ago, after young Mr. Kersey died."

Ashley nodded, touched his hat again, winked at Eric, and rode on. The Kersey name had been mentioned. This was where they had belonged, where they had been known. This was where she had lived. She had ridden and walked along this driveway perhaps a thousand times. And she had lived in the house that was coming into view again. There would be signs of her inside. Unless decisions had been made after Alice's death without his having been consulted, many of her possessions would remain in the house. He could almost feel her presence already.

He shivered.

13

Lady Sterne and Emily had agreed between them during the carriage journey to London — though Lady Sterne did all the talking, of course — that for the first week they would stay at home preparing to launch themselves into all the busy activities of the Season.

And so Lady Sterne had all the delight of summoning her mantua maker and of spending two long days having Emily's measurements taken and choosing patterns and fabrics with her and convincing her that she needed many more clothes than Emily had first thought.

She had the delight too of spreading the word that the sister of the Earl of Royce, the sister-in-law of the Duke of Harndon, was in town to take in the Season. She made a particular point of having it known that Lady Emily Marlowe was totally deaf and without speech but that she could read lips.

And that her beauty surpassed even that of her sisters, who were remembered as great beauties. Had not one of them snared Harndon, the most handsome, the most discriminating, the most eligible bachelor of his time?

"Egad, but you are happy, Marj," Lord Quinn said to her when the week was almost over. "I have not seen you so happy in a long while."

"Of course I am happy," she said, smiling sleepily at him. " 'Tis the effect you always have on me, Theo. And it has been three whole weeks. An eternity. You were especially good today, dear."

Discretion and the strictest of good manners had kept them apart at Bowden, but now that both had returned to London, they had resumed the weekly trysts that had brought them together for years. They were lying in each other's arms, lazy after lovemaking.

Lord Quinn chuckled. "Only because you were happy and especially eager, Marj," he said. " 'Tis the gel. You are enjoying having her. How the devil you are to launch her when she is stone deaf and has none of the pretty conversation the bucks all enjoy, I do not know. But the very impossibility has you enjoying yourself immensely, by my life."

He kissed her lips.

" 'Tis one last chance," she said. "I thought 'twas lost, Theo, when she was to marry Lord Powell. And I was glad for Anna's sake that all was settled. But I cannot pretend to be sorry that I could bring her with me. She is going to have all the young blades prostrate at her feet."

Lord Quinn chuckled again. "I'll not forget," he said, "how we schemed to bring my nephy together with your goddaughter eight years ago, Marj. They were married within a week, and as I predicted then, she was brought to bed exactly nine months later."

"With a daughter," she said. "You said 'twould be a boy, Theo. But we did do rather well, did we not? Dear Anna. She is still happy with him. And the boy came later — boys. Three of them." She sighed and wriggled a little closer to him.

"By my life, Marj," Lord Quinn said, "I believe we should try it again."

Her head went back and she looked into his face.

"With that scamp of a younger nephy of mine and your little gel," Lord Quinn said.

Lady Sterne looked at him consideringly for a long time. "Why did it happen, Theo?" she asked at last. " 'Twas not ravishment, I

282

am happy to say for Lord Ashley's sake. But why, then? She seemed fond enough of Lord Powell."

"Marj, m'dear," he said, "I thought 'twas women who were the romantics."

She looked at him long and hard again. "Do you believe so?" she said. "Do you really believe so?"

"Egad," he said, "but only one thing bothers me. If she loves the lad, why would she not have him? Perhaps I am wrong."

"Oh, pshaw!" Lady Sterne said. "That should be as plain as the nose on your face, Theo. And as plain as the nose on mine. I would have seen it sooner if I had but crossed my eyes. Why else would she refuse him? Of course she loves him. Why else would she have said no?"

"There it is," Lord Quinn said, his brows knitted into a frown. "Female logic. I never could get the hang of it, by my life. But you agree with me, Marj?"

"Faith, but you have deflated all my hopes," she said. "I brought her here to find her a husband, Theo, despite all the odds. But if she loves Lord Ashley and will not have him, she will doubtless not have anyone else either." She sighed.

"Then perhaps, m'dear," he said, "we had better do what we did before. We had better bring them together."

"Lud, but how?" she said. "He has offered and she has said no. He has gone off to Penshurst and she has come to town. How can we bring them together? With Luke and Anna 'twas easy. They were to attend the same ball; all we had to do was arrange it so that they took a good look at each other."

"Egad, but 'twas more than that," he said. "There was Luke swearing he would never marry. There was Anna swearing that *she* never would. But marry they did. We have to get the boy to London, Marj."

"How?" she said. "He has just gone to Penshurst, nursing a broken heart over that poor dead wife of his. Doubtless he is also nursing a sense of shame over Emily. Does he love her, do you suppose, Theo?"

"He will," Lord Quinn said. "But we have to bring him here to see her enslaving all the other young bucks, Marj. I can think of one sure way."

She gazed at him. "You are looking positively sheepish, Theo," she said. "Whatever are you plotting?"

" 'Tis like this, Marj," he said. "I believe 'tis time I made an honest woman of you, m'dear."

Lady Sterne stared at him with incredulity for a few moments, and then she tipped back her head and laughed. "Theo," she said when she was able, "you have been making a sinner of me for longer than twenty years. We have agreed on a number of occasions that 'tis better so, that neither of us fancies the shackles of matrimony."

"If we were to get shackled, Marj — in St. George's, of course, with all the fashionable world in attendance — my nephy would have little choice but to come too."

"We would marry," she said, "merely to bring Lord Ashley to town, Theo? 'Twould be the most eccentric reason for marrying I have ever heard."

He tightened his arm about her and kissed her hard. "The fact is, Marj," he said, "I have been a bachelor all my life and have never thought of loneliness — till recently. But with the creeping of the years, I find myself with a hankering to have someone to wake up to in the nights and in the mornings. And someone in the chair on the other side of my hearth in the mornings and the evenings."

"You have been eyeing the crop of young girls this Season," she said. But she was blinking her eyes hard to keep the tears at bay.

Lord Quinn chuckled. "I am old enough to value comfort, Marj," he said. "I am comfortable with you, m'dear."

"Comfortable?" Her eyebrows shot up.

"Egad," he said, " 'twas not well expressed, by my life. You know I love you, Marj. I loved you in those days when you were married to Sterne. I loved you after you were widowed. I still love you. There has never been another woman for me. Never will be."

She turned her face in to his shoulder. "But to marry in order to promote another match, Theo," she said. "You must mean soon, do you?"

"We could have the banns read for the first time next Sunday," he said. "You see, Marj, I have thought of how you will be after the gel has gone. She *will* be gone, y'know, either back to Bowden or off to Elm Court when summer comes. Or else she will marry someone, though I cannot see it happening. But the gel is not my main concern. You are. You will be unhappy, m'dear. You will be lonely. Again. You think I have not noticed in the last year or two that some of the sparkle has gone out of you? Perhaps you need a new life, a new challenge, one that will be a little more permanent than finding a husband for Anna's young sister. I'll be a challenge. I promise to be a challenge."

286

"Oh, Theo," she said, her face still against his shoulder. "Lud, but I am tempted. 'Tis ridiculous."

"After the Season is over," he said, "I would be able to take you to France, Marj, and to Italy and Austria and all the other places you always say you would visit if you but had the chance. Harkee, we could be young again, m'dear. Not in years — I have no wish to be young in years again. But young in hope. Egad, I like the sound of it. Marry me, woman."

"And Lord Ashley will come to town for the wedding, and we will convince him that he loves Emily," Lady Sterne said, laughing, "and convince Emily that he loves her. And then we will attend their wedding. 'Tis the wildest of wild schemes, Theo."

"We will do it," he said, raising himself on one elbow and leaning over her. "Now say yes, Marj, and kiss me. Without any more delay. There is still time to have each other again at our leisure. You know I hate to be rushed. Let us waste no more time, then."

She sighed audibly. "Yes, then," she said. And she raised her head to meet his lips with her own.

Emily had never had any desire to go to London, to enter society. She might have done so with Anna and Luke, who occasionally went to town. She had always shuddered at the thought of being away from the countryside, of being forced to dress and behave as a lady all day and every day, of having to be in company with people who would look on her as a kind of freak. She had made sure before deciding to take Lord Powell's courtship seriously that he was the sort of man who spent most of his time on his own estate. Luke had understood that when choosing her suitors.

But now she found herself in London, preparing to enter society with Aunt Marjorie, subjecting herself to long sessions with a mantua maker and lengthy shopping expeditions to purchase shoes and hats and caps and fans and a dizzying array of other frivolities. It was the Season in London and she knew that they would attend fashionable entertainments every day, sometimes more than once a day. She would meet polite society. Soon — just one week after her arrival.

It was madness. It was impossible.

She faced it all with a sort of wild excitement. All of her carefully planned future had been thrown to the winds in exchange for a moment of foolish indiscretion out at the falls. The seemingly inevitable consequences had been defied and denied when she had refused to marry Ashley. And the stifling net that had been about to fall over her head in family plans for the remainder of her life had been avoided at the last moment — she had not been forced to go to Victor's or Charlotte's.

She felt incredibly free. She felt as if the whole world, the whole of life was awaiting her. She felt as if she had not lived thus far in her two-and-twenty years. She felt as if she had a great deal of living to do and as if at last she had all the opportunity in the world to do it.

She would not look ahead. Had she done so, she would have known that the Season would come to an end, that she could not live with Lady Sterne for the rest of her life, that eventually she was going to have to be dependent again on her family, and that perhaps she would not be allowed to determine her own very limited fate. She refused to think about it. She had not gone to London with any intention of finding herself a husband, though she knew that Lady Sterne had hopes of her doing so. She would never marry. Partly it was because she could not. She was no longer a virgin, and she knew that virginity was a man's primary requirement in a bride. But mainly it was because she had no wish to marry. She had given herself once to Ashley. She would never give herself again.

Yet even the fact that she was not in search of a husband was freeing and exhilarating. There was no ulterior motive to her coming to London for the Season. She had come merely to enjoy herself. She had no idea how that was to be accomplished, but she did not much care. She reveled in every moment of the week of preparation.

"I have never known a young lady more patient or more docile through such lengthy fittings, my lady, I declare," Madame Delacroix, the mantua maker, said to Lady Sterne while Emily watched her lips.

But Emily wanted to be transformed. She wanted to be as fashionable, as beautiful as she could be. She wanted to forget everything else — her deafness, her differentness, her guilt, the mess she had made of her life. She wanted to be a new person. A *normal* person. She wanted to forget the world in which she had always been trapped.

"And I have never known one more beautiful," Madame Delacroix added.

Doubtless she said the same things to every young lady client of hers, Emily thought, smiling at her image in the glass. But it was impossible not to be warmed by the compliment.

"Let me look at you." Lady Sterne had stood up when Emily entered her drawing room, and now she clasped her hands to her bosom. "Lud, I thought you lovely, child, on the evening of Harndon's ball. You are ten times lovelier now. What say you, Theo?"

"Egad," Lord Quinn said. "If my head does not swell to twice its size tonight with two such lovely ladies to escort, 'twill be a wonder."

Emily pirouetted slowly. They were to attend Mrs. Cadoux's ball on Berkeley Square. It seemed madness that her first appearance should be there when she was deaf and would be unable to hear the music or dance — she tried to forget the one occasion when she had been foolhardy enough to try it. But she had readily agreed to attend when Lady Sterne had held the invitation aloft and said she thought it might be the perfect start.

Her gown was blue, the sack dress, fitted tightly at the front and flowing loosely behind, opened down the front and trimmed with elaborately ruched robings. The petticoat, of a slightly darker blue and worn over large hoops, was well covered with flounces and furbelows. Her stomacher was trimmed with fashionable ribbon bows of diminishing size. There was lace at her bosom and elbows. Her hair, dressed rather high in front and elaborately curled at the back, was carefully powdered. A lace confection of a cap had been pinned to the back of it, its lappets fluttering freely to her waist. For the first time she wore cosmetics — rouge and coloring for her eyelashes — and a small black heart-shaped patch on one cheek, a frivolous concession to fashion.

She opened her silver silk fan and plied it gently before her mouth, laughing over the top of it at Aunt Marjorie and Lord Quinn.

"Lud, child," Lady Sterne said. "Those eyes are deadly weapons."

"There will not be a gentleman present who will not be slain by them, by my life," Lord Quinn said. "Ladies?" He offered them each an arm after making them an elegant bow.

In truth, Emily found a scant half hour later, as their carriage inched its way forward for a chance to deposit its occupants before the well-lit doors of the house on Berkeley Square, this was not going to be quite as easy as she had anticipated. Her heart was beating painfully with excitement and fear. How could she meet a whole ballroomful

— a whole houseful — of strangers? But it was too late now to turn back.

She looked about with wide eyes when she entered the house on Lord Quinn's arm and ascended the stairs slowly to the ballroom and the receiving line. And she had thought the ball at Bowden a crowded and splendid affair! This ballroom, she discovered when she was finally inside it, was surely too crowded to allow for dancing. There were people conversing in groups, couples promenading about the edge of the space kept clear for dancing, people — mostly gentlemen — standing and looking. She felt dizzy and frightened. This was more than madness.

And soon there were people converging on her own small group — ladies come to greet Lady Sterne, gentlemen come to wish Lord Quinn a good evening. And gentlemen come with the express purpose of being presented to her. Emily suspected after the first few moments of surprise that it had been arranged thus, that both Lady Sterne and Lord Quinn had been busy ahead of time seeing to it that she would have partners, if not for dancing, then at least for strolling and conversing. Certainly none of the gentlemen who came seemed surprised to find that she could not speak and could hear them only when she could see their lips.

Emily smiled and nodded and shook her head in appropriate places and even laughed. She plied her fan against the heat of the ballroom and smiled over the top of it. And when a young gentleman came and talked with Lord Quinn and was then presented to her and showed surprise at her handicap, she knew that finally she had attracted someone who had not been persuaded ahead of time to take notice of her. She smiled all the more brightly.

Viscount Burdett secured her hand for the first set and directed her toward a sofa that was just being vacated by a couple who intended to dance.

It was the beginning of a strange, delirious sort of evening. The sofa became the place from which she conducted her court, to use the phrase that Lord Quinn used in the carriage on the way home. She did not know quite what the attraction was, but gentlemen sat beside her, stood beside her, hovered in her vicinity. All had secured introductions through either Aunt Marjorie or Lord Quinn.

They talked with one another. Sometimes they talked to her, using such precise lip movements that she laughed at them. They seemed amazed when she nodded or shook her head at appropriate times and they realized that she really had understood. She suspected that they saw her as some sort of amusing curiosity. She did not care. *They* were amusing curiosities. She was amused. She was wildly happy — or wildly enjoying herself at least.

" 'Tis hardly to be wondered at that you are a success, child," Aunt Marjorie said in the carriage, patting her hand. "You were not only beautiful, child — you sparkled, I do declare. And gentlemen can never resist sparkle. All those poor girls who are instructed to look bored lest they be accused of rustic enthusiasm are badly advised."

"Egad," Lord Quinn said, " 'twould be strange indeed, m'dear, if you did not acquire a large and permanent court. Burdett asked if you and Marj intend to be at home tomorrow afternoon. And a dozen other young bucks listened avidly to the answer."

Emily laughed.

"Theo," Aunt Marjorie said, leaning forward to set a hand on his knee, "shall we tell Emily?"

Emily looked across the carriage at him. She was still smiling.

"You will be the first to know, m'dear," he said, catching Aunt Marjorie's hand as she was about to remove it and bringing it back to his knee. "Marj here has done me the great honor of accepting my marriage offer. We are to be married, here in London, as soon as the banns have been called. At St. George's, with half the world present."

Emily bit her lower lip. She did not know which one of them to hug first. She looked from one to the other with shining eyes. She had known them both for a long time and loved them both. And she had always thought that there was a fondness between them stronger than mere friendship.

"I daresay all your family will come to town for the occasion," Aunt Marjorie said. "My only relationship to any of you is as Anna's godmother, but you have all been kind enough to call me aunt. I want you all present when I marry."

She would see Anna, Emily thought. And Anna would see how happy she was. She had been so worried that London was not at all the place for her youngest sister.

"And all my family too," Lord Quinn said. "Doris and my sister are already in town. Luke will come from Bowden and Ashley will come from Penshurst."

Emily's insides performed a complete and

uncomfortable somersault.

"You may think it quite unseemly at the age of fifty, Emily," Aunt Marjorie said, patting Emily's arm with her free hand, "but 'tis going to be the happiest day of my life."

Ashley would come from Penshurst. As soon as the banns had been called. For the wedding. Within a month. She would see him again.

Ashley would come.

Emily closed her eyes and rested her head against the cushions. Her eyes ached. Did other people's ears ache from incessant conversation the way her eyes sometimes did? She longed suddenly for solitude and the sweet, undemanding companionship of nature.

But she had stepped out of that life into the real world. She had come to enjoy herself. She *was* enjoying herself.

She opened her eyes determinedly and smiled, first at Lord Quinn and then at Aunt Marjorie, both of whom were regarding her silently but rather intently.

Ashley would come.

14

There was no separate breakfast parlor at Penshurst. All meals were taken in the huge dining room, with its gilded paneled walls and its coved and painted ceiling. The massive oak table had been made especially for the room.

Ashley sat in lone state at the head of the table, eating his breakfast and reading his mail. There was nothing from Bowden. He had leafed through the pile first to ascertain that. Of course, the news, if and when it came, might not come from Bowden. She had gone to London with Lady Sterne. Luke had already mentioned that in an earlier letter. Emmy in London, with the very sociable Lady Sterne. It was difficult to imagine. Poor Emmy!

He had been at Penshurst for almost three weeks. She would probably know by now, or at least suspect. Would she tell anyone immediately? Would she even understand?

Emmy was such a curious mixture of wisdom and innocence that it was impossible to know. But the suspense was weighing heavily on him. And he could not at all decide if he wanted it to be so or not. Emmy with child — with his child — and forced after all to marry him.

Part of him hoped fervently that it would not happen. He did not want her in that way, and he did not want her forced into doing something she so clearly did not want to do. But part of him wished that she would be forced into allowing him to do the decent thing.

And part of him longed just for her, for her closeness, her companionship, her unconventionality, her — but he could never put into words exactly what it was about her that he longed for.

And part of him longed for a child. Son or daughter — it would not matter. A child of his own body. His first.

There was a letter from London, but it was from his uncle Theo and not from Lady Sterne. Theo would hardly be the one elected to send for him. Sometimes he considered going on his own. To London. It was the Season. He was newly returned to England. It would be easy to excuse his going there for a week or two. Just to see that she was in good health and good spirits. Just to see if she needed him.

He had always been the one to need her, not the other way around, he realized. It was quite the contrary to what an outside observer might have been led to believe. Emmy had always been the strong one, the independent one. Right to the end.

He looked down at his uncle's bold handwriting when he had broken the seal of the letter. He read the short note twice and then smiled and chuckled. The old rogue! It was an open family secret that Theo and Lady Sterne had been lovers for as far back as Ashley could remember. Finally they were to be married. And they were not going to creep quietly off to the nearest clergyman with a special license. They were going to have a grand wedding at that most fashionable of all London churches, St. George's, in the presence of as many members of the fashionable world as could be packed within its pews.

He wished them well. He had no doubt that they would be happy together. They knew each other well enough — in all possible ways, Ashley did not doubt. It would never be said of them that they had rushed into marriage after a mere few weeks of acquaintance. The smile faded from Ashley's face.

And then the implication of what he had read struck him. The letter was more than an announcement. It was an invitation.

Ashley folded the paper and set it down. He drummed his fingers slowly on it. He had told himself that he would not go to London. She would not wish to see him. There was work to do here — he was still in the process of getting to know his new estate and of gradually taking charge of its administration. And there were invitations to honor from the neighbors who had been calling on him.

But the temptation to go had been strong even before the arrival of Theo's invitation. He found the house oppressive despite its still very new splendor. It was a feminine house. There were signs of Alice in every flounced drapery and every frilled cushion, in every delicate landscape painting and in every porcelain ornament. He was reminded powerfully of how she had transformed his own very comfortable home in India and of how she had raged against his habit of leaving books and garments and snuffboxes lying around. And here at Penshurst there was one particular set of rooms that drew him like a magnet though he hated setting foot inside them. And yet he found himself unable to give the order to have them cleared out. Alice's rooms, still full of her personal possessions, still with the distinctive perfume she had always worn clinging to the clothes in the wardrobes.

If only she had died naturally, he had thought one day, standing in the middle of her sitting room, his eyes tightly closed, or if only she had died in an accident for which he could not possibly feel personal blame, perhaps he would not feel so fettered by all this. She had been no wife to him. She had never even tried to deny that she had lovers. She had given birth to a red-haired child fourteen months after the only time she could possibly have conceived the child with him. She had told him they would be from home the night of the fire.

But nothing he had been able to say to himself in more than a year of mental torment had ever been able to convince him that he must not blame himself. While they were at home alone, dying in that fire, he had been taking repeated and delighted pleasure in the bed of a married woman — ironically his only foray into adultery.

And so, as Roderick Cunningham had predicted, he punished himself with the house which almost breathed her presence

— and longed for an excuse to be away from it.

There was another reason for wanting to be in London. An illogical reason, perhaps merely the exchange of one form of self-punishment for another. Lady Verney, his closest neighbor, had called on him with a couple of other neighbors. She was a lady of late middle age. She talked of her son and daughter, both of whom were in London for the Season. She referred to them several times as Henry and Barbara. He had dreaded meeting Sir Henry Verney — Alice's lover, the man she had loved almost fanatically. Verney, Ashley believed, had blighted her life. If she had not loved him, if he had not for some reason abandoned her, perhaps she would not have been so driven by self-hatred. For that was what had motivated Alice. He was convinced of it. Though he had often hated her, he had pitied her too.

He did not want to meet Verney, he had thought. And yet now, finding the man absent, he discovered that part of his reason for coming here must have been to see Verney, to try to piece together exactly what had happened here five years or so ago, to try to wrest some meaning out of the turbulent events of the past three years. He was still seeking that peace he had blindly sought on his return, he realized, though with his rational mind he knew that he would never find it. He was too wrapped about with his own sin and guilt.

His steward was doing a quite capable job on the estate, even though Ashley had his own ideas for change and improvement. And the housekeeper and butler were managing the house perfectly well. His neighbors would understand his reason for canceling or postponing his promised visits. There was no reason not to go to Theo's wedding.

And if he went, he would escape the house for a while. He would be able to call upon the Verneys. And he would see Emmy.

He would see Emmy. He rested his hand flat on his uncle's letter and closed his eyes. He could picture her sitting cross-legged on the soaked grass at Bowden, the front of her dress dark with wetness and clinging to her, her bare feet covered with grass, her hair loose and untidy and damp and brushing the ground behind her. She was frowning in concentration and touching her fingertips to his throat. He could hear her strange, low, curiously attractive voice saying *yass*.

Emmy. He would see her if he went to
304

London — *when* he went. There was really nothing to decide. He could not possibly absent himself from the wedding. And he had no wish to do so.

He would see her again.

It was a warm night, fortunately. She had hoped for it for all of the week past, a week during which the weather had been cloudy and somewhat chilly. But tonight was perfect. There were moonlight and starlight to sparkle off the surface of the River Thames as they crossed it by boat. She raised her face to the light for a few moments and was aware of the vast mystery of the universe.

And then they stepped out of the boat — Viscount Burdett took her hand and held it firmly and smiled at her while Lord Quinn helped Aunt Marjorie and the Earl of Weims helped Doris. A few moments later they were standing inside the entrance to Vauxhall Gardens, and she was looking around at the place she had been told about and had dreamed of seeing. The famous pleasure gardens, the great rival of Ranelagh Gardens, which she also longed to see. Both were said to be magical by night.

To their right, extending away into the distance, was a long colonnade with an arched, Gothic roof, hung with golden and red lamps. Ahead were the trees she had heard about, the grove, and the numerous shady walks. The trees were hung with festoons of lamps. Along the wide central path, farther in among the trees, she could see a brighter blaze of light. That would be the rotunda, the place where orchestras played and famous singers performed and people danced, the place where the more wealthy patrons sat in boxes and ate and drank while they enjoyed the spectacles around them. Viscount Burdett had hired a box there tonight.

"Lady Emily." Her arm was resting on his satin sleeve. He touched his fingers briefly to hers. "Do you find it pleasing?"

It was magical, spectacular. It was hard to believe that this was a park, with trees and grass, with sky above. She wondered briefly what it must be like in the daytime, when there would be no lamplight to mask reality, or what it would be like with the lamps unlit and all the crowding masses gone. But she pushed the thought aside. She did not want to know.

She smiled dazzlingly at the man who had conversed with her at several balls during the past weeks and had called upon her at Aunt Marjorie's and walked with her in the

Mall of St. James's Park. He was the most constant among a startlingly large number of gentlemen who paid her attention wherever she went. She did not know what the attraction was, unless perhaps there was novelty in paying court to a woman who could only smile and nod no matter how outrageous their compliments or how tedious their conversation. Almost always there was a group of them, who spoke with one another and did not therefore find her silence tedious. The crowds also released her from the necessity of concentrating every moment of every evening on other people's lips.

Lord Quinn said the attraction was that she was the loveliest young lady in London — or in England, for that matter. Emily laughed at him. Aunt Marjorie said it was that she sparkled and doubled her beauty with each smile. Emily laughed at her.

The almost reckless sense of freedom and gaiety that had taken her in its grip as soon as Aunt Marjorie had made her unexpected proposition in the garden at Bowden had not released her in the weeks since. She had not lived until now, she told herself. She was happy. And she knew now that she would never have to relinquish that freedom and that happiness. She had been a little afraid for herself when she learned that Aunt Marjorie was to marry Lord Quinn. But both had assured her that they had every intention of staying in London until the end of the Season and that then they would probably travel and wanted her to go with them. A lady needed more company than a man could provide, Lord Quinn had said. Gentlemen needed sometimes to be alone, Aunt Marjorie had said, as did ladies. But ladies did not have the freedom that men did to be quite alone. They needed companions. She would need Emily.

They were sitting in their box at the rotunda a few minutes after their arrival. They were just in time to watch the ballet, the viscount explained. He had deliberately chosen a night when there would be visual entertainment for Lady Emily as well as just music. She smiled at him. But before the ballet began, some gentlemen called at their box to pay their respects to her and to try to guess what message she was sending tonight by the design and positioning of the black patch she wore on one cheek. There had been much hilarity last night over the small heart she had worn close to the corner of her mouth. Tonight she wore a star high on her cheekbone, near the outer corner of her eye. There was no message, of course, but it amused her to see how inventive the gentlemen could be and how much they enjoyed themselves at her expense. She always laughed with them. Sometimes she even stopped listening and looked about her instead. They did not seem to notice her inattention. None of them, she realized, though she never dwelled on the thought, were really interested in *her.* None of them knew her or realized they did not. She did not care.

She was laughing and tapping Mr. Maddox on one arm after he suggested that she was Venus and was rivaling the stars in brightness when someone else joined the group. Someone who made her insides jump even before she looked at him. She had known he was coming to London, of course, but she had not known that he had arrived. Still, she told herself, she should have been prepared.

Fortunately she was locked safely inside the mask she had chosen to wear since her arrival in London. She turned her dazzling smile on him.

Unlike every other man present, he wore no wig. Neither was his hair powdered, as hers was. His hair, correctly rolled at the sides, neatly tied back, and bagged in black silk behind, looked startlingly dark. His face was still thinner than it should have been, angular, ascetic, handsome. He was dressed in dark blue velvet, a contrast to the pastel-shaded silks and satins of the other gentlemen.

It had been less than a month. It seemed an eternity. It was difficult to believe that those events at Bowden had really happened. She had come to feel that they had happened to a different person, someone who was no longer herself.

"Hello, Emmy," he said. His eyes were soft on her, though he did not really smile.

She raised her fan to her nose and kept her eyes sparkling. He turned to greet his sister and the other occupants of the box, then accepted an invitation to step inside and seated himself between Aunt Marjorie and Lord Quinn.

"Egad," one of her followers said just as she turned her eyes on him, "someone who has been granted the privilege of addressing you familiarly. Shall I call him out, Lady Emily? Or shall I put a bullet through my brain?"

Emily tapped him sharply on the arm.

"Do you not know Lord Ashley Kendrick, Max?" Viscount Burdett said. "Harndon's brother?"

"Ah," the other young man said. "Merely

family. I will live on to hope, then." He held one hand theatrically over his heart.

But there were too many participating in the conversation. It was too dizzying to try to watch the right one. And they had nothing important to say. Emily smiled brightly and looked around her — everywhere except at *him.*

"If you will pardon us," Viscount Burdett said, taking Emily's hand and setting it on his sleeve again, "the ballet is about to begin. I would appreciate it if my invited guests could watch the dancing unobstructed."

The other gentlemen all grumbled good-naturedly and moved off. Emily looked at Lord Burdett, who pointed at the orchestra. They were tuning their instruments. She had never seen ballet, and had been looking forward to it. She directed her eyes at the stage and resisted the urge to remove her hand from the viscount's arm.

Ashley had moved to Aunt Marjorie's other side, so that he was in the far corner of the box. He leaned back in his chair rather than forward as most people were doing as they waited for the performance to begin. He was watching her. She did not turn her head by even a fraction of an inch, but she had felt his every move. And she felt his eyes.

Something inside her threatened to crumble. Everything that she had built so determinedly and so eagerly during the past weeks. She was not going to let it happen. It was herself she had created since coming to London — her free and happy self. She refused to crawl back into misery and slavery to a love that had held her in thrall for eight years and had brought her precious few moments of happiness. She was happy with this new life. More than happy.

She realized suddenly, with something of a jolt, that the ballet was in progress and had been for some time. Her eyes had watched it but had seen nothing at all. She thought for one moment that her smile had slipped, but it had not. She turned it briefly on the viscount and he returned it and touched her hand again with his free one.

The visual spectacle of the ballet was magnificent. It was music for the eyes. The dancers moved with precision and grace to a silent melody. For a short while she felt the same connection she did when she was alone with nature.

But she also felt Ashley watching her.

He had arrived in London late in the morning and had called upon his uncle just an hour later. Ashley was staying at Harndon House, which had been opened in imminent expectation of the duke's arrival with his family. Luke had written to invite him to stay there, and after a brief hesitation he had accepted. He would not cower from his family like a whipped schoolboy. What was past was past — as far as his relations with his family were concerned, anyway.

His uncle had pumped his hand and slapped his shoulder and shown every sign of being delighted to see him. Ashley had wondered if the invitation had been a mere courtesy, if perhaps they would have preferred it if he had refused. He must pay his respects to Lady Sterne without delay, he was told, but the gels — his uncle's quite inappropriate word for his betrothed and Emmy — were to attend a private garden party during the afternoon. They were all going to Vauxhall that evening, though, as guests of Viscount Burdett. Ashley must come too — his uncle would send around to Burdett's to make the arrangements.

A note was delivered to Harndon House later in the day expressing the viscount's wish that Lord Ashley Kendrick would honor him by being one of his guests for the evening.

Who the devil was Viscount Burdett? Ashley wondered. And he wondered too if Emmy was one of his guests. But she must be, he reasoned, if Lady Sterne was to be there. Poor Emmy. He did not like the thought of her being dragged about to all the social entertainments. She would not like them.

He found himself aching to see her again. To see what he had done to her. She must have felt obliged to take herself away from Bowden and away from her brother and sisters for a while, he mused, and so she had come here, to exactly the wrong place for someone like Emmy. He expected to find her lost and wan and listless. Perhaps she would be ready to listen to another marriage offer. He was not particularly happy at Penshurst, but he could offer her countryside there, hills, a river, trees.

He went alone to Vauxhall and found his way to Viscount Burdett's box. He was not the first to arrive. He spotted Doris and Weims. The other occupants were blocked from his view by the press of men in front of the box. It was only as he drew closer that he saw what the attraction was — or who.

She looked much as she had looked at Luke's ball — fashionable, elegant, and quite extraordinarily beautiful. Except that

314

there she had not worn cosmetics. Or a small black patch placed just where it would draw attention to her eyes. And there, though she had smiled and shone with delight at the occasion and at her first minuet, she had not been exuberant and laughing and — coquettish. She was tapping some foppish-looking gentleman in lavender on the arm and drawing to herself all the foolery of flattery and mindless gallantry. Burdett — it must be he, Ashley figured — who sat beside her, looked like the cat who had drunk the cream or caught the canary or some such cliché. Emmy was flirting with the lot of them.

Ashley's first instinct, thankfully contained, was to lash about him with his fists.

She became aware of him. He expected her smile to soften on him. She had refused to marry him, but they had parted on affectionate terms. He remembered that last hour they had spent together, both rashly sitting on the soaked grass, almost knee to knee, while she learned to speak her first word. And he remembered too that at the ball he had known as soon as he looked into her eyes that she was Emmy.

Her eyes — her very shallow eyes — continued to sparkle as she smiled at him and raised her fan to her nose. She looked wonderfully happy. But her smile chilled him. She did not look like Emmy. He was sorry he had come. To Vauxhall. To London.

He entered the box and sat between his uncle and Lady Sterne after nodding to Doris and Weims and exchanging a few pleasantries with them. He congratulated Lady Sterne on her betrothal, kissed her hand, concentrated all his attention on her. But just as all the gentlemen clustered outside the box began to move away and the orchestra began to tune their instruments so that the ballet might begin, Lady Sterne leaned toward him and tapped him on the knee.

"I will change places with you if I may, dear boy," she said, "and sit next to Theo."

Ashley was briefly amused. The two of them had been lovers for twenty years or more and had always behaved with perfect good breeding in public, and yet it was important to them now to sit next to each other? He almost expected to see them linking hands. But his amusement soon waned. From the chair that Lady Sterne had occupied, he had no choice but to look across the box and see Emmy.

He might have turned his head, of course, to watch the ballet — it was rude to stare at one of the box's occupants. But he could not stop himself from doing just that.

She was watching the ballet, but she did not look absorbed, with the look of wonder he would have expected to see in her eyes. She still had the smile on her face, the coquettish smile that was not Emmy's at all. And her hand lay along Burdett's arm, her fingers splayed on his wide cuff. Her chin was lifted in a gesture of pride.

Was this what he had done to her?

He remembered — it was when he was dancing with her at Bowden — asking her if it was a disguise she wore or if that was what they had done to her. *Have they tamed you and your heart has not cried out for the wild?* he had asked her. *Do they have you singing prettily here, like a linnet in a cage?*

No, they had not done that to her. She had still been free. The next morning she had been out at the falls, painting, looking like his little fawn. She had painted the life force, bursting passionately through every living thing and out into the universe itself. It was he who had now done it to her. He had tamed her spirit and caged it.

There was an ache in his chest and his throat. He felt like crying.

Viscount Burdett rose and bowed over her hand and took her walking along one of the lamp-lit paths after the ballet was over. Lady Sterne looked at Doris and raised her eyebrows, and she and Weims followed them to offer chaperonage. Ashley stayed where he was. Soon, he saw, there were other gentlemen walking with Burdett and Emmy.

"Lud," Lady Sterne said, "but 'twas the best thing I ever did to bring Emily to town, Theo. She is enjoying herself immensely and has almost the largest court of any lady here this Season. I am in daily expectation of offers for her hand."

" 'Twould not surprise me, Marj," Lord Quinn said. "She is the loveliest gel here, and she has those speaking eyes. Burdett has been marked in his attentions. A viscount too, egad. She could do worse."

Ashley clamped his teeth together and said nothing, though the conversation continued on the same subject for a while longer — almost as if the newly betrothed couple had forgotten both his presence and the fact that if Emmy was ever to marry, he was the only possible candidate for her hand.

15

She had been shopping all morning on Oxford Street and Bond Street with Lady Sterne. She had spent money quite unnecessarily on a cornflower-trimmed straw hat. She had enough hats already to wear for a month without wearing the same one twice, she was sure. She also had scarcely slept the night before — for the first time since she came to London. And there was a connection between the purchase of the hat and the sleepless night. Ashley was going to take her walking during the afternoon in the Mall.

He had not spoken a word to her at Vauxhall after his initial greeting, not until he took his leave, early, before the rest of them. She had just returned from her stroll with Viscount Burdett, Doris, and Andrew. He had bowed over her hand after standing and speaking with the others first. She had thought he was going to leave without speaking to her at all. But he had.

"I have asked Lady Sterne if she will be at home tomorrow afternoon, Emmy," he had said. "I will call and take you walking in St. James's Park, if I may?"

She had smiled and nodded. In that moment there had been only Ashley and no consideration at all of the wisdom of being close to him. He had left before she saw the annoyance on Viscount Burdett's face. But he had no reason to be annoyed. She did not belong to him and did not intend to. Besides, she walked and drove with other gentlemen. She liked it that way.

"Lord Ashley Kendrick is a member of your family, Lady Emily?" he had asked her, leaning toward her so that, she guessed, no one else in the box would hear what he was saying. "A type of brother?"

She had smiled, opening her fan and cooling her face with it.

"Then I take it unkindly in a mere brother to monopolize your time for a whole afternoon, madam," he had said. "How will I live with the disappointment?"

She had laughed at his foolish gallantry and stretched out her arm to fan his face for a few moments.

But she had slept very little all night. Less than a month ago she had expected never to see him again. And then Aunt Marjorie and Lord Quinn had decided to marry, and she had known that Ashley would come for the wedding. She had been dismayed. She had not wanted him to come to London, just as a little more than a month ago she had not wanted him to come home to Bowden. Her life had to be lived without Ashley, and it was just too painful to see him.

Especially now. All last evening, after he had joined Viscount Burdett's party, although she had not once looked at him until he took his leave of her, she had felt him with every part of herself. Not just with her heart. Not even just with aching arms and yearning lips. She had felt him with a throbbing in her womb and lower, where his body had known hers. It had been not so much desire she had felt as — knowledge.

He should not have asked her to walk with him. It was unfair. He wanted to resume the relationship with her that had always been comfortable for him. He wanted to be her brother, her friend. Did he not know now, as she had always known, that such a relationship was impossible? Would he be a friend and a brother during their walk? Or would he try again to persuade her to marry him? But surely not that. He must have seen at Vauxhall how happy she was, how much she was enjoying the Season and the company of other gentlemen. He should not have asked her.

And so she tossed and turned more than she slept during the night. And so too she went shopping during the morning and bought a new straw hat.

Before going to Lady Sterne's, Ashley had a call to make on South Audley Street. It was one he had told himself all the way to London and again all morning that he need not make and should not make. Even though Lady Verney had given him her son's address when she knew he was going to London and had urged him to leave his card there — Henry and Barbara would be honored by such a marked courtesy, she had told him — there was really no compulsion on him to call on complete strangers.

But curiosity got the better of him. He wanted — no, it was almost as if he *needed* — to see the man Alice had loved and lain with before she went to India. Perhaps if he could understand that relationship, he thought foolishly, he would somehow be able to put to rest the terrible memories.

He would see if Sir Henry and Miss Verney were at home, the butler told him after he knocked on the door at South Audley Street and deposited his card on a silver tray. Ashley almost hoped that they were not, or that they would choose not to be. Verney might well wish to avoid *him,* after all. But the butler returned within a couple of minutes, bowed, and asked if his lordship would follow him up to the drawing room.

A man and a woman were rising to their feet as Ashley followed the butler's announcement into the room. The man came striding toward him, right hand extended. He was a powerful-looking man of about his own age, Ashley guessed. He was not as tall as Ashley, but he was broad-shouldered and wide-chested and gave the impression of size though he was not in any way portly. He was fashionably, though not foppishly, dressed. He wore his own fair hair tied neatly at the neck. His face was good-humored and smiling.

"Lord Ashley Kendrick," he said. "What an honor this is. I had heard from my mother that you had returned from India and taken up residence at Penshurst. I was sorry to be from home and unable to call on you to pay my respects. And so you have called upon me instead. May I present my sister, Barbara?"

Ashley shook the offered hand and bowed

to the lady, who curtsied and smiled at him. She was somewhat darker than her brother in coloring, but she shared his quiet elegance and air of good humor. She was not pretty, but then she was not quite plain either.

"Madam," he said. "Verney. You will be pleased to hear that I left Lady Verney in good health. She sends her affectionate regards."

"How kind of you to bring them. Do have a seat, my lord," Barbara Verney said. "I have given directions for the tea tray to be sent up."

Ashley sat. The suffocating hatred he had begun to feel had taken him completely by surprise. He had expected a dark, brooding, morose-looking man, the sort of man one could easily imagine to have seduced and abandoned a woman who was besotted with him. He had not expected this smiling, genial man, who would perhaps be attractive to women more for his personality than for his looks. He could almost have forgiven wariness and surliness. He could only hate the warm hospitality.

"It must be admitted," Sir Henry said, seating himself after his sister had settled into a chair across from Ashley's, "that we have been curious to meet the man Alice married. Have we not, Barbara? We were devastated, by the way, when news reached us a few months ago of the tragedy that befell her and your son. We wrote to you immediately, not realizing that you were on your way to England. May we express our heartfelt condolences now?"

"Yes, indeed," Miss Verney said.

If he could have throttled the man and remained civilized, Ashley thought, he would have done so. There was not a flicker of shame or guilt on his face. "Thank you," he said. But he was curious. He addressed himself to the sister. "You knew my wife well?"

"We grew up together," she said, "Alice, Gregory — her brother, you know — Henry, and I."

"And Katherine Binchley," Sir Henry added. "Daughter of Kersey's steward. You may have met her, though she is Katherine Smith now."

"Yes, and Katherine too," Miss Verney said. "We were all close as children. But we grew up and grew apart. 'Twas inevitable, I suppose. Though Henry and Gregory remained close friends. But Gregory died and Alice went to India and Katherine went away to marry Mr. Smith — all within a few months. Everything was changed."

"But you wanted to hear about your wife as she was before you met her," Sir Henry said. "She was always beautiful, was she not, Barbara, even as a child? Small and dainty and exquisite. By the time she was sixteen she had the whole of the county on its knees to her. The fact never went to her head. She favored no man. She was very discriminating." He smiled.

Very discriminating. Because she had ignored the attentions of all the young men in the county except those of Verney himself?

Barbara Verney was pouring the tea. She smiled as she handed Ashley a cup. "I do believe Mama had hopes at one time that Alice and Henry would make a match of it," she said. "Happily for you, it did not happen."

"But then," Sir Henry said with a laugh, "neither did you make a match with Gregory, Barbara. Sometimes, Kendrick, as you may know from personal experience, mothers have tidy visions of their children's lives that in no way match what their children want for themselves. I was pleased when I heard that Alice had married you, a man with impressive connections and a respected colleague of her father's. She was a very unhappy young lady when she left Penshurst."

He had no feelings of regret or guilt at all, Ashley decided. He had been *glad* to hear of her marriage to someone else. Would *he* feel glad to hear of Emmy's marriage to another man? Would he be able to look the other man in the eye some years in the future and tell him he had been pleased to hear of her marriage? When he himself had had carnal knowledge of her? And did Verney wonder if he knew? Did his smile hide a certain contempt for the man who had taken his leavings? But he did not wish to think of Alice like that. He had not loved her; indeed, he had in many ways hated her. But she had been a person, and a desperately unhappy person.

"Yes," Ashley said. "She had recently lost her only brother. I gather they were close, though she rarely talked about him. I understood it was too painful for her to do so."

Brother and sister exchanged glances. "Yes," Sir Henry said. "They were close. His death was a dreadful shock to her, as it was to all of us."

Gregory Kersey had been shot in a hunting accident. That much Ashley had learned from Sir Alexander Kersey, long before he met Alice. She herself had almost never mentioned her brother.

"How did it happen?" Ashley asked.

For the first time Verney looked uncomfortable. He scratched his head and looked at his sister.

" 'Twas early in the morning," she said. "He was out shooting with several other gentlemen from the neighborhood."

"Myself among them," Sir Henry added.

"Yes," she said. "They had decided to finish for the day, and were all beginning to make their separate ways home when there was a shot."

"None of us paid it any heed," Sir Henry offered. "Someone had seen a bird and had been unable to resist one more shot, we all thought. 'Twould not have been unusual. Binchley found the body at noon. Alice had sent him to discover why Gregory had not come home from hunting."

"No one remembered having fired that late shot," Barbara Verney said.

"Or no one would admit it," her brother added. "Doubtless it was an accidental shooting. Greg had no enemies. But 'twould be difficult to face the fact — and to admit publicly to it — that one had shot and killed a fellow human."

"Where?" Ashley asked. "Where was he shot?"

"In the hills north of Penshurst," Sir Henry said. "Inside the park."

"Through the head," Miss Verney added quietly. " 'Twas what his lordship meant, Henry. 'Twas dreadful. Suspicion attached to almost every man in the neighborhood. Henry included. Henry was his closest friend."

Had Gregory Kersey found out about his closest friend and his sister? Ashley wondered unwillingly. He pushed the thought aside. He had not intended to wade into waters as deep as this.

"Hearing about Alice and her son — your son — was like a nightmare," Sir Henry said. "It seemed almost as if that family had been doomed. But we become morbid. I am sure you have done enough grieving in the past year and more to last you a lifetime. You have come to town to take in part of the Season?" He smiled.

"For that reason," Ashley said, "and to attend the marriage of my uncle."

The conversation proceeded into comfortable, impersonal topics. They talked about weddings and fashions and entertainments and even the weather.

Sir Henry Verney was a man who had

taken pleasure but felt no guilt, Ashley thought as he left South Audley Street a half hour after arriving there. An essentially shallow man. It was difficult to understand why Alice had been so fanatically attached to him. But then love was difficult to understand. It was not always a rational thing.

It seemed almost as if that family had been doomed.

The remembered words were chilling. And yet, Ashley thought, there could not possibly have been any connection between the tragic accident that had taken Gregory Kersey's life and the one that had taken Alice's four years later. It was merely a disturbing coincidence. But he could not shake those words from his mind.

It seemed almost as if that family had been doomed.

She was wearing her new blue and white striped silk open gown. Beneath it, in the newest fashion, she wore not hoops but a white silk quilted petticoat. Her hair was braided and coiled at the back of her head. The coils were covered with a lace cap. Over all she wore her new straw hat, tipped forward to shade her eyes, secured with a ribbon bow at the back of her neck.

She wondered if he would like her appearance. It did not matter except that she wanted him to see how she had changed, how very happy she was. If he had come with any sense of guilt still remaining, with any lingering conviction that he owed her marriage, she wished to reassure him. He had done her a favor, she thought. If he had not come home, she would have married Lord Powell and spent the rest of her life in the country fighting to assert herself over his mother — probably an impossibility. She would not have discovered, at the very elderly age of two-and-twenty, how much life had to offer even a deaf woman.

Emily leaned forward and looked closely at herself in the glass of her dressing room. She would smile at him and he would know that she did not need him at all. Yet when she caught her eye in the glass, she looked away quickly, concentrating on every part of her appearance except her eyes.

He was waiting in the hallway with Aunt Marjorie when she went downstairs. He was early. He wore a dark green skirted coat, fashionably pleated at the back with a matching waistcoat beneath, and buff breeches. His hair, as usual, was unpowdered. He held his three-cornered hat beneath one arm. His blue eyes smiled at her. She was becoming accustomed to his thin face. It made him look quite impossibly handsome.

"Emmy." He made her a formal bow. "You look quite lovely."

She gave him the full force of her dazzling smile.

"Lud," Aunt Marjorie said, "you will quite turn her head, Lord Ashley. I have heard nothing but compliments for Emily since I brought her to town. You will be fortunate indeed if you find time for any private conversation in the park with her."

He smiled at Emily while Aunt Marjorie spoke, but she had looked to see what was being said about her. She blushed. Not that her head had been turned, she thought. All those silly compliments — those that she bothered to watch being spoken — meant nothing to her. Except that they amused her and kept her mind firmly off — no, *on*. They kept her mind on her newfound happiness.

She looked about her during the drive to the park, watching the people they passed, the elegant pedestrians, the hawkers, who were clearly yelling out news of their wares, the darting children, two dogs on leashes. It struck her suddenly that it could be very frightening indeed to be alone in such a setting — very different from the countryside, where she was rarely if ever afraid. But she had never been alone here. She was not alone now. She smiled and felt Ashley's eyes on her. She would not look to see if he had anything to say.

Ashley. There was a sinking feeling in the pit of her stomach, but she fought it with every ounce of her being.

He offered his arm when they had descended from the open carriage and begun to walk. She loved the straight, tree-lined Mall, with its crowds of strollers and groups of people in conversation together. Sometimes she liked to look up to see the branches and the leaves against the sky. But more often she preferred to watch the people and to feel at one with them. Today she could seem to feel only the muscles in Ashley's arm and the warmth of him. Finally she looked up at him from beneath the brim of her hat. He was looking at her, that smile in his eyes. A smile that did not touch his lips.

"You are happy, Emmy?" he asked her.

She told him with sparkling eyes how happy she was. She gestured about her. How could she not be happy?

"Penshurst is rather lovely," he told her. " 'Tis in a valley with a broad park stretching from the house to the road. Between the house and the village to one side of it there is a broad river with a river walk inside the park, which was constructed for maximum beauty and seclusion. And behind the house are wooded hills, mostly quiet and shady but with the occasional and unexpected prospect over miles of quiet countryside. There is a summerhouse up there. 'Tis even furnished, though it has not been touched in years, I believe."

Penshurst. It was where he lived. Where he belonged. Where Alice had lived. Where he would have lived with her and their son if they had not died.

"You would like it, Emmy." He had bent his head closer to her and touched his hand to hers. "I wish you could see it."

For a moment she felt dizzy with yearning. But for only a moment. No, she told him. She laughed and indicated with one arm again the formal elegance of the walk ahead of them and the fashionable splendor of their fellow strollers. This was where she wanted to be. This was where she belonged.

He brought her eyes back to his face. "Do you speak the truth?" he asked her. They were both signing, she realized, with one hand each. "It makes me sad to see —"

But she did not catch the rest of his

sentence. She did not learn what it was that made him sad. Two gentlemen had stopped before them and were smiling and making their bows to her. Two gentlemen who were part of her usual group. They complimented her on her appearance, asked her if they would see her at this evening's ball, bowed to a silent Ashley, and proceeded on their way. She smiled brightly at Ashley.

"I do not wonder at your success," he said. "But is it what you want, Emmy?"

Of course it was. Could he not see it? She told him so with her free hand and her smiles. Then she thought of something else. "Yess," she said, her eyes sparkling into his. Her one and only word. Her full repertoire.

"I could have taught you the rest of the dictionary, Emmy," he said. "I still could. And you could have taught me —"

But Mr. Maddox, a young lady on his arm, was making his bow to her and asking her how she had enjoyed the ballet last evening.

She would not look at Ashley after they moved on. She could not. She could feel her defenses, like a very thin veneer, in danger of crumbling. She had not even admitted to herself until now that they were just defenses, that she was not really enjoying herself at all. That her heart was all broken up inside her. And she knew too that Ashley had found no peace since she had last seen him, and probably never would. He did not need to use words or sign language to tell her that.

He touched her hand again and squeezed it, and she had no choice but to look up at him. "I felt sorry for Powell," he said, "that morning out at the falls when you would not look at him, Emmy. Now you are doing it to me."

She gazed at him and realized with some surprise that her mask had not deserted her. She was smiling.

"Emmy." He bent his head very close. She guessed that though he was moving his lips he was making no sound at all. "Is there still a chance that you are with child? *Are* you with child?"

She was not. She had been late, and then she had found her hands shaking out of control with relief when she had discovered she was not. And later, after she had tended to herself, she had thrown herself across her bed and cried. But not necessarily with relief.

Her smile had gone. No, she told him. There would be no child. Any obligation he still felt toward her was over. He was free to think of her merely as a sister again. But she could not tell how relieved he was. His eyes merely gazed back into hers until she lowered her own to his cravat. Yes, there had been the possibility. For two days she had thought . . . But it had not been so.

And she had been sorry. How foolish and irrational emotions could be. If she had been with child, she would have had to marry him. To marry the man who was dearer to her than her own heart while she was merely a dear sister in his eyes. It would have been intolerable. Far more intolerable than this was.

She raised her eyes and smiled at him.

And then she was distracted by another couple who had stopped before them. She turned to look, but she did not know them. They were both smiling at Ashley.

"We meet again so soon," the man said while the woman laughed.

Emily looked at Ashley. He was nodding in acknowledgment of them. She saw his hesitation, but then he looked down at her.

"Emmy," he said, "may I present my neighbors at Penshurst, Sir Henry Verney and Miss Verney?" He looked at them. "Lady Emily Marlowe, sister of the Earl of Royce and of the Duchess of Harndon."

She smiled brightly at them. His new friends, part of his new life. And she liked them. It was foolish, perhaps, to make such snap judgments, but they both looked thoroughly amiable. Miss Verney merely smiled back. Sir Henry made her a bow.

"Of Bowden Abbey," he said. "I saw it once during my travels. A beautiful place."

Yes, she told him with a nod. Home. It was more home than Elm Court had ever been, she mused.

"Ah, is that so?" Sir Henry said to Ashley, to whom his eyes had moved for a moment. "Yes, I can tell that you read lips, Lady Emily. I could see that you heard my comment about Bowden Abbey and agreed with it."

"It must be a strain upon your powers of observation," Miss Verney said. "But 'tis said that any affliction can be used to strengthen character if one is willing to accept it as a challenge. Would you agree, Lady Emily?"

She was not sure that her deafness had strengthened her character. She was not even sure she had met a challenge. A silent world was as natural to her as a noisy one must be to them, she reflected. But people tended to assume that deaf persons could function as people only if they learned to conform to a world of sound. What about the challenge of silence? Very few people of hearing ever accepted it or even knew that there was a challenge there. People of hearing feared silence, she suspected. But she could not explain all that. Miss Verney was being kind, friendly. Emily smiled, then turned in time to see what Ashley said.

"Emmy is very modest about her accomplishments," he said. "She is going to dance with me at tonight's ball."

Emily laughed.

Am I? she asked him with raised eyebrows when they moved on a minute or so later.

"Now, on what matter am I being interrogated?" he asked her. "My presumption in presenting you to strangers? Or my presumption in telling you rather than asking that you will dance with me?"

Yes, that, she told him with a signing hand. *Am I going to dance?*

"But you will, Emmy," he said, laughing. All the austerity went from his face when he laughed. It would not be good for her to see him thus too often, she warned herself. "Because you love to dance, remember? Because you have always wanted to dance. And because only I am reckless enough to accept the challenge."

She laughed again.

"Will you?" he asked her with his hand and his eyes as well as with his lips. "Dance with me? Will you, Emmy?"

Yes, she would. Even in front of all the fashionable world. Of course she would.

It was only as he handed her back into his carriage and she arranged her skirts while he came around to the other side and climbed in that she realized something had changed. She was smiling, laughing, bubbling with happiness — as she had been for a month. But there was a difference. The mask had slipped and had been replaced, for the moment at least, by the real thing.

It was a frightening thought.

16

"You were quite right," Sir Henry Verney said to his sister as they continued their stroll along the Mall. "There is quite a marked resemblance. I am surprised I did not notice when he called earlier."

"He is a little taller and more slender," Barbara Verney said. "Perhaps not quite as dark. And considerably more handsome, I believe. But undeniably like. We were both surprised to hear that Alice had married, and wondered what manner of man had persuaded her into it. Now we have our answer."

"I wonder," he said, "how happy she was. One cannot somehow imagine Alice being happy. Not surprisingly, I suppose. There must have been —"

But his sister cut him off. " 'Tis better not to discuss it," she said. "I am sorry I aroused old memories by commenting on the likeness. She came to a terrible end, poor woman. One can only hope she is now at peace. But poor Lord Ashley lost a son as well. 'Tis no wonder that there is a somewhat haunted look about him. Did you find him charming, Henry?"

"A trifle reserved," he said. "I read a certain coldness in his eyes. But I suppose that making the acquaintance of people who grew up with his wife must have put a strain upon him. It must have taken some courage to call on us. It was a courtesy I appreciate."

"A coldness?" she said. "I think not, Henry. He has the most soulful blue eyes. But no, you need not look at me like that. I have not conceived a passion for Lord Ashley Kendrick or for anyone else. Did you admire Lady Emily Marlowe?"

"She is a beauty of the first order," he said, "and has a sparkle that makes her quite irresistibly charming."

Barbara laughed. "You do not find her inability to converse a deterrent?" she asked.

"On the contrary," he said. "Any man would consider it an exhilarating challenge to keep those fine eyes concentrated on his lips and to keep that dazzling smile focused on himself."

"Henry." She laughed again and squeezed his arm. "You are straying, I do declare."

"Not so," he said, chuckling too. But he sobered and sighed. "No, absolutely not, Barbara. I could only wish there were something definite from which not to stray. Am I foolish to be so constant to a dream? But enough of that. Tonight's ball that Kendrick referred to is Lady Bryant's, do you think? Perhaps I will try to engage Lady Emily for a set — if she is willing to lower her gaze to a mere baronet, of course."

"Any lady should consider herself fortunate," she said.

Ashley was somewhat later than he intended at Lady Bryant's ball. Luke and Anna and their children had arrived at Harndon House early in the evening, and he was caught up in all the bustle of greeting them and of adjudicating a fight between young George and James and then wrestling with both the boys, who had united against him while Luke was attempting to soothe a very cross and red-faced Harry and bend an ear to Joy's advice at the same time, and Anna and the nurse were inspecting the nursery rooms with the housekeeper to see that all was in order.

He felt almost cheerful as he stood in the doorway of the ballroom and looked about. He saw Emily immediately. The music was between sets, and she stood close to Lady Sterne, surrounded by gentlemen, as she had been at Vauxhall last evening. She was laughing and plying her fan, flirting with her eyes over the top of it. As had been so last evening, her hair was elaborately styled and powdered and her face was painted with cosmetics. She wore a patch close to one corner of her mouth. She looked quite magnificent in a gown that appeared to be all silver. Only her fan was a different color. It was crimson.

He did not like to see her thus. He remembered his initial reaction to her at Luke's ball, when he had singled her out as the loveliest lady in the room before he had known who she was. It had been one-tenth admiration he had felt, and nine-tenths pure lust. And when he looked at her now, it was hard to see past the outer appearance to the reality within. It was hard to see her as Emmy. He did not like the stirring of desire he felt when he saw her like this. And yet, he thought before he could push the memory away, she had not looked like this when he had possessed her. She had been Emmy then, his wild, reckless sprite.

But he was feeling almost cheerful. She was not with child. She had quite firmly rejected his marriage offers at Bowden. That episode, then, could and must be put behind him. He could safely return to the old relationship with her. It gladdened him that they no longer needed to dread seeing each other. It cheered him to think that he could actively seek her out as he had always done — though only to keep her on the periphery of his life, instead of at its center as he had done when she was a girl. He would avoid drawing her again into his darkness.

He watched her laugh at something one of her followers said to her. And there was pain again — yes, definitely, even though everyone else in the room might look at her and wonder at her total and vivid gaiety. He would have preferred to see Emmy where she belonged, to be who she really was. He smiled slightly and remembered the quite inexplicable disappointment that had warred with relief in him this afternoon. That she was not with child by him. That she would not be forced into marrying him. Relief had won — relief for both their sakes.

And then her eyes met his across the room. He had not been in her direct line of vision, but she had sensed his presence. She smiled her coquettish smile at him; then the fingers of the hand that was not holding her fan beckoned in a gesture that probably only he noticed. She was surrounded by admirers, but for the moment she was ignoring them.

Do join me, she was telling him.

And then she touched her fingertips to her heart.

I really want you to.

Ah, Emmy.

"Lud, but 'tis working, Theo," Lady Sterne said, touching her betrothed's arm and patting it. "He did not like it at all when he discovered that she was engaged for the next two sets after his arrival. He went slinking off to lick his wounds until this set began."

"He went to the card room and watched young Heyward lose a small fortune," Lord Quinn said. "Looking as cool and as disapproving as Luke himself can appear, Marj. He has changed from the days of his wild and reckless youth, I warrant you. He has eyes for no one but the gel now."

"And did you have a word with him this afternoon as you promised?" Lady Sterne asked. "I did think of mentioning the matter myself when he came to escort Emily to the park, but I thought 'twould seem too contrived if you then gave him the same hint."

"Egad, but it felt wicked, Marj," he said, "after we have assured the gel that our mar-

346

rying will make no difference to her prospects. But the more I think of it, the more I like the idea for *myself.*"

She tapped him on the arm with her closed fan. "The thought of a private wedding trip to the Lakes for two weeks has an irresistible appeal," she said. "But why should we not do it, Theo, and enjoy it too? The idea was not conceived selfishly, after all. 'Twas designed for dear Emily and Lord Ashley's sake."

" 'Tis not sure yet, though, Marj," Lord Quinn said with a sigh. "I merely dropped the hint. Luke and Anna are not far from Kent now that they have come to town from Bowden, I said. Anna must hope to spend a week or two with her sister after being away from her for a month, I said after taking time to discuss the weather. I sighed, m'dear, after talking about my visits to White's this morning, and remarked that a short wedding trip would have been pleasant if it had not been the middle of the Season and if you had not taken on the duty of bringing out dear Lady Emily — not that you consider it a duty, of course, I hastened to add. But even so . . . And then I sighed piteously. One can only hope now that my nephy will conceive the idea, entirely on his own, you understand — of inviting Luke and Anna and Emily out to Penshurst for a week or two."

"Lud, 'twill be the very thing," Lady Sterne said. "Look at them, Theo. The very best-looking couple at the ball, and dancing the minuet as if they were unaware of anyone else's existence. Who would guess that she is deaf, except for the fact that she dances almost *too* perfectly? Dear Emily."

"If the lad has not had her to the altar by the end of the summer and had her brought to bed of a boy before the beginning of next summer," Lord Quinn said, "he is no nephy of mine, by my life."

He was not quite sure how she did it. He tried to imagine having to perform the steps of the minuet if he could not hear the music. It seemed impossible. But she danced perfectly in time to the music. More even than just that. She danced with grace and a sense of rhythm, as if she held the music inside herself, as if it was the other side of silence.

He smiled at her as he performed the elegant steps with her, and she smiled back. Emmy's smile, happy, exuberant, and yet serene too. No longer coquettish.

And that was it, he thought. She did have music inside her, and beauty and peace and harmony. There were levels on which their two worlds could converge, and strangely, this was one of them. There was the music he could hear and the silent music she could feel. He remembered her painting and her explanation of the feeling of life and exaltation she had tried to reproduce with her brush and her paints. There was a beauty and richness of character and experience about Emmy far deeper than the powdered hair and the rouged cheeks and the provocatively placed heart-shaped patch she wore close to her lips.

An idea flashed into his mind — a desire to see Emmy in the hills behind Penshurst and on the shady walk beside the river. More than a desire — almost a yearning.

Despite his pleasure at once again being so near to Emmy, Ashley was not able to fully enjoy the dance. When he had returned from the card room to claim this set, he had found Emmy surrounded by the usual group of young men — plus Sir Henry Verney and his sister. Miss Verney had been talking with Lady Sterne until she was led away by a gentleman into the set that was forming. Verney himself had been talking with Emmy — and had been soliciting her company for the set following the minuet.

The thought of Verney, of all people, so

much as touching Emmy made Ashley want to scoop her up into his arms and carry her forcefully off to a place of safety. Verney had better not consider becoming a regular member of her court, Ashley thought angrily; not if he knew what was good for him. And yet Ashley's mind could not refrain from making the parallel. Ruined and abandoned — Alice by Verney, Emmy by himself. But there was a difference, he told himself. Alice had loved Verney passionately. His abandonment had destroyed all hope of future happiness for her. Emmy had not really been abandoned — he must not add that burden to his conscience. She had abandoned him.

"Thank you," he said, bowing over her hand when the minuet was at an end and offering his arm to escort her back to Lady Sterne's side. The wedding was only a few days off. Once it was over, he would have no further excuse to remain in town. There was work to be done at Penshurst. And yet the thought of returning there was chilling. That large and empty house was too new to give off any sense of history, but held only the presence of its most recent occupants. Alice was everywhere in that house. If he could fill it with guests . . . even perhaps with children . . . If Emmy were there . . .

He was forced to stand and make conversation with Verney, who had come early to claim his time with Emmy. He was forced to watch the two of them smile at each other and apparently like what they saw. And after a few minutes he was forced to watch Verney lead her away, presumably to find a couple of chairs or a sofa to sit upon. His eyes followed them all the way to the French doors, which stood open onto a veranda. It was bright with lamplight. He could see them strolling back and forth outside the doors for a couple of minutes, then could see them no more.

Verney had taken her down the steps into the garden, which had been made available to guests. There were lanterns among the trees, and seats. Ashley had been out there earlier while waiting for his set with Emmy — only now did it strike him as strange that he had not considered dancing with any other lady.

Certainly there was no reason why a man should not take his partner into the garden for a stroll. The night was warm and the ballroom almost uncomfortably hot. But Verney was not any man. And Emmy was not any partner. Ashley could feel the tension building inside himself, and then the anger. His uncle and Viscount Burdett were standing on either side of him, making conversation. But fury became like a steady hammer blow against Ashley's eardrums, blocking out both the sound and the sense of what they were saying. He excused himself after five minutes had passed and made his way toward the French doors.

She liked Sir Henry Verney and felt she could relax in his company. Unlike most of the gentlemen who crowded about her almost wherever she went, he did not ply her constantly with compliments and meaningless gallantries. With him she did not feel the constant necessity to smile dazzlingly and to flutter her fan.

Smiles seemed to come easily to Sir Henry Verney, as if they were his natural expression. Looking at his wide-spaced gray eyes, she thought that before many more years had passed, he would have permanent wrinkles at their outer corners. But they would be attractive. They would be laugh lines. He was an attractive man, large and solid, with a pleasant face. He was a man to be comfortable with. A man to trust, she thought, though she did not know him at all.

" 'Tis hot in the ballroom," he said, "and you have been dancing. Would you care for a stroll outdoors, Lady Emily? The garden is lighted and there are other people there. I have Lady Sterne's permission to take you strolling — if 'tis what you wish."

He was making sure that she would not feel uneasy about agreeing to something that sounded so heavenly, Emily reflected. He had even spoken with Aunt Marjorie. She smiled and nodded and set her arm along his very solid one. She would be glad to go outside, where it would be darker and less crowded and cooler — and where she would not see Ashley. Her mind and her heart were still in an uncomfortable turmoil after their dance. There had been the wild exhilaration of dancing again, of feeling form and rhythm and movement. And part of the wildness and of the exhilaration had been the sight of Ashley, tall and slender and more than usually elegant in a wine-colored velvet skirted coat with silver embroidered waistcoat and gray knee breeches and sparkling white linen and lace. In addition, his hair was powdered tonight.

She would have suffocated if she had had to remain in the ballroom, she thought.

He lived near Penshurst in Kent, Sir Henry told her as they strolled on the veranda. He lived with his mother and his sister, though he often came to London for a few weeks at a time. His sister liked to shop and visit here and they both enjoyed the entertainments of the Season. He liked to travel more extensively too, he told her as he led her down the steps into the garden, though most of the time now he stayed in the British Isles so that he would not be too far from his mother if she had need of him. He had made the Grand Tour of Europe, of course, as a very young man.

Emily smiled at him and invited him to tell her more. He was not a talkative man. There had been welcome silences between the things he had told her. He seemed to realize that silences were not as awkward to her as they seemed to be to most people, that sometimes she appreciated moments without conversation so that she could turn her head from looking at her companion's lips in order to look about her and relax. The garden was pretty, its trees and lawns intersected with several paths, all converging on a central fountain which spouted water that looked multicolored in the light of the lanterns.

They arrived at the fountain and stood gazing into the spray for a whole minute. Emily could smell the water. Although none of the spray touched her, she could feel the dampness and knew that the merest breath of a breeze could send droplets against her face and hands. She half closed her eyes and saw the lantern light filtered through a million drops of water. She could almost imagine herself back in the country. But Sir Henry leaned slightly toward her and she turned her eyes to his lips.

"I always think there is no sound more soothing than that of flowing water," he said.

She smiled, allowing amusement to show in her face.

"Zounds. Pardon me," he said, looking stricken. "That was unbelievably tactless of me."

But she laughed and pointed to her eyes. She indicated her nose and breathed in, and rubbed her fingertips over her thumbs.

"You use your other senses and find them just as soothing," he said. "And I am forgiven, Lady Emily?"

She shrugged her shoulders and smiled as she nodded, to indicate that there was nothing to forgive. The ballroom had become uncomfortable with the heat of so many people. She had felt the discomfort. Did it also become uncomfortable with the noise of so many people? she wondered. If so, then she had been spared that annoyance. She set her arm along Sir Henry's again so that they might resume their stroll.

But before they could do so, before she could turn her head to concentrate on his account of his Grand Tour, she had that familiar feeling again. He was close by. Closer than the ballroom or even the veranda. Her eyes found him standing some distance away, slightly to one side of the foot of the steps down into the garden. He was alone. Why had he come? she wondered. Was he merely hot and in need of air? Lonely? Unhappy?

But her partner had been about to speak. She turned her head and her attention determinedly toward him.

"I was away from England for longer than a year," Sir Henry said, "completing my education. That is the polite way of saying that I enjoyed myself enormously, Lady Emily, doing all that was wild and extravagant. But perhaps I was learning too. 'Tis through wildness and extravagance that we learn the value of steadiness and moderation, I often believe. Are you sure you wish me to bore you with the tale of my adventures?"

She nodded, but she laughed to tell him that it would be no bore. He must have been to Paris, where Luke had lived for ten years. He must have been to Italy and seen all the riches of architecture and painting and sculpture, and to Switzerland and seen the

356

mountains and the lakes. He must have been . . . She did not know of any other places. She knew so little.

She watched his lips intently and lived his experiences in her imagination. And yet all the time she knew that Ashley was not leaving the garden. He stayed at the foot of the steps for a while and then strolled the paths. He stood at the fountain, leaning back against the stone wall that surrounded it. He watched them. She was sure he was watching them, though he did not come close or so much as lift a hand in greeting.

"Ah," Sir Henry said at last, raising one hand and cocking his head in a listening gesture, "the music draws to an end. 'Tis the end of the set and I must return you to the ballroom. You are an excellent listener, Lady Emily." This time he did not apologize, though he did wince when he realized what he had said. He laughed, and Emily joined him. "I have enjoyed our half hour together. Perhaps we may repeat it some time?"

She nodded as he led her to the steps and up onto the veranda and into the ballroom. She did not turn her head. She did not need to. She knew that Ashley had remained at the fountain.

There had been nothing to worry about.

Not as far as Emmy's physical safety was concerned anyway. But Verney had touched her, taking her arm along his. He had bent his head toward her as they walked. He had talked to her, smiled at her, laughed with her. She had given him her attention, her smiles. She had looked as if she enjoyed his company, as if she understood what he said.

And all the time Ashley had visualized him with Alice. Seduction? Rape? Had it been that? No, hardly. She had loved him, been obsessed with him. He would have used that smiling charm he was now using with Emmy. In order to win her love, in order to seduce her. He had had all the time in the world — they had been neighbors all their lives. And then he had abandoned her, the daughter of his neighbor, sister of the man he had called friend. And that friend had died in circumstances that were mysterious if not downright suspicious. Had there been a confrontation after the other hunters had dispersed that morning?

Ashley watched them return to the ballroom when the interminable set finally came to an end. He dropped his head and closed his eyes. If Verney was going to start taking an interest in Emmy, then there was another reason to —

A sudden crunching of gravel caused him

to lift his head to see who was approaching.

"I feel compelled to ask," Sir Henry Verney said to him, "though perhaps it is impolitic to do so — was I being watched during the past half hour?"

Ashley considered his reply. He had not quite made up his mind to have a confrontation. But he supposed it was inevitable.

"Yes," he said.

Sir Henry was silent for a while, apparently expecting an explanation. "Might I be permitted to know why?" he asked at last.

"Lady Emily Marlowe, despite her age, is innocent in the ways of the world," Ashley said. "And she has no voice with which to draw attention to herself."

The amiable face of his neighbor tightened with noticeable anger, though he kept it well under control. His right hand, though, Ashley noticed, moved and came to rest on the hilt of his dress sword.

"I find that explanation insulting," he said. "I must remember, however, that you stand somewhat in the nature of a brother to Lady Emily and that her affliction has perhaps made her family overprotective of her. I am a gentleman, Kendrick. In future, if I seek out the company of the lady, with her chaperon's permission, and if the lady herself chooses to accept my company, I would expect you to refrain from appointing yourself her watchdog."

So he was going to start paying court to Emmy. Probably deliberately so, now that he knew his attentions would annoy the man who had married Alice.

"I know about you," Ashley said quietly.

Sir Henry stood motionless. His hand was still on the hilt of his sword, though he did not grip it.

"Did you think my wife would have told me nothing?" Ashley said. In fact, she had told him almost nothing, but Verney did not need to know that. He knew all that was essential to know. Verney had to understand his fears for Emmy. "She told me everything."

Sir Henry said nothing for a long time, though his hand fell away from his sword. "Ah," he said at last. "I wondered, of course. You must have loved her very dearly. You do not wish to see Lady Emily acquainted with someone who was involved with that ugliness. I believe I can understand that. But I will say nothing, you know, to sully Alice's name. I never have and I never will. I am glad you know, though. I would always have wondered and would always have felt somewhat awkward in your company."

Somewhat awkward? But he would not feel it now? "Zounds!" Ashley came up to a full standing position from the fountain wall against which he had been half reclined. His hand clapped on to the hilt of his own sword. "You will say nothing to sully her name? *You* will say nothing, sir?"

In another moment he would have scraped his sword free of its scabbard. In another moment Sir Henry Verney would have done likewise, his hand having returned to his sword hilt. But someone laughed not far off, someone who was strolling along one of the paths with a companion. And Ashley, facing toward the house and the ballroom, became aware of his surroundings again — and of the fact that Emily was standing at the foot of the steps to the veranda.

"If you wish to meet me," Sir Henry said, letting his hand drop to his side once more, "perhaps we should go through the proper channels, Kendrick. I see no reason for a meeting, but I will not cry off if you wish to make a formal challenge."

"No," Ashley said, concentrating on letting the tension flow out of his body. "No, 'twould be ridiculous. The events to which we refer happened long before I met Alice. But I would make it clear that I will protect Lady Emily Marlowe's honor with my life,

361

if necessary."

Sir Henry made him a half bow. "I abhor violence," he said. "I choose to read no personal insult into those last words. Lady Emily's honor is perfectly safe with me. But I see now that I misunderstood the true nature of your concern for the lady. Good evening, Kendrick."

He turned and strode away in the direction of the ballroom. Emily, Ashley saw, was no longer standing at the bottom of the steps. She had moved to one side and was hidden to Verney's view behind a tree. She stood where she was after he had disappeared into the ballroom.

Like Verney, she had come out to talk with him, Ashley realized. And talk she would, with her hands and with those eyes of hers. He was not sure he was equal to looking into them.

I see now that I have misunderstood the true nature of your concern for the lady.

He walked toward her.

17

She had not seen Sir Henry Verney go back outside. But she had not seen Ashley come inside either, and she wondered what he was doing in the garden, why he had gone there, why he had been alone. She shook off her followers by smiling at Lady Sterne and making her way pointedly toward the ladies' withdrawing room. But she did not go there. She went out onto the veranda instead and down the steps into the garden.

And she found that he was still at the fountain, talking with Sir Henry. Quarreling with him. She was not close enough to read lips, but she could see Ashley's face and she did not fail to notice how his hand went to his sword. For one heart-stopping moment she expected to see him draw it. She instinctively hid herself a few moments later when Sir Henry came striding along the path toward the steps.

But Ashley had seen her. He came toward

her, a curious half smile on his lips.

"Come, Emmy," he said when he was close enough for her to read his signing hands. "Walk with me." And he took her hand and drew it through his arm and held it firmly against his side.

She would not look at him while they walked. Had they been quarreling over *her*? But why? For once she wished desperately for speech. At one side of the garden there was a small rose arbor, separated from the rest of the garden by a trellis over which the plants had been trained. There was a wrought-iron seat inside and lanterns hanging from the trellises. There was no one else there. He led her inside and indicated the seat. She sat down and he took the place beside her. She turned to look at him.

"Emmy." He took one of her hands between both of his. "You came out here to scold me, as he did? For acting as a watchdog? I ask your pardon. I remember, you see, how someone took advantage of your innocence just a month ago when you were out of doors alone with him. I feared for you."

She snatched her hand away and stared at him incredulously. He made it seem — *sordid,* what had happened between them. And how dared he suggest . . .

He reached for her hand again and held it tightly while he closed his eyes and dropped his head.

"I feared for you," he said again when he lifted his head. She could see torment in his eyes. "Emmy, stay away from him. Anyone but him. Stay away from him — for my sake?"

From Sir Henry Verney? *But why?* she asked with her free hand. He was such a very amiable gentleman. She liked him better than any of the other gentlemen who partnered her and conversed with her. She frowned.

"Zounds," he said, "you will not be deceived by a lie and you will not accept an appeal without a full and truthful explanation, will you? Sometimes I wish you were as other women are. Do you see more deeply because you are undistracted by sound, Emmy?" He raised her hand briefly to his cheek.

No, she would not be lied to. She would always know if he lied.

"My wife was once fond of him," he said. "No, more than fond, Emmy. She loved him. He encouraged her and then cruelly rejected her. She never quite recovered her spirits."

Ah. For a while her mind did not quite

grasp what she had just been told about Sir Henry Verney — her heart was too fully occupied. Alice had never fully returned Ashley's love, then. She had always pined for a lost love. And now Ashley had been forced to meet that man.

"And so you see," he said, "why I fear for you, Emmy. He has the sort of looks and charm that I can imagine might be attractive to many women. But he is a cruel man. Stay away from him. Promise me?"

But she was frowning again. Sir Henry Verney deliberately cruel? Taking pleasure out of luring a woman into loving him only to dash her hopes and turn away from her? Oh no, she could not believe it. There had to be some other explanation. Unrequited love, for example. He and Alice must have known each other for a long time. They had probably grown up together. And he *was* an attractive man. Perhaps she had fallen in love with him but he had been unable to return her feelings. Perhaps she had exaggerated the truth when telling Ashley — and why, for that matter, *had* she told him? How could she have been so cruel? That must surely be the explanation, though. After all, she herself knew all about unrequited love. But she would never have given Lord Powell reason to suspect the truth if she had married him.

"You do not believe me," Ashley said. "You must believe me, Emmy. He can hurt you."

No. She shook her head. Sir Henry Verney could not hurt her even if what Ashley said about him was true. Her heart could never be hurt by Sir Henry. Or by any other man. It was that fact that had enabled her to enjoy the past month so well — except for the past day. It was hard now to realize that Ashley had come only last evening. *No,* she told him with her hands. *I am happy. I am me.* She was not vulnerable the way he feared.

He gave up. He sat back on the seat beside her and drew her arm through his again. The evening was almost chilly when one was sitting still. She felt the warmth of his arm and side against her arm and of his shoulder touching hers. She ached to let her head fall sideways to rest against his shoulder. A long time ago she might have done just that, but no longer. She had a sudden memory of lying naked against his clothed body, his cloak snugly about her. She remembered the intense tiredness that had succeeded the shock of what had happened to her just before that. She remembered sleeping in his arms. Yet now she could not even put her head on his shoulder.

He moved then, turning slightly toward her and setting an arm about her shoulders. "You are chilly," he said.

She shook her head. She did not want this moment to end, even though she knew she should go back to the ballroom. Aunt Marjorie would wonder where she was. But stillness and silence were so important to her, and there had been little of the former lately. She had reveled in busyness — just as if the gap really could be bridged, as if she really wished it to be. Did she? Did she want to be like others but inferior because of her deafness?

He sat still and silent with her for a long time, as if he felt her need, or perhaps even shared it. But he spoke at last, touching his fingers lightly to her chin so that she would look.

"Emmy," he said, "after the wedding, Luke and Anna will be coming to Penshurst with me for a week or two. At least I believe they will come once I have asked them." He grinned engagingly. "Anna will not want to leave you so soon. You have not even seen her yet. They arrived this evening, you know, before I came here."

Oh. She smiled. Just a few weeks ago it

had been a relief to get away from Bowden and all her family. But suddenly a month seemed an age. She could hardly wait to see Anna.

"And there are only three days to the wedding," he said. "Emmy, have you considered that Lady Sterne and my uncle would probably enjoy some private time together, perhaps even a short wedding trip? For a week or two, perhaps, before they resume all their usual social activities?"

But Aunt Marjorie had assured her that her new marriage would not in any way interfere with the social activities she had planned for Emily. Emily must never feel she was in the way, Aunt Marjorie had said. And Lord Quinn had echoed her words.

"You need not look so dismayed," Ashley said. "Of course they love you. But of course too they will be newly wed. Be kind to them, Emmy. And to Anna and yourself. And to me. Come to Penshurst too. Just for a week or so, until Theo and Lady Sterne return to town — though she will be Lady Quinn by then, will she not?"

Emily felt such a surge of yearning that for a moment she felt almost robbed of breath. It was so very foolish to want him. She had refused the opportunity to spend the rest of her life with him, because she knew the misery of seeing him and of being close to him like this when there could never be anything between them except friendship.

"I want you to see Penshurst, Emmy," he said. " 'Tis a magnificent, almost new place. But I did not enjoy being there alone. I found it cheerless. I want my family there with me. And you. I want you to see the river walk and the hills. I want to see you in the summerhouse. I want to see you happy. You are not really happy here, Emmy. And you must not deny it. Not to me. I know you too well."

How could she be happy — at Penshurst? But she had read the description of the place on his lips and had a mental picture of it as his home — as the place where he had been, where he would be for the rest of his life. How could she ever be happy if she never saw it for herself?

"Say yes," he said. He grinned at her again. "*Say* yes, Emmy."

"Yess," she said.

He had moved his head forward so that he was looking directly into her face. "Thank you," he said. "You will not regret it. I will give you a happy time there, I promise. And I will teach you more words. A vocabulary of one word is nothing to boast about, by my life. Not for your teacher, that is. I shall teach you whole sentences."

She shrugged and laughed.

"Emmy," he said. "Ah, Emmy. And you shall teach me — more than I will ever teach you. Please, Emmy — teach me."

Even as her heart lurched at the strange plea, he leaned forward and set his lips to hers and kept them there for several moments. They were warm, gentle, quite without the passion with which he had kissed her at the falls. His arm was still about her and she found the side of her head coming to rest against his shoulder after all. She felt warm again, and very sad. She closed her eyes and kept them closed for a few moments after he had raised his head.

He was looking at her with a matching sadness in his own eyes when she opened hers. "I am so sorry," he said.

They gazed at each other in sadness. She wondered for what he had apologized. She did not think it was for the kiss — it had not been a passionate embrace.

"Come," he said at last. "I must return you to Lady Sterne and all your admirers." He touched a finger to the small black patch she wore close to her mouth, and smiled. "I have just realized something tonight, Emmy. I cannot hold you back from being all grown up, can I, no matter how dearly I wish to believe you are still that girl I knew. My little fawn."

No. No, he could not. But she knew that he would never really see her as anything but that girl — despite what had once happened between them.

He got to his feet and offered her his hand.

"Lud," Lady Quinn said, seating herself on the empty chair beside Anna and fanning herself vigorously, "there is nothing like a wedding — one's own wedding — to make one feel like a giddy girl again. It seems almost indecent for people our age to have such a crush of guests." She smiled fondly at her groom, who was talking with Luke and the Earl of Weims and a few other gentlemen some distance away.

"You look very happy, Aunt Marjorie," Anna said with a smile, and she leaned over impulsively to kiss her godmother's cheek. " 'Tis what I have hoped for for years. I am so very fond of Uncle Theodore."

"And you look like a giddy girl, Aunt Marjorie," Agnes said with a laugh.

"Mercy on me," Lady Quinn said.

"Or perhaps 'twould be better to say you

look like a young bride," Charlotte said.

"A *lovely* young bride," Constance added.

Lady Quinn laughed heartily and turned her attention to a wedding guest who had come to speak with her. The wedding had taken place a mere few hours before at St. George's, which had been packed with fashionable members of society. And at the duke's insistence, the wedding breakfast had been eaten in the ballroom of Harndon House. Now the guests were relaxing in the ballroom or wandering out to the garden or into other rooms while an army of servants discreetly cleared the tables.

Lady Quinn turned back to Anna. "Faith, child," she said, "you must think me totally lacking in a sense of duty. I undertook to bring Emily to town for the Season, yet I have married in the middle of it and now Theo is whisking me away to the Lake District for two weeks. But I would not have consented, Anna — and Theo would not have suggested it — if Emily had not assured me that she wishes to go to Penshurst with you and Harndon. Oh mercy on me, he is my nephew now and told me but an hour ago that I must call him Luke. Emily wrote me *three* letters, child. I had to believe that she really wishes to go."

"She does, Aunt Marjorie," Anna said.

"She wrote to me too. She wants to spend a couple of weeks with me and the children. She misses us, I daresay, as we miss her. But she will come back for the rest of the Season. I can scarce believe the change in her." She turned her head to look across the ballroom, and all the ladies with her did likewise.

Emily was sitting on a low chair near the French doors, looking elegant and lovely and flushed and very slightly disheveled. Charlotte's baby was in her arms and showing persistent interest in her pearl necklace. Anna's Harry was sitting on the floor at her feet, beating some toys with the flat of his hand. Joy was standing at her shoulder, disentangling the baby's hands from the pearls. Agnes's youngest was straddling Harry so that he could look Emily directly in the eye and hold her attention while he told her some lengthy tale.

"I cannot imagine, Anna," Charlotte said, "why you are allowing Emily to go to Penshurst with you. 'Tis most improper. Jeremiah even calls it scandalous. If she is to go there at all, it should be as Lord Ashley Kendrick's bride. 'Twould be more seemly under the circumstances for her to come home with Victor or with me while Lady Sterne — Lady Quinn — is away."

"Victor and I would be very happy to have her, Anna," Constance added.

"Emily is of age," Anna said firmly. "It is her decision to go to Penshurst. It will be entirely proper. Luke and I will be there with her."

Lady Quinn looked away from gazing at Emily and saw with some satisfaction that Lord Ashley — no, he was simply Ashley to her now — was leaning against a corner of the mantel at one end of the room, not a part of any group or conversation. He was watching Emily, a brooding look on his face — with a little imagination, one might almost have construed it as a somewhat lovelorn look. And the girl really was showing to best advantage today, Lady Quinn thought, dressed as she was in all her new finery, the sparkle of happiness still in her face, but the warmth of real pleasure back there too as she amused the babies and listened patiently with her eyes to the confidences of the other children.

The situation might just work out well, Lady Quinn mused. And it might well justify the sacrifice she and Theo had made in marrying and arranging a wedding journey right in the middle of the Season.

Some sacrifice! Lady Quinn turned her attention to her new husband. It was difficult to see him objectively as a man of advanced middle years. To her he was still the dashing, handsome, rakish young gentleman with whom she had fallen painfully in love when still married to Sterne. And who had unbelievably — and really quite uncomfortably — fallen in love with her. His eyes met hers across the room and they smiled at each other.

Just like young lovers, she thought fondly, impatient to be alone together.

It was the sleepy time of day. And a sleepy kind of day. It was a sunny afternoon, and the inside of the carriage was warm. Anna was nursing Harry, a shawl wrapped discreetly about her shoulders. When Emily glanced at her, she saw her lips moving and a dreamy expression on her face, and figured she must be singing a lullaby. Their mother must have sung her lullabies when she was an infant, Emily thought, before she lost her hearing. She could almost remember — almost, but not quite.

The children were supposed to be traveling with their nurse in the carriage behind, but none of them were. James, who was sometimes troubled by the attention his mama gave the baby, was curled up on the seat opposite, fast asleep. Perhaps the lullaby had been intended for him more than for Harry, who never seemed to need lulling. The other two children were riding, Joy up before Luke on his horse, George with Ashley.

It was a cozy family party that made its way toward Penshurst. And Emily was not without an awareness that the ties might have been even closer — she might have been Ashley's wife by now. She set the side of her head against the comfortable cushions of Luke's traveling carriage and gazed out the window. She wished Aunt Marjorie and Lord Quinn had not decided upon a wedding trip. She wished Ashley had not come to London. She wished her life there could have continued for the rest of the Season. She had been wildly happy — or at least had fully convinced herself that it was happiness she felt. If it had continued longer, perhaps self-deception would have become true reality. She was not sure now that she would be able to go back in two weeks' time.

Viscount Burdett, knowing that she was leaving town for a few weeks and disturbed by the fact, as several other of her gentleman acquaintances had claimed to be, had made her a marriage offer just the evening before. He had wanted to talk with Victor this morning, before Victor left for home. But she had shaken her head quite firmly while smiling fondly at him. He had seen the smile and the fondness and had vowed to renew his courtship when she returned. She had not realized that he believed what they had was a courtship. What a foolish man he was — he had never been alone with her for longer than a few minutes at a time. He could not know if he would find her silence tolerable. He really did not know her at all. She wondered what the attraction was. Novelty?

Anna touched her arm suddenly and pointed through the window on her side of the carriage. In the distance, across a broad park, stood a large and elegant mansion, flanked on each side by equally elegant smaller buildings. Behind them rose wooded hills. When Emily leaned slightly across Anna, careful not to disturb Harry, who was asleep with his mouth open, she could see the spire of a church farther to the east of the house and a cluster of houses that she assumed made up the village.

She sat back in her corner, her head turned so that she could see the house as they drove onward to the village. They would approach it from the side, she realized, not from the front. She had not been quite prepared for the churning of pain and emptiness — and excitement — inside. It was his home. It was where he belonged, where he would be happy. No, where he would have been happy if Alice had returned with him, and Thomas. Ashley would never be fully happy again. This was where she had lived, where she had been a child. And he had loved her and blamed himself for her death. He must find the house more of a punishment than a pleasure, Emily thought sadly.

But this was where he belonged. And for ever after now, she would be able to picture him in his own proper domain. Wherever she was for the rest of her life — on the Continent with Aunt Marjorie, at Bowden with Anna, at Elm Court with Victor — she would have only to close her eyes and see this lovely house and the quiet, peaceful scenery surrounding it. And she would know loneliness. Things might have been so different, she reflected with regret. She might have spent her life here with him, if only the marriage he had offered her had been offered for different reasons.

It was a pretty village, centered on a village green, of which a wide river formed one side and the churchyard another. The houses looked well cared for. Some people on the streets stood still and watched them go by. Several curtsied or raised hands in greeting to Ashley, who was riding just ahead of the carriage, in Emily's line of vision. Of course, he was already known here. And probably already liked. Most people smiled.

The carriage turned to cross the river, the sun sparkling off its surface. Anna turned her head.

"Beautiful!" she said. Emily could tell from the look on her sister's face that the word had been spoken with fervor.

The gates into the park were just ahead. But the carriage slowed and then stopped before reaching them. There was a cottage beside the road with a small but lovingly kept garden. A young woman was doing something with the rosebushes at one side of the house. She straightened and looked toward the carriage, though she did not smile or make any sign of greeting. But there were two other people on the path in front of the house, an older man and a young boy, who was standing on the lower rung of the wooden gate. Ashley was talking to them, presenting Luke and turning to the carriage. Emily drew down the window.

They were Mr. Edward Binchley and his grandson, Eric Smith. The woman was Mrs.

Katherine Smith, Eric's mother. Eric, Emily estimated, was about four years old, a handsome child with dark hair and blue eyes. He was not unlike George, with whom he was exchanging interested glances. They might easily have been brothers.

"Mr. Binchley was the steward at Penshurst before his retirement," Ashley was saying. "He is a store of useful information on the estate and neighborhood, as I have already discovered over several mugs of ale here."

Emily looked at Mrs. Smith, who had made no move to come closer. She stood still and watched. She was very young — not much older than herself, Emily thought, and very lovely. She must be a widow if she and her son were living with her father, Emily reasoned, then found the woman's eyes on her. She smiled warmly and for the first time Katherine Smith smiled — briefly.

They drove on.

The house was indeed rather new, Emily saw as they drove past the stable block and drew up before the broad steps leading to the huge double doors at the front of the house. It sparkled almost white in the sunshine. Whoever had built it had liked wide-open vistas. The view to the front stretched for miles over the park and the river and the road and distant farmland.

Luke lifted a drowsy and grumbling James from the carriage, and Ashley helped Anna descend with Harry. He grinned down at the baby, who was oblivious to everything about him. And then he turned back to Emily.

She set her foot on the top step, her hand in his, but he did not wait for her to climb down. He released her hand, set his hands at her waist, and lifted her to the ground, bringing her close to his body as he did so. Luke and Anna, preoccupied by their children, were not looking.

His eyes were smiling. Although the suffering was still there, far back in his eyes, Emily could see that for the moment he was enjoying himself. "Welcome to Penshurst, Emmy," he said. "And welcome back to the countryside, where you belong, little fawn."

Her hands had come to rest on his shoulders. Her body was arched inward, almost touching his. For those few moments she felt utterly happy. She felt foolishly as if she were coming home.

"Sir Alexander Kersey must have been a man of considerable good taste," Luke said. "In design, the house and park are exquisite, Ash."

Ashley had seen the dubious glances Luke had cast at the frills and pastel shades that dominated several of the rooms in the house. But the library, at least, was an entirely handsome room. They sank down onto leather chairs at either side of the unlit fireplace, Ashley with a brandy, Luke with his customary glass of water. Luke had just returned from the nursery, where he had as usual read a bedtime story to his children, helped Anna tuck them into their beds, and listened to them say their prayers. Anna was still giving Harry his night feed. Emily had withdrawn after dinner in order to spend a quiet evening in her own room.

"The sad part is," Ashley said, "that he built it all for his descendants."

"There will be some," Luke said quietly. "Not direct descendants, perhaps, but in spirit. From your letters I gathered that you were fond of him and he of you. He approved of you as a son-in-law?"

Ashley nodded and stared moodily into his glass.

"Give it time," Luke said. "Be patient with yourself. And at the end of the day forgive yourself."

Ashley half smiled.

" 'Tis none of my business," Luke said, "and you may consign me to the devil if you wish, Ash. But why did you invite Emily here? I got the distinct impression that we were invited here because you wanted to invite her — not the other way around, as you have explained it to numerous people. Why do you want her here?"

Ashley turned the glass in his hands and still half smiled. "She is mine," he said. "I cannot see other men pay court to her without wanting to break all their noses and smash all their teeth. She is mine."

"By right of ownership?" Luke asked, eyebrows raised. "Or for more tender considerations, Ash?"

Ashley did not answer for a long while. "You did say I might consign you to the devil," he said at last.

"Quite so," Luke said, sounding infinitely bored. "Tell me some of your plans for Penshurst, Ash. Knowing you as I do, I will not believe that you intend to allow it to be run by your steward, no matter how capable a man he might be."

18

Ashley stood at his window looking out across the park and the river. There was a farmer's cart moving at a leisurely pace along the distant road. The birds beyond his window, hidden among the leaves of the trees, were in full chorus.

He felt almost relaxed this early-morning hour. He felt almost that he liked — or even loved — his new home. Just a few rooms away, Luke and Anna were sleeping. Their four children were asleep in the nursery, watched over by their nurse. Emmy was in the house.

He had gone into Alice's rooms again the night before and had stood in her sitting room for a long while, not touching anything, feeling her presence, smelling that faintest suggestion of her perfume. He had almost made up his mind to give the order to have everything of hers cleared out, given away, or burned. *Forgive yourself,* Luke had said — just as Roderick Cunningham had said it before he left India. But Luke did not know the whole of it. He did not know that his brother had hated his wife — hated and pitied her — and had a dozen times wished her dead. And Luke did not know that on that fatal night he had not been at a business meeting but in another woman's bed. Or that mingled with his terrible grief over the loss of the child he had loved had been a guilty relief at knowing that he no longer had as his heir another man's child. He even knew the man's identity — a handsome, red-haired army captain who had left India long before his son was born.

This morning Ashley had still not made a final decision about those rooms, but this morning he felt that perhaps after all it was possible to live again. *I see now that I have not understood the true nature of your concern for the lady,* Sir Henry Verney had said to him almost a week before, and the words had repeated themselves in his mind over and over since then. And since then he had accepted the undeniable fact that Emmy was a woman. She was a girl no longer. She was a woman.

He smiled suddenly and leaned forward, his hands on the windowsill, bracing himself. He might have guessed it. In fact, he felt that he had been almost expecting it, waiting for it. She had emerged from the house and was hurrying off in the direction of the river. The sun was scarcely risen. He doubted that many of the servants were even up yet. The only disappointing detail about her appearance was the fact that she was dressed as if for the park in London. She was even wearing a hat, prettily tilted forward over her lacy cap.

Ashley hurried into his dressing room.

She was on the river walk, standing still and gazing at the water, when he caught up to her. She was watching a mother duck with a string of little ones bobbing along behind her on the surface of the river. She was smiling. The smile did not fade when she saw him approaching. She pointed at the birds. *Beautiful,* she told him, kissing her fingertips and extending her hand toward the river.

He had been a little afraid that she would resent his presence as an intrusion on her solitude, but she did not look resentful. This was all so very beautiful, she told him again with one all-inclusive sweep of an arm. Despite the fashionable dress and the cap and hat, which made her look deliciously pretty, she looked more like the Emmy he loved. Her hair — what he could see of it beneath the hat — was unpowdered. Her face was clear of cosmetics and patches. Her smile was without the forced gaiety that had chilled him at Vauxhall.

"Yes," he said, using his hands as well as his voice. "I told you you would love it, Emmy. And there is so much more to see."

He found himself wondering if she would have looked so happy in this place and at this moment if she had married him, forced into it by propriety and the pressure both he and their families had exerted. They would have been together now for more than a month. They would have been lovers for that long. His mind, which had shied away from the memories and had shuddered at the very idea of thinking carnally of her, considered the thought somewhat sadly now. She had not wanted to marry him and had been strong-minded enough to hold out against all the persuasions.

He had brought her here to woo her. But he must not be over-confident, he knew. And he must do nothing to lose her friendship. Emmy's friendship, he was realizing anew, was all he had to cling to. All that could turn his life around and give him occasional moments of peace. It had once been very much a one-way thing. He had talked at her, used her for his comfort —

and felt superior because he could hear and speak and she could not. But friendship was a two-way process. Both friends had to give, both had to receive. Emmy had much to give — not through words or the inadequate substitute for words they had devised and would continue to devise, but through silence. He needed to listen to the silence. And he had much to give — acceptance, understanding, the willingness to recognize the validity of her world. Love. But friendship first and foremost. If that was all he could have of her for the rest of his life, then he would be very careful not to forfeit it.

He drew her arm through his and strolled with her, not even attempting for several minutes to talk. Conversation was really not necessary, he realized, when one could share quiet companionship with a friend. The river flowed quietly to one side of them. Trees and shrubs, most notably rhododendrons, carefully placed and selected, closed them in on the other side, so that there was an air of utter seclusion and peace. It all now seemed complete with Emmy there. And more lovely than it had ever seemed before.

"Did you bring your painting things with you?" he asked her at last, touching his fingers first to her chin so that she would turn her head.

Yes, she told him.

"But you have not used them since you were at Bowden?" he asked.

No, she had not.

"Why not?" he asked.

I, she told him with her hands and her whole body and with the bright smile she had used in London, *have been too busy enjoying myself to think of painting.*

"Yes," he said, "I know you have been busy enjoying yourself. But painting is important to you, Emmy."

Yes, she admitted after a few moments, with obvious reluctance.

"Enjoyment for the sake of itself becomes less enjoyable as time goes on," he said.

She frowned in incomprehension.

"You would not enjoy that life forever," he told her.

She admitted the truth of that only by directing her eyes downward. He left her to her thoughts for a while — but he had to persist. He had the uncomfortable feeling that his violation of her body had jolted her out of the world she had created from her own silence. It had been a happy world for which she had found no comparable substitute. If he could do nothing else for her, he would give her back her world.

"Emmy?" He touched her hand and brought her eyes back to his face. "Will you do something for me?"

She looked wary.

"I invited you here," he said, realizing the truth of his words even as he spoke them, "so that I could offer you freedom. You took freedom in your own hands when you refused to marry me. 'Twas incredibly courageous of you, when your whole family was united with me against you. But you have used your freedom to deny yourself, to deny all that is most beautiful and most meaningful in your life. You are deaf, Emmy, and mute, even if you have learned to say one word and may in time learn more. You cannot live the life that women with hearing live — not without giving up all that is most precious to you. I want to give that back to you — here, with this." He gestured to the river and the park around them. "Do you understand me? Have I hurled too many words at you?"

She had stopped walking. She drew her arm free of his and looked at him with troubled eyes. But yes, she told him with a sign he recognized. Yes, she had heard him.

"Emmy," he said. "Let me give you something of real worth. I want you to feel free here to do as you will. If you want to wander here or in the hills, do so. If you wish to absent yourself from any visits I will organize for your sister and Luke, then do so. If you want to let your hair down or go barefoot, do it. And most of all, paint. It is your way of speaking — without the encumbrance of words. Take your easel and your paints to the summerhouse if you will. Will you please accept this gift from me?"

For a moment her eyes filled with tears, but she blinked them back. And she nodded. "Yess," she said.

And the thing was, he thought, that he had meant the word *freedom*. He wanted her to be free, just at the time when he also wanted to clasp her tightly to him and never let her go. But one could never clasp Emmy close without crushing all the life out of her, he realized. She was a free spirit and would never flourish in captivity. She would never have been happy if she had married him at that particular time and under those particular circumstances. The realization was infinitely saddening. Perhaps the time and the circumstances would never be right.

Selfishness could not help but intrude. "Emmy," he said, "may I join you — just occasionally? Not all the time. Not even often. Just sometimes? You will never know how much nourishment I have drawn from just being near you."

She lifted one arm and cupped her hand very gently about his cheek. She nodded.

"I may?" He held her hand where it was and turned his head to set his lips against her palm. "Are we also going to make a talkative woman out of you?"

She smiled sunnily and shrugged, turning both hands upward. *Why not?*

"Now?" he said. "Can we double your vocabulary, do you suppose?" They both laughed. "What word will you try? No?"

No, she told him quite decisively, and pointed one finger at his chest.

"Ashley?" he said. "Try it, then."

She blushed and bit her lower lip. But he could tell as soon as she spoke his name that she must have been practicing before a looking glass. The lip movements were precise and perfect. He doubled up with laughter and she punched him on one shoulder. She was frowning in vexation when he caught her eye, but then she laughed too.

"Not Ahzhee," he said. "Ashley."

That is what I said, she told him with impatient hands and shoulders.

"Sh-sh-sh," he told her, taking one of her hands by the wrist and holding it in front of his mouth while he set the fingertips of her other hand against his throat. "Not zh, but sh-sh-sh."

"Shhhh," she said obediently.

The *l* sound was more difficult to show her. He had not realized how many sounds must be invisible to the beholder. This one, he discovered, was formed with the tongue behind the teeth. He began to have more respect for her skill in being able to read lips so well.

"Ahshley," she said at last, after they had stood face-to-face for every bit of five minutes.

He should tackle that first sound, he thought. But his name spoken thus in her low, sweet, toneless voice sounded just too charming.

"Yes," he said, smiling warmly at her. "Yes, Emmy."

"Yess, Ahshley," she said, and covered her face with her hands and laughed.

He took her by the shoulders and drew her against him, then hugged her tightly and rocked her as they both laughed. Her eyes were dancing with merriment when she tipped her head back and looked up at him.

"Yess, Ahshley."

He rubbed his nose back and forth across hers. "At this rate," he said, "you will learn three hundred and sixty-five words in a year,

Emmy. One extra in a leap year."

Spare me, she told him with a mock grimace.

"Naow," she said.

He grinned. "Oh-oh-oh."

"Oh-oh-oh. No."

"You have been teaching yourself," he said, drawing her arm through his again. "You have been making my services as a teacher redundant."

"No." She pulled her arm free and her hands went to work. "Naow. Oh-oh-oh. Ahzhee. Sh-sh-sh. L-l-l-l." She pointed at him.

He chuckled. "Very well," he said. "I can still correct your pronunciation." Except for the opening sound of his own name, he reminded himself.

"Yess." She smiled sunnily at him. "Yes, Ahshley."

They grinned at each other, thoroughly pleased with themselves.

"And now you must teach me," he said. "Let us stroll onward in silence. Noise — the need to make noise in conversation — causes us to miss so much, Emmy. Teach me."

"Yess," she said again.

Conversation really was unnecessary, he discovered over the next half hour or so.

They shared a pleasure in the morning just as surely as if they had spoken of it.

By the time they returned to the house, he felt almost at peace. Almost happy.

She loved Penshurst. She had always loved Bowden more than any other place she had ever been, even Elm Court, where she had been born and had lived for her first fourteen years. She had always felt that Bowden would feel like her home for the rest of her life. But Penshurst, even before she had made a full exploration of either the house or the park, left her with a strange feeling somewhere in the pit of her stomach. A feeling of almost painful longing.

Perhaps, she thought, it was because Penshurst was his. Ashley's.

They all went outside later in the morning, after breakfast, when the air was warm. At first they strolled with the children about the more cultivated part of the park and Ashley pointed out various features — a lime grove, a small artificial lake, views over the surrounding countryside. But soon enough the children demanded more by way of entertainment, and Luke and Ashley played ball with them while Emily sat with Anna on the lawn and Harry sat too and bounced his palms on the grass. Then Ashley was galloping about with a delighted James on his back and Luke was raising his eyebrows and telling his brother that he would have warned him if he had been given a chance. And so poor Ashley found himself having to gallop George and Joy about too. He collapsed onto the grass afterward in mock exhaustion while Joy and James simultaneously wrestled with Luke.

George had come running over to his mother. "Mama," he said, "I want to go and play with the little boy." He pointed off in the direction of the village.

"The little boy?" Anna frowned. "At the cottage, do you mean? Eric? But perhaps he is busy, George. Or perhaps his mama has taken him somewhere."

"I want to go and see," George announced.

"He *is* a sweet-looking child," Anna said. "But Papa and Uncle Ashley are looking after Joy and James" — James had just jumped onto Ashley's stomach and was being rolled in the grass — "and Harry is going to be hungry soon. I will have to take him inside. You cannot go alone. Perhaps this afternoon."

But George was in no way daunted. "Aunt Emily can take me," he said.

Emily smiled and nodded. She would

enjoy the walk. And if Eric Smith lived alone with his mother and grandfather, perhaps he would enjoy having a new playmate. She got to her feet and brushed the grass off her petticoat.

"You are too good, Emmy," Anna said. "You will be sure he does not outstay his welcome? Children know woefully little about etiquette."

George ran on ahead when they were close to the park gates. He could see Eric swinging on the garden gate outside the cottage. The two of them were in earnest conversation by the time Emily came up to them. She smiled at Eric.

"George has come to play," he told her. "I am four years old. What is your name?" He transferred his attention to George and then looked back at her. "Oh," he said, "you cannot hear or speak? Can you understand me?"

Emily nodded. But Mrs. Smith had appeared in the doorway. She was wiping her hands on a white apron.

"Mama," Eric called, keeping his face turned toward Emily, "George has come from the house to play with me. This lady cannot hear and cannot speak. But she can understand. You have to look at her, though."

Mrs. Smith looked embarrassed. She beckoned Emily. "Please come in," she said, mouthing the words clearly.

And Emily suddenly felt embarrassed too. She had been used to wandering about Bowden, where people knew her and made allowances for her. These people would be dreadfully put out. And so would she. What if they talked and she could not understand? What if they did *not* talk and looked very uncomfortable? But it was too late to think of such things now.

Mrs. Smith smiled when Emily came through the gate and approached the cottage door. "You are Lady Emily Marlowe? Have I remembered your name correctly? How kind of you to bring the little boy — he is the duke's eldest son? — to play with Eric. He is frequently lonely, but he has a wonderful imagination." She flushed. She had been speaking very slowly. "Do you really read lips?"

Emily nodded and smiled.

The cottage was plainly but neatly furnished. Mr. Binchley was coming downstairs as Emily stepped inside. He was clearly a gentleman, as his daughter was clearly a lady, though Emily guessed that they were by no means wealthy. He made her a bow and smiled warmly.

"This is an honor, my lady," he said. "And how do you like Penshurst?" He turned away and appeared to be offering her a chair. He was not easy to understand. And then he turned toward his daughter, appearing startled, and finally looked at Emily. "Really?" he said. He seemed acutely embarrassed.

Emily smiled at him.

Mrs. Smith disappeared into the kitchen, perhaps to make tea.

Emily sat with Mr. Binchley, who looked about as uncomfortable as a man could possibly look. There was no one to break the silence — and Emily knew that people who could hear were always distressed by silence. She could say *yes* and break it, she thought, but though the idea amused her, she was not feeling comfortable. Far from it.

Mr. Binchley caught her eye and they smiled weakly at each other. His hands fidgeted in his lap. Emily lifted hers and beckoned with her fingers. When he looked at them, she made flapping gestures and beckoned again. *Speak to me.* She felt remarkably foolish.

"I never knew of any deaf-mute reading lips," he said.

She smiled with genuine amusement and tapped her chest. *I can,* she was telling him, and then laughed.

The laugh must have done it. He visibly relaxed and started to talk, a little more slowly than he had at first. She found to her relief that she could understand much of what he said. He told her about Penshurst and the neighborhood, and about how pleased everyone was to have the new owner living at the house at last. He had been steward at Penshurst for many years, he was telling her when his daughter returned with the tea tray, until his retirement after the death of Mr. Gregory Kersey, Sir Alexander Kersey's son.

But Katherine Smith looked up at him tight-lipped and Emily turned her head in time to read her lips. "Must you always keep alive that myth, Papa?" she said. "You did not retire. You were replaced."

"This is neither the time nor the place, Katherine," he said. He got to his feet and bowed to Emily again. "I will leave you ladies alone." He smiled kindly at her. "Thank you for calling, Lady Emily, and for bringing the child. He is the Marquess of Craydon?"

Emily nodded.

Mrs. Smith spoke to her about Eric, about the sadness of the fact that he had no brothers or sisters. Her husband had died — she looked down at her hands for several moments before continuing. She spoke about growing up at Penshurst. She had lived in this cottage, though she had been at the house a great deal. She had been educated with Alice Kersey. They had even been friends — when they were children, she added pointedly. Emily was left with the impression that they had no longer been friends once they had grown older.

She found Katherine easier to understand than her father. Nonetheless she decided she would not stay too long, reasoning that it must be a strain on strangers to entertain her when they had to bear the burden of conversation alone. And it was a strain upon her to be the only guest — to have to concentrate upon everything that was said and nod and smile in the right places. But as she was leaving, and after Mrs. Smith had called to George, the woman turned to her and smiled.

"I do thank you for coming," she said. "You are very easy to talk to. You seem to be part of a conversation even though you say nothing. Do come again — if you wish, that is. You are staying at Penshurst for a while?"

Emily nodded, took her leave warmly, then walked back to the house with George, feeling that she had made a friend. Someone who had not smiled at either Ashley or Luke yesterday but who had smiled at her both then and today. Someone who felt anger over the fact that her father had been dismissed from his position as steward at Penshurst after the death of Mr. Gregory Kersey. Alice's brother. Who had dismissed him? Sir Alexander Kersey, who had been in India at the time? Alice, who between the time of her brother's death and her own departure for India must have been in charge at Penshurst? But why? And Katherine Smith had not liked Alice. At least, that was what her one comment had implied.

But Emily had no real wish to know about the past. Even though she knew she would look back on these two weeks and feel pain because they were over and would probably never be repeated, she was going to enjoy them anyway. She was going to enjoy Ashley's friendship and the freedom he had offered her. She was going to enjoy being here in this place, for which she felt such a strange and strong affinity. And it was such a relief to be back in the countryside, to look forward to the prospect of time alone with nature. Ashley had even permitted her to absent herself from visits, to leave off her hoops and her shoes, to paint . . .

Ashley, she thought, understood her more than anyone else, even Anna and Luke. Ashley understood that though handicapped, she was a whole person.

Ashley . . .

She sighed. She had to remember that in two weeks' time she would be leaving again. Leaving Penshurst.

Leaving him.

19

For three days she explored the huge park about Penshurst.

The more cultivated parts before the house she walked through with everyone else, including a few of Ashley's neighbors who called upon them while the weather remained fine and warm. The other parts, the wilder, more extensive parts, she roamed over alone. She slipped out in the mornings, sometimes even before the sun rose, and in the afternoons after they had eaten if there was no visit planned, or immediately afterward if they went somewhere or someone came to call on them. Once she went out in the evening instead of staying to help entertain the visitors Ashley had invited to play cards.

The river walk extended for a whole mile and was very beautiful. But Emily discovered that the riverbank beyond the walk was even lovelier, with its long, sometimes coarse grass and myriad varieties of wildflowers. The hills behind the house, which did not look high from in front, were nevertheless wooded and secluded. And the artfully planned clearings afforded wonderful views over rolling, pastoral countryside. The summerhouse Ashley had referred to overlooked the river and miles of empty farmland. The house and the village were hidden from view behind the trees. She suspected that whoever had built it there had wanted to feel utterly secluded, utterly alone. It was, as Ashley had said, sparsely furnished. But she knew as soon as she set foot inside it that he had had it cleaned and spruced up. There were even clean, soft cushions on the worn sofa and a folded-up blanket.

On the third morning she took her painting things up to the summerhouse, though she did not try to do anything with them. She did not know yet what she wished to paint. Although she felt all the beauty of this new part of the country, it had not yet spoken to her soul. But she knew it would. She had to give it time. Time, real time as opposed to human time, could not be rushed or forced. She was content to sit on the sofa and gaze out the low window opposite — out and down the hill and across the river and the countryside beyond.

On that third morning Ashley came to her. She had left the door of the summerhouse open, and she became aware after several minutes had passed of a shadow in the doorway. He was leaning against the door-frame, his arms crossed over his chest, smiling at her.

"I knew," he said, "that you would look at home here, Emmy." He glanced toward her easel. He used his hands to speak. "I am glad you are going to paint again. And I am glad to see my sprite back."

She had not brought any of her oldest clothes from Bowden. But she had put on her simplest gown this morning without either hoops or padded petticoat. She had tied her hair back loosely with a ribbon. She was barefoot. She had forgotten until these last three days how much she needed that contact with the earth.

"May I?" he asked, indicating the seat beside her on the sofa.

She nodded and he came inside and seated himself. He took her hand in his. But he said nothing more. For half an hour or perhaps longer they sat side by side, hand in hand, looking at the view, watching early morning turn into definite day. There was no more perfect communication than silence, Emily thought. Perhaps that was an easy paradox for her to learn, but she felt that Ashley was learning it too — as he had asked to do. Perhaps she really did have something to teach him, something to give him. He was giving her speech and she was giving him silence.

She had wanted to give him comfort when his emotions had been too tempestuous for there to be any comfort. Perhaps she could give him some comfort now. And perhaps she could weave memories for herself to take with her into a lonely future.

"I shall leave you, Emmy," he said at last after squeezing her hand to draw her eyes to his lips. "Stay here as long as you wish. Thank you for allowing me to share some of your time here." He leaned over her and kissed her softly on the lips. Then he was gone.

She wondered if it would be easier if he did not like her at all. If in his own way he did not love her. If he had not invited her here. If she had not come. She closed her eyes, blocking out the beauty of the view. No, she could not be sorry that he felt a fondness for her. And she knew that she would never be sorry that she had come here. Somehow, in some strange way, she knew it had always been intended that she come here. It was a puzzling thought, and a restful one.

Except that in less than two weeks' time she would have to leave again and return to London. And not see him again for a long, long time.

If ever.

On the fourth morning she went in a different direction, away from both the river and the hill, which were a strong lure in her search for solitude and peace. But she wanted to see all there was to see, and so she went in the opposite direction from the river and the approach to the house. She went across lawns and past the lime grove and in among the trees until she came to the edge of the park. It was marked by a hedgerow, with the road beyond.

It seemed sad not to go farther. The clouds, which had brought rain during the night, were moving off, and the sun was just rising. The air was fresh and cool. The grass and soil underfoot had made her feet tingle with cold. But she could not go farther — not looking the way she did. And not in a neighborhood where she was not well known and would not be able to communicate with anyone she met. She shook her head and closed her eyes, feeling the wind blow her hair out behind her. She had not even tied it back this morning.

There was a gap in the hedgerow into which a wooden stile had been built. She climbed over it and sat on the top rung, facing out over the fields and meadows beyond the road. It was lovely, she thought. There was not the obvious beauty of the river here or the seclusion or the panoramic views of the hill. There was just a basic unspectacular loveliness about it. It was England. It was home.

She was rather sorry she had not brought her paints and her easel. She rather thought she could paint here — the wonder of the ordinary. Though even the seemingly ordinary could appear extraordinary when one opened one's eyes and one's heart to it.

But her reverie was interrupted. She could feel someone else's presence. She jerked her head to one side to look along the road to her right. For the merest moment she felt a surging of gladness. He had come again. But she knew even before she saw the man that he was not Ashley. Something inside her always seemed to know unerringly when he was close by.

He was sitting on horseback a short distance away, handsomely dressed in riding clothes with a cloak for warmth and highly polished boots. His three-cornered hat was tipped slightly forward over his eyes. He was grinning appreciatively at her.

A stranger.

He raised his eyebrows. "I thought you must be deaf," he said.

He must have been speaking to her before she became aware of his presence. She smiled at him, feeling some amusement as well as some embarrassment at his words. He was a young man, rather dashingly handsome.

"Egad," he said, "but I am glad I took to the road early this morning. Have you escaped from your milking chores, wench?" He dismounted from his horse as he spoke and led it closer to her.

Oh. She felt her smile fading as she shook her head. What a wretched embarrassment to be mistaken for a milkmaid. This would teach her to stay well within the confines of the park when she was dressed thus. And she could not even explain.

He laughed and said something she could not see. But he continued. "You would be wasted squatting on a milking stool caressing udders," he said. "I could put your hands and your . . . derriere to far more pleasurable use." Brown eyes roamed over her from head to foot, pausing suggestively with the pauses in his speech. He abandoned his horse to graze on the grass at the side of the road and strolled closer to her.

Emily shook her head firmly and lifted her chin. Her heart began to beat uncomfortably fast. It was just the sort of situation that sometimes appeared in her nightmares. In reality she was rarely alone in a place where a stranger might come upon her. She wished desperately that her legs were on the other side of the stile. She mentally calculated how long it would take her to swing them over. He was not a particularly tall man, she noticed, but he was very solidly built, and he had an indefinable air of command about him. He looked like a man accustomed to having his own way.

"I have rendered you speechless?" he said, laughing at her again. "Come, wench, I would taste of those lips. And perhaps of something else too. Yes, undoubtedly of something else, though I would do more than taste there — I would delve deep for a sweeter feast. The road *is* deserted, I am happy to see, and the hedgerow in yonder field is quite secluded."

She did not see every word. She did not need to. She was desperately frightened.

Ashley. *Ashley.* For the moment fear

paralyzed both her body and her mind. All she could do was silently scream out his name and wish for a miracle.

The stranger took another step toward her.

"No." She held her hands palm out in front of her. "No."

"No?" He became instantly haughty, though the laughter was still there in his eyes. "No, wench? But I say yes. I will give you the chance to earn half a sovereign for yourself before breakfast. A princely sum for a truant milkmaid. But perhaps I will judge that you have not earned even half a farthing if you protest."

Her brain was beginning to function again. She half smiled and kept her eyes on him as she swung her legs over to the other side of the stile. He stood still in order to watch her.

I am Lady Emily Marlowe. I am a guest at Penshurst. The Duchess of Harndon is my sister. But there was no point in wasting time verbalizing the words in her mind that she might have written down if she had had the chance. It was impossible to speak them. Her mind, still terrified but mercifully released from its paralysis, worked frantically.

"Ah," he said, obviously believing that she moved in compliance with his suggestion, "the offer of half a sovereign has done the trick, has it? This will be rare sport, wench, money or no money, I warrant you. I daresay you enjoy a good rutting as well as I."

He was within arm's reach of her. She started suddenly with surprise, her eyes as wide as saucers, gazed beyond his shoulder at the imaginary rider who was not approaching down the road behind him, and pointed with one dramatic arm. She hoped — oh, she hoped and hoped she could say it right.

"L-l-look!" she said.

And then, when his head went back over his shoulder, she hurled herself down from the stile and began to run. The grass was slippery among the trees, but her toes gripped it surely. She knew that she had only a few seconds' grace. It would not take him long to climb over the stile, and surely he could run faster than she. Her back crawled with terror and for once the silence was menacing, but she dared not waste a moment in looking back. She tried to decide whether it would be better to weave among the trees, hoping to lose him, or to run a straight course through them, as she was doing. She tried to decide what she would do when he caught her. Panic was robbing her of both breath and rationality. And finally she could deny the panic no longer. She turned her head to look back.

She could still see him, though he was not close. He was only just on her side of the stile. He was down, one knee bent, the other leg stretched out ahead of him. He must have skidded on the wet grass. He touched his right hand to the brim of his hat in a mocking salute. He said something, but she could not read his lips at that distance. She turned her head again and ran on.

Ashley was not at home. She entered the house at a run, looking neither to left nor to right. She raced upstairs and hurled herself at the door of his bedchamber and through it. He was not there. Nor was he in his dressing room. She gripped the back of a chair there for a moment, gasping for breath, setting a hand to the stitch in her side, not sparing a single thought to wonder how she even knew where his room was. Then she raced downstairs and into the breakfast parlor. It was empty.

The footman in the large tiled hall looked at her impassively. Not by the flicker of an eyelid did he show any reaction to her disheveled appearance. But he had come closer to the door of the breakfast parlor.

"His lordship is out riding, my lady," he said with careful lip movements, "with his grace. Her grace is, I believe, with Lord Harry in the nursery."

Anna. Luke. She stared blankly at the footman. She had not even thought of running to either one of them for help. But Luke was gone anyway, and she would not disturb Anna, who she knew must be feeding Harry. She nodded to the footman and turned back to the stairs.

She paced in her room, with the door firmly shut, for several minutes, stopping frequently at the window to peer downward. But she did not know where he had gone or from which direction he would return. And she could not see the stable block from her window. She finally threw herself facedown onto the bed. She wanted his arms tight about her. She wanted her head against his heartbeat. She wanted the strength of his body enclosing her. She wanted to climb right inside him. She gathered fistfuls of the bedcover into her hands and held tight. And then she turned onto her side and drew up her knees, curling as nearly as she could into a ball. She started to shake so uncontrollably that her teeth chattered, but she could not even reach out to pull the cover over herself for warmth and protection.

Ashley, she thought, *come home. Please*

come home.

After a long time she felt enough in command of her body to get up again. He must not see her like this, she decided. Her hair was wild and tangled. She could see a twig caught in one lock that lay over her shoulder. Her hands and feet were dirty. Her dress was torn at one side. She could smell her own perspiration. She spread her hands in front of her. They were still trembling. So were her legs, now that she was standing on them. She rang the bell for a maid and stripped off her dress.

She felt hardly any better half an hour later, though she was clean and neatly dressed and had had her hair braided and coiled at the back of her head beneath her lace cap. She had deliberately chosen one of her favorite new gowns, an open gown of spring green, its robings embroidered with spring flowers, the petticoat beneath a slightly lighter shade of green. She wore stays and small hoops. But she did not really feel better. She descended the stairs at a sedate pace, her chin up, her expression serene. She had made enough of a spectacle of herself for the servants earlier.

She was not sure she could say the word properly. It began with that invisible sound. "Lord Ahshley?" she asked the footman.

"His lordship is in the library, my lady," the footman said with a bow. "He is with —"

But she had turned away from him and was hurrying despite herself in the direction of the library. She felt the panic of pursuit again, the crawling sensation at her back. She was almost safe. But not quite. She did not wait for the footman to catch up to her but flung the library doors wide for herself and hurried inside.

He was standing not far from the door, his back to her, but he turned at its abrupt opening, a look of surprise on his face. She hurried straight into his arms, her eyes closing even before she reached her destination, her face burying itself against the solid safety of his chest. She wrapped her arms about his waist even as she felt his arms come about her. She breathed in deeply the warm, safe smell of him. She was safe at last. At last. She sighed and relaxed her weight against him.

But he would not allow her to cling to the safety for long. He set his hands on her shoulders and moved them firmly away from him so that he could see her face. His head dipped down and his eyes searched hers.

"Emmy?" he said. "What is it? What has

happened? 'Tis all right, my love. I am here. I have you safe."

She could not see beyond the blessedly safe circle of his face and chest and shoulders and arms. But her mind had caught up to her panic. And she realized that he had not been alone in the library when she had entered it. She released her hold on Ashley, stepped back, and looked beyond him. Luke was standing close to the window, his hands clasped at his back, his eyes intent on her. And there was someone else by the fireside. She could not for the moment turn her eyes to look at him. She jerked her head back in Ashley's direction.

He looked at her with silent concern for a moment, but he must have felt some awkwardness in the situation. Her mind had not quite begun to grasp it. "Emmy," he said, "I have had an unexpected pleasure this morning. Here is my particular friend home from India with his regiment and come to visit me. Meet Major Roderick Cunningham. Rod, may I present Lady Emily Marlowe, the Earl of Royce's sister, Luke's sister-in-law?"

Her eyes moved to him at last. And she could see that in the same moment as she recognized him, he recognized her. But his reaction was as controlled as she hoped hers was. He smiled slowly and made her an elegant bow. "Lady Emily," he said, " 'tis my pleasure and my good fortune to arrive here at this particular time."

Instinct had her making him a curtsy in return. Ashley must have been saying something, but now that she had finally looked at his visitor, Emily could not look away from the man who had wanted to ravish her for half a sovereign just a couple of hours before. She could feel Ashley's hand resting lightly against the back of her waist.

"Indeed?" Major Cunningham said after a pause. "One would never have guessed. Remarkable. But do you not tire of always watching lips, Lady Emily?" His smile lit up his face and was suggestive of deep charm.

The hand at her waist turned her slightly. Ashley's eyes were still full of concern. "But what frightened you, Emmy?" he asked. "What happened?"

She shook her head. She was not sure she was not going to faint or vomit, but perhaps she would do neither if he but kept his hand against her. This man was his friend? He was an army officer, a man bound by the code of chivalry and honor? And he had come to visit? To stay? She smiled.

Ashley's eyes went beyond her for a moment and then looked back. "Yes," he said,

" 'twill be best. Luke will take you to Anna, Emmy. I will talk with you later, or any time you have need of me. I am going to see Roderick settled. I will twist his arm and persuade him to stay for a week or so. What a very pleasant week this is going to be." His smile was warm and happy.

Luke was beside her then, drawing her arm firmly through his, turning her in the direction of the door.

She was very naive, Emily admitted to herself. Despite her month in London, she knew very little about life as it was lived beyond the confines of a sheltered country estate. But she did know that many men — perhaps most men — did not live celibate lives. She was even aware — or thought she was aware — that many men thought any woman beneath the rank of lady fair game for their gallantry, a strangely euphemistic word. Was it possible that there had been nothing so very heinous about Major Cunningham's behavior, given the misunderstanding engendered by her appearance?

Oh, but there had been, she thought. There had. She had said no — she had even spoken the word aloud — and he had been in the process of ignoring her refusal. He had been about to ravish her. Surely he had been about to ravish her.

"My dear." Luke paused on the first landing of the staircase, a private place, and set a hand over hers to bring her eyes to his face. "You were very frightened."

She stared mutely at him.

"Something happened to terrify you," he said. "You went to the library to the protection of Ashley only to discover that he was entertaining a newly arrived guest. 'Twas unfortunate. Will I do as a substitute? Will you tell me what frightened you? Shall we find pen and paper?"

Luke had been both brother and father to her for eight years. She loved him dearly and trusted him utterly. She swallowed. And remembered that Major Cunningham was Ashley's friend. And that perhaps that sort of behavior was not considered so very reprehensible among gentlemen. But it would be seen as reprehensible if they knew the major had treated *her* so. They would have to do something about it, both Luke and Ashley. There would be dreadful unpleasantness. Ashley had looked so very happy to see his friend again.

She shook her head and then shrugged and smiled. *It was nothing,* the gestures told Luke.

Luke's cool gray eyes could be the most

fearsome things. They probed hers for a long while.

"I will bring you to Anna," he said at last. " 'Tis time for us to take the children outside. You will come with us, my dear, where you will feel safe. And where you will *be* safe. I will not allow any harm to come to you."

She smiled at him as he patted her hand and looked deeply into her eyes again. She was safe now, she thought. And would be safe even though he was to be a guest here for the next week. She would be safe now that he knew who she was.

She did not feel safe. The normally comfortable silence was full of unknown terrors.

20

He felt for the rest of the day that he had failed her in some way. She had needed his help — quite badly needed it, to have come hurtling into the library and hurling herself against him as she had when, even without the presence of Luke and Roderick in the room, there had been a footman coming up behind her and standing gawking in the open doorway, until he had withdrawn hastily at Ashley's pointed look and closed the door behind him.

She had come for his help and he had been unable to answer her need because he had been entertaining. He had solved the problem by sending her away with Luke in order to find Anna — though he had not doubted that Luke would try to handle the situation himself. He had failed — she had been unwilling to confide in either him or Anna, Luke had told him later. She had pretended that all was well.

And she had told him the same thing when he had drawn her aside briefly after their midday meal. She had told him with shrugs and sunny smiles and blank eyes that all was well, that nothing had really been wrong in the first place. And she had run upstairs for her straw hat so that she might accompany Anna on return visits to ladies who had called during the past few days.

She had been smiling and serene when she returned and during dinner, at which they had other guests in addition to Roderick, and for an hour in the drawing room afterward. She retired early, disappearing quietly from the room. Perhaps only he noticed. They had had a silent conversation across the room before she went, using one of their oldest agreed-upon series of hand gestures.

Are you uncomfortable? he had asked, spreading his hands palms down in his lap and shaking them slightly.

Yes. A simple nod.

Do you want me to sit beside you? Hands pointing to his chest and to the seat beside hers.

No. A shake of the head. *I am going to leave.* Hands pointing to her bosom and to the door behind her.

It had all been very unobtrusive. No one

else had known that they conversed.

Go, then. A smile and a hand wafted toward the door.

Thank you. Fingers touching her lips.

He had watched, troubled, as she left. The serenity she had displayed all evening had been a thing of the surface, rather as her gaiety had been in London. She had shut herself off behind the calm, smiling eyes.

He had failed her, he thought, frowning at the closed door. He should have left Luke to entertain Rod this morning and taken Emmy aside himself. He could not but remember that she had had eyes for no one but him when she had come running into the room, that it was to him she had come, burrowing against him for safety and protection.

And he had a niggling suspicion that he knew what might have happened. Or if not that, at least who it was who had upset her. The imagination could only boggle over the exact nature of the encounter if she had been that frightened by it.

He and Luke had ridden through the village and beyond it. When they were returning, there had been a horse tethered to the fence of Ned Binchley's cottage. And the owner of the horse had been stepping out through the door as they drew abreast of the gate. Verney. Ashley had not known of his return from London. They had nodded stiffly to each other and exchanged pleasantries. Luke had conversed more easily, both with Verney and with Katherine Smith, who came out of the house behind him. Eric had darted out ahead of them.

"I am to go with Uncle Henry," he had announced. "I am going to see the horses and the puppies. And Aunt Barbara and Lady Verney," he had added as an afterthought.

Sir Henry had mounted his horse and lifted Eric up in front of him, and they had all gone their separate ways.

Ashley could not push from his mind the thought that somehow Verney and Emmy had met this morning, and something had happened. He had no evidence, no proof. But he did have a strong prejudice against the man and a conviction that he fancied Emmy. And the knowledge too that he had seduced and irreparably hurt Alice.

He slipped from the room soon after Emily had left it. She was nowhere to be found in any of the rooms where she might have taken refuge for a short while. He climbed the staircase and stood outside the door of her room for a few moments before lifting a hand and knocking. He knew it was a foolish thing to do, of course, when she would not hear him. But perhaps there was a maid in there with her. There was no sign of a light beneath the door, though. After a short while he turned the handle and opened the door gingerly. The room was dark and empty, as he had expected it to be.

She had gone outside, then. It was perhaps a strange thing to do when something — or someone — had undoubtedly frightened her just this morning. And already it was dusk outside. But Ashley knew that Emmy did not always behave as other women did. She drew nourishment and peace from the outdoors. It was quite conceivable that she would have gone out there. Up onto the hill, at a guess. To the summerhouse.

He wondered if she would resent his following her there. Perhaps not. She had come to him for comfort this morning. Granted, she had fought against his concern all day, but probably only because it had been more or less publicly offered each time. Perhaps in the quietness of the summerhouse she would be thankful to lean on him for a while. Besides, he did not like to think of her there alone. Verney would have to have brought Eric Smith back home sometime . . .

He took candles and a tinderbox with

him. He had not thought to take any there before. The sky was clear and would in all probability be lit with stars and moon when full night came on. But even so, he reasoned, the inability to see was undoubtedly disturbing to someone who could also not hear.

It was not quite the thing to abandon his guests, he thought, even though he had had a quick word with Luke. But Luke and Anna were quite capable of being substitute hosts, and Rod's easy charm had made the gathering a very merry one.

Ashley had gone to India as a very young man, eager to enjoy his work, eager to like the people with whom he would associate there. He had made numerous friends, but none had been as close or as loyal as Roderick Cunningham. He had gone out of his way, it had seemed, after his arrival with his regiment in India, to be presented to Lord and Lady Ashley Kendrick and to establish a close friendship with Ashley. The friendship had never really extended to Alice. She had disliked him.

Roderick was perhaps the only one of Ashley's friends who had known about his marital problems. Not that Ashley had ever talked of them and not that Rod had ever openly intruded. But there had been quiet sympathy and support. He had excused her when she had deserted Ashley at a ball and gone home alone one night — an embarrassing situation, as she had intended. Rod had reminded him that life had been hard on her, with the still recent deaths of her brother and father. And after Thomas's birth, he had commented good-naturedly on the fact that heredity often skipped a generation or two before reasserting itself. Somewhere in Ashley's ancestry or in Lady Ashley's, he had said with a laugh, there was a redhead. Alice had been even darker in coloring than he, Ashley, was. Yet Thomas had been undoubtedly red haired.

It was Roderick who had first told him that Mrs. Roehampton fancied him and meant to have him. They had laughed over that fact and over Rod's jealousy — he fancied the woman himself, he said, but she would talk about nothing but his friend. And they had laughed over the numerous provocative, suggestive, erotic messages she sent via Rod. Messages that, unknown to his amused friend, had begun to have their effect on a celibate Ashley. Until he had maneuvered a meeting with the lady at a party.

She had looked him almost defiantly in the eye when they had come face-to-face. "Yes," she had said.

"Yes?" He had looked back at her in some surprise.

"I can bear it no longer," she had said. "You have won, my lord. Yes."

They had made an assignation to meet the following evening — the evening and night that would forever be etched on Ashley's memory. It had been a night of lust and pleasure and guilt — on both sides, it had seemed. The lady had seemed almost bitter.

"Persistence does sometimes win the prize, you see," she had said to him at one point. "Your words are as seductive as your body, my lord."

He had been too caught up in the pleasure and the guilt to question her words.

Rod had known they were together. But he had not uttered a word of censure, even after the disaster. He was the one to come for Ashley, who had had to get out of the woman's bed to hear the news. He had been a pillar of calmness and strength and efficiency. He had made all the arrangements. He had spoken all the possible consolations. He had provided the alibi — Ashley had been with him all night; they had sat talking and drinking, since Lady Ashley had expressed the intention of staying the night with her friend and had taken her son with her. And finally he had been simply a friend.

"Go home to England, then, Ash," he had said. "Go to Penshurst. Punish yourself for a while. But not forever. 'Twas an accident. A tragic accident. Eventually you will accept that and forgive yourself. Move away then. Sell the place. Marry again and have a family. Live again."

And now, soon after his return to England, he had come visiting. It was good to see him again. To know that he was a true friend, that he cared.

Ashley stopped when he came in sight of the summerhouse. The dusk was deep now, almost darkness. But the door was open. She was sitting quietly on the sofa, he saw when he came closer.

It was strange how the mind and the emotions could be so much at variance, she thought. All day her mind had told her that she was perfectly safe — Ashley and Luke, and Anna too, had kept a close eye on her; in fact, she had found it something of a strain to smile and relax and appear perfectly normal for their sakes. And all day her mind had told her that she had met Major Cunningham under unfortunate circumstances, ones that had shown him in the worst possible light. All day he had been friendly and charming. He had seemed a worthy friend of Ashley's. Luke and Anna obviously liked him. The neighbors who had come for dinner were clearly delighted with him.

And yet her mind could not persuade the rest of her to put the morning's incident behind her, to forget about it, to feel convinced that it could not happen again. All day her imagination had reenacted the scene — as it had been, as it might have been. As it might have been . . . Terror had lurked all day only just behind the calm, cheerful facade she had assumed so that she would not be confronted again with questions.

And all day she had debated with herself the desirability of confiding in someone — not Ashley, perhaps, but Anna. Or Luke. Perhaps they could help her decide if what had happened was something Ashley should know about, or if the telling would merely damage a friendship unnecessarily. It horrified her to think that such behavior might be commonplace among gentlemen. But she could not tell Anna. Her sister would be dreadfully upset — and she had upset Anna more than enough not much longer than a month ago. And she could not tell Luke. He might do something as drastic as challenging the major to a duel. Luke had once had the reputation of being a deadly swordsman, but Major Cunningham was an army officer. Fighting was his job.

All day she had kept her secret and hidden her irrational fears. But by the evening they were threatening to show themselves again. It was ridiculous really, she told herself. She was surrounded by people. There were guests in the house, and even when they left there would be Ashley and Luke and Anna — and *him.* But as the light began to fade beyond the drawing room windows, she could think of only one thing. *There was no lock on the door of her bedchamber.* And her mind seemed quite powerless to tell her quite sensibly that he would not try to press his attentions on her any longer now that he knew who she was and now that he was beneath Ashley's roof.

She had to get out, she knew. Outside where she would be safe. It was another irrational notion. The opposite was surely true. But she could not control the urge without giving in to panic and becoming hysterical in front of her family and Ashley's guests. And so against all reason she slipped from the drawing room after making her silent excuses to Ashley and up the stairs to her room, where she changed into a plainer gown, removing her stays and her padded petticoat as she did so, and brushed out her hair. She drew a warm cloak about her even though she guessed the night would be warm, and slipped down the servants' stairs and out through a side door.

She would go to the summerhouse, she decided. She could calm herself there, find peace there. Perhaps she would stay there all night so that she would not have to face the terror of that unlocked door. She felt no fear of the lonely hillside or of the fast-approaching darkness, even though she realized as she climbed that she had not thought to bring a candle with her.

The summerhouse was very warm; the heat of the day was still trapped inside. She left the door open and draped her cloak over the back of an upright chair. And she sat on the sofa and gazed out on the darkening scene beyond the window. After a few minutes she felt herself begin to relax. It was the first time she had relaxed since early in the morning when she had been sitting on the stile, wishing she had brought her paints with her.

Tomorrow, she thought, she would paint.

And then she felt the presence of someone else. Strangely, she felt no alarm. She turned her head and smiled. He was saying something, but the light was too dim for her to see. It did not matter. She did not want to talk. She did not want him asking her questions, discovering the answers in her eyes. She reached out one hand to him.

He sat beside her and held her hand. She could not have asked for more, she thought, than to be sitting here with him like this, quietly, peacefully, as they had done . . . was it just yesterday? Today seemed to have been a week long, a month long.

But the feeling did not last. Perhaps it had not been such a good thing for him to have come after all, she thought. Now that he was here, now that she was not alone to fight her own fears, she felt the return of terror, of the panic that had sent her hurrying through the library door and into his arms this morning. She leaned sideways so that her shoulder leaned against his arm. She rested her cheek against his shoulder.

He must have read the language of her body, she thought, as he could always read the language of her eyes and hands. He turned to her, transferring her hand from his right to his left, setting his right arm firmly about her shoulders, dipping his head close to hers. He was speaking again. She could not see what he said. She did not want to know. He had set two candles and a tinderbox on a small table as he came inside. She knew as soon as he moved that he was going to reach for them. But she grabbed his arm.

"No," she said. "No, Ahshley."

She did not want to talk. She wanted to hide, to be held close. She wanted to be a part of him, part of his strength. She did not want him to see her eyes. She closed them. She put an arm around his neck, urging him closer, and sought blindly for his mouth with her own.

His arm was firmly about her. His body was warm. His mouth was comforting, gentle. It was not enough. She parted her lips and touched his with her tongue. He drew his head sharply back and said something and got to his feet, drawing her up with him. She fit more comfortingly against him when they were standing. She linked both arms about his neck and leaned her whole weight into him. She could feel the barrier of his splendid satin evening coat and the heavily embroidered waistcoat beneath, and of his shirt and breeches. His arms were about her waist, his cheek against hers.

She realized she was sobbing only when he lifted his head and feathered soft kisses on her mouth. She could feel that he was talking or whispering to her. She pressed her mouth hard against his. Safety was close. So very close. A door had opened. All she had to do was step inside. But there was still the chance that the door would slam in her face or that danger would snatch her away from behind.

He held her with an arm while he caught up the folded blanket from one end of the sofa with his other arm and spread it on the floor. He tossed cushions at the end of it, then took her down with him until they were lying on the blanket, face-to-face. He held her close. She could feel the vibrations in his chest that told her he was still speaking.

He held her very close to him for a long time while she clung tautly, her eyes tightly shut. Then he turned her onto her back, sliding her almost beneath him as he leaned reassuringly over her. She could scarcely see his face in the darkness, but his hair was back, the length hidden inside the black silk bag, a ribbon bow holding it closed behind his neck. She pulled on the ribbon and freed his hair, so that it spilled about her face. He was lifting her skirt, removing undergarments, opening the front of his breeches.

For a moment she was reminded . . . And for a moment her mind touched upon sin and propriety and scandal. But only for a moment. She linked her arms loosely about his neck beneath his hair, and drew his mouth down to her own. His hand had parted her legs and his fingers were stroking her very lightly, very skillfully, so that the panicked need to make herself part of him, to hide in him, took on an ache of longing to be filled, to have the emptiness taken away.

"Ahshley." She did not know if she had produced any sound to accompany the movements of her lips against his. "Ahshley."

There was memory then. Memory of the hardness pushing slowly inside her, stretching her, of the man's body covering her own, much of his weight pressing down onto her. Memory of her own body becoming part of someone else's. Ashley's. Memory of the depth of penetration. Memory of pain. But there was no pain this time. She lay safe beneath him, felt him still and deeply embedded in her, and closed inner muscles about him.

And then there was memory of the movements, of the repeated thrust and withdrawal of the body joined to hers. Movements that had hurt and hurt that first time, but this time did not hurt at all. She lay still, feeling safe, feeling cherished. Feeling the sheer physical pleasure of rhythm. It was slow and steady. Deep. Her hands played with his hair, her fingers twining themselves into it. She braced her heels against the floor and lifted to him and used her muscles again to match his rhythm. And the ache was back that his fingers had created. Except that now it was a raw pain that centered in the place where he worked and shot upward to tauten her breasts and farther upward into her throat. She moved her hips, urging him onward — and then her head lifted from the cushion to bury itself against his shoulder as the ache got beyond her. She felt every muscle tighten in her body before shuddering and shaking into a fall toward safety.

He was moving slowly again when she recovered herself. Ashley, making love to her. In the summerhouse. Still clad in all his evening finery. Making love to her because she had begged for it, demanded it. Because all day she had been terrified and lonely. Because this might have happened this morning with a stranger. It was not happening with a stranger. It was happening with Ashley because she had needed him and he had answered her need — as she had answered his more than a month ago.

She was warm, languorous. He felt good. So very good. He smelled good. He was Ashley. She pictured him behind her closed eyelids. The man who was so much a part of her heart that there would be nothing left of it if she ever tried to tear him away from it. She pictured him splendid and smiling as he had been this evening, dressed in a glorious shade of kingfisher blue with silver embroidery, his dark hair unpowdered, as she liked it best. He had looked not quite so thin, not quite so haunted tonight. It was he who was joined intimately now with her own body. He was Ashley.

She wondered what the morning would bring. Another offer of marriage? She would think of the morning when it came. She lifted her legs to twine about his. She would not be ashamed about this, though she knew he would be sorry. And she would always cherish the memory of this and the knowledge that it had been utterly wonderful. She would be able to put aside the memories of pain and soreness, and of guilt. And of failure. She had meant to comfort and had brought only suffering — to several people. This time she had been comforted. She would not feel ashamed.

His rhythm grew faster and he set a hand between them to touch her so lightly that she felt the effects more than the touch itself. There was that desire again, and that ache again. And the cresting and release of pain again — though it had not been exactly pain. But this time it was not quite mindless. She felt him hold still in her. She felt the gush of heat deep within. And she felt him relax his full weight on her.

She let herself slip into peace.

21

He held her for perhaps an hour. He did not want to risk waking her. She had been so very distressed, and now she was sleeping peacefully. He wondered if she had realized, or if she would realize when she thought back, how reluctant he had been to do this to her. He had tried to soothe her, to comfort her, without violating her. He had tried to cling to what he had told her only a few days before, that he had brought her here to see her happy, to set her free. He had not wanted to enslave her again.

She had been distraught, clinging and sobbing, and yet she had been unwilling for him to light a candle. She had not wanted to talk. He had talked to her, but of course she had not heard. She had not wanted to talk about whatever it was that had frightened her. Finally he had known that only one thing would bring her any comfort. And so he had given her what she had given him at Bowden. He had given himself.

If there was one consolation, he thought as he held her afterward, it was that her fear could not have been occasioned by what he had begun to suspect. She would surely not have taken him into herself so eagerly if she had been violated just this morning.

He edged away from her at last, sliding his arm from beneath her head. She grumbled in her sleep and turned her head farther into the pillow. He found the tinderbox and blew a flame gently to life so that he could light one of the candles. He set it on the table and sat down on the sofa after covering her with her cloak.

There were going to have to be some answers, he thought, looking down at her. Tonight if possible. Definitely tomorrow. He was beginning to think that he carried his punishment with him wherever he went. His punishment was to watch all who were dear to him hurt by his presence, even when he was trying to show them love. Perhaps it was fitting that it was happening here at Penshurst. He should not have brought Emmy here.

There were answers that must be gathered, he thought. Answers about Alice's relationship with Verney. Answers about Gregory Kersey's death. Answers about Ned Binchley's retirement — why had he retired so soon after Kersey's death when he was a comparatively young man and had clearly loved his job, and when his retirement appeared to have impoverished him? And there must be answers about today. What had happened to Emmy?

There seemed to be no relationship among the questions, he thought. And he was not sure what could be gained from learning the answers — except that knowing the last would help him know what he must do for Emmy. He certainly could not see that there was any connection between what had happened here over the years, culminating today, and what had happened in India.

And yet, he thought, sitting here in the summerhouse, surrounded by darkness and silence and gazing down on a sleeping Emmy, something deep inside him seemed to be telling him that everything *was* connected. It was an absurd thought. What could possibly connect the horrifying accident in India to Emmy's fright today? Or to Binchley's retirement? Or to Kersey's accidental death?

God, he thought, gazing down at Emily, her face and shoulders all but obscured by her tangled hair. God, but he loved her. And another long-suppressed memory surfaced in his mind. He remembered saying good-bye to her when he had been on his way to India. It had been on the driveway at Bowden. She had been leaning back against a tree and he had been standing in front of her. Touching her with his body. Kissing her lips. And feeling desire for her. He had been horrified at the time — hence the repression of the memory. He had felt like a man lusting after a child. But she had not really been a child. She had been halfway to womanhood. She had been fifteen years old.

Even then, he thought, part of him had known that he loved her totally — as a friend, as a brother, as a man. Most of all as a man. He had been afraid of such a vast, all-encompassing love. And so he had repressed it. Until now.

She was looking up at him. He did not smile at her or she at him.

"I will not allow harm to come to you, Emmy," he said, not at all sure he was capable of keeping such a promise. He used signs along with the words. "I will always protect you, even with my life. Will you not trust me?"

Yes, she told him with a slight nod of the head.

"I do not like to see you frightened and vulnerable," he said. "I have come to see

446

you as a woman of strong character and indomitable will, Emmy. I have come to believe that you are stronger than I. 'Twas seductively sweet to be able to comfort you tonight as you comforted me not so long ago. But I would rather take away the source of your fear if I might. Something happened this morning?"

No, she told him with a slow shaking of the head.

"But something *might* have happened?" he asked her. "You escaped from it?"

Still the shaking of her head. But her eyes told him this time that she was lying. Her eyes had become opaque — deliberately so. Why would she not tell him? Or even Luke? Was she afraid of causing trouble? Among neighbors, perhaps? Did she think it better to keep her secret and contain her fear as best she could? It would be so like Emmy to do that.

"I begin to realize," he said, "that I should have stayed in India, or that at least I should have come here and stayed away from Bowden. You would have been happy, Emmy. You would have been preparing for your wedding to Powell."

She sat up sharply, reached out a hand, and touched his knee. She was shaking her head. "No," she said. "No, Ahshley." He

447

must not blame himself, her eyes and her hands told him. He must not blame himself.

"Well." He patted her hand. "Come then, Emmy. I will take you home."

No, she told him. No, she was going to stay here.

"All night?" he asked her, frowning.

"Yes."

He might have expected it, of course. Where would one expect Emmy to go if something had upset or frightened her? To where there was the comfort of other people? Certainly that had happened this morning — she had come running to him. But it was more likely that she would go running to the source of all that had brought serenity and happiness to a life that most people would have found impossibly difficult. Yes, it made sense when one knew Emmy to understand that she would spend this night up here in the hills rather than in the safety of her room at Penshurst.

"Very well." He curled his fingers about hers. "Then I will stay here with you, Emmy."

She did not argue. She got to her feet and drew him to his. She led him outside. As he had anticipated, the sky was bright with moon and stars. The moon was shining in a bright band across the river below them.

They stood outside the summerhouse for a long time, gazing at the sky and the land, holding hands until he released hers and set an arm loosely about her shoulders and she rested her head on his shoulder.

He wondered if the love she undoubtedly felt for him could possibly grow the one extra dimension. But it was not something deeply to be wished for, he supposed. He had not earned forgiveness and perhaps never would. His life was still full of darkness and perhaps always would be. He seemed to have been a blight on those he loved since his return from India and was perhaps incapable of ever bringing happiness to another person. Especially to Emmy.

Though, of course, he knew he must offer her marriage again. Once more there was the chance that she would be carrying his child. He did not know if he hoped more that she would accept him or that she would reject him.

But tonight was something of a time out of time. He turned his face into her hair and kissed the top of her head. She sighed. Tonight, he thought, she was in love with him because she had needed him and he had brought her comfort — and pleasure. He had never had a woman take that kind of pleasure from him before tonight. He had been awed by it. Tomorrow would be different. Tomorrow would bring back the safety of daylight and would be a new day. Tomorrow she would be strong again. She would love him in her own sweet, strong way again.

But tonight was a time out of time. A time to be silent and at peace. Silent . . . Silence, he realized, was more than an absence of speech. One could be silent and yet have one's mind so teeming with words that the silence was loud with inner noise. True silence involved a letting go of words, both spoken and thought. It involved abandoning oneself to one's senses. It involved . . . merely being.

He stood with Emily for a long time while the inner noise and turmoil gradually ceased their clamor and he became part of the beauty of the night with her. Part of the beauty of being.

"Let us go back inside," he said to her at last with a sigh, tipping her head back with a hand beneath her chin so that she would see his lips.

"Yes," she said.

He knew that she was consenting to a night of love. No frenzied reaching for comfort by either of them for the rest of the night. Merely a mutual giving and taking. A night of love, even if tomorrow brought denial and a harsher reality.

As bad fortune would have it, Roderick Cunningham was wandering in the garden early in the morning and saw them returning, even though they had headed for the side door rather than the front entrance.

Ashley, who had an arm about Emily's waist, felt her tense and shrink against him. But it was impossible to cover up the truth. He tightened his arm reassuringly, kissed her swiftly on the lips, and opened the door for her.

"All will be well," he said quietly to her before she turned and disappeared up the stairs. "There is nothing to worry about."

Poor Emmy. He would have saved her from the embarrassment and humiliation if he could have. She would not realize, of course, that Rod was the soul of discretion. Ashley turned to look rather ruefully at his friend, who was smiling back at him.

"If there had been a tree to duck behind, Ash," he said, "I would have discreetly availed myself of its services. I trust you have had a good night's . . . sleep?"

Rod did not understand. "She had need of me," Ashley said more curtly than he had intended. "I do not know what happened yesterday. She does not frighten easily.

Something happened. We are not involved in any sordid affair."

Major Cunningham looked instantly contrite. "I never for one moment thought you were, Ash," he said. "She appears to be a sweet lady. 'Tis too bad she suffers from such an affliction. She has been unable to explain what it was that happened?"

"Not unable," Ashley said. "Unwilling. I mean to wring some answers from someone else today, though. It will mean deserting you for an hour or two this morning, Rod. I trust you can amuse yourself?" He grinned. "But help my brother and sister-in-law keep an eye on Emmy, if you will be so good."

" 'Twill be my pleasure," the major said. "She is relaxing on the eye, Ash. Perhaps she will confide in me, a virtual stranger. Does she have any means of communicating?"

"She can write," Ashley said.

"If I were you," his friend said, looking him up and down, "I would follow Lady Emily through that door, Ash. *I* might believe that those clothes are suited to a morning ride, but I am remarkably gullible."

Ashley slapped him on the shoulder and laughed. "Right," he said. "My brother is decidedly not."

He let himself in through the side door,

looked about to make sure there was no one in sight, and ran up the stairs.

The Duke of Harndon was reclining comfortably on a nursery chair, watching his wife suckle his youngest son. He had been there for only a few minutes.

"All is well," he said. "They have returned."

"All is well!" She looked up and met his keen gray eyes. "Were we foolish, Luke, to agree to bring her here?"

"As I remember it, my dear," he said, raising his eyebrows, "Emily was invited to come here and accepted and we were invited and accepted. We did not bring her as we brought Joy and George, James and Harry."

"Oh, Luke," she said, "you know what I mean."

"I do." He rested his elbows on the arms of the chair and steepled his fingers. "But it has come to my notice, madam, that Emily is not one of our children. Or a child at all, in fact. And that Ashley is no longer a boy in need of my guidance and discipline. They are adults, both of them."

"But —," she began.

"We cannot bear the burdens of other adults on our own shoulders, my dear, much as we love them. I cannot escape from the conviction that Theo somehow maneuvered this — with his lady as an eager accomplice. And I cannot help wondering if they have not been wise. There is something between those two, Anna, something they must work out between them. Happily, 'tis to be hoped."

"Oh, Luke," she said. "If only —"

"But we can do nothing," he said firmly. "Our son is going to grow fat if you continue to so indulge him."

She smiled fondly down at Lord Harry, who was sucking lustily. "You have said that of each child," she said. "But none of them are fat."

"Given the fact that I have been envious of each of them at this stage of their existence, madam," he said, "perhaps I can be forgiven for indulging a little spite."

She laughed.

Lady Verney wished to discuss her health and inquire after that of each of Ashley's houseguests. Barbara Verney conversed about London and the entertainments of the Season in which she and her brother had participated. Sir Henry Verney sat silent except for uttering the barest of courtesies. Ashley turned to him at last. He, after all, was the object of this visit.

"I wonder if I might have a private word with you," he said, "on a matter with which I would not wish to bore the ladies." He smiled at them and felt rather sorry for the insult to the intelligence of Miss Verney that his words had implied. She was a lady he liked and respected.

"La, if 'tis business you wish to discuss, Lord Ashley," Lady Verney said, "Henry will take you out into the garden or into the study. Such matters give me the headache."

Sir Henry suggested the garden, since the day was sunny and warm. They strolled along a secluded path that took them about the perimeter of the small park. A couple of dogs — a collie and a terrier — were soon ambling at their heels and making the occasional detour among the trees to sniff at roots.

"It is the dogs who are the main attraction for Eric Smith," Sir Henry said. "There is one more in the stables with a litter of puppies. The boy scarcely moved from them yesterday." It was his first attempt at conversation, though he was making no great effort to ingratiate himself, Ashley noticed. He was glad there was no pretense of friendship between them.

"Yesterday," he said quietly. "You were early at Binchley's cottage. Did you encounter anyone on your way there?"

Sir Henry looked at him consideringly. "It is no idle question, is it?" he said. "I cannot remember without giving the question concentrated thought if I met anyone or not. Is it important that I go through that process? Perhaps you would like to tell me whom you suppose I met."

"Lady Emily Marlowe," Ashley said. He watched his neighbor closely and despite himself felt sorry that he had come to Penshurst so burdened. If he had known nothing about this man before he came, they might have been friends. But then he might have been deceived in the friendship. Something had happened to Emmy yesterday.

"Ah." Sir Henry said no more for a while. His voice was decidedly chilly when he did speak. "I understand, Kendrick, as I understood when we were in London, that you are a jealous and a possessive man. I do not know if your claim to Lady Emily's affections is real or imaginary, but either way, the lady has my sincerest sympathy. Have you confronted her too? Expressed your displeasure or your cold disapproval to her? Do you imagine that because I was abroad early and because she presumably was out too, we must therefore have enjoyed a clandestine meeting? And would my denial make any difference to these suspicions of yours?"

"Are you denying it?" Ashley asked.

"No," Sir Henry said. "Nor am I admitting it. Unless you can assure me that you are betrothed to the lady, Kendrick, or married to her, I do not recognize your right to question either her movements or mine in relation to her. I was prepared to welcome you to this part of Kent with all the courtesy and even amiability due a neighbor and possible friend. I believe that you absolved me of any such obligation the last time we met in London."

They were trading civil insults. The thought of becoming openly uncivil was markedly unpleasant, especially in broad daylight and in the civilized surroundings of Verney's park. But Ashley had come for answers. He remembered the night before and the desperation in Emily that had drawn him into a repetition of his indiscretion at Bowden. "I am neither married to Lady Emily nor betrothed to her," he said. "But I will protect her, as I hope I would protect any lady, from harm and from terror. Moreover, she is a guest in my home. I mean to discover what happened to her yesterday morning. I need to know to what extent you assaulted her." It was as well to call a spade a spade.

"Terror? Assault?" Sir Henry had stopped walking and stood facing Ashley, with a coldness and a tension in his manner to match Ashley's own. "I am a gentleman, sir. By my life, instinct directs me to slap a glove in your face, since clearly you believe I have been responsible for both. Good sense, however, tells me that perhaps I should answer your earlier question after all. No, I did not meet or even set eyes on Lady Emily Marlowe yesterday morning. I have not seen her since I walked in the garden with her at Lady Bryant's ball."

Ashley stared hard at him while the dogs circled them, obviously eager for them to move onward. Dammit, Ashley thought, he believed the man. And yet he surely could not expect an instant admission even if he were guilty. Verney's open, honest face was perhaps his greatest asset. Alice must have trusted it, after all. "I must accept your word as a gentleman," he said.

"But with the greatest reluctance," Sir Henry said, lifting one eyebrow, "and with only a grain of trust. Very well, then. But I am sorry in my heart that something appears to have happened to upset Lady Emily. If she is unable to tell you the cause of her terror, then I can understand your concern. I can even perhaps excuse the conclusion you appear to have jumped to, since I *was* out riding early and was alone until I took Eric up with me. But I did not see her. Perhaps it will help you to know that my affections are otherwise engaged and have been — to the same lady — since I was a boy. And that at last it appears I may be having some success in engaging the lady's affections."

Ashley's head went back, almost as if he had been struck. Zounds but the words were wicked. Deliberately so? Verney had loved another woman since boyhood? He had never cared at all for Alice? Well, he had come for answers and he would not be diverted. "Why did you treat my wife so badly?" he asked.

Sir Henry stared back at him before breaking eye contact and bending to pat one of his panting dogs on the head. He began to walk onward and Ashley fell into step beside him.

"I have regretted the harshness with which I spoke to her and the coldness with which I treated her during that final month before she left for India," Sir Henry said. "I was perhaps unjust. Certainly I was hasty. I should have taken more time for consideration. Undoubtedly she was devastated by the power of her own feelings, and my words only made matters worse for her. At the time I did not care. Any fondness I had ever had for her was forgotten. I cared for Katherine — and for myself. And yet a part of me, a guilty part of me, could not help being secretly glad of the gift Alice had presented to me. And so I lashed out at her to cover my own guilt. I am sorry — woefully inadequate words. Did I do her lasting damage?"

"I believe," Ashley said, "your question must be rhetorical, Verney." He had abandoned her — apparently quite abruptly and quite cruelly — for Katherine Binchley. And Katherine in her turn had abandoned him in order to marry Smith. It seemed hardly just that Verney was now having a second chance with her.

Sir Henry sighed. "The answer is apparently yes," he said. "Your coldness to me is understandable, then. But I cannot help but wonder if any permanent damage to Alice's happiness was not caused more by personal guilt than by anything I said to her."

Guilt? Guilt at having lain with her seducer, the man she had loved? The man she had been unable to forget? Ashley knew what it was to see red at that moment. His fist beneath one side of Sir Henry's jaw caught the man unprepared. He reeled backward and only just kept his footing. His hands balled into fists and he glared with anger. But he did not use his fists, Ashley was disappointed to find. He would have welcomed a good fight.

"She was your wife," Sir Henry said, breathing hard. "I must remember that. I am sorry. Sorry for the whole sordid mess and for your doubtless painful attempts to come to terms with it. But perhaps 'twould be as well, Kendrick, if we kept our distance from each other in future, maintaining merely a distant courtesy as neighbors."

"Perhaps," Ashley said coldly, "it would. Answer one more question for me before I take my leave. Did you kill Gregory Kersey?" The question hung between them almost like a tangible thing. But he would not withdraw it if he could have, Ashley thought. Verney was correct: Ashley was trying to come to terms with the past, though he doubted that knowing the full truth would help ease him of his own guilt. Perhaps he felt somehow honor-bound to understand the wife he had been unable to save better than he had ever understood her while she lived. Had she known that her lover was also her brother's murderer? Had that knowledge added to her torment?

Sir Henry blanched and the hand that had been rubbing at his jaw stilled. "Did I kill Greg?" he said in little more than a whisper. He closed his eyes. "Oh, God. Is that what she told you?"

" 'Tis a possibility that has struck me," Ashley said. "Did Kersey find out the truth? Did he confront you?"

"He had always known," Sir Henry said. "We quarreled bitterly over her, yes. There was a marked coolness between us up to the time of his death, though we had been close friends for too long and were still too close as neighbors to be fully estranged. We were shooting together that morning — along with several other neighbors." He paused to draw a deep breath. "No, I did not kill him. I wonder if Alice believed I did. She never accused me of it. But if she did believe it, then that would mean . . . Ah, who knows? The past is best left in the past, buried with the two of them."

"Why did Ned Binchley retire so abruptly after the death of Gregory Kersey?" Ashley asked.

Sir Henry sighed again. "You would have to ask him," he said. "Though it was not retirement. Alice dismissed him."

"Why?" Ashley frowned.

"I believe," Sir Henry said, "that she did not realize he owned his cottage. Sir Alexander had made it over to him after a number of years of good service. I suppose Alice thought dismissing him would be a good way of ridding herself permanently of Katherine. There — I have answered your question after all."

"Yes," Ashley said curtly. "Yes, I see now." And he did, too. Alice had been in love with Verney and he, unable to win Katherine Binchley's affections, had taken advantage of Alice's devotion and had lain with her. That fact had caused a quarrel and a deep rift between her brother and her lover. And then, after all, Verney had abandoned her for Katherine. Had Katherine Binchley teased him — held back from him one moment, encouraged him the next? Alice's brother had died — perhaps at Verney's hands — Verney had abandoned her, and Katherine was still at the cottage with her father, the steward at Penshurst. And so Alice had tried to get rid of them, and failing at that, had gone to India to join her father. It was little wonder that she had been emotionally scarred for life.

"I have comforted myself with the thought that they are both now at peace," Sir Henry said. "Alice and Greg, I mean. The thought would not bring you so much comfort, of course. You did not even know him, and Alice was your wife. And, of course, there was the child, your son. I am sorry. I wish you would believe that. But I understand that you blame me for some things and can never be disposed toward me in any friendly manner. I am sorry for that too. Can we agree at least to be civil?"

"Yes," Ashley said curtly. It was all they could do. And he knew he must let the matter drop now. He had the truth, or as much of it as he would ever have. He had to learn to live with past unhappiness, past guilt. Somehow he had to live on and find some new meaning in life. He thought of Emily. She deserved better. She deserved light and wholeness. He had so little that was of any value to offer her. Even the gift of freedom he had given her less than a week ago had turned sour. There had been their night of intimacy, a night during which he had bound her to him bodily over and over again. He had to offer her once more the protection of his name. And of a love that weighed heavily upon him because there was no real honor to offer with it. He had lost his honor during a certain night in India.

Sir Henry Verney was holding out his right

hand. Ashley had been looking at it, unseeing — until almost too late.

"No," he said sharply as he watched the hand close upon itself and begin to drop to Sir Henry's side. "Please." He extended his own hand and they shook. "The past is, as you say, past."

He was on his way back to Penshurst a few minutes later, not sure if anything had been accomplished. Of one thing he felt sure, though — perhaps foolishly. It was not Verney who had caused Emmy's fear. Someone else had done that.

22

"Henry?" Barbara Verney stepped out onto the terrace as Ashley rode away from the stables. She looked at her brother with some concern.

"I walked into a tree," he said ruefully, touching his jaw.

"I suppose his fist met the same fate," she said. "What happened? He was so very pleasant with Mama and me, but I could not fail to notice the way the two of you glowered at each other."

"I could cheerfully run him through with my sword," Sir Henry said, "and yet I cannot help feeling pity for him, Barbara. He has come here a year after Alice's death to try to fit the pieces together, to make sense out of them. It was, perhaps, a difficult marriage. One does not know exactly what she told him — what truths she withheld, what lies she might have told. He asked me if I had killed Greg."

"Ah," she said, grimacing.

"I had to choose my words with great care," he said. "I am not at all certain that he understands the central truth."

"Ah," she said again. "Perhaps he merely suspects, Henry. Perhaps he finds it difficult, if not impossible, to ask the question outright. Perhaps that is why there is a look of tension about him. He must need to know. Perhaps you should have told him."

"How?" he said, blowing out his breath from puffed cheeks. "We cannot even be quite certain ourselves. And 'tis not something you should even know is possible, Barbara. You are a lady."

"And should delicately swoon at far less," she said. "Nonsense. But there is an unaskable question . . ." She took his arm and walked away from the house with him. "I have never been able to ask you. But I have always wondered. And now the question has been raised in a different form by Lord Ashley. Do you believe *she* killed him?" She bit her lip now that the question was asked.

"Egad!" he said. "I have no proof. I am not sure I would want proof. 'Tis unthinkable — though I did accuse her of it in the first flush of shock."

"Or suicide," she said. "Murder was spoken of, though never with Alice as a possible suspect. Suicide was whispered of at first as a possibility, but no one could think of a motive. There was a powerful one, of course."

" 'Tis best not spoken of, Barbara," he said. " 'Tis best forgotten about. They are both dead."

"But poor Lord Ashley is alive and troubled," she said. "Perhaps you should not have chosen your words with such care, Henry. Which ones did you choose more rashly? The ones you spoke just before colliding with a tree?"

Her brother thought for a moment. "I believe I said something about her having felt guilty," he said. "I said that if she was unhappy in India, perhaps 'twas guilt that made her so."

"Ah," his sister said sadly, "then he does suspect, Henry. Poor man."

"We must keep out of it," he advised. " 'Twere well to keep quiet, Barbara. 'Tis none of our concern after all. It never was."

"Except that Gregory was your friend," she said, "and you loved Katherine."

" 'Twere best to leave the past in the past," he said.

She examined his jaw closely. "I wonder if Mama will believe the story about the tree," she said.

"She will when I tell her I was chasing the dogs," he told her.

She laughed.

Emily was relieved to find when she left her room that Anna had not gone riding with Luke and the children. It was unusual for her not to do so. But her reason for staying at home was soon obvious, though she did not state it. She merely said that she wished to walk to the village and wanted Emily to accompany her.

Of course. Ashley had gone out alone, probably on some estate business, and the children had been eager for their usual morning outing with their parents. But Anna had decided — or had been appointed — to stay to watch over Emily. They all knew that something had frightened her yesterday.

Emily was relieved, even though she had never before feared solitude. And a walk, she thought, would be just the thing. She was tired, and part of her would have liked nothing better than to stay in her room or to find a secluded corner somewhere so that she could relive the events of the night — the repeated and glorious lovemakings interspersed with periods of relaxation and even sleep. Part of her wanted to consider the meaning of what had happened and its implications for the future. She was not sure if last night had changed everything or nothing. But part of her did not want to have to confront the issues — or to be afraid of what, or who, might be lurking behind her. The exercise and air and the company of her sister would help to clear out her head.

But it was not to be as pleasant a morning as she had hoped for. As she and Anna were preparing to leave the house, Major Cunningham came upon them, discovered their purpose and destination, and offered his escort. Anna smiled warmly and agreed. And so, when they set out on their walk, the major stepped between them and offered an arm to each.

In addition to everything else, Emily thought, taking his arm though she inwardly cringed, he had seen her and Ashley this morning, and it would have been evident even to an imbecile that they had been returning from a night spent together. Ashley had still been wearing his rather crumpled evening clothes. And his arm had been about her waist. She could feel power in the major's arm and sense it in his military bearing. He frightened her even as he smiled and conversed pleasantly with Anna, even as he turned to her occasionally with some polished gallantry that needed no verbal reply.

Eric Smith was swinging on the gate outside the cottage, apparently a favorite activity with him. He waved and started prattling as soon as they came within earshot. He wanted to know where James and George were. Emily did not see Anna's reply.

"I am going to have a dog," he announced. "Uncle Henry and Aunt Barbara said I might have one of the puppies if Mama and Grandfer would say yes. Uncle Henry took Mama into the garden last night when he brought me home, and when she came back, she said yes."

Uncle Henry and Aunt Barbara must be Sir Henry Verney and his sister, Emily thought, taking the opportunity to disengage her arm from the major's in order to step forward to ruffle Eric's hair and to bend and kiss him on the cheek. They must have come home from London, then. Her stomach fluttered when she remembered what Ashley had said about Sir Henry at Lady Bryant's ball. She hoped the two men would not come face-to-face any time soon.

Katherine Smith had come outside. She smiled fleetingly at Emily, but she was looking very pale and tense. Anna presented

Major Cunningham. Mrs. Smith curtsied slightly, but she barely looked at him. She did, however, invite them inside for a cup of tea. Mr. Binchley met them at the door and ushered them into the sitting room.

The visit was rather longer than it might have been. Soon after Mrs. Smith had returned from the kitchen with the tea tray, Major Cunningham remarked on the beauty of the garden behind the house, visible through the window, and asked her if she would be so good as to show it to him. She rose silently and led the way without inviting either Anna or Emily to join them.

Anna was telling Mr. Binchley about Bowden Abbey. Emily watched their conversation, though she used Anna's presence as an excuse to allow her attention to wander. She also watched the two in the garden. She hoped Major Cunningham had not taken a fancy to Katherine Smith, that he did not imagine that because she lived here with her father in genteel poverty she was therefore fair game for seduction. The man made her flesh crawl.

"— did not dream you would come here," Katherine Smith was saying. "And to Penshurst instead of here." The sun was on her face, making it very easy, despite the distance, to read her lips.

The major had his back to Emily.

"How can you be his friend?" Mrs. Smith asked. Her face was still pale. Her eyes watched him intently. "Does he know?"

Major Cunningham made a gesture about the garden with one arm.

"They cannot hear," she said. "The window is closed." But she turned her head away and they strolled together about the carefully plotted flower beds.

Emily watched, the sitting room and its occupants forgotten. Katherine Smith and Major Cunningham knew each other. How peculiar that they had allowed Anna to present them to each other as strangers. And then the major was facing toward the window.

" 'Twere better that you asked no questions," he said. " 'Twere better that you know nothing. They died acc—" He turned his head away.

Accidentally? Who had died accidentally? They moved out of sight and at the same moment Anna got to her feet and was taking her leave of Mr. Binchley. Emily did likewise, and within a very few minutes they were continuing on their way toward the village. Anna had promised Eric, after asking Mrs. Smith's permission, that on their return journey they would call for him and he might come to Penshurst to play with the children.

Emily watched Major Cunningham comment to Anna on the charm of the cottage and the hospitality of its occupants, but she did not try to follow the conversation.

Mrs. Smith had asked him why he had come to Penshurst instead of to the cottage. *How can you be his friend?* His? Ashley's? *Does he know?* Know what? And who had died accidentally? Why was it better for Mrs. Smith to know nothing? Major Cunningham had been in India and had become Ashley's friend there. He had been there presumably when Ashley's wife and son died. They had died accidentally. What was it that Ashley might or might not know? That his friend also knew Katherine Smith?

But if they knew each other, why had they been careful not to acknowledge the acquaintance to her and Anna?

Emily's mind puzzled over the questions for the next hour, while they looked around the church and the churchyard, talked with the rector and his wife, who came out to the gate of the rectory to bid them a good morning, and purchased a few items from the village shop.

It was a relief to Emily finally to be on their way back home. When they reached the cottage and Eric came tripping out to meet them, Emily walked with him, holding his hand while he talked without pause, and allowed Major Cunningham to walk on ahead with Anna.

"Thank you." Ashley held out his right hand to Major Cunningham. "You are a true friend, Rod. I know that a stroll to the village and a call at a neighbor's cottage is not the way you might have expected to spend your first full morning here. But 'tis a relief to me to know that she had the company this morning not only of my sister-in-law, but also of a man well able to defend them both from any danger that might have presented itself."

The major shook his hand, and they both stood looking out of the library window at Emily, who was patiently throwing a ball alternately to George and Eric and watching them catch it perhaps twice out of every ten attempts.

" 'Twas my pleasure," the major said. "I had a lovely lady on each arm. What more could any man ask of life?"

Ashley laughed.

"She means a great deal to you," his friend said quietly.

"Yes." Ashley was picturing her playing

thus with her own children. His. Theirs. It was a thought that warmed him and troubled him.

"You are ready to live again, Ash. I can see it," the major said. "Did you learn any answers from your morning visits? Did you discover what happened yesterday?"

"No," Ashley said. "No to your second question. Yes to the first. There were some facts I needed to know. Some things from the past. Some things I needed to know if I am ever to let go of the past and move on into the future. Now I know. But the fact remains, of course, that somehow they were at home when they were not supposed to be there and that I was not there when I should have been. I might have saved them. That poor innocent baby! But I was busy satisfying my lust in the bed of a married woman." He laughed harshly.

"There is always forgiveness," the major said. "Even for the worst offenses, Ash. And there is always redemption. Yours is playing on the grass out there with those two little boys."

Yes, he had come home looking for redemption, Ashley thought. From Emmy, though he had not known it at the time. But it was too simple an answer. And if he drew redemption from her, what would she gain in return? He had so little to offer beyond material things. He had nothing else to offer except a wounded soul.

"You need to marry her," his friend said, "and have babies with her. But not here, Ash. You need to leave here, put behind you everything that would remind you of the late Lady Ashley. 'Twould not be fair to the new Lady Ashley to keep her here."

Ashley drew a deep breath. Perhaps that was part of the problem, he thought. Perhaps he should go. Perhaps there could be happiness for both Emmy and himself if he left here, started somewhere else. And yet . . . And yet he had the deep inner conviction that this thing could not be run from. And that it should not be run from. What he would be running from was deep inside himself. He must confront it if there was to be a future. If there was to be Emmy.

"Sell Penshurst to me," Major Cunningham said. "Sell it and go elsewhere and forget it."

Ashley was so deeply immersed in his thoughts that it took a moment for his friend's words to register on his consciousness. He turned his head and looked at him rather blankly.

"What?" he said. "You would buy Penshurst, Rod?"

The major looked rather embarrassed. "I like it," he said. "And I have been giving serious thought to selling out of the army and settling at home. You know I am a gamer. I have amassed a tidy fortune and would as soon buy land with it as lose it all again at the tables. I like Penshurst. And it has occurred to me that I could do myself a favor and do my closest friend a favor at the same time by purchasing it."

Ashley's look was still rather blank. Roderick had come to Penshurst as his guest, and after a day he was offering to *buy* the place? "But it is not for sale," he said.

The major shrugged. "I am rather impulsive," he admitted. "I ought not to have said anything, Ash. Certainly not yet. But I will not change my mind. I am convinced of that. Think about it. And think about her." He nodded in the direction of the window. "If you change your mind, we will talk business. I will make you a definite offer."

Ashley laughed. "You are doing this purely out of friendship," he said. "How extraordinary you are, Rod. You would regret it within a month — selling your commission, settling on an estate you do not know in a part of the country with which you are unfamiliar. And yet I know you would do it in a moment if I said yes. I value your friendship more highly than to say the word. Penshurst is not for sale."

The major shrugged again. "I am going out riding," he said. "I want to explore this countryside, which is, as you have said, unfamiliar to me. Would you care to join me?"

"If you will forgive me, no," Ashley said. "Luke and Anna have taken the other children out."

"And you would not leave the Lady Emily unguarded," his friend said. He chuckled. " 'Tis commendable in you." He slapped a friendly hand on Ashley's shoulder and made for the door.

"Rod," Ashley said before he reached it. "Thank you."

He wondered how he would have coped with the tragedy and the guilt if Rod had not been there for him in India. He had always been the best of friends. He had seemed to value Ashley's friendship, had sought after it and cultivated it. And it seemed to Ashley now that his friend had always given more than he had received, and that he was continuing to do so. There could be no other explanation than friendship for his extraordinary offer to buy Penshurst.

It was a tempting offer.

He could not accept it, though. Not ever. Somehow, he felt, if salvation was to be had, it was to be had here. He could not explain the feeling to himself. He had not even fully realized he felt this way until Roderick had offered him a way out. But it was so, he was sure. And so he was even less sure about Emily.

He turned to the window to watch her with the children. But they were coming toward the house, the boys running on ahead, looking flushed and excited. She was smiling. Ah, Emmy, always sweetly serene. Or almost always. What had happened yesterday to take away the serenity? Was it something that might recur? He would have to be very careful to see that she was properly protected for the remainder of her stay at Penshurst — perhaps forever, if she would listen to what he knew he must again say to her.

She was painting. It was not coming easily, but she persevered. It was a different scene from any she had ever tried before. Although she was on the hill and there were numerous trees to paint, she knew she could not paint any of them. Her spirit had always been uplifted by trees, but today the trees were strangely silent. It was the flat farmland below that called to her. But she did not know the message and for a long time her brush did not know how to express it.

But finally she was absorbed. So absorbed that she knew when she finally felt his presence that he had been there for some time. Leaning against a tree, his arms crossed over his chest. Far enough away not to intrude upon her privacy or her creative need to keep her work unobserved. He smiled at her when she turned her head to look at him.

She felt desire deep in her womb, though she knew it was not entirely a physical thing. It was love that put the slight unsteadiness in her legs. A love that had now manifested itself in every way. She had decided after leaving the boys in the nursery to play at highwaymen and heroes that she would no longer fight to keep her love suppressed. Not for what remained of her two weeks at least. She would accept this time as a gift. It had been a freeing decision.

"Hello, Emmy," he said. He strolled a little closer. "May I see?" He was signing as well as speaking the words.

"No," she told him aloud, looking briefly at her painting. And then, very daringly, "Naht yet."

He grinned at her. "You have been learning words in my absence," he said. "And learning them wrongly. O-o-o, not ah. Not."

"O-o-o," she said, obediently lifting her jaw a little higher. "Not yet." She felt her throat quickly with one hand. Yes, the vibrations were there. It was not so difficult after all to produce sound. It was almost, she had thought when practicing before the mirror in her room, as if she remembered . . .

He sat on the grass a short distance from her easel, but in such a position that he could not see her painting. He reclined sideways on one elbow and plucked a blade of grass to set between his teeth.

She thought at first that she would not be able to concentrate with him sitting so close. She expected him to be restless, curious. But he was as he had been last night when they had stood together outside the summerhouse. He was still and relaxed. He was very like the soul partner she had always dreamed of having. After a minute or two she forgot about him again with her conscious thoughts and found that at last her brush was speaking the meaning that had been lodged deep within her.

He was gazing off down the hill when she looked at him again. He seemed peaceful. She stood gazing at him for a while, enjoying the luxury of watching unobserved.

"Now," she said at last, forming the word carefully.

He did not correct her pronunciation this time. He merely looked up at her, smiled, and got to his feet, then looked at her painting for a long time in silence, his expression unreadable. She looked for ridicule or amusement or even simple puzzlement, but she saw none of them.

"Everything is horizontal this time," he said, also signing with his hands — he was doing that more often, she noticed, making up new and easily interpreted signs, as if he had decided that it was unfair to expect her always to listen to and speak his language when visual communication was better attuned to the workings of her mind than verbal — "instead of vertical as in the other painting I saw. Everything stretches sideways rather than upward, with the colors of fields and sky intermingling. Not fields down here and sky up there, but all part of one another. Explain to me, Emmy. What have you seen that I have not? I envy your ability to see with an inner eye."

She showed him with her hands and with her bare feet and with her expressive face that the earth was beneath them, the nurturing component of life. Soil and grass and crops. It was through the earth, she attempted to demonstrate, that one must learn all there was to learn about the mystery of life and growth and measureless time and patience. And love and peace too. It was not up there, as she had thought before and told him before. The meaning of it all was not up there, beyond one's grasp, always to be yearned for, never to be attained. It was all here and now, if one only recognized it and accepted it. Not in the future, but now. Not in the distance, but here, within one's grasp. She tried to tell him in words too because she knew she was not communicating quite clearly.

"Naht — not there," she said, pointing upward. "Here. Now."

"Emmy." He took her busy hands in his finally and held them both against his heart as he closed his eyes tightly. "Emmy," he said after a while, and she could see that there were tears in his eyes. "Is it true, then? Is peace not so very far away after all?"

"No," she said.

They spoke to each other without words, without images. They spoke to each other in the silence. It was one of the most precious moments of her life.

He kissed her lips softly before releasing her hands and folding her easel while she cleaned her brush and tidied her paints and paper. Then they walked in silence back to the summerhouse. A silence that was both sweet and sad to Emily. She knew she was dear to him. She knew too that peace was still just beyond his grasp. She wondered if it could ever be possible to know peace after the person one had loved most in the world had died in circumstances that one might have prevented or at least shared.

She turned to him in the summerhouse after setting down her things. He was looking at her. It was the most natural thing in the world to take the couple of steps into his arms, to lift her mouth for his kiss, to set her own arms about his neck. She was not going to analyze. Not until she was away from Penshurst again. And she would not allow conscience or any notion of sin to intrude. Perhaps she was rationalizing, she thought. Perhaps this was what people did when they consciously committed one of life's great sins. But she could not yet feel that this affair she was sharing with Ashley was wrong.

He sat down on the sofa after they had caressed each other with lips and hands and had felt the need to be closer still, and she stood before him and watched as he unbuttoned the front flap of his breeches and then lifted her skirt and drew down her undergarments.

"Come," he said, setting his hands on her hips and drawing her toward him.

She knelt astride him and watched his face as he first positioned her and then returned his hands to her hips and brought her firmly down onto him. He looked at her, his head against the back of the sofa, his eyes half closed.

"Emmy," he said.

She had learned something the night before. Two things, perhaps. She had learned that physical love was intensely pleasurable. And she had learned that it really was love, that in the physical act, which could be called sin when performed outside marriage, as now, love bonded to love and was a thing of the heart and even of the soul as well as of the body. She loved him totally as he began the already familiar rhythmic dance of physical love and as she matched her movements to his — she loved him with her body and with every part of herself enclosed by her body.

She watched his face and saw that he was watching hers. Watching each other's pleasure. But seeing deeper than pleasure. Watching the essence of each other, deeply penetrating each other. Not just in the physical masculine-into-feminine sense, but in every way possible. Masculine, feminine; feminine, masculine — they did not matter. Each was both, and each was both giver and receiver.

He loved her during those minutes, she knew. During the intensely felt minutes of the act of love. Memory would come back to him afterward and set up the barrier again. But for now there was no barrier. Oh no, she would not fight this or see it as sin. Or ever regret it.

He drew her head down to his and set his mouth on hers, his tongue coming deep inside as his other hand held her firm and she felt the hot rush of his seed. She sighed out her own release and relaxed down onto him. It seemed so natural, so right to love him thus. She set her cheek against his shoulder and sank for a few minutes into sleep.

23

"Emmy," he said. She had been sitting quietly beside him on the sofa, her head on his shoulder. But he could not talk to her thus. He sat forward slightly so that the weight of her head was transferred to the crook of his elbow and he could turn for her to see his face.

She looked back at him with smiling eyes and he caught his breath again at the expression in them, far deeper than the smile itself. It was the expression she had worn as he had loved her, deeper than the physical passion she had obviously felt. It was Emmy's usual look of serenity and peace. It was her usual look of deep affection. It was the look of a woman who had just received the seed of a man who loved her body. It was — ah, it was far more than any one of those, or even of the sum total of them. He would not verbalize even in his mind what her expression told him.

"Emmy." He touched his lips very lightly and briefly to hers. "I am not going to say the obvious — not yet. We have been lovers, last night and today. We both know what that might mean and what it should mean. You may well be with child, and even apart from that possibility we should both now do what is right and proper. But I have learned from you since last time. I have learned that there is something far more important than what society tells us is proper."

She touched her fingertips to his lips. He was not sure there was not a tinge of sadness in her smile.

"I want to tell you some things," he said. "I want to burden you with knowledge that should be mine alone. I want you to know the man to whom you have opened your greatest treasure as a woman. The man who will offer himself to you for life some time soon — unless you indicate that under no circumstances can you accept me. You knew me once better than anyone has ever known me, I believe, little fawn. You no longer know me. You care for me. Perhaps you believe you care enough to marry me. But you do not know me, Emmy. And so I must tell you."

"I know you," she said, indicating with

her hand that it was heart knowledge of which she spoke. But she said the words aloud.

It was still a shock to hear her speak, her words slowly and distinctly spoken, her voice low and toneless and yet strangely sweet.

"There are so many things about me you do not know," he said. "There were seven years when you did not see me, Emmy. So many things."

"No, no, no," she said. She set one hand flat over his heart. "I know you, Ahshley."

Why was it, he wondered, that he so often found himself fighting tears when he was with Emmy, even though she could also bring him closer to happiness than he had thought ever again possible? He had shed no tears after the death of his wife and her son.

Tell me, then. She spoke now with her hands and her eyes.

"Not here." He got to his feet and took her hand in his. He had to make this more real to her. She had to understand that he was not the man she had loved more compassionately than his own sister had ever loved him. It seemed that she must marry him now. But he needed her to understand how unlovable he was, how despicable. He could not even offer himself to her again with all the darkness shut up within. She had a right to know.

He did not talk to her as they descended the hill and approached the house from the side. They did not see anyone on the way, for which fact he was thankful, and the servants' stairs were deserted too. He paused for a moment outside the door of Alice's suite and took Emily's hand firmly in his own.

"These were her rooms," he said when they had stepped into the dressing room and he had shut the door firmly behind them. "As she left them. No one cleared them out when she died because no order to do so was ever given. I have not given that order since my own arrival here, though I have wanted to and have been on the verge of doing so numerous times. These were her clothes." He had released her hand in order to open the double doors of a large wardrobe. "You can breathe in her perfume if you take a deep breath."

She did so, then stood very still. He opened the door into the bedchamber and she followed him inside.

"She was a very feminine woman," he said. "As you can see, she loved pinks and lavenders — and frills and flounces and

491

fussiness. She was very beautiful — small and dainty and seemingly fragile. She aroused all of a man's protective instincts. Men routinely fell in love with her."

She touched the frilled satin bed hangings, a look of deep sadness in her eyes.

"Come," he said, beckoning her toward the door leading into the small sitting room. "This is where she sat and wrote letters and sewed. It has all the daintiness one would expect of Alice's personal domain."

He watched her run a hand over the inlaid wood pattern on top of the small escritoire. She slid open a desk drawer, something he had never been able to bring himself to do. She reached in after a few moments and drew out two oval picture frames, hinged together in the middle, then turned them over and stood looking down at the two pictures. He took a step toward her and drew in a slow breath as he looked over her shoulder.

"Alice," he said, though she did not look up to see him speak. Alice, looking as lovely and as vital as she had looked before they married, when she had nursed him, when he had been weak and in need.

Emily looked up at him. She was pointing to the other portrait. She pointed at him and then back at the picture. *Like you,* she was telling him.

He was a young man, dark like Alice, blue-eyed. He must be her brother, Gregory Kersey, Ashley reasoned. And yes, he thought, there was perhaps a slight likeness.

"Gregory Kersey," he said. "Alice's brother."

She set the portraits back inside the drawer as she had found them and closed it carefully. She looked up at him.

"I hated her, Emmy," he said.

She gazed at him, her face without expression.

"We fell in love in great haste," he said. "She was my nurse when I was very sick. I was her patient when she was grieving and adjusting to life in a new country. We married before we really knew each other. I repulsed her. She would — make no attempt to like me. She was repeatedly unfaithful to me. I suppose I was much to blame. Rarely is the fault all on one side in a failed marriage. I grew to hate her. A hundred times I must have wished her dead."

"No," she said aloud.

"My mind shied away from the wish," he said. "But 'twas there. I longed to be free of her, to be free of the endless nightmare of being bound to her for life."

Her eyes were wide with shock.

"Thomas was not mine," he said. "I would tell no one else this, Emmy. I would defend the honor of his memory with my life if anyone were to challenge his legitimacy. I acknowledged him as mine. He had my name. He was an innocent child whom I loved."

She frowned.

"Emmy," he said, "the 'business meeting' that kept me from home the night of the fire was no such thing. I spent the night in the bed of a married woman." He wondered suddenly if she had understood his torrent of words. He had not even tried to sign any of the meaning to her. But it appeared she had understood.

She closed her eyes and tipped back her head. He waited for her to look at him again. When she did so, her eyes were filled with pain. Pain for herself? Pain for him? Knowing Emmy as he did, he did not doubt there was plenty of the latter.

"There was nothing between Alice and me after our wedding night," he said. "The night of the fire was my first adultery, though I do not suppose it would have been my last. 'Tis no excuse anyway: Adultery is adultery. My wife and the child I loved died while I was committing it."

Her face had lost all vestiges of color. He wondered if she would faint. But he would not step forward to support her. He kept himself rigidly apart from her.

"Now tell me," he said quietly, "that you know me, Emmy."

She closed her eyes again and swayed on her feet. But after several moments she took a few hurried steps toward him, wrapped her arms tightly about his waist, and pressed her forehead to his cravat.

"I know you," she said in words.

Why did her words feel like absolution? Like forgiveness? She did not have the power to forgive him. No one had that power. Perhaps not even God, whom he had never asked. There was no forgiveness.

He set his arms like iron bars about her, buried his face against her hair, and wept. Wept with deep, painful, racking sobs. For a long time he could do nothing to bring them under control. For a long time he touched the very bottom of despair. But he held on tightly to Emily, who leaned warmly and softly into him. And he knew that he was clinging to the only hope he might ever have of pardon and peace.

It was a damp and misty morning. The grass was wet and chilly beneath her bare feet.

But she walked up onto the hill anyway, not even trying to see down into the valley or ahead of herself into the trees. She walked to draw tranquillity from the morning.

He was far more troubled than she had ever realized. The burden of his guilt was far heavier than he had indicated. And yet she could not feel totally dejected this morning. He had not loved Alice. It was a selfish thought to delight in, but she could not help repeating the thought over and over in her mind. He had not loved Alice. His terrible suffering had not been caused by grief over a lost love.

She remembered the look in his eyes as he had made love to her the afternoon before. And his determination that she know all before he offered her marriage again. He had not tried to excuse his own guilt. He had tried to show himself to her as he saw himself — evil and unforgivable. She remembered how he had cried in her arms as if his heart would break, perhaps because she had tried to tell him that he was still Ashley, that he was no different now than he had been seven years before. Only more wounded. Deeply wounded.

There was hope this morning. Hope for him. Hope for herself. She knew that when he asked again, she would say yes. Happiness was by no means assured them. But unhappiness was certain if they parted — for both of them, she believed. He needed her as she needed him. It was the dependency of love. Neither needed the other as any sort of crutch. They needed each other because they cared for each other, because the world was a more meaningful place when the other was close.

He had seemed quite genuinely cheerful last evening when they had all attended a soiree at a neighbor's house. It was true that he had avoided being in close company with Sir Henry Verney, though the two of them had been civil to each other. But he had treated Miss Verney and everyone else with his old amiability. Perhaps in time this new home and this new neighborhood, despite the fact that Alice had lived here, would bring stability and peace to his life. Perhaps she would be able to help. She breathed in the clean, damp smell of the air. This morning she was beginning to believe that this would be her home for the rest of her life. And the thought was deeply pleasing to her. She was no longer haunted by Alice's ghost.

She had even lost her fear of Major Cunningham. Not her dislike, it was true; she doubted she would ever grow to like him. But perhaps that was unfair. He had contrived to speak privately with her last evening. He had sat beside her a little apart from most of the other guests, who were grouped about the pianoforte listening to the musical offerings of several of their number.

"Lady Emily," he had said, a look of frank apology on his face, "will you ever be able to forgive me?"

She had not known quite how to react. A swift glance had shown that both Ashley and Luke were not far away.

"My behavior was unpardonable," he had said. "Even if you had been what I mistook you for, 'twould have been unpardonable. I will not even try to justify what I said and what I suggested. I can only ask humbly for your pardon, without any expectation that it is my right to receive it. Will you forgive me?"

It had been a handsome apology and she had been able to see nothing but shame and sincerity in his eyes. She had nodded her head quickly.

"My sincerest thanks," he had said. "And my sincerest good wishes. Ashley is my dearest friend, but it does not take the intuition of friendship to see that he has conceived a deep affection for you. May I hope for his sake that you return it?"

She would not answer that. It was none of his concern.

"I ask only," he had said, "because 'tis my dearest wish to see him happy again, and I believe you are the lady to make him happy. But not here — at Penshurst, I mean. Always here the memory of his late wife would come between you, Lady Emily. Pardon me for speaking so frankly about what seems not to concern me. But friends must always wish the best for each other. I have offered to purchase Penshurst. I like it. So I am somewhat partial, you see." He had smiled. "Persuade Ashley to accept my offer. 'Twill be for your happiness and his." He had looked apologetic again. "And mine."

It had not been easy to understand every word; he was undoubtedly unaccustomed to talking to a deaf person. But she had understood the main message, she believed.

She still felt surprise. He wished to buy Penshurst. Was he not an army officer? She hoped Ashley would not sell. She had felt a strange attachment to Penshurst almost from her first sight of it.

But at least this morning she could feel a certain respect for the major. She would work on growing to like him. After all, people constantly did unforgivable things.

Why would forgiveness be of any value if it were reserved only for forgivable offenses? And didn't Ashley wrongly believe that *he* had done something unforgivable?

The mist was lifting in places. She stood still to gaze downward at a short stretch of the river that had for the moment come into view. The mist had made her hair damp. She lifted a hand to push it back behind one shoulder.

And then she felt such a piercing dread that she became momentarily paralyzed. There was the quite irrational terror that her heart had stopped and would not start beating again. She seemed to have forgotten how to draw breath into her lungs.

She did not know where the terror came from. And for those few moments she was unable even to turn her head to find its source. There were only mist and trees and hillside — and a wide bloody swath across the back of her lifted hand.

She stared at it as if it were someone else's hand, someone else's wound. Several moments passed before she recognized that the main focus of her feelings was pain. Her eyes turned to the tree trunk directly behind her and gazed at it. Her mind must be working very sluggishly, she suddenly thought with great lucidity. She had been staring at the bullet embedded in the trunk for several seconds before she really saw it. Now she stared for several more seconds. And then again down at her hand, from which the blood was dripping onto her skirt.

Panic took her then and she hurtled blindly downward through the mist, wailing loudly without realizing that she was doing so. The silence was a ravening terror at her back.

A footman in the hall of the house gaped at her, but he did not have to react further. Luke was on his way downstairs. He paused for a moment before hurrying toward her. She collided with his chest and clawed at him.

"Hush, hush, hush," he was saying, but she did not look at his mouth. He lifted her chin and held her head steady. "What have you done to your hand? It appears to be bleeding rather copiously. Hush now. Hush, Emily. I shall take you to your room and we will have it seen to."

But she clawed at him again without seeing his words. And then other hands gripped her shoulders tightly from behind. She did not hear herself scream.

"She has cut herself rather nastily," Luke was saying. "She is also in shock."

One of the hands on her shoulders moved

down her back to behind her knees. The other circled her shoulders. Ashley lifted her into his arms.

"Try not to struggle, love," he said, "or I may drop you. Luke, will you bring Anna to her room? We will have to see if a physician is needed. Hush, love. Shh."

She was still wailing. She buried her face against Ashley's neck as the concerned face of Major Cunningham came into view.

Ashley had been in his study, writing some letters before breakfast. His pen had made an ugly squiggle across the page and spattered it with ink blots when he had heard her. The sounds had been chillingly inhuman, more like those of an animal in pain than of a woman. Yet he had known even before flinging back the door and striding out into the hall that it was Emmy.

"Shh, love. Shh," he said to her as he carried her up the stairs, though he knew she could not hear him. The horrible wailing continued. Luke hurried ahead of them, presumably to fetch Anna. But it was not necessary. She was running down from the floor above, her eyes wide with alarm.

"Merciful heaven!" she exclaimed. "What has happened? Emmy! What has she done?"

"She has cut her hand," Luke said, "and

is deep in shock." He hurried on ahead to open the door to Emily's room.

Ashley set her down on the bed, but she clutched at him with renewed panic. The sounds had not abated at all.

"Hush, love," he said, and heedless of his brother and sister-in-law, who were both in the room, he followed her down onto the bed and gathered her against him, rocking her, crooning to her.

"Emmy." Anna's voice was shaking. "Emmy, what happened?"

Luke was talking to a maid, for whom he must have rung or who had been sent up. He was directing her to bring warm water and cloths, soothing ointment and bandages. His voice, as one might have expected of Luke, sounded reassuringly firm and calm.

It was a raw and nasty cut, Ashley saw when he looked down at the hand that clutched his frock coat. And still bleeding. It must hurt like the devil, he thought. But she was too distraught even to feel the pain at the moment. He forced her head back from his chest and held her chin firmly.

"Emmy," he said. Her eyes were clenched tightly shut. He kissed each in turn and then her mouth. "Emmy."

Her eyes, when she opened them, were

blank with terror. Oh God, and he had looked out of his window this morning, seen the weather, and assumed that she would not think of going out. He had not been there to watch over her.

"Hush, my love," he said. "I have you safe. No one is going to harm you now. You see? Anna and Luke are here too." Why was it that he could never seem to protect the women in his life?

The wailing stopped finally. She stared blankly at him and then looked over his shoulder at her sister and Luke.

"Emmy," Anna said. "Oh, Emmy, what happened?"

"Set them down beside the bed," Luke was instructing the maid. "Then you may leave."

"I am going to let you go, love," Ashley said, "and get up so that we can attend to your hand."

Her eyes moved to it and stared blankly. He eased away from her and stood up beside the bed, but her hysteria did not return. Her face and even her lips were chalk white. She winced but did not make a sound when Anna spread a towel beside her and gently spread her hand on it.

"Oh, Emmy," she said.

"It looks worse than it is," Luke said, setting a hand on Anna's shoulder. "When the blood is sponged away, my dear, you will see that 'tis no mortal wound."

Anna was dabbing with a damp cloth about the long gash across the back of Emily's hand.

"Emmy?" Ashley said when her eyes found him. "You fell?"

No, she had not fallen.

"You scraped it?" he asked. "Against a tree? A rock? A building?"

No. It suddenly occurred to him that a mere cut incurred in such a manner, even if rather a deep one and even given the amount of blood lost, would not have sent her into such deep shock anyway. Not Emmy.

"What happened?" he asked. "Can you tell me?"

She stared at him for a long time. Then she lifted her free hand, seemed not to know quite how to explain, and finally formed it into the unmistakable shape of a pistol and pointed it at the window opposite.

"Zounds," Luke said.

"Someone *shot* at you?" Ashley felt suddenly as if all the blood had drained out of his head. "You *saw* him, Emmy?"

No. She shook her head.

She would not have heard a shot. How

505

could she know, then? Ashley wondered. But cuts like that did not simply appear from nowhere. "How do you know?" he asked her. Anna, he could see, had looked up from her task, her face as white as her sister's.

There had been something behind her. Something big.

"A tree?" he asked.

Yes, a tree. And something small and round — she formed it with her forefinger curled into the base of her thumb — against the tree.

"A bullet," Luke said quietly. She was not looking at him.

"A bullet?" Ashley asked.

Yes, a bullet. Lodged in the trunk of the tree behind her. It had cut a swath across the back of her hand. No more than a few inches from her body. From her heart — it was her left hand that had been hurt. Someone had shot at Emmy and had missed killing her by only a few inches.

"But you saw no one?" he asked her. "Either before or after it happened?"

No, no one. She winced again. Anna was crying and dabbing at the cut. Luke squeezed her shoulder and reached for the jar of ointment.

"Move aside, my dear," he said. "I will

finish this and bind up her hand. Some laudanum would not be amiss, I believe."

"Emmy," Ashley said, "we are going to need to know what happened to frighten you two mornings ago. We need to know who wishes you harm."

Who could want to harm Emmy? Ashley asked himself. Verney? But why? Had Verney shot Gregory Kersey after all? In the same hills? With the same gun? But why Emmy?

Her eyes closed and her teeth bit into her lower lip as Luke applied a liberal dose of ointment to her hand and began to bandage it.

"I believe a physician's services will be unnecessary," he said, "unless the shock has still not worn off after she has slept. But the questions will have to wait, Ash."

"I need to know," Ashley said. "I am going to kill him, whoever he is."

"I shall help you," Anna said fiercely.

"You will stay close to your sister while she has need of you, madam," Luke said quietly and gently, "and to our children, who have a right to your attentions."

"And leave the serious business of guarding our safety to the men in the family," she said sharply, her eyes flashing. " 'Tis always the way of the world. And what if the men fail?"

Ashley watched in some astonishment as his brother and his brother's wife, the models of marital love and affection, proceeded to quarrel. Luke, his task completed, looked coolly at Anna.

"To my knowledge I have not failed you yet, madam," he said.

"But once you needed my help," she said. "Once I helped you kill a man who needed to be killed."

Luke raised his eyebrows and pursed his lips. "And so you did, madam," he said.

"Then do not tell me that I have no further use in life than to comfort my sister and play with my children," she said.

Luke had killed Anna's kidnapper years ago, after Ashley went to India. He had not heard before now of Anna's having had any part in that killing.

"I ask your pardon," Luke said. "If you wish to continue this difference of opinion, Anna, I shall be at your service later in the privacy of our own rooms."

She flushed, opened her mouth, and closed it again.

Ashley sat on the side of the bed and took Emily's good hand in his own. She opened her eyes and looked at him.

"You are in pain?" he asked. "I shall have some laudanum brought up."

She shook her head.

"But you will stay here and sleep?" he asked her.

She nodded, but her hand tightened about his.

"You must not fear," he said. "I shall see that someone is always with you, night and day. I shall have a maid sent to sit with you." He would have stayed himself, but there were proprieties to be observed. He wondered what Anna and Luke had made of his lying on the bed with her when he had carried her in. And had he not been calling her his love? For Emmy's sake, he did not wish to arouse their suspicions. Perhaps she would still refuse to marry him when he next offered.

"I shall stay with her, of course," Anna said. "I intended to do so even before I was informed that 'tis my function in life." There was a definite edge to her voice. "Harry will not need me for a few hours."

"I have a strong premonition," Luke said, sounding both bored and haughty, "that I have just fashioned a scourge with which I am to be whipped mercilessly for the next eternity or two."

"Anna will stay with you," Ashley told Emily. "Both Luke and I will be in the house — and Roderick too, I daresay. He will be waiting to hear what happened. He is a military officer, well experienced at defending people in danger. And there are many servants here. You are quite safe. Do you believe that?" If she did not, then he would stay himself and to hell with propriety.

She nodded.

He raised her hand to his lips. "Try to sleep," he said. "Later we will talk and get to the bottom of what has been happening here. I will put everything right for you so that you will never have to fear again." It was perhaps a rash promise, he mused. "I swear it, little fawn. On my honor."

She smiled — a mere ghost of a smile — for the first time since he had picked her up downstairs in the hall and carried her up here to her room. And she closed her eyes.

Luke, looking somewhat grim about the mouth and eyes, was holding the door open for him. He closed it behind them after they had left the room.

Roderick Cunningham was pacing back and forth in the corridor outside, a look of deep concern on his face.

24

Anna was suckling Harry, who had been crying lustily when she arrived in the main room of the nursery. He had been playing happily with his sister until his stomach suddenly told him that his mama was late and he was hungry. He was now contentedly sucking. The housekeeper was sitting with a sleeping Emily, who had been persuaded after all to take a small dose of laudanum to ease the pain in her hand.

Anna did not look up when the door opened and closed or when her husband seated himself in a chair close to hers. She was quite out of charity with him — especially over the fact that he had had to point out to her in his usual oblique way the distasteful nature of quarreling in public.

"Your only function in life is not to care for my children, Anna," he said after several minutes had passed in silence. "Or even to bear them. Nor is it to give pleasure to my bed. Though you perform all of those functions superlatively. You are the joy of my heart and half of my soul. Yet your function is not even to be those things. 'Tis merely to *be*, as a person worthy of my respect, regardless of your gender or your relationship to me."

"Oh." She still refused to look up. She watched Harry pull on one of his ears as he sucked. "You were always magnificently clever with words. And you have *rehearsed* this speech. 'Tis not fair."

"Rehearsals take time and effort," he said. "And commitment and conviction. I belittled you and I hurt you and I beg your pardon."

She looked at him and her lips quirked. "I wish your Paris acquaintances could hear you apologize to a woman," she said. "To your own wife."

"They would assume that I had been corrupted by English beef and English ale," he said. "They would be immensely saddened. Forgive me?"

She smiled, but she sobered instantly. "Someone is trying to kill Emmy," she said. "Who could possibly wish to do such a thing?"

"Perhaps," he said, his elbows on the chair arms, his fingers steepled, "someone who knows that she is precious to Ashley."

She frowned and lifted Harry against one shoulder so that she could rub his back and pat it to dislodge the wind he never failed to swallow. "But who would wish to hurt Ashley?" she asked. "No one here has even known him for long."

"He was Alice's husband," he said. "Ashley tells me that Alice dismissed Mr. Binchley as steward here before she left for India. Mr. Binchley and his daughter now live in near poverty outside the gates of Penshurst. Someone appears to have shot Alice's brother. The verdict was that 'twas an accident, though no one ever admitted to doing the shooting. Ashley believes 'twas murder. And now soon after Ashley has returned, someone has been frightening the woman he loves."

"Trying to kill her," she said.

"I doubt it." Luke considered for a moment. "It was misty this morning. Whoever did the shooting must have been close. Emily's deafness would enable him to draw quite close without much fear of detection. Unless he was a very poor shot, 'tis surprising that he hit so far from his mark, assuming that he was close and that his mark was her heart. I believe the intention was merely to frighten her. If so, then 'twas brilliantly successful."

Anna shuddered. She set Harry to her other breast, the wind having been quite audibly dislodged. "But who?" she said. "And why? What does Emmy — or Ashley — have to do with what happened here before he even met Alice?"

"We will have to hope, my dear," he said, "that Emily can enlighten us as to the nature of the first frightening experience she had. If she saw someone and can tell us his identity — or *her* identity, for that matter — then perhaps we can proceed further."

"Was Ashley serious when he said he would kill the man responsible?" she asked.

"Were you serious," he asked, looking steadily at her, "when you said you would help?"

"Yes," she said after a pause.

"I believe, my dear," he said, "that Ashley has a stronger motivation even than yours to stake his life on Emily's protection."

She said no more but lowered her gaze to Harry, who was beginning to tire and lose some interest in his meal. Luke sat quietly watching them. Wisely he did not reflect aloud on the fact that a man would willingly die to protect the peace and safety of his woman and of the children they had begotten together in love.

■ ■ ■ ■

"Come with me, Rod?" Ashley asked. The two of them were sitting in the study, waiting. Waiting for Emily to wake up, Ashley supposed. There was little else to do. He had walked about on the hill behind the house with his friend while Luke had stayed at the house at his request, and it seemed to him that they had looked at every tree. They had found no bullet. And what would have been solved if they had, he did not know. Now his butler had brought word that Sir Henry Verney and Miss Verney had come to call on her grace and Lady Emily and that he had shown them into the visitors' salon. Ashley's first instinct had been to send word back simply that the ladies were not receiving.

"Of course. It would be my pleasure." Major Cunningham got to his feet. But he clapped a hand on Ashley's shoulder before they reached the door. "But 'twould be as well to keep a cool head, Ash. Despite what you have told me, there is nothing to prove that Verney has any reason to wish Lady Emily harm, or you either. Besides, I like the man."

Barbara Verney was rising to her feet when

515

they walked through the doorway of the salon. Sir Henry Verney was standing before the window, his back to it. Both looked somewhat surprised to see neither Anna nor Emily.

"Miss Verney." Ashley made her a bow. "Verney. This is a pleasure my sister-in-law and Lady Emily will regret having missed."

"Oh," Miss Verney said, after curtsying to both him and the major, "they are from home. What a disappointment. You see, Henry? I told you this was rather a late hour of the morning to be paying a call."

"Please do have a seat," Ashley said, indicating the one she had risen from at his entrance. "I shall have some tea brought in. They are not from home. Lady Emily is indisposed and her grace is tending her."

Both looked instantly and politely concerned. "I hope 'tis not a serious indisposition," Sir Henry said.

"No," Ashley said. "Not serious."

"I do believe," Major Cunningham said, smiling appreciatively at Barbara Verney, "that I must have been from England altogether too long. The styles of ladies' hair and hats are far more becoming now than they used to be. Or perhaps 'tis just that the few ladies I have seen since my return have superior beauty and taste."

Miss Verney laughed. "If you flatter the enemy as you flatter my sex, Major," she said, " 'tis no wonder France was defeated in the recent war."

But the major insisted that she describe to him how ladies succeeded in dressing their hair so high and keeping its height.

"Pads," he said after she had explained. "Ingenious, madam, and altogether enchanting."

They drank their tea and conversed on a wide range of topics, all decidedly frivolous and all directed by Major Cunningham.

" 'Tis a good thing, Henry," Miss Verney said, setting down her cup and saucer and signaling an early departure, "that you did not leave me at the door as you suggested in order to go about your own business before returning for me. I would have been an embarrassment to Lord Ashley."

"Not at all, Miss Verney," he said. "I would have been pleased to show you the park and the river walk. Are you familiar with them?"

"From childhood," she said, getting to her feet. "I am sorry about Lady Emily. You will convey our good wishes to her for her restored health, my lord? We would have called earlier this morning, but Henry was from home from first light until little more than an hour ago. 'Twas most provoking when he had promised to escort me on several visits in addition to this one." She smiled at her brother to indicate that she was teasing rather than seriously scolding.

Ashley drew a slow breath. "Where were you?" he asked Sir Henry.

"I beg your pardon?" Sir Henry looked back at him with raised eyebrows.

"I asked where you were this morning between first light and one hour ago," Ashley said. "I ask again. Where were you?"

"Ash —," Major Cunningham said, touching him lightly on the arm. They were all on their feet.

Ashley jerked his arm away. "Where were you?" he asked again.

Sir Henry's eyes narrowed. "I am not convinced that I owe you or anyone else an explanation for my movements, Kendrick," he said. "And if you will excuse me, there is a lady in the room. I will escort her home."

"I believe," Major Cunningham said, "it might be wise to tell them what happened this morning, Ash."

" 'What happened'?" Miss Verney was looking bewildered and rather pale. "What *did* happen this morning?"

"Perhaps *you* can tell us," Ashley said, not taking his eyes from Sir Henry.

"Ash." The major's voice had taken on a note of authority. "Sit down. Miss Verney, please do seat yourself again. Lady Emily was shot at this morning up on the hill."

Barbara Verney pressed both hands to her mouth.

"Fortunately," the major said, "apart from a badly grazed hand and badly shocked nerves, she is unharmed."

"And you think I did it," Sir Henry said almost in a whisper. "Egad, you still think I killed Greg Kersey. And you think now I tried to kill Lady Emily. Do you believe I make a career of shooting people, even when they have done nothing to offend me? I will meet you for this, Kendrick." He drew an audible breath through his nose. "But this is not for a lady's ears. Come, Barbara. I will take you home and deal with this later."

"No," she said, her voice shaking. She sat down. "Let us deal with it now and without foolish talk of duels. Lord Ashley is upset, Henry. Lady Emily is his guest here, and we all know that even besides that point he has an affection for her. And all he did was ask you a question — which you refused to answer. I believe 'tis time for some plain speaking."

"Bravo, madam," Major Cunningham

519

said. "Sir Henry, sit down, if you please. Sit down, Ash. Perhaps you would prefer that I leave?"

"No," Ashley said quickly. "Stay, please."

"You must tell Lord Ashley what you believe, Henry," his sister said.

"It concerns your late wife," Sir Henry said stiffly. "Perhaps you should hear it alone."

"No," Ashley said. He had seated himself again. Sir Henry did not sit. "Whatever you have to say can be said in Major Cunningham's hearing."

" 'Tis my belief," Sir Henry said, "that Gregory Kersey's death was not accidental. He might have taken his own life. He had a gun with him and it had been recently fired — as had all our guns, of course. He had motive — perhaps. But I believe 'twas murder." He drew a deep breath. "I believe Alice killed him."

"What?" The word came out as a whisper. Everything had blackened about the edges of Ashley's vision.

"But why?" Major Cunningham's voice, sounding strangely calm, broke into the ensuing silence.

"He was to marry Katherine Binchley the very day he died," Sir Henry said. "He had the special license and had made the arrangements for the ceremony to be performed quietly in a different parish."

Ashley could do nothing but stare at him.

"And you believe that Lady Ashley — Miss Kersey — killed her brother merely because she was about to be supplanted as mistress of Penshurst?" the major asked. "It sounds a trifle extreme, does it not?"

"Not for that reason." Sir Henry was looking at Ashley. "I believe you understand, Kendrick. She told you all — except perhaps the incriminating details I have just mentioned."

But he did not understand at all. Not at all. He felt as if he must have walked into some bizarre dream.

"Tell me," he said.

Sir Henry looked acutely uncomfortable. He glanced at Major Cunningham and at his sister.

"I know already, Henry," she said. "I guessed and you did not deny it, remember? You need not worry now about my sensibilities."

"She was upset at the whole idea of his marrying," Sir Henry said. "She was fond of him." He cleared his throat nervously. "She was overfond of him."

"Egad," the major said.

But Ashley's eyes had closed. Into his

consciousness rushed a detail that perhaps he had kept at bay ever since meeting Sir Henry Verney. Ashley had reminded her of her lover, Alice had told him on the morning after their disastrous wedding night. That was what had attracted her to him. He had reminded her of her lover — Sir Henry Verney. But Verney looked nothing whatsoever like himself. And one of Emmy's signed messages just yesterday echoed loudly in his mind, as if she had spoken aloud. *Like you,* she had indicated. She had been pointing to the portrait of Gregory Kersey, set in a twin frame with Alice's portrait. *Like you.*

"She was an unhappy woman when Gregory started paying court to Katherine," Sir Henry said. "As unhappy about it as I was."

"But you were her lover," Ashley said without opening his eyes.

"Katherine's?" Sir Henry said stiffly. "No. I behaved with honor toward her."

"No," Barbara Verney said. "He means Alice's, Henry."

"Alice's?" Sir Henry looked shocked. "I was Alice's lover? Is *that* what she told you? Egad. 'Tis not true, as I live."

But Alice had not been a virgin. *She had not been a virgin.*

"I can see," Sir Henry said, "that all of

this is new to you, Kendrick. I am sorry. Truly sorry. I assumed when you told me Alice had told you all that she had told you the truth, even if she had withheld the most violent and incriminating part of it."

"Your quarrel with Kersey," Ashley said, "was occasioned by the fact that you both loved the same woman. 'Twas not because he knew you had debauched his sister."

"Dear Lord God," Barbara Verney said.

"No," Sir Henry said quietly.

"Her attachment to her brother was so strong that she would kill him rather than lose him to another woman?" Major Cunningham asked. "Do you have any proof that she shot him, Verney? Or is this a wild guess?"

Yes, her attachment was that strong, Ashley thought with certainty. *They had been lovers.* Her eyes had been fiercely fanatical when she had told her husband of twenty-four hours that she still loved the other man, that she would always love him. *Always.* Yes, she had loved him enough to kill him. And to live in torment ever after.

"She was on the hill," Sir Henry said. "I saw her fleeing downward when I stopped and looked back after hearing the shot. She denied having been there when I confronted her, and then admitted it. She claimed to have been coming to join the shoot — she did sometimes — and to have heard the lone shot and to have seen her brother down. She claimed to have been too filled with horror and panic to go close. She had run back to the house for help. But there was a firmness, an intrepidity about Alice that made that explanation ring not quite true. Besides, she did not send Binchley to look until hours later. Do I have proof that she killed Greg? No. Perhaps I have always been glad that I did not. I kept my mouth shut. Even Barbara has only guessed these things until this morning. She is now hearing for the first time, as you are, that I saw Alice."

"Why might it have been suicide?" Major Cunningham asked. "Why might Kersey have killed himself on the morning of his wedding?"

Ashley's elbows were on his knees, his face in his hands.

"His — love for Katherine was a sudden thing," Sir Henry said, an edge of bitterness in his voice. "And he was an unhappy man. We had always been close friends. But there was a barrier there between us even before he took Katherine from me. There was something he was not willing to talk about. Something I could only guess at. 'Twas only later that I discovered Barbara had made the same guesses."

"He was trying to make his life more . . . normal, then?" the major said.

"I believe so." Sir Henry had gone to stand at the window, his back to the room.

"Henry has been puzzled and hurt by the extent of your hostility," Miss Verney said quietly to Ashley. " 'Tis clear now that there has been a huge misunderstanding. I think we should take our leave, Henry. Major? He looks in a state of near collapse."

"I shall see to him, madam," Major Cunningham said. "I am his friend."

"Yes," she said. "I can see that. Come, Henry."

Ashley was aware of Sir Henry Verney's stopping beside him on his way to the door. For a moment a hand rested on his shoulder.

"I am sorry," Sir Henry said.

Ashley kept his head down, his face resting on his hands. His wife's brother had also been her lover. She had killed him because he had been trying to break free of an incestuous relationship by taking a wife.

"Henry," his sister said as their carriage drove away from the house, "he did not know. That poor man!"

"There is one thing no one seemed to think about," he said, "though I daresay Kendrick will think about it soon enough. The person who killed Greg cannot be the same person who shot at Lady Emily this morning — not if our suspicions are correct. So who did shoot at her? And why?"

"I thought all unpleasantness concerning Penshurst was at an end when Alice went away," she said with a sigh. "Now it seems to be back again. But can there possibly be any connection? What *were* you doing all morning?"

His smile was rather crooked. "Are you wondering if I was on that hill?" he asked.

"Of course not," she said briskly. "I am just curious."

"I was riding for most of the time," he said. "If you were to ask me exactly where I rode, I would be unable to answer. I do not remember. I went to see Katherine earlier. I often do, you know, before Eric rises and she has no time for me. I offered for her at last — I finally got up the courage. She refused me."

"Oh, Henry," she said, and she leaned across the space between their seats to lay a sympathetic hand on his arm. "But why? She has always been fond of you. I used to think she loved you. I have thought recently that she loves you again — if she ever stopped."

"She said no." He set his head back against the cushions. "She would offer no explanation. Just no."

"I am so sorry," she said.

But when the carriage reached the gates to the park, Sir Henry turned to rap on the front panel for his coachman to stop outside the Binchley cottage. Eric was, as usual, swinging on the gate. He was smiling and waving.

"What is it today?" Barbara called to him after pulling down the window. "A horse? A ship?"

"A cloud," he said. "I am riding across the sky. Grandfer told me a story about a god who rode his chariot across the sky. But I am riding a cloud."

"Eric," Sir Henry said, "ask your mama if she will step outside for a moment."

Eric went skipping off up the path.

"I will not intrude upon her," Sir Henry explained when his sister looked at him in inquiry. "But I very much need to talk to her."

She came, wiping her hands on a clean white apron as she did so. She did not look at the carriage but somewhere on the ground before her feet. She looked as if she might have been crying.

"Katherine," Barbara said, "you are busy as usual, and as usual you make me feel like an idler."

"Kathy," Sir Henry said, "we have come from Penshurst. Lady Emily Marlowe was shot at this morning by an unknown person for an unknown reason."

Her eyes looked up at him, wide with dismay.

"She was not badly hurt," he said. "She is suffering more from shock than from her wounds, I believe. I tell you only so that you will be careful. So that you will stay close to the house unless your father is with you. And so that you will watch Eric. Promise me?"

Her face had blanched.

"Kathy?" he said.

"You have frightened her," Barbara said. "There is no reason whatsoever to fear, Katherine. Only to be a little cautious, perhaps. How lovely all your flowers are. You are so very clever and industrious."

Katherine Smith had set her arms around her son from behind. She lowered her face to kiss the top of his head.

"Kathy," Sir Henry said. He sighed in frustration. "Be careful." He signaled his coachman to drive on.

She stood for a long while with her arms about Eric, looking after the carriage. Eventually he protested and she released him so that he could continue with his game. She stared sightlessly around at the flowers.

25

Emily came downstairs for tea. Apart from a slight pallor and her heavily bandaged hand, one would not have known that anything was very wrong with her, Ashley thought, bowing over her good hand in the drawing room and seating her beside him on a sofa. She was dressed prettily and fashionably in spring green with delicate flowers embroidered onto her stomacher and the robings of her open gown. Her hair was neatly dressed beneath a frothy little wing cap. He resisted the need to sit closer to her than propriety would allow and to draw her arm through his.

She answered all inquiries about her health with a smile.

"She refused to lie abed any longer," Anna said, "or to take any more laudanum. The hand must be very painful, though."

"Sometimes pain is preferable to the feeling of being drugged," Luke said. " 'Tis but a cut, Anna, though a nasty one to be sure."

"Lady Emily's courage is to be much commended," Major Cunningham said. "Many ladies of my acquaintance would cower in their rooms for days or even weeks after such an experience."

Emily smiled her way through tea. Ashley noticed that she made little attempt to follow the conversation.

It had not taken Ashley long after the departure of Sir Henry Verney and his sister to realize that the mystery of what had happened to Emily that morning and two days before had deepened. Only she herself could enlighten them — but now seemed hardly the time.

Luke and Anna thought that they should take her away, back to Bowden, at least until Theo and Lady Quinn returned to London. Ashley could not help but agree, though with the greatest reluctance. He wanted to marry her. He was half convinced that this time she might be prevailed upon to accept his offer. But how could he marry her if she must leave Penshurst? If it was not safe for her?

There was only one answer, of course, and Roderick Cunningham had provided it in private, after the four-way conference on Emily's safety had been concluded over luncheon: Ashley must live elsewhere with her. The offer to purchase Penshurst was still open.

It was an offer Ashley hated to consider seriously. Penshurst was his. He already felt the attachment of ownership. He and Emily had loved here and found happiness together here — lasting happiness, he hoped. He wanted to settle with her here, have children with her here, grow old with her here. He did not want to be driven away. He did not want to fear to bring her into this part of the world. And who knew for sure that the strange assaults would not follow her elsewhere? He would far prefer to find her assailant than to run from him — or her.

But he had told Roderick that he would think about selling.

His friend had laid a hand on his shoulder. "I know 'twould wrench your heart, Ash," he said. "But I know that giving up Lady Emily would shatter it. Think about my offer. There is no hurry, no pressure. We are friends."

"Come for a walk, Emmy?" Ashley asked now, setting a hand on hers to draw her attention. "The rain has stopped. Will it frighten you too much to leave the house? With me at your side?"

No, she told him, she was not afraid. She left and came back with one of her attractive wide-brimmed straw hats perched forward over her brow and secured with a wide ribbon bow at the back of her neck beneath her cap.

But he stopped her in the hall before they stepped outside. He made sure that he was not within earshot of any of the footmen, then said, "Emmy, answer some questions before we leave. We may need pen and paper. You did not see the person who shot at you this morning. Did you see the person who frightened you two days ago?"

He could see she had, though she was obviously reluctant to say so. But she did nod eventually. He breathed an inward sigh of relief and satisfaction.

"Who?" he said. "Tell me who."

"No," she told him, biting her lip.

"Emmy." He caught at her upper arms and bent his head closer. "Let us go into the study. Write the name for me. I must know. I must be able to protect you from further harm."

"No," she said, frowning.

He drew a deep breath and let it out on a sigh. "Tell me, then," he said. "Do you believe there is any connection between the two incidents?"

She was very firm in her answer. No, there was no connection. But how could she be certain? he wondered.

"Are you very sure of that?" he asked her. "Sure beyond any doubt at all?" He searched her eyes.

"Yes," she said.

And so his final hope was gone. It was frustrating not to know who had frightened her so badly, but she seemed quite convinced that whoever it was had not also tried to kill her that morning.

They strolled along the river walk, her arm drawn firmly through his. Though he usually wore it only for evening dress occasions, he was wearing his sword beneath his skirted coat. And in one pocket of his coat he carried a loaded pistol. It was not a good way to be in one's own home, he thought. Perhaps in a different home he would feel more in control, better able to protect his woman.

"Emmy," he said, dipping his head so that she would see him beneath the brim of her hat. "Luke and Anna wish to take you home to Bowden. Perhaps even tomorrow."

She stopped walking and stared at him with wide eyes.

"I cannot fight them on it," he said. "I do not have the right. And I am as concerned for your safety as they are. What is your wish?"

She spoke very carefully. "You wahnt it?" she asked him. He could tell by her lifted brows that it was a question, not a statement.

Love made him selfish. He hesitated, but he shook his head finally. "No," he said. "But you have been very badly frightened here, Emmy. Perhaps you ought to go. I can come to Bowden when I have settled a few things here."

"No," she said.

"You would not want me to come?" he asked her.

She tipped her head to one side and looked reproachfully at him. *I will stay here,* she told him firmly with her hands.

"I will make Penshurst safe for you, then," he said. "I promise you, Emmy. And then you can live here without fear — forever, if you wish."

It was the wrong time to say more, though he yearned to do so. And her eyes appeared to tell him that she wished it too. It just seemed to him that his life was still too full of tangles — or perhaps fuller of tangles now than it had been even the day before.

He bent his head and kissed her.

She woke up with a feeling of deep dread. The room was dark despite the fact that the curtains were pulled back both from about her bed and from the window. It was still. Not a shadow moved. But why would she expect one to do so? And why this feeling?

It was only when she gripped the bedclothes covering her and felt the bandage on her left hand and winced with the pain of the sudden movement that she remembered. She did not like the helpless feeling that fear brought. All her life she had fought it. Because she was deaf, she was perhaps more susceptible to fear than most people. But she had never been willing for fear to master her. She had fought hard to be in control of her emotions, to make peace the dominating force of her life. She had tried again when she came to bed earlier. She had refused to have either Anna or a maid sleep in her room with her. She had even refused to allow herself to leave the candles burning.

It seemed that since coming to Penshurst there had been nothing but one fear following another. Perhaps she ought to do what Anna and Luke wished her to do and what even Ashley advised. Perhaps she should leave Penshurst and go home to Bowden. But she did not want to leave. She wanted to stay with Ashley. He had mentioned forever during their walk by the river. She wanted forever with him, or at least the rest of their lives. She even dared to hope that he was coming to love her as she loved him. Besides, she did not want to run from her fear. If she ran now, perhaps she would find herself running all her life. She would start seeing herself as a handicapped person.

She had given in to the temptation to take a small dose of laudanum again at bedtime, she remembered. Her hand had been stinging beyond her power to ignore. The effects of the drug had worn off. Doubtless it was the disorienting effect of emerging from her drugged state that had caused her to wake up in the state of panic that still had her heart thumping uncomfortably against her rib cage. The fear was so very hard to shrug off. She dared not move. But why?

She deliberately turned onto her side, wriggling and squirming to find a comfortable position. She would conquer this fear soon, she decided. She would close her eyes and go back to sleep.

But her eyes focused on the small table beside her bed. The familiar contours of the candle in its ornate candlestick were obscured by something larger. She tried to remember what it was. Her small prayer book was at the edge of the table where she had placed it last night. What was the larger object? Her mind puzzled over it, tried to remember — entirely without success. Finally she was forced to sit up in order to lean over and touch it. She picked it up and still could not remember. It was heavy, a picture frame. No, two picture frames, hinged together.

And then she knew. The feeling of dread returned, redoubled in strength. *How had it come here?* It had not been here when she went to bed.

She scrambled out of bed, clutching the frames to her bosom. She looked wildly about her for her night robe. It should have been over the back of the chair beside the fireplace, but it was not there. She could not remember where she had put it. She set down the picture frames on the bed and went searching in her dressing room. But her mind was too distraught even to remember what she was looking for. She opened the door into the corridor outside and fled along it.

His door was unlocked. She opened it in a hurry, rushed inside, and closed it behind her. She stood with her back against it, trying to catch her breath, trying to calm her mind, trying to remember why she had come. And where she was.

And then her eyes focused on the bed. He was getting out of it and coming toward her. He was naked, she could see in the near darkness. His hands were on her shoulders. He was talking to her, she knew, though she could not see his lips clearly. His hands gripped tightly and pulled her against him. She shuddered into his warmth.

She was on the bed then without knowing how she had got there. It was soft and warm from his body heat. He was sitting on the edge of the bed, close beside her, lighting a candle. He had pulled on a red silk robe, though she had not seen him do so.

"Emmy?" He leaned over her. "My love, what is it?"

Her teeth were chattering. She was in his room, she realized. Why? His fingers were smoothing through the hair at her temple.

"You woke up and were frightened?" he asked. "You should have allowed Anna to stay with you, or at least one of the maids."

Yes, she had woken up frightened. And alone. There had been a shape . . .

His mouth was on hers, warm, comforting. "Shall I send for Anna?" he asked her.

His eyes suggested something else.

No, she told him without words. No, she could not move again. She could not go back *there.* But where? And why could she not go back?

"Are you in pain?" he asked. "The laudanum must be wearing off. It has left you disoriented."

Her hand was throbbing. She became aware of the fact only when he asked. It was not unbearable. She did not want any more laudanum. Laudanum made her strange, filled her with fears. She hated being afraid. She was still afraid from the last dose. She could feel her teeth chattering.

"No."

He stood up then, undid the belt of his robe, and let the whole garment slide to the floor. He bent to blow out the candle. He was so very beautiful, she thought, even if he was somewhat thinner than he should have been. He was still well muscled, and possessed a graceful masculinity. He lay down beside her and held her close so that she could draw on his warmth and his strength and eventually relax into them. When he finally made love to her, he lay heavily on top of her and pushed swiftly and deeply inside without first loving her with hands and mouth. He moved with hard, firm strokes. It was as if he knew her need to lose herself in him, to become one with his strength and virility. She did not participate. She lay relaxed and open and grateful. She felt him pressing at her core and gladly on this one occasion allowed him to master her.

Sleep came almost at the same moment as the hot gush of his seed.

Holding her asleep in his arms in his own bed and in his own home as he did now brought stark reality to his mind. She was unmarried, yet very possibly she was with child by him. She was a guest under the protection of his roof. Her sister and his brother were under that same roof. Yet she was in his bed. He had been inside her body. It would not do. He could not simply allow matters to continue like this.

She would have to go away from Penshurst. That was quite evident now. And if she must go, then he must too. He could not live without her. And he would not do so unless she was very adamant in her refusal. He did not believe she would be. Besides, her choices were very limited now. He did a quick mental calculation of the number of times he had put her in danger of conceiving. She had to go away. And so would he.

He held her and held himself from sleep. He would not take her back to her room before daybreak. But he would have to take her there before any servants were abroad. No one could know that she had spent several hours of the night here.

He stared into the darkness. He hated to see what had become of Emmy. He hated to see her cringing with fear even when there was no foundation for it — she had been safe in his home tonight. She had tried to be brave. They had all pressed her to allow someone to sleep in her room with her, but she had been stubborn in her refusal to show such weakness. Dear Emmy. He longed to see the serenity and the peace back in her life. The strength.

It had not escaped his notice earlier that she had not made love, that she had merely surrendered her body to his penetration. And her mind and all her emotions too. He had felt almost as if she had abandoned herself to ravishment, as if she had given up the very essence of herself to his male domination. He had not enjoyed the lovemaking. He had given her what she had so obviously wanted and needed, but he had not enjoyed it. He had grieved for the person she had denied — for Emmy. For his little fawn.

He still grieved for her.

He waited for light to dispel the last shadows of darkness before kissing her on the lips and blowing gently against her ear. She stirred sleepily and tried to burrow against him. He quelled desire.

"Emmy," he said, kissing her again. "Wake up." She would not hear him, of course, but his kisses, and his finger running lightly up and down her spine, would wake her.

Her eyes were blank. She looked at him and then about the room. It was as he had guessed: she had woken from her laudanum-induced sleep frightened and disoriented, and had come scurrying to him without consciously knowing it. Perhaps she would not even remember that he had made love to her.

"You came to me for comfort," he told her. " 'Tis all right, Emmy. I will always be here for you. As you were there for me when I first returned to England. I will take you back to your room before anyone is up and about. 'Twould not do for anyone to know you had been here."

She got obediently out of bed and waited while he belted his robe about him. He opened the door and made sure the corridor was empty before setting an arm around her and taking her to her room. The bed was unmade, as she had left it when she came to him. He drew her close to him and kissed her.

"You will be all right on your own?" he asked her.

She nodded.

"Promise me you will not go out this morning?" he asked.

She nodded again.

"Go back to bed," he said. "Sleep some more, Emmy. You are quite safe here, I promise you." He let her go and was about to turn back to the door. But there was something lying on her bed. Something he instantly recognized. His eyes stilled on it. He felt suddenly cold.

"How did Alice's portrait get here, Emmy?" he asked.

She turned her head to look at it and her eyes widened. Her face paled. She looked bewildered when she turned back to him.

"You brought it here?" he asked, signing to her. "Why?"

She frowned.

Why had she gone into that room? Why had she brought Alice's portrait here? It was on the bed, hinged to the matching portrait of Gregory Kersey. On the bed she had got out of last night in order to come to him.

She had been terribly frightened, her eyes large with terror, her teeth chattering.

"Come," he said gently, picking up the double picture frame and looking for something to set about her shoulders. But there was no shawl or robe in the room. He put his arm around her and drew her close.

The door to Alice's dressing room was wide-open. So were the doors into the bedchamber and the sitting room. The bedclothes were drawn back, the sheets creased, the pillows dented. A satin night robe was flung across the foot of the bed.

Emily's arm came up. Her hand was trembling. She indicated the robe and herself. *Mine,* she told him by the gesture.

Inside the sitting room the drawer of the escritoire where the portraits had been was wide-open. He set them back inside and closed the drawer.

He turned Emily toward him and lifted her chin. She was very pale. "Laudanum has terrible effects on some people," he said. "You must not be upset, Emmy. You are not going mad, I do assure you. I am going to take you back to your room and leave you there for a very few minutes. I am going to fetch Anna to you. You are not going to be alone again until you leave Penshurst. I cannot see you like this, always frightened, always pale. I will send you away, and after I have sold Penshurst, I will come for you."

She moaned.

"I will see you happy again and at peace again," he said before drawing her close for a few moments. "I swear it, my love."

He took her back to her room and hurried to knock on Luke's door. He was going to dress after talking to them and sending Anna to Emmy, and then he was going to talk to Rod, even if it meant waking him up at this early hour. They had business to discuss — the sale of Penshurst.

26

"Kathy?" Sir Henry Verney removed his three-cornered hat when she opened the cottage door. It was very early in the morning. "You wished to talk with me?"

She had sent word the night before with his steward, who had spent the evening visiting her father. He had had the message last night, but it had been too late to come then. He had slept scarcely a wink all night. But if he had expected to be given hope by the first sight of her face, he was disappointed. She looked almost haggard.

"Yes." She leaned against the door. "I did not know to whom to talk. Papa would be merely upset. It was you or Lord Ashley Kendrick. But I cannot go to him or ask him to call upon me here. He might tell —" She stopped and looked at him with troubled eyes.

Ah, so she had not changed her mind. She had not summoned him to make him the happiest of men.

"Fetch a shawl," he said, "and we will walk. Eric is still asleep?"

"And Papa too," she said.

He offered his arm as they walked toward the bridge and was relieved that she took it. They crossed the bridge and turned to walk along the footpath beside the river, on the opposite side from Penshurst park.

"What is making you so unhappy?" he asked her after she had had time to compose herself. "How can I be of service to you, Kathy?"

"I do not know where to start," she said, looking up at him with liquid brown eyes.

"Wherever you wish," he said. "I have all morning, all day to give to you if necessary."

She drew breath a few times. Finally she spoke. "I always assumed that we would marry," she said. "You and I, I mean. I did not believe the difference in our stations would hold you back and I was . . . fond of you."

"Yes," he said. "I always assumed it too. I loved you."

"I do not know quite what it was with him," she said. "With Gregory. Suddenly he seemed to — to need me. I do not believe he loved me, but he pressed his attentions on me with single-minded determination. I do not know why I responded as I did. I was flattered, perhaps. He was from Penshurst, after all. Papa *worked* for him. Or I felt his need and responded to it. The love you and I seemed to share was a quiet thing. I did not fully realize until afterward how — how deep it was. I — I do not know why I responded to him."

"I thought," he said, and he could hear the hurt in his own voice, "that you had stopped loving me, Kathy. That you had grown to love him."

"I think I persuaded myself 'twas so," she said. "I knew 'twas not even before he died. Henry, there was no Mr. Smith. I have never been married."

"I know that," he said quietly.

"You knew?" She looked up at him and bit her lower lip.

"Before you even returned here," he said. "And if I had not known, I would have realized it as soon as I saw Eric."

"He does resemble Gregory, does he not?" she said sadly.

"Kathy." Hope stirred painfully in him again. "Was that why you refused me yesterday? Did you think I did not know? Did you believe I would not want you if I knew you had never been wed? If I knew of Eric's illegitimacy? These things do not matter to me at all. You would be my wife. He would be my son."

"I think," she said, her voice shaking badly, "I am guilty of terrible things. Much worse than these."

"Tell me, then," he said. " 'Tis time. You used not to be as quiet, as unhappy as you have been since your return. He is a lovely child, Kathy, and you are a good mother to him. There seems to be no reason for lasting unhappiness. What are these dreadful things you mention?"

"I went to stay with my mother's family," she said. "They took me in and were kind to me. I was very fortunate. But I was angry and bitter. I had ruined my life, turning to him in his need and away from everything that would have led to my permanent happiness. And even my chance for respectability had been snatched away at the last moment when he died on our wedding day. My son, who would have been heir to Penshurst after his father, was instead a bastard. And Papa — poor innocent Papa, who had always taken such great pride in his work — had been dismissed. All because of *her.* I do not know why she hated me so, unless it was that I was merely the daughter of her father's steward. But I was a lady. Papa is a gentleman. After all, Gregory would have

married sooner or later. She must have realized that. But she did hate me. And I think
she hated him too after he told her about
me. I think — Henry, I have always thought
that she killed him. Is it wicked to suspect
such a thing?"

"No," he said.

"Is it true, then?" She stared at him with
wide eyes.

"Yes," he said. "I believe so, Kathy."

"There was a man," she said. "My cousin's
friend. He was enormously wealthy, having
inherited money from several relatives,
though he was rather unhappy about own-
ing no land of his own. He was handsome,
charming, sympathetic, attentive. I was
soothed by his interest. Gregory was dead, I
had lost you — I was grateful to him. I
poured out all my bitterness to him, all my
hatred, all my suspicions."

"Perhaps it was not in the best of taste to
do so," he said when she paused in obvious
distress. "But 'twas understandable, Kathy.
I wish you had come to me."

"No," she said, "you do not. You were hard
and bitter, Henry. You were unkind to me
— not that I blame you. If I had told you
afterward that I was to have his child . . ."

"Yes," he said quietly. "Yes, you are right.
I hated you for a long time."

"I did not know," she said, "that he was conceiving a passion for me, that he was becoming angry on my behalf, that he was plotting revenge on my behalf. Oh, he talked about avenging the wrong that had been done me. He was an army officer and he thought it possible that his regiment would go to India, where of course Lord Kersey was living, at some future time. He said he would see to it that one day Eric would live in his rightful home and that I, as his mother, would live there too. 'Twas all a game to me, a gleeful, spiteful dream. I encouraged him."

"To India," Sir Henry said quietly.

"And then," she said, "long after I had forgotten about it, and about him too, we heard of Alice's and her son's horrible deaths. And only a few days after that there came a letter from him, telling me that he was in India and enjoying his duties there. Nothing more. Nothing about Alice. The suspicions have gnawed at me ever since. I have wondered about it, worried about it, had nightmares over it."

" 'Twas a coincidence, Kathy," he said, covering her hand with his own. " 'Twas a coincidence, by my life. You must forget it. Alice and her son died accidentally in a fire."

"But he is at Penshurst," she said quickly.

"He is Lord Ashley's friend, Henry. His friend from India. Major Roderick Cunningham."

"Zounds," he said, his reassuring touch turning to a grip.

"He has talked to me," she said. "He has told me that soon Eric and I will be living at Penshurst — with him. I am terrified of him, Henry. What has he done for my sake? And what is he planning to do — for my sake? Yesterday morning Lady Emily Marlowe was shot at. By whom? Why? I fear I know the answer to the first question at least."

"You have done the right thing in telling me," he said. "I shall handle it, Kathy."

"I am afraid even for you," she said. "What if he sees me walking with you? I should not have come out with you like this."

"You must not fear for me," he said.

"But am I guilty of murder?" she asked him. "If he did . . . Am I?"

"Of course you are not." He turned her to him and held her firmly by the upper arms. "Of course you are not, Kathy. I will have to tell Kendrick what you have told me. May I?"

"You do not think that he would say

something to Major Cunningham?" she asked.

"No," he said. "I do not. I have had reasons not to like the man particularly well, but he is no villain. Kathy, why did you refuse me yesterday? Because you were frightened? Because you felt you were guilty of some villainy? Because you are an unmarried mother? Or because you do not want me?"

Tears welled in her eyes. "Perhaps for all except the last reason," she said.

"I will ask you again then," he said, "after this thing is settled."

"Henry," she said, "what are you going to do?"

"I am going to consult with Kendrick first," he said. "But one thing I promise you, Kathy: Cunningham will not be frightening you again. I can wager Kendrick will say the same for Lady Emily Marlowe."

"You will not —" She gripped the edges of his coat beneath his cloak. "I could not bear it if you were hurt."

He kissed her for the first time in years. She clung even more tightly, pressing her lips hungrily back against his.

"Just one thing," he said when he raised his head. "You will not be living at Penshurst. But you might start wondering if you might like to live at Willowdale Manor. And if you think Lady Verney a prettier name than Mrs. Smith. And if you think Eric Verney sounds like the name of a successful lawyer or businessman or clergyman."

"Henry," she said, "be careful. Oh, do be careful."

Luke, Ashley, and Major Cunningham took the children riding and amused them outdoors for an hour afterward. Anna stayed at home with Emily, conversing cheerfully as she sewed. Afterward the two of them went to the nursery to play with James and Harry. Luke was there too, helping Joy practice her penmanship, listening to George read aloud.

Emily let James ride her around the nursery like a horse. She sat beside Harry, making his face light up with merriment and his arms flap and his legs kick with excitement. She looked at Joy's writing when it was brought to her and smiled her approval. With her one good hand she helped James build a castle with his wooden bricks.

They were to go home to Bowden tomorrow. If it had not been for the difficulty of organizing all the children and their baggage as well as their own, Anna had assured her, they would go today. But she would see to it that Emily was not left alone for a single minute. Tonight she would sleep in Emily's room and when Harry needed her, she would simply have his nurse bring him from the nursery.

None of them mentioned the incident of Alice's room, though Emily was sure Ashley must have told them. It was too embarrassing and too disturbing to think about. She must have been sleepwalking from the effects of the laudanum. But she had actually *lain* on that bed. She had brought those portraits back to her own room. And then she had gone to Ashley's. She could not remember going there. She could remember only being in his bed there this morning, warm and comfortable and safe, and unwilling to wake up. There was only one isolated memory of the night before. She could remember his making love to her.

It was hard this morning to smile, to watch people's lips instead of withdrawing into her own very solitary silence, to give her energy and her cheerful attention to the children.

She hated feeling like this. Frightened, out of control, haunted. Guarded. She hated thinking of Anna and Luke as guards, robbing her of privacy and curtailing her freedom. She was afraid to be alone, afraid to go outside, afraid to run up the hill to the summerhouse. And yet she wanted to do all three. She resented her fear. And irrationally she resented the people who protected her from it. The very people she loved most in the world.

She hated the feeling.

And she hated the thought of going. And of Ashley's leaving Penshurst for her sake. Had he been serious this morning when he had talked of selling it? He must not do so. Not for her sake. She must persuade him not to do anything so foolish. But he would never be willing to bring her back here. And she would probably always be afraid to come. If he did not sell, then . . .

She did not believe she was going to be able to live without him. She had thought so before. She had thought so when he left for India, and again over a month ago at Bowden. She had lived without him for seven years. She had lived without him for that month in London. Yes, she told herself firmly, she would be able to do it again. But the very thought threatened to pitch her into a black void of panic.

And then she laughed as the tall, thin tower she had been building for James finally collapsed — and looked up to find that Ashley was there. He snatched James up, tossed him toward the ceiling, and set him down on the floor again. He was smiling, but she could see weariness and tension in his face.

"I shall be with Emmy for the next half hour," he was telling Luke. "I have to go out then — Verney has summoned me on some business that apparently cannot wait beyond today. But when I return, we will all go out for a drive. The children too. We will take food and drink with us and have our tea in the outdoors. Rod is belowstairs now, charming my housekeeper and my cook and arranging it all for me. We must enjoy your last day here."

Emily took his offered arm and allowed him to lead her to the library, where he seated her in a soft leather chair and perched on the arm beside her. He took her good hand in his.

She felt embarrassed with him. What must he think of her having gone to Alice's room last night? Of her having lain in Alice's bed? Of her having taken Alice's portrait to her room? What must he think of her for going to him in his room during the night? She raised her eyes to his.

She saw a deep tenderness there.

"Somehow," he said, "I am going to make all this up to you, Emmy. I am going to see you happy and at peace again. Perhaps I can atone for some of the great wrongs in my life if I can do this for you."

She tried to smile at him.

"I am going to ask you a question," he said. "One I have asked before. I will hope that this time the answer will be different. But I will not ask it yet. Not here. This has become an unhappy place for you — and therefore for me too. I am going to sell Penshurst, Emmy. I will buy another home and hope that it will be happier — for you as well as for me."

"No," she said, shaking her head. "No, Ahshley." She would have liked to say more so that he would understand.

He kissed the back of her hand. "Rod is going to purchase it," he said. "We have already come to an agreement between ourselves. It needs only for our lawyers to arrange the actual business details. He seems genuinely happy at the prospect of living here. And 'twill make me happy to know that it will be owned by a friend."

She did not understand all that he said, but the main point was clear. Despite her efforts, she still could not like Major Cunningham. She could not bear the thought of Ashley's selling Penshurst to him of all people.

"No," she said.

"He will be happy here," he said. "There are no memories, bad or otherwise, to spoil it for him. He is a stranger here. He does not know this part of the country or anyone in it except me. This will be the best way, Emmy, believe me."

"No." She frowned. No, that was not true. She remembered the visit she had paid to Mr. Binchley's cottage with Anna and the major. She remembered watching Major Cunningham and Mrs. Smith through the window as they walked in the garden. How could she say it? And why was it even important that it be said? But she did not want Ashley to sell Penshurst. Especially not to the major.

"He knows Mrs. Smith," she said very slowly. She was never sure when she spoke that sound came out. But he had evidently heard something.

"Who does?" he asked. "Rod?"

"Yes," she said.

"Impossible," he said. "He has never been here before. Unless he met her when she lived elsewhere with her husband, of course. But 'twould be strange that he has said nothing. Are you sure?"

"Yes," she said.

"Strange," he said. "I must ask him about it."

But she remembered that Major Cunningham and Katherine Smith had not openly acknowledged their acquaintance. They had gone out into the garden, like hostess and guest, and talked there. The window had been closed. No one in the house would have heard their conversation. But she had seen it. For some reason those two did not want it known that they were acquainted. Emily felt a wave of the now almost familiar dread and panic.

"No," she said, clutching the wide cuff of Ashley's coat. She shook her head firmly. "No. No. Do not ahsk."

He lowered his head and looked closely into her face. "Emmy," he said, and now there was a frown on his face too, "you do not like Rod. Why?"

She dropped her hand and deliberately made her face expressionless. She shook her head.

"I will say nothing, then," he said. "I must take you back to Anna and Luke. Sir Henry Verney wishes to speak with me. I would take you with me, Emmy, to visit Lady Verney and Miss Verney — you like them, do you not? — but Verney particularly requested that I come alone. I will be as quick as I can so that we can have a long afternoon outing. You look as if you need fresh air."

She smiled.

He leaned his head down again and kissed her warmly on the lips. He spoke carefully with his hands and his face as well as with his voice. "Emmy," he said, "you are the most precious treasure of my life. You have been since the day I met you, but I have not fully realized until recently how all-encompassing is your influence on my life and your importance to my happiness. How blind one can be! And how foolish!"

He gave her no chance to reply. He got to his feet, took her hand, and drew it through his arm. Then he took her back to the nursery, where Luke was holding Harry above his head and making him laugh while Anna read a story to the other three.

They sat in Sir Henry Verney's library, one on either side of the fireplace, like two old friends exchanging news and views and gossip. But Sir Henry had done most of the talking. And finally they sat in silence.

"I mean to marry Katherine," Sir Henry said at last. "I mean to give her son my name. I mean to call out Major Roderick

Cunningham for the guilt and the terror he has forced into her life."

"Then you will have to wait your turn," Ashley said, breaking his long silence.

"Yes," Sir Henry said. "I guessed that I might. I seem to have been nothing but the bearer of disturbing news in the past few days. I am sorry."

Ashley looked steadily at him. "I owe you so many apologies," he said, "that I scarce know where to begin. But they must be said now lest after today I am forever prevented from saying them."

"We will take them as spoken and accepted," Sir Henry said. "Under similar circumstances I would perhaps have behaved with less restraint and courtesy than you have shown. 'Tis altogether possible that we will be neighbors for many years to come. Is it possible we can also be friends?"

Ashley got to his feet and held out his right hand. Sir Henry stood up too and took it. Despite the fact that they clasped hands quite firmly, there was some awkwardness between them. But there was the will on both sides to put the past behind them and to begin their acquaintance anew.

Ashley took his leave without further conversation. For the moment there was nothing else to say. Both knew that they might never meet again.

27

Emily had gone to her room to rest for a while before the picnic. At least, that was the reason she had indicated to Anna. She had also signaled her that she did not need company. It was broad daylight. There could be no danger. Anna, dubious though she had looked, had allowed her sister to be alone.

But it was not rest Emily had needed. She needed to be alone so that she could think. She had become a prisoner to fear. She had become dependent for safety on Anna and Luke, and on Ashley. They had taken charge of her life. She was to return to Bowden — because she was afraid to stay at Penshurst. Ashley was going to sell Penshurst because — well, because he was going to offer for her again, and because he believed he could not have both Penshurst and her.

She hated the fear. She hated the dependence. And she hated the thought of

Ashley's selling Penshurst. Somehow, she felt, he needed to stay here, to make it his home, to find his peace here. And she loved it too, despite everything.

How could she fight her fear? How could she overcome whatever it was that was causing it? It was that last point that had finally sent her in search of solitude. She needed to think. Or rather, she needed to analyze the strange, confused conviction that had come to her since talking with Ashley: Major Cunningham was the cause of her fear — *all* of it.

He was the original cause, of course. He had tried to ravish her when he had mistaken her for a servant. But it was not just that. He had shot at her. He had come into her room last night. He had brought the portraits and taken her dressing gown. She still had only very vague memories of the night, but she was almost sure she had woken up to see the shape of the portraits on her bedside table. And she was almost sure she had looked for her dressing gown before fleeing to Ashley and forgetting everything else in the sense of safety she had found as soon as his arms came about her. Major Cunningham had a previous acquaintance with Mrs. Smith — one that both of them wished kept secret.

She had proof of nothing. She understood nothing. But she *knew.* She had nothing to take to Ashley. He would either not believe her at all or he would become suspicious of his friend without provable grounds. She could tell him about that first morning, of course. That was grounds enough to send the major away and to keep Penshurst. She could tell Ashley, or she could —

She felt the familiar hammering of her heartbeat in her throat, the familiar terror. Gazing from her window, she could see Major Cunningham walking about down by the stables and carriage house. He was organizing transportation for the picnic.

It would be madness to go down there. He had *shot* at her. She would be unable to confront him with words. She was shaking with fear. She could accomplish nothing — because she was a woman and a deaf-mute. No, she was *not* mute. And though she was a woman, she was also a person who had always confronted the shadowy places in her life and brought them into the light. Her handicap could have made her passive and submissive and timid and dependent. She had made it into her strength. Until now.

No, even now.

Major Cunningham was alone in the carriage house when Emily arrived there, running one hand over a wheel of the open carriage. He looked up, startled, smiled, and bowed.

"Lady Emily," he said. "Are you ready for the picnic?"

But she did not smile. She shook her head. Her heart was thumping.

"You are alone?" he asked, looking behind her. "I am surprised at your sister and his grace for allowing it. Permit me to escort you safely back to them." There was nothing but kindly concern in his eyes.

Emily shook her head again. "I know," she said slowly. It was so very important that she get it right.

"By Jove." He grinned. "You can talk. I did not imagine it that first morning."

"I know," she said again, "about you." She hoped she was saying the words right.

"About me?" He touched a hand to his chest and raised his eyebrows.

She had set herself too great a task. She knew that. How she longed for words. But somehow she would convey her meaning. "You." She formed the shape of a gun with one hand and then pointed to her wounded hand. "You." There was no sign he would recognize. "Lahst night. You. Mrs. Smith."

Something happened to his eyes. Perhaps

people who had ears did not know how eloquent the eyes were. But she knew from his eyes that she had not made a mistake.

He smiled. "I do assure you, Lady Emily," he said, "that you are mistaken. I would perhaps be angry if I did not realize that the manner of our meeting put a lasting suspicion in your mind. But —"

She was shaking her head firmly, and he stopped speaking. "No," she said. "I know. I know you."

" 'Tis to be hoped," he said, "that you will not go to Ash with these quite groundless suspicions, Lady Emily. Zounds, he might believe you. And he is my dearest friend in this world."

"Go," she told him, making broad shooing gestures. Ah, it was too long and too hard to tell him that she would not allow Ashley to sell Penshurst to him. "Go." She made an even wider gesture with her arm to show that she meant away from Penshurst — forever.

"By Jove," he said, "you mean to frighten me."

No, *he* had meant to frighten *her*. She understood that. He could have killed her with that shot — he was a soldier. He might have murdered her in her bed last night. He wanted to frighten her so that Ashley would sell Penshurst to him and take her away.

"Go," she told him again.

He stood smiling at her. She read a certain reluctant admiration in his look. She lifted her chin and kept it up.

"Are you not afraid now?" he asked her. "Alone with me like this?"

She was about to shake her head. But of course she was afraid. She was almost blind with terror. And she scorned to lie to him. "Yes," she said. "Go."

He could kill her now, she realized. There was no one else in sight. If he wanted Penshurst as passionately as she guessed he must, he might very well kill her, knowing she could tell Ashley and spoil everything for him. How foolish she was to have come. And yet she knew even as her knees trembled under her that she had had no choice. Life was more than just breathing and eating and sleeping. Life had to have quality and dignity.

"Ah, but you are merely an hysterical little deaf girl," he said. "One who walks in her sleep and is obsessed with her lover's dead wife. One who runs to him for protection every time she is frightened — and she is always frightened. Go back to the house, Lady Emily. Your charges are absurd." He turned back to examine the wheel again.

She returned to the house, her back prickling with terror the whole way. He was right. Even if she could write everything down quite coherently, she had no modicum of proof for anything. And she *had* become hysterical. But she would do it anyway. She was not going to let Ashley sell Penshurst. And she was not going to let Luke and Anna take her back to Bowden tomorrow.

She was going to stay and fight. For Ashley and for herself.

The footman in the hall and the butler who joined him there on Ashley's return did not know where Major Cunningham was, though they believed it was somewhere outside the house. The butler thought he was probably in the carriage house, personally supervising the preparations for the afternoon's drive.

"You will find him," Ashley said curtly, "and ask him to meet me in the ballroom at his earliest convenience." He turned toward the staircase and took the stairs two at a time.

Some minutes later, as he was leaving Roderick Cunningham's room, he came face-to-face with Luke.

"Ah," Luke said, "the wanderer has returned. And the revelries are about to begin." His eyes lowered to the sword Ashley held in his hand and moved to the other sword he wore at his side. He pursed his lips and raised his eyebrows. He looked thoughtfully at the door to the major's room.

"I am on my way to the ballroom," Ashley said. "He is to meet me there. Go to the ladies, Luke, if you will be so good, and keep them well out of the way."

"I trust," Luke said, looking again at the swords, "that there is good reason?"

"*Every* reason in the world," Ashley said.

"Then I shall be present in the ballroom too, my dear," Luke said. "After I have given my instructions to Anna and to Emily, that is." He turned and walked away without another word.

Major Cunningham was already in the ballroom when Ashley arrived there. He was standing in the middle of the floor looking up at the high-coved ceiling.

" 'Tis really quite magnificent, by Jove," he said, half glancing at Ashley. "I did not particularly look up when you gave me the tour of the house, Ash. Are you planning to give a ball here? A farewell ball, perhaps? I would be delighted to assist you."

"No," Ashley said.

"Then why the summons here?" His friend looked at him with a grin. "It had a dash of mystery to it. The ballroom in the middle of an afternoon." But his eyes had lighted on the sword — his own — clutched in Ashley's hand. Then they moved to take in the sword at Ashley's side. And finally they looked up to Ashley's grim face. "Ah, Lady Emily has spoken to you already then?"

"I have been your dupe," Ashley said.

"No, Ash." Major Cunningham did not move from where he stood. "You have been my friend. You still are."

Ashley saw the major's eyes move beyond his shoulder and guessed that Luke had come into the ballroom. He did not look back and Luke made no move to intrude.

"You killed my wife," Ashley said. "And my son."

"He was not your —"

"You killed Thomas Kendrick, *my son*," Ashley said. "You killed Lady Ashley Kendrick, my wife."

"Ash." Major Cunningham spread his hands to his sides. "She was a wicked woman. You have learned that for yourself during the past week. She killed her own brother, for whom she had an unnatural passion, to prevent him from marrying a woman she thought beneath him and to prevent that woman's child from becoming his heir. She made you miserable. Do you think I did not know that? I was your *friend*. I released you from a life sentence."

" 'Twas why you befriended me," Ashley said. "So that you could get close to her."

"But I soon felt a genuine friendship for you," Major Cunningham said. "I did for you what you could not even dream of doing for yourself, Ash."

"Why was she at home that night?" Ashley asked.

The major shrugged and looked apologetic. "She disliked me," he said. "Much can be made of dislike, Ash. Attraction can come of dislike. She found me attractive."

"And you knew I would be safely from home for the night," Ashley said. "Did you arrange that too?"

"A few words supposedly from Mrs. Roehampton to you, a few words supposedly from you to her . . ." The major shrugged. "I merely enabled the two of you to recognize a mutual attraction, Ash. Forgive me for the pain you felt afterward. I know there has been a great deal. But I rescued you from a great evil. I am glad you have discovered the truth. Yes, I truly am. Now you will be able to let go of your damnable sense of guilt. You will realize that you were not in any way to blame for what happened."

"You murdered my wife and son," Ashley said.

"Murder," the major said softly. " 'Tis a harsh word, Ash. I am a soldier. I have killed a hundred times — more. I have never thought of myself as a murderer. And if 'tis any consolation, they died quickly, the two of them, and the nurse — they were dead before the fire. I did that much for them."

"You tried to kill Lady Emily Marlowe yesterday morning," Ashley said.

"Oh no, Ash." Major Cunningham raised a staying hand. "I am an excellent shot. I was close. I was careful to hit the target I had set myself. If she had only been capable of hearing, I would not even have had to graze her skin."

"And last night?" Ashley asked. "You have been deliberately trying to terrorize her. You were in her room. You took her night robe. You put the portraits there. Why? But I need not ask that, need I? You have correctly divined my feelings for her. You have thought to drive her away and therefore to drive me away. You very nearly succeeded."

"You could not be happy here, Ash," the

major said. "Not with your wife's ghost haunting you every day of your life. Not with the knowledge that young Eric should be living here as the rightful owner. A few hours more and his mother would have been married to his father. Sell to me. I will marry Katherine and make the boy my son. He will be where he belongs, and so will she."

"Just tell me what happened on the morning of your arrival," Ashley said. "What did you do to frighten Lady Emily so?"

"She has not told you?" Major Cunningham laughed rather ruefully. "My apologies, Ash. I saw her in what I now realize is a common guise. But at the time I mistook her for a milkmaid. No harm was done — fortunately for all of us, she is rather fleet-footed. Since discovering her true identity, I have been the soul of honor. Besides, I have other interests of a more serious nature than that aroused by milkmaids. Come, Ash, shake my hand. There is no point in making a damned quarrel of all this." He held out his right hand and took a step forward.

"One of us is going to die here today," Ashley said. "If 'tis me, my property will become Harndon's. He will discuss with you how he wishes to dispose of it. If 'tis you, I will bury our friendship with you and consider that the deaths of my wife and my son and the nurse as well as the terrorizing of Lady Emily Marlowe have been justly avenged. I have brought you your own sword, as you see."

"This is very foolish, Ash, and very unnecessary," Major Cunningham said. "I have no wish to kill you."

"Then you must stand and be killed," Ashley said. "I suggest we strip down to shirts and breeches."

He set down the major's sword on the floor and walked away to prepare himself. Luke was standing motionless inside the door, looking tight-lipped and rather pale.

"Ash," he said quietly as his brother removed his skirted coat, "let me do this for you. I have a reputation as a swordsman that has been well earned, I believe."

Ashley's smile was somewhat grim. "I had to do something for physical exercise in India," he said. "I practiced swordplay. Besides, Luke, they were my wife and my son. And Emmy is my woman."

"Yes," Luke said rather sadly. "I love you, brother."

Ashley grinned. "Zounds but I will hold those words over your head for the rest of your life," he said, setting his long waistcoat down on top of his coat. He was no longer smiling when he straightened up and withdrew his sword from its scabbard. "Luke, tell her I love her. Care for her if she is with child."

"Yes," Luke said. "For your sake and because she is almost my sister and almost my daughter. She will always have my love and my protection. So will any child of hers — and yours." He strode away then to the middle of the ballroom to talk quietly with Major Cunningham, who was ready in his shirtsleeves, drawn sword in hand. After a minute or so, Luke looked across at Ashley and nodded curtly.

" 'Tis, as I understand it," he said when Ashley had approached and the two men stood face-to-face and had crossed swords, "a fight to the death. Nevertheless you will not begin until I give the signal and neither one of you, for honor's sake, will hit the other from behind or stab the other when he is down."

Ashley had not noticed that Luke too was wearing his sword. But he had it drawn now and set it beneath their crossed swords. Major Cunningham's eyes were on Ashley's, cool, calculating, rueful. He was a friend, Ashley thought, who had betrayed him during every moment of their friendship. A friend who must now die or who must kill him. This was no moment for sentiment, for regrets, for hurt feelings of betrayal.

Luke's sword came up, and with a clash of steel the swords of the combatants were separated. "Begin," he said.

Major Cunningham was solidly built, strong, and fit. He was a soldier. As an officer, he habitually carried a sword. He led his men into battle with drawn sword. But that did not necessarily make him an expert in its use during single combat. Ashley was slender in comparison, taller, also fit. He had never been in a real sword fight. But, as he had just told Luke, he had learned and practiced the art of swordplay.

And Ashley had the advantage of motivation. His anger was cold and controlled. Alice had been many things. Perhaps — even probably — she had been a wicked woman. Certainly she had been a tormented woman. But she had been his wife and under his protection. Thomas had been another man's son, conceived in sin. But he had been an innocent baby, and a baby to whom Ashley had given the protection of his name. Emily was simply his love. He fought for all three of them, so that the two might finally rest in peace, so that the third might again live in peace. And he fought, though he did not consciously think of it, for the restoration of his honor, lost when his wife and child died while he was in the arms of another woman.

Swordplay, he discovered, was very different from serious combat. Swordplay was conducted according to strict rules of gentlemanly etiquette and honor. Combat was not. And in combat a hit drew blood. Major Cunningham drew first blood after several minutes of circling and clashing swords and sizing each other up. He did something with his left hand that drew Ashley's attention away from his sword for a mere fraction of a second and in that time was past Ashley's guard and had pricked him on the right shoulder.

There was pain, shock, and a fast-spreading stain of red in the corner of Ashley's vision.

"Enough, Ash," Major Cunningham said, his voice breathless. "You have made your point. Honor has been served. Enough now."

"To the death," Ashley said coldly. Though it was painful, the wound did not incapacitate him. Instead it made him cautious. It made him grimly aware with his whole body of what his mind already knew — that one of them was to die. He ended the momentary lull in the fighting and bore his opponent back with the force of his attack.

They fought to what seemed an inevitable stalemate. They fought for long minutes until it seemed that exhaustion must end the fight before death did. But Major Cunningham lost his patience first. He lunged forward into what was only an illusory opening. A mere turning of Ashley's body sent the major's sword harmlessly past. But Ashley's own sword, firmly held, impaled his enemy.

The major went very still as his sword clattered to the ballroom floor. He stared into Ashley's eyes, and a peculiar twisted smile distorted his lips. A line of blood oozed from one corner of his mouth and trickled down to drip off his chin. Ashley pulled his sword free, and the dead body of his erstwhile friend crumpled at his feet.

Ashley looked down at the red sword in his hand and dropped it to the floor. There was no feeling of relief at being the survivor. There was no feeling of triumph at being the victor, or of guilt at having killed a man. There was no feeling at all. He stared downward.

"You will need to have that shoulder tended to, Ash. You are losing blood." Luke's voice. Cool and calm, as might have been expected of him.

"Yes," Ashley said.

" 'Twas a fair fight. And a necessary one," Luke said.

"Yes."

"And if I ever again see you for one hairbreadth of a second take your eye off the sword of your opponent, even in a friendly bout," Luke said, his voice shaking, "I will personally thrash you within an inch of your life, Ash. With a horsewhip."

"Yes," Ashley said.

"I shall see to everything here," Luke said. "I shall have the nearest magistrate summoned and the body attended to. Go and have that blood stanched, Ash. Anna is stouthearted. Go to her in Emily's room. I instructed them to wait there. She will not have disobeyed my instructions. Do you need help with your coat?" He was again the cool, practical Duke of Harndon.

"No," Ashley said. He walked to his discarded clothes and pulled on his coat, heedless of either the pain or the blood. He turned to leave.

"Ash," Luke called.

Ashley looked back.

Luke said nothing for a moment. He merely nodded his head. "I meant what I said earlier," he said. "Just in case you are ever in doubt."

Ashley left the ballroom.

28

The sky was cloudless. It was going to be a clear blue when the sun rose. It was going to be a warm day. She walked first along by the river, looking across its smooth glassy surface, watching another mother duck — or perhaps the same one — lead her babies in a line down the very center of their highway. Then she walked up the hill, wandering in no particular direction, touching the bark of tree trunks, feeling grass and soil beneath her bare feet, breathing in sweet, cool air.

She stopped at one particular tree and saw that the bullet was still lodged there, just below the level of her eyes. She did not even look over her shoulder. She did not feel afraid any longer. Last night she had slept alone in her room, despite Anna's pleadings. She had not felt afraid.

Yesterday had been a horrid day. First the threat of having to leave Penshurst and of knowing that Ashley planned to sell it for her sake. Then her foolhardy confrontation with Major Cunningham. Then Luke's coming to them — to her and Anna — with set face and that look of authority that even Anna dared not defy, and commanding them to go to Emily's room and to stay there until he or Ashley came for them. And the long wait, during which they had both known that something was dreadfully wrong. Then Ashley's coming, white-faced, to tell them that all was well, that there was nothing more whatsoever to fear. Then he had stumbled forward, grabbed at a chair, overturned it, and landed on his knees. They had seen the blood.

Major Cunningham was dead. Ashley had killed him. Neither he nor Luke had given any great detail, but they had said that the major had killed Alice and Thomas and that in his determination to own Penshurst he had terrorized Emily, hoping that fear would drive her away and convince Ashley to sell.

She had helped Anna half lift, half drag Ashley to her bed and had helped remove his stained coat and cut away his blood-soaked shirt. But she had cleansed and bound the wound herself while he had watched with half-closed eyes.

She hated to think of the sword fight in

which Major Cunningham had died. But she was not afraid any longer. She looked upward and turned about and about. The world was a beautiful, spinning place. Especially the natural world. If one remained a part of it, merely one creature among many, one's feet firmly resting on earth, great happiness was possible. And peace. She was happy this morning. She felt at peace with the world.

She wanted to watch the sun rise across the river. She wanted to see the colors of dawn reflected in the water. Perhaps one day she would paint the scene. But not today. Today there was too much beauty to behold in nature itself to spoil it by getting out her paints and analyzing the meaning of it all. This morning she was content merely to watch and to feel. Merely to be. She made her way toward the summerhouse.

She was standing in front of it, gazing down the hill and across the fields to the horizon, when she sensed that her morning was going to be complete. She turned her head and smiled. He was wearing his arm in the sling she had fashioned for him yesterday. But he had lost yesterday's pallor. And his eyes, smiling back at her, were clear of the suffering and the darkness that had lurked there since his return from India.

She could see that at last he was at peace with himself.

He came to stand beside her, and set his good arm about her waist. She rested her head against his shoulder and together they watched the sun come clear of the horizon in a blinding burst of glory. She looked up at him and smiled. His eyes reflected the brightness of the sun. Not a word had passed between them. The peace, the silent communion, was perfect.

They had not spoken a great deal yesterday. Both he and Luke had spent a long time with the magistrate who had come to the house to investigate the death. Then they had spent an almost equally long time with Sir Henry Verney, who had also called. And finally Luke had played stern elder brother and implacable head of the family — his own words — and had sent Ashley off to bed early.

But Emily was glad there had been little chance for words. Yesterday had been the wrong time. They had needed this new day. Her heart began to beat faster, and despite herself, despite what deep down she knew to be the truth, she was anxious.

"Emmy," he said, shrugging his shoulder and turning his head so that she could see his lips — so very close to her own — " 'tis a clear, bright, warm morning. It feels like the first morning that ever was. Is this how Adam and Eve felt, do you suppose? Is this Eden?"

She loved the warmth and the merriment in his smile. Everything else was gone. She touched her fingers to his cheek.

"At last I feel that perhaps I have something to offer you," he said, gazing back at her, his eyes softening to such unmistakable tenderness that she felt her anxiety melting away as if by the warmth of the newly risen sun. "My honor. I will not say that I was guiltless. I have confessed to you that I committed adultery. 'Tis a grievous offense. But there can be pardon for such sins, I do believe. I no longer feel so very responsible for their deaths, and I have avenged them. I feel that I have reclaimed my honor."

"Yes," she said. Foolish man — she had loved him anyway. But she knew that he had been unable to forgive himself and that therefore her love would never have been enough for him. They could never have been fully happy.

"My love has always been yours," he said. " 'Tis a strange thing to say, perhaps, when I almost completely forgot you during my years away. But that very fact tells me that unconsciously I had deliberately erased you from memory because my feelings for you disturbed me. You were only fifteen, Emmy. Even after my return I fought my love for you. In my mind those years had not passed — you were still a child. But you have always been a woman, have you not? Even when we first met? When you were fourteen?"

"Yes," she said.

"Ah, Emmy." He kissed her warmly, and for a while nothing else mattered except that they were together in sunshine, with no shadows at all to darken or chill. "Emmy, my love. Forgive me for forgetting you. Forgive me for denying your womanhood."

She set her hands on either side of his face and smiled at him. "Yes," she said. She was not sure she could say it, but she would try. "I love you." She knew that he was still unsure of himself, unsure of his worthiness for happiness and peace. "I love you."

His smile softened and was again untroubled. He set his hand over one of hers — it was her injured one, still rather sore now that she had removed the bandages, but she stopped herself from wincing — and turned his head to kiss her palm.

"Thank you." He grinned at her. Ashley's grin, all mischief and sparkling eyes and happiness. "If you wish," he said, "you may tell me all the ways you love me so that we can make a speech lesson out of this."

She laughed, and he hugged her and rocked her with his good arm.

"Ah, Emmy," he said, releasing her sufficiently that she could see his lips. "You have the most infectious laugh I have ever heard. My love, marry me. Will you? Not because you have lain with me and may be with child by me. But because 'tis the only thing in the world we can do to be complete and happy. Will you marry me?" His eyes were anxious once more.

"Yes," she said. "Ahshley."

They simply smiled at each other for a long while. She could see no clouds behind his eyes, no troubles, not even any remaining doubts. Only a happiness and a peace that matched her own. His face was lit up by the sunlight.

"Will we stay at Penshurst?" he asked her. "I will sell it if you wish, Emmy. We can live elsewhere. It does not matter where as long as we are together."

But she had set her fingertips over his lips before using her hands to speak. *No,* she told him. *We will live here. This is home.*

And after he had searched her eyes and had seen that she meant it, he looked happy

again. Bad things had happened at Penshurst, Emily mused. They had culminated
in the death of a man yesterday. But they
were over and done with. Penshurst was
merely a place, a beautiful house in natural
surroundings with congenial neighbors, a
few of whom would become close friends
— Sir Henry Verney and his sister, Katherine Smith, Mr. Binchley. It was a place she
and Ashley would make home, a place in
which their children would be born and
raised, a place where they would grow old
together. They would make of it a good
place with good memories.

"Yes," he said, using his free hand to sign
to her as well, "it is home. Because you are
here with me, Emmy. But I am going to
send you to Bowden tomorrow."

Her smile faded and her eyes widened.

"We should marry at Bowden, not here,"
he said. "And we should marry soon, Emmy.
Because we wish to and because we must.
We will send for your family and mine
today, and tomorrow when you go to
Bowden with Anna and Luke, I will go to
London for a special license. We should be
able to marry within two weeks."

She bit her lip. She would be two weeks
without him?

"An eternity," he agreed, smiling ruefully.

"This arm sling is mere decoration, you know, worn to arouse sympathy and to invite people to wait on me hand and foot. It does not incapacitate me for any of the important activities of life."

She watched him remove it and drop it to the grass before flexing his shoulder and grimacing only slightly.

"Making love, for example," he said, looking at her with a curious mixture of playful smile and smoldering eyes.

"Yes." She touched one hand to his cheek again. "Yes." It seemed important that they make love this morning. Not because of any fear or need for comfort, motives that had clouded their past lovemakings. But purely for the sake of love and sharing and joy.

He took her by the hand and led her into the summerhouse. It was flooded with the bright light of early morning. He turned and drew her against him. They smiled at each other before his mouth found hers.

"Faith, child," Lady Quinn said, kissing Anna warmly on both cheeks, "you will think us mad. Lud, we *are* mad."

"This is a grand place, I warrant you, lad," Lord Quinn said, rubbing his hands together and looking about the hall of Penshurst. He was addressing Luke. "I told Marj 'twould look magnificent by the light of the morning sun."

"But he has never seen the place before," Lady Quinn said, tossing her glance upward. "The moon and the stars were bright last night, Anna, my love. We were watching them." Lord Quinn chuckled. "And Theo concocted the notion that we should leave town almost as soon as we had returned there and come here for breakfast. We have traveled half the night."

"And are hungry, by my life," Lord Quinn said. "I could devour an ox. Now, where is that youngest nephy of mine? Not up yet to welcome his aunt and uncle to his own home? Pox on it, but I have a good mind to go up and turn him out of bed with a pitcher of water over his head. If I but knew which direction to take." He gave vent to a short bark of laughter.

"Ashley is outside, Theo," Luke said, "taking the air."

"At this hour? A lad after my own heart," Lord Quinn said.

"And how is my dear Emily?" Lady Quinn asked. "I can scarce wait to bring her back to town with me, I vow. Unless —" She looked hopefully, first at Anna and then at Luke. "Unless she has something more important to do with her time, that is."

Luke looked at his wife, who was smiling back at him, and raised his eyebrows. He pursed his lips. "By some coincidence, Aunt," he said, "Emily is out taking the air too."

Lord Quinn slapped his thigh with the three-cornered hat he had removed from his head. "Egad," he said, "it worked, Marj, m'dear. You did not marry me in vain." He roared with laughter.

"Theo," his wife said, "you will be putting strange notions into dear Anna's and Luke's heads, I do declare. We merely thought that *if* we married and went away on a wedding journey, and *if* Emily came here with Anna for a fortnight, and *if* Ashley was not a dreadful slowtop . . ."

"They did not go out *together* this morning," Anna said. "Luke saw them both, but separately," she added, flushing. "Still, we are hoping . . ."

"I have been set to spying on my own brother and sister-in-law as an occupation suited to my dotage," Luke said in his haughtiest, most bored voice. "My duchess has encouraged me."

Lord Quinn slapped his thigh again. "And has there been much to spy upon, lad?" he asked.

"Oh, most assuredly," Luke said. "We had

better take you in to breakfast, Aunt Marjorie and Theo. If we await the return of Emily and Ashley, we might well be here until dinnertime. We might well all starve. Madam?" He bowed elegantly and offered Lady Quinn his arm.

"Dear Emily," she said with a sigh. "And dear Ashley."

"I warrant you, Marj," Lord Quinn said, roaring his comment after his retreating spouse as he gave his arm to Anna, "she will be brought to bed of a boy come nine months from today."

"Nine months from the *wedding day*, 'tis to be hoped, Theo," his wife said placidly while Anna blushed and Luke raised his eyebrows and pursed his lips again.

Luke had discouraged him from coming to Bowden Abbey until the day before his wedding. And family members, Ashley had discovered to his chagrin, moved about England with tortoiselike speed. Despite the fact that he had acquired a special license the very day after Emily had agreed to marry him, more than two weeks passed before he was finally permitted to go to Bowden to claim his bride.

And when he finally arrived there and finally saw her again, it was to find her ringed about, *walled* about with sisters and sisters-in-law and assorted other relatives, so that all he could do was bow formally over her hand, inquire formally after her health, and converse formally about the weather and other such scintillating subjects. And then she was whisked off to spend the night at Wycherly with her sister Agnes. Anna and Charlotte followed her there early on the morning of the wedding day.

His wedding day!

"Zounds, I feel like a damned Paris beau," he said when he was ready to leave for the church. He frowned at his image in the pier glass of his dressing room. He was resplendent in silver embossed satin skirted coat with silver embroidered waistcoat, gray breeches, white stockings and linen, and heeled and buckled shoes. His hair was powdered white, carefully rolled at the sides and bagged in black silk behind.

Luke met his eyes in the mirror. "You have something against Paris beaux, Ash?"

Ashley grinned. As usual on dress occasions, Luke, all in rich green and gold and white, would turn heads even on Paris's most fashionable boulevard.

They were early at the church. Or Emmy was late. He did not know which. But it seemed that he waited an eternity at the front of the village church, trying to look dignified, trying to feel calm. What if she had changed her mind? What if she did not come at all? Would she send a message? Or would he stand here like this, feeling the eye of every guest in the pews on him, until noon came and went, until dusk descended?

And then she was there.

She looked incredibly beautiful. He watched her as she came closer down the aisle, her hand resting on Royce's sleeve. She wore an elaborately trimmed sack dress of palest gold, with a train. The heavy robings down the edges of the open gown were of a darker gold and matched the color of her frilled, flounced petticoat and of her heavily embroidered stomacher. The two deep lace frills at her elbows were also trimmed with gold lace. Her hair was piled rather high over pads. Gold rosebuds and green leaves were entwined in it. It was unpowdered.

She was the other Emily. The one he had first seen and admired without knowing who she was on the night of his return to Bowden. The one he had seen and admired in London. And yet when her eyes met his and when she smiled — her bright, warm, serene smile — she was his Emmy too. His little fawn of the loose dress and the bare feet and the wild mane of fair hair. She was each and both and all. She was everything. He smiled back at her.

The service began, the marriage service that would make them man and wife, that would bind them together with love for the rest of their lives. The Reverend Jeremiah Hornsby led them through it with a slightly pompous competence until it came Emily's turn to make her vows. She was to watch Hornsby's lips and nod her acceptance of the words as her own. But a look passed between Hornsby and Emily, a look of mutual understanding. Almost a look of conspiracy.

"I, Emily Louisa, take thee, Ashley Charles," Hornsby said.

"I, Emily Louisa, take thee, Ahshley Charles," Emmy said.

Ashley guessed that they had practiced it endlessly, the two of them. He knew she would speak the whole of it, that she would pledge herself to him in words for him to hear, for the whole world to hear. He knew too that they must have practiced in secret — he was half aware of the distinctly audible gasp and murmuring from their gathered relatives. But he did not look at them. He looked only at her, deep into her eyes, each time she turned back from watching Hornsby's lips. He tightened his grasp of her hands.

And he smiled at her.

"Until death do us part. So help me Gahd."

He would tease her about that pronunciation later.

"God," she said, correcting herself and then smiling in triumph.

Ashley heard nothing else of the service until Hornsby was telling them and the world that they were man and wife. She was his — for the rest of his life. How could he possibly have come to deserve such happiness? But of course he had not. All he had done was love — and allow himself to be loved. So simple — so complex.

He lowered his head and kissed her. His wife. His love. His serenity and peace and joy.

Her eyes, when he raised his head again, said all the same things back to him.

They were married.

They had decided to stay at Bowden Abbey for the night and leave for Penshurst early enough in the morning that they could make the journey in one day.

They had retired early to Ashley's old

suite of rooms amid the knowing smiles, the tears — from Anna, Agnes, and Constance — and the mildly ribald comments of Lord Quinn. They had gone immediately to bed and had made love with lingering slowness and exquisite sweetness. And Ashley had called her his wife, whispering the words against her mouth — at least, she guessed that that was what he had whispered when he lifted his head and apparently repeated the words so that she could see them in the candlelight.

They had lain quietly in each other's arms and then made love again and relaxed once more — until he had told her that there were no more sounds, that he was convinced everyone, even down to the last servant, was in bed. They had smiled conspiratorially at each other as they had got up and dressed and slipped down the stairs and outside.

And now they were where they had planned to come ever since they had been alone together for a few minutes in the carriage after their wedding. They were at the falls, standing side by side on the highest rock, the one that jutted out over the water. Their fingers were entwined. It was a beautiful, warm night. The stars seemed almost close enough to touch. They were like lamps in the sky, so that even without the moon, which was almost full tonight, it would have been nearly as bright as day.

"Well, little fawn," Ashley said, turning her to him and taking her other hand in his free one. "We are back where it all started."

"Yes," she said. They had first met in Luke's drawing room, but this was where they had first talked, sitting together on this rock, her feet dangling in the water. She thought of him as he had been then — very young and handsome and restless. And of herself focusing on him all the love and devotion of her girl's heart. She thought of lying here facedown, alone, living through the terrible pain of his departure for India. And of his return and all that had followed it.

"But not where it will end," he said. "Tomorrow we will go home. To Penshurst. To our new life. I have had those rooms cleared out, Emmy. All is gone. And I want you to change everything else that does not suit you. I want it to be your home. Ours. There will be a wedding to attend soon — Henry Verney is to marry Katherine Smith. And I am encouraging my steward to desert me — as he phrases it — in order to move back to the north of England, where he comes from and which he misses. I will offer his position to Binchley."

She smiled at him, then used their private language to reply. *I am very happy,* she told him.

I am very happy too. He spoke to her without words. He pulsed a lightly closed fist against his heart. *I really mean it. I feel deeply.*

But there was something else she wished to say in words, though she could have signed it to him. She wanted to *tell* him.

"Ahshley," she said.

"Emmy." He smiled. "I love my name on your lips more than on anyone else's in the world."

"Ahshley," she said again, using her hands too. "You. Me. A baby."

She was not quite certain, of course, and she had felt unable to ask Anna. But she was almost certain — with her body. With her heart she knew it beyond a doubt.

She watched his eyes brighten with tears. He bit his lip. And then he caught her up in his arms and held her very close. He was talking to her, she knew. But it did not matter that she neither heard nor saw the words. Words were not important.

She kept her eyes open and looked up at the vast sky and at the stars. The whole sky and the earth too, the whole universe was singing. Did it matter that she could not hear? The melody, the dance, the joy were in her heart. And in his.

And then she could neither see nor hear. His mouth found hers and she closed her eyes.

There was only a silent melody.

ABOUT THE AUTHOR

Mary Balogh grew up in Wales and now lives with her husband, Robert, in Saskatchewan, Canada. She has written more than one hundred historical novels and novellas, more than thirty of which have been *New York Times* bestsellers. They include the Slightly sextet (the Bedwyn saga), the Simply quartet, the Huxtable quintet, and the ongoing seven-part Survivors' Club series.

The employees of Thorndike Press hope you have enjoyed this Large Print book. All our Thorndike, Wheeler, and Kennebec Large Print titles are designed for easy reading, and all our books are made to last. Other Thorndike Press Large Print books are available at your library, through selected bookstores, or directly from us.

For information about titles, please call:
(800) 223-1244

or visit our Web site at:
http://gale.cengage.com/thorndike

To share your comments, please write:
Publisher
Thorndike Press
10 Water St., Suite 310
Waterville, ME 04901